Praise

'Elegant, thoughtful and powerful'
Daisy Buchanan

'A cobweb of a book: beautifully intricate and delicate'
Veronica Henry

'A truly beautiful story of love, desire, identity and courage
– Julie Cohen is at her spellbinding best'
Rosie Walsh

'Wonderfully written and evocative'
Woman & Home

'Beautifully written and thought-provoking'
Kate Eberlen

'Loved every page!'
Claire Dyer

'Simmering with passions, it is a testament to the
enduring power of love'
Sunday Mirror

'Poignant and heartfelt'
Prima

'Wonderfully evocative'
Woman's Weekly

'A must read from Julie Cohen'
Good Housekeeping

Julie Cohen grew up in the western mountains of Maine and studied English at Brown University and Cambridge University before pursuing a research degree in nineteenth century fairies. After a career as a secondary school English teacher, she became a novelist. Her award-winning novels have sold over a million copies worldwide. *Dear Thing* and *Together* were both selected for the Richard and Judy Book Club.

Julie is a teacher of creative writing, a Vice President of the Romantic Novelists' Association, a founder of the RNA Rainbow Chapter for LGBTQ+ authors, and a Patron of literacy charity ABC To Read. She lives in the south of England with her son and a terrier of dubious origin.

Twitter: @julie_cohen
Website: www.julie-cohen.com.

SUMMER PEOPLE

PEOPLE

JULIE COHEN

ORION

First published in Great Britain in 2022 by Orion Fiction,
This paperback edition published in 2023 by Orion Fiction,
an imprint of The Orion Publishing Group Ltd
Carmelite House, 50 Victoria Embankment,
London EC4Y 0DZ

An Hachette UK Company

1 3 5 7 9 10 8 6 4 2

A CIP catalogue record for this book is
available from the British Library.

ISBN (Paperback) 978 1 4091 9015 8
ISBN (eBook) 978 1 4091 9016 5

Typeset at The Spartan Press Ltd,
Lymington, Hants

Printed and bound in Great Britain by Clays Ltd,
Elcograf S.p.A.

www.orionbooks.co.uk

For my mom, who bakes me blueberry pies, and my dad, who lets me beat him at cribbage.

Part One

—

Summer, 2015

Chapter One

Vee

The ferry goes from the mainland to Unity Island and back three times a day in summer and twice in winter. To reserve your spot from the mainland or the island during high season, you have to call the night before. These facts are so well known to the residents of Unity Island that they have the ferry number programmed into their phones next to the numbers of their family and friends, and every summer evening at seven, islanders instinctively glance at the clock and think 'Do I need to go inland tomorrow?' knowing if they don't book a place they could miss their dentist appointment, their job interview, their back-to-school shopping, their aunt's birthday, their best friend's funeral. During peak season, impetuous visitors or ignorant summer people who wander up to the grey-shingled ticket office on the mainland, credit card ready, to book a place for a day trip often find themselves watching the ferry disappear without them.

There's no website for the Unity Island Ferry Company, which has been run by the Lunt family for generations, since back when it was a single fishing boat pressed into double duty. There's a sign outlining the rules, but it's long-winded and bleary with salt and almost nobody reads it, and the result every weekend from June to October is a few milling New Yorkers, Canadians, people from Augusta or Bangor or other inland places, pacing the waterfront, squinting at the island in the distance, readjusting their plans.

People who live on Unity Island know that plans aren't adjustable. You make a decision and live with the consequences.

Mike had booked the tickets the night before. He'd called while they were waiting for their chowder in the restaurant in Rockland, because Vee had told him to. 'By phone?' he'd said, incredulous. 'Not online?'

'Yes,' she'd replied, and told him the number by heart. 'Do it now, before the appetisers turn up.' Even now, all these years later and wherever she was, she still caught herself checking the clock at seven, unprompted by anything but instinct, a pull in her belly.

Vee sat on her suitcase behind the ticket office. She had a cast on her left arm and she held her phone in her right hand. The only place she could get signal was here at the edge of the parking lot, which was basically a field. The smell of diesel and seawater, the sound of gulls and New York accents and engines, brought her back so many years that she could almost taste the pink peppermint lip gloss she used to wear, the Wrigley's gum she used to chew to mask the scent of cigarettes. She didn't want to read any of her emails, but deleting spam was a distraction from the memories of the last time she'd been on this shore, passing through in the other direction, carrying whatever she could pack. Then, she'd had no intention of ever returning.

Now here she was.

'Do you think it will be safe here?' Mike said, joining her.

'Yeah there are hardly ever any ferry accidents,' she said, not taking her eyes from the screen. 'Not since the seventies.'

'I meant the car. It's so open. There's no CCTV cameras, and it's not even paved.'

'It'll be fine.'

'For two weeks?'

She looked up at this, but not at her husband. Instead, she gazed at the parked cars in the field. When they were young, Sterling's dad used to take the two of them across some afternoons in the early season just to wander through the cars parked in the ferry lot. Row upon row of Cadillacs, Mustangs, Porsches. Mercedes, BMWs, Audis. All of them glossy, free of dings and dents. Even their tyres were spotless, as if the roads between Maine and New York were clean as a carpet. Tom Ames always took them to the summer people's cars first, showing them off as if he personally had brought them here. Their licence plates were from New York, New Jersey, Connecticut, Québec; as far away as South Carolina or even Texas. But for Sterling and Vee, the islander's cars were almost as exotic, even though they were four-wheel-drive trucks, battered sedans, wood-sided station wagons, all with mud flaps and salt spatter and rust, veterans of Maine seawater and snow. They were things from another world.

There were no cars on Unity Island, only two or three trucks that stayed there full-time, running the same ruts in the road. When Sterling and Vee got old enough to learn how to drive, they took lessons on the mainland after school in Mr Grenier's green Buick.

Vee shook her head. God. Was it going to be this way all the time while they were here: ambushed by memories?

'They don't even have a fence,' Mike was saying. He jingled his keys in his pocket. Distantly, their Audi beeped its recognition. 'I could hotwire one of them right now and drive away with it.'

'Nobody steals the summer people's cars,' Vee told him. 'Some kids might take one of the trucks for a joy ride, but not the summer cars. It would be an incredibly stupid thing to do. Everyone here depends on the summer people. They depend on *us*,' she added, because she could say that now.

Mike wore a white linen shirt, with the sleeves rolled up. Artfully distressed jeans, white Adidas with no socks, sunglasses, thick gold wedding band, Omega watch. Vee had a matching watch, ladies' model. He'd given it to her for her birthday, because she'd complimented his when he bought it for himself. She already had a perfectly good Seiko that she preferred, but Mike liked to see people enjoying his gifts, so she wore the Omega.

Looking at him, the picture of easy privilege, the sort of person who parked his car with all of the other expensive cars in the field, she thought: *Maybe this will be okay*. Maybe she was enough like him now, that she could just enjoy his gift.

'It's like a different world,' Mike said cheerfully, sinking down on his haunches beside her. 'It's harder to take this ferry than to take a plane.'

'You don't have to take your shoes off and empty your water bottle to get on the ferry.'

'You know what I mean.'

'There's no safety video. Or little packets of pretzels. Or seat belts.'

'But you have to carry your own bags.'

'Actually,' she said, 'maybe not. As kids we used to pick up some extra cash in tips by meeting the ferry and carrying the bags up the dock. Some of those bags were twice as big as I was.'

'They're still twice as big as you.'

'You mean twice as big as *you*, shortarse.' It was a well-worn sliver of banter between them, as automatic as checking the clock at seven. Vee used to think their teasing meant nothing, but lately she had begun to wonder if it meant everything instead. If it was all there was. They'd been trading verbal ripostes since the day they met. If they stopped now, what would they have to talk about?

'The ferry leaves in ten minutes and there's no sign of anyone near it. Why do you think we had to turn up an hour early?' He checked his watch again. 'I should have got some coffee. I think there's still time. I can be back here in ten, fifteen. Want some?'

This was the world they lived in and were leaving: where takeout coffee was never more than ten minutes away, where he placated her by getting it. She stood. 'We don't have time,' she said, and bent to pick up her suitcase. It was pushing the fifty-pound limit. Last night in the hotel she'd had second thoughts about packing so many shoes, when the island only had one road and nowhere to go on it. But by then it had been too late.

He looked around and seemed to notice what she saw: the line of people edging closer to the dock, fellow passengers standing up, taking the handles of their bags, tucking drink bottles into backpacks. 'How'd you know?' he said, taking the suitcase handle from her, reaching for his own.

'I think it's something you're born with.'

Mike's smile never got any less charming, even though she'd seen it so many times. Sometimes she hated how charming it was, how little effort it took him, how little it cost him. He leaned over and kissed her cheek.

'I'm excited about coming here with you,' he said to her and, hoisting both bags as if they weighed almost nothing, started round the building to the boarding point. Vee grabbed the two cabin bags and her oversized handbag and followed him. The Unity Clipper was white and smaller than she remembered it, with an enclosed passenger cabin and seats on the open fore and aft decks. The morning fog had burned off and sun dazzled on the water. Gulls danced in the air, looking down with stern eyes, hoping for scraps. A man, squat and bald, hauled baggage from the walkway into the hold. She knew he was a Lunt because all the Lunts had always looked like that. He seemed incurious about the tourists, but Vee pushed up her sunglasses and ducked her head anyway. She and Mike left their bags for him and walked onto the ferry.

'Let's go on the bow so we can see everything,' Mike said, and when he took her hand and squeezed it she could feel the edge of his wedding ring against her fingers. It felt smooth and warm. He found them a place near the railing. 'Where's the island?'

'That way.' She pointed east, to the flat water horizon.

He pushed up his sunglasses and squinted into the distance. As the ferry pulled away from the dock, Vee didn't look at where they were going, or back where they'd been. She looked at her husband, who was both of these things.

It was 8.05 in the morning of Tuesday, the eighteenth of August. It was their last chance.

The ferry terminal consisted of a dock on pilings, a rusty crane, and a pitted road leading upwards past mounds of lobster traps. On top of the hill, to the left, the first building anyone ever saw when they came to the island, was Ames' General Store. As the ferry docked Vee noticed the new sign, carved out of wood and painted with gilt capital letters that were one hundred per cent made for visitors, because natives knew that the white clapboard store was Ames' General, and had been for nearly two hundred years. Instinct made her think of cherry vanilla ice cream melting on her tongue, cold ginger ale, Billy Joel on the radio, the flare of a match, the scent of fog, home.

'Where are the waiters bearing champagne and lobster?' Mike asked, and Vee said, 'Let's get one of the kids to put the bags in a truck and we can walk to the house.'

'You know where it is?' Around them, passengers were standing up, turning away from the rail.

'Just grab a kid, tell him the name of the house, and give him a big tip.' In the line for the gangway she found her hat rolled up in her handbag and put it on, pushing her hair up underneath it. 'I'll meet you up near the school.'

'Where's that?'

'You'll see it,' she told him, and slipped through the crowd on the gangway, onto the dock. Her trainers sounded familiar on the boards; her feet knew the way. Head down, she hurried up the road and passed the store without looking at it, its ice machine with the blue words ICE, dripping painted icicles, and its wooden benches and chairs in front next to the green-painted barrels of perennials, the lobster pound built on the side, and the grey-shingled house standing next to it, a little back from the road, which might still have marks on the porch steps from her own careless feet.

She passed the chatting tourists and the empty golf carts, the people who had come to see the ferry arrive because not much else was happening, the enterprising summer kids selling lemonade and cookies on homemade stands. She headed towards the red-painted school with its belfry and white picket fence. Most of the day passengers would wander the town, go to the store, walk towards the beach on the south end. The residents and summer people would disperse to their houses, maybe get a cold drink first at the store, trade some news. She hadn't had a cigarette for ten years, not even when she was teary drunk, but she wanted one now.

At some point since she'd left, the school had been turned into a museum. There was a sign saying UNITY HISTORICAL SOCIETY. Shoulders hunched, she pretended to be reading the noticeboard outside: opening hours, a poster about a lobster boil, a poster about fire risk, a poster about taking your litter with you. She dared to look up. Nobody was watching her. Over the years she'd pictured being back here but she'd never imagined the actual arrival, the smelly ferry, the crowd of summer people and their sun cream, the waiting teenagers, one of which might be his, who knows. She'd thought somehow that the mere touch of her foot on Unity Island soil would cause some sort of earthquake, a reverberation like the engine made under the deck of the ferry, or the way the walls of their flimsy house used to shake during a Nor'easter.

She hadn't thought about how she'd look just like the summer people. How no one would notice: Vivian Gail Harper, back at last, a completely different person.

'Hey,' said Mike, coming up behind her, hands in pockets, sunglasses flashing, smile on his lips. 'This place is adorable. It's so *quiet*. Did you really go to school here, right here in this building?'

'Until sixth form.'

9

'It's like stepping back in time. I can see you with your pigtails and your pinafore.'

'You've just named the two things that I definitely never had.' She looped her arm through Mike's. They *were* summer people. That was her life now. 'Come on, the house is on the east side.'

'I want to rent a golf cart.'

'Next time. We need to stretch our legs.'

He pouted, but not too much. He was still trying to please her, to be pleased with everything. A couple of golf carts passed them, and then the loaded truck with their baggage. It beeped a greeting, and a hand waved from the open driver's window, but Vee couldn't see the face of whoever was driving. She and Mike started walking up the road. There was only one, so it didn't need a name; it was a loop around the perimeter of the island. On Unity, you could only travel in two directions: clockwise, or counterclockwise. Today they were walking against the clock.

'You said you know where the house is?'

'There are only so many. So yeah.' She was sweating, despite the breeze coming off the ocean. The air was never still on the island. Glimpses of silver and blue water flashed between the trees. She wiped her top lip with her wrist. 'This one was built while I was living here. I've never been in it, though, not since it was finished.'

'Really? I'd have thought with so few people living here, everyone would be in and out of each other's houses all the time.'

'The residents don't pay social calls on summer people.' The road rounded a corner and there was the gatepost with the sign: Daybreak. The drive curved out of sight, behind pines. Rich people got privacy. Definitely a perk.

'Finally,' said Mike. 'I need coffee basically pumped into my veins at this point.' He started down the drive, but Vee stayed for a moment looking at the sign. She remembered when it went up, when they'd torn down the old Douglas farmhouse with machinery ferried over from the mainland, and started building.

She and Sterling had sneaked into the site after dark, to watch the progress of the new house. Mr Douglas had moved to a nursing home in Rockland and his son had sold the land to summer people. The new house was only a frame at that point, no outer walls, no inner walls or roof, a skeleton pointing up at the inky sky. It seemed impossibly vast, taking in the whole island, the glittering ocean, the stars.

'I'm going to live in a house like this one day,' Vee had said, climbing up on a pallet of stones.

'What, not finished?' teased Sterling. He was trying to figure out where the bathroom would be, where the lines to the septic tank ran underneath the poured concrete foundation. At this point he was obsessed with plumbing. Vee could only assume it was a boy thing.

'No, finished. With marble floors and silk curtains. But somewhere else. Somewhere far away.'

He'd said something in reply, but Vee didn't remember it. Sterling had always known where he was going to live when he grew up. He'd travel the world and then, once he'd seen everything, he'd come back to the same place he'd been born. He didn't like it when Vee talked about moving away permanently, so he probably hadn't said much. They'd been in total agreement about the name of the new house, though. It was stupid. But most of the rich people house names were stupid: West Wind. Nor'easter. Early Mist. Eagle Point. Dunroamin. Rich people lived in a fantasy world. The houses of the year-round residents were sensibly named for the people who lived there or the purpose of the building. Some of them had signs, like Ames' General; most of them didn't, like Vee's grandfather's place which people called 'Old Harper's'. You didn't need a fancy sign when everyone knew where you lived anyway.

Vee said she wanted a mansion; privately she thought she'd be happy with a house that had a number. A house with a number like lots of other houses. It would be a place to live, not a trap.

'You coming?' Mike called from up the drive.

She'd been staring at the cursive of the sign, blue on white background. 'On my way,' she said, and hurried to catch up with him, so when they emerged from the cover of trees and she saw the house finished for the first time she was holding Mike's hand.

The drive ran up to the back of the house, which was painted grey with white trim around the windows. It was shorter than it had looked from its skeleton: two storeys in a wide V shape, with a steep-pitched roof with dormers. When she was a teen, she'd pictured something like a castle; this looked like a normal, albeit large house. Big, but not intimidating. On either side, she could see that the wide green lawn sloped down to the water.

The truck had been and gone; as if by magic their bags were lined up next to the back door. The bags said, *This place is yours now*.

'Wait till you see inside,' said Mike. 'I'm sort of glad now that you didn't look at any of the photos, because you are going to love this.' He dug in his pocket for the key – a strange thing to see on Unity, where residents never locked their doors.

They stepped inside and Vee saw immediately that the back of the house had not prepared her, the skeleton of the house had not prepared her, her childish dreams had not prepared her. It was light, all light: floor-to-ceiling windows stretched the length of the ocean side of the house, double-storeyed in front of her, with wooden beams soaring. The wooden floors squeaked under her feet, shiny as ice. But the view: green grass, blue sky, blue ocean, stretching out forever, the same view she'd seen a million times but it was completely different when framed by glass and polished wood. The house was merely a shell, a trap for all that outdoors.

Beside her, Mike was vibrating with excitement. He got like this with any new toy, like a kid. He took her hand and breathlessly gave her a tour, announcing each room as if he'd built the house himself rather than merely browsed the brochure and then paid the rent: open-plan living room with its white furniture, rough-hewn fireplace; dining area to seat twelve, an artfully bleached sculpture of driftwood as a centrepiece; kitchen of stainless steel and granite. The bedrooms were in the side wings, single-storeyed, with walls of glass. 'The gym is in an outbuilding,' he told her. 'Steam room and sauna. There's a clay tennis court somewhere, we can work on your serve. And look, come on, we've gotta see this, the best part.' He tugged her outside through a glass door, across a wide patio with Adirondack chairs and a dining area, down the steps and over lawn that had been groomed by someone else.

'It's a private cove and our own dock,' he said, hurrying them onward. On Unity, sometimes the surrounding ocean was a solid grey mass, sometimes a crawling creature, sometimes only a noise of ceaseless breathing. Today it was blue and dazzle, sapphire perfection. She pushed down her sunglasses, squinted her eyes. 'There she is,' said Mike, stopping, with reverence in his voice. He pushed up his own sunglasses. 'That's a beauty.' A white-hulled sailing boat was moored to the private dock, name inscribed in blue cursive to match the house sign: *Dawntreader*.

'Twenty-two-foot sloop,' he said, scanning the boat. 'Handmade just up the coast from here. Perfect for day sails. We can explore all the islands. We'll make a sailor of you yet.'

'I prefer dry land,' she said, watching him, knowing she'd lost his attention for the next half an hour, at least. She checked her watch. 'I'll go and see if there's any coffee.'

'The house should be fully stocked,' he said, but he stepped onto the deck and exclaimed about something, lost in his own world of admiration, so she went back up towards the house. From the back Daybreak had seemed a little awkward, even apologetic, but from the front, the coast side, it sat on its land with spotless authority, wide lawns spread either side, glass shining. This island is mine, said this house, and Vee stopped on the lawn to remind herself too. *This house is mine. Rented, but I earned it. This summer, I live here. I belong here, not the old me but the new one.*

A deep breath of sea air. Yes, she'd earned it. She'd earned everything.

She made herself a coffee from the sleek espresso machine. Perched on a kitchen stool, her arm with the cast resting on the granite island, she leafed through the thick binder with all the house information. She wasn't surprised that their happy-couple togetherness had lasted only until Mike discovered his new toy. Maybe she was even a little relieved. This was a lot to process.

All the pages in the binder were written in a sort of breathless excitement, and they were in plastic sleeves, which told her it had been put together by the agent, not the owner. She skimmed information about the house's features, the heating and lighting controls, the rainwater collection barrels, the island's rules for recycling and trash and fires, and paused at the page headed LOCAL AMENITIES.

Ames' General Store is the only food store on Unity Island, though you can buy local lobsters and clams directly from boats, and eggs from Howards' Farm. In addition to groceries, Ames' functions as the island's post office, transport hub (you can rent golf carts and bicycles and arrange a dinghy ride to moorings), delivery service, hardware store, fishing and boating supply store, bakery, lunch counter and ice-cream parlour. Most importantly, it's the place where all the locals meet to talk and trade news, especially in the winter months, when the island population shrinks to less than 60. Ames' was founded by Robert Sterling Ames in 1820, the same year that Maine became a state, and the building has

'Hey, where's my coffee?' Mike's arms wrapped around her from behind.

'I didn't make you one because I thought it would go cold.' She quickly shut the binder, hiding the names.

'That's all right,' he said, kissing her cheek. 'Let's see what else we have around here.' He went to the huge stainless-steel refrigerator. 'Ah,' he said, emerging with a bottle of Moët. 'Even better.'

'It's not even noon.'

'And we're officially on holiday.' He unwrapped the foil, and Vee got up to look for glasses. She heard the pop behind her, the shout of laughter as the champagne foamed out of the bottle and down Mike's arm. She hurried over to hold out a glass, catch the flow. It dripped onto her fingers.

'To us,' Mike said. He licked his arm, and held up his glass. 'New beginnings. A second honeymoon.'

'New beginnings,' she echoed, chimed her glass with his.

'Let's find a bedroom, Mrs Ellis.' He looped an arm around her waist, pulled her closer, nuzzled her neck.

'Nobody calls me that except for salesmen. Even they don't say it twice.'

'Mrs Ellis,' he crooned, kissing her under her ear. 'Let's bring this champagne to bed.'

When she woke up, the light had changed. The water outside was navy rather than sapphire. She lay there watching the dip and swoop of gulls outside the window. Mike was still asleep. Their clothes were on the floor. She pulled on his shirt, rolling up the sleeves, and brought the empty bottle into the kitchen. Her muscles felt pleasantly achy, her chin pink, her hair tangled. A champagne headache lingered behind her eyes, but it was fuzzy, benevolent. She drank a glass of water, checked her phone for the time, thought about getting dressed, remembered their suitcases were outside by the back door. When she opened it, next to the suitcases were two cardboard boxes, plus a large cooler and a small one. A note sat on top of the cooler, held down with a rock. She glanced around, saw no one, picked up the note.

Hi, welcome to the island! I knocked but there was no answer and I didn't want to disturb you. If you need anything else just come by, or give us a call.

She didn't recognise the handwriting – it was a fluid scrawl, big capitals and curly slanting 'I's that looked like 'J's, written in pencil on a torn-out lined notebook page. Not Sterling's print, not his mother's Palmer-method. Nothing like her own. Not Unity Island handwriting, learned from the letter cards that circled the one-room schoolroom. It was probably summer help. Maybe the store had changed hands. Maybe nothing was what she expected it to be any more. She opened the big cooler and saw milk, orange juice, lettuce, butter. The small one held two live lobsters. They clambered over each other, their brown claws held shut with blue elastic bands. Their eyes were small black beads, reflecting nothing.

Chapter Two

Sterling

He met his mother at the midday ferry. As usual, she was the last one off. Arnie Lunt helped her across the gangplank and she was leaning on him quite a bit, which told Sterling that today wasn't one of her good days.

'You should've rested at home,' he said, kissing her cheek when she transferred from Arnie's arm to his.

'Oh, I'm fine. I just don't have my sea legs any more.' Sterling took her big quilted handbag, and Brenda accepted her cane from Arnie, thanking him and saying, 'I've got homemade cookies in that bag, so come on up to the store when you've finished here and have a couple.'

'Do you want me to get a cart for you?' Sterling asked.

'Don't be ridiculous, it's only a few steps.' But they took those steps slowly, as Brenda told him about the people she'd spoken to on the ferry: the Collinses, the Coopers, the Kuhns. Sterling half-listened, thinking about how much frailer she seemed this summer than last. They didn't talk about it, though. It was as unspoken as the resemblance between them: same grey eyes, same short-palmed hands, long legs, thick unruly hair, his brown and hers silver. He'd started finding silver strands in his own hair, in the mornings in the mirror.

She greeted every single person they passed, and told them to come and get some cookies. From the weight of her bag, she'd baked several dozen.

'Do you want to go up to the house?' he asked her.

'I think I'll sit here in front of the store for a little while, and then come up and visit with Rachel.' He helped her to one of the green-painted Adirondack chairs in front of Ames', and noticed the sigh of relief as she sat.

'So,' she said, patting the chair next to hers. 'Tell me the news.'

He didn't sit. 'It's pretty busy right now.'

'That summer kid can handle it while you talk to your mother.'

He glanced at the store, which wasn't too crowded. 'Well. There is one piece of news. I'm not sure what to make of it.'

'Is it about the Showalters and their new grandson? I asked them to make sure to tell you when they were coming, so I could come over and meet the baby. I need that new baby smell in my life.'

'I'll get you a cold drink,' he said, and left her there while he went into the store. He breathed deeply as he filled a cup with ice and lemonade from the big glass jar near the coffee stand.

When he came back, she said, 'I'm sorry, Sterling. Sometimes I forget. I never mean anything by it.'

'It's okay,' he said, as he always did. 'I guess I'll have one of those cookies.'

As suspected, she pulled out a huge plastic bag of homemade cookies from her handbag. She gave him two, and he sat beside her.

'How's Rachel?' she asked.

'She's fine.' He kept his face pleasant, because there was no point in going into it. Sometimes he didn't understand Rachel at all. It was if she lived in an entirely different world than anyone else – still did, even after a couple of years on Unity. 'She's covering the store and says she'll meet you at the house in a little while.'

'What's the big news you were talking about?'

'Jacob thinks he saw Vee this morning.'

The expression on his mother's face was unalloyed delight, and that irritated Sterling as much as her talk about babies. Even more, because it wasn't what he expected. Why couldn't she understand his point of view? The *obvious* point of view?

'She's back?' his mother said.

'The guy she was with told Jacob that they were at Daybreak, but he didn't get a really good look at her. He thought it was her, though. It looked like she had her arm in a sling.'

'Daybreak.' She raised her eyebrows. 'If that's her, she's done well for herself.'

'Why would she come back now?'

'This is a wild guess, but maybe she's … on holiday?'

'Mum. I thought you'd understand. Rachel doesn't have a clue. I told her and she shrugged.'

'You know I always felt you were too hard on Vee, Sterling. You could have let bygones be bygones years ago.'

'She never gave me a chance. She never called, never wrote. It's not like I've gone anywhere. She knew where to find me. And if she's here now, why wouldn't she come straight to the store?'

'This has really ruffled your feathers, hasn't it?'

He'd broken one of the cookies in half, and chocolate chips and crumbs were all over his lap. 'I'm not ruffled, I just don't know what she's up to. I don't have feathers.'

She reached over, tousled his hair. 'Would it be so bad if you saw her again?'

'Mum, you remember what she did. How she left. *When* she left.'

'Yes, but you used to be so close and there's so much water under the bridge.'

'That's exactly the attitude that got me in trouble in the first place. I used to forgive her for everything.'

'Well, a lot can change.'

'I don't think anything has changed. You can't betray someone like that and then *change*.' He swept the crumbs into his palm and tipped them into his mouth. 'You're too nice to everyone.'

'That's the reason I've got so many friends. Face it, you love me for it.'

'That's not the only reason,' he said, standing up. He pointed to Arnie Lunt, who was making a beeline for Brenda, along with Wendy Howard. 'I need to give P.J. his break. Are you okay to stay here for a little bit?'

'Of course. I'll catch up on everything.'

She'd learn even more than he had about Vee Harper, he thought, as he went back inside. His mother and her homilies. It drove him crazy, always dancing on the surface of everything, always pretending that everything was fine, that life was a sugared pastry, that it could all be solved with cookies. She literally never saw the bad in anyone: you could show her a documentary about a serial killer and she would bemoan the poor monster's unhappy childhood. Not that she would ever watch anything like that; she hated anything 'nasty' on television. She thought *Saturday Night Live* was a little too mean. The evening news caused an hour-long wince.

And then there was Rachel.

The shop had a few customers, people from off the ferry buying picnic supplies or sun cream. He greeted them all as he walked by, spent a few minutes talking about the weather with Marjorie Woodford, who was picking up her mail (islanders could talk forever about the weather; they had a saying that if you didn't like it, all you had to do was wait a minute, and everyone always laughed as if that were the first time they'd heard it), told a couple who was looking at the 'Made on the Island' display that he had a few more hand-stitched pot holders in the back, if they didn't see a pattern they liked. Islanders were said to be standoffish, even more so than Maine people in general, who were never known for effusiveness. But his father had taught him this: if a person walks into your store, that person, within your own four walls, is your family.

The wooden floor creaked in its familiar spot. P.J., his summer hire kid, was behind the till, feet up on the shelf, scrolling his phone. Family or not, sometimes he wished he'd never shared the wifi code. 'Where's Rachel?' he asked, and P.J. took his feet off the shelf and put his phone in his pocket, having the good grace to look ashamed.

'She said she was going to take the orders in the truck.'

So much for finding out if Vee was on the island. One of those orders was for Daybreak, and he'd planned on getting a good look while he was dropping it off. Now he'd have to wait until she was more reliably spotted or until she walked into his store. Would she have the audacity to do that? Probably – one thing you could say about Vee Harper, she had balls.

He didn't know what he would do if she walked in. How he would treat her, what he would say. Whatever his mother thought, Vee was the one person in the world, including strangers, who had forfeited the right to be treated as family within his own four walls.

Anyway, there was no use thinking about that now. If it happened, it happened. He'd deal with it.

'Go ahead and take your break,' he said to P.J., and took his abandoned seat. It was the same wooden chair that had sat behind the till for as long as Sterling could remember. The seat was cracked green leather. 'You were born for this chair,' his father had told him when he was younger than P.J. was now, when he was just a little kid, standing on the leather seat and stacking up all his pennies so he could pretend to sell Swedish fish to himself, one by one. His father always let him put his pennies back in his pocket even though he'd eaten all the candy fish.

Walter Beotte came in the door and before he'd even made it all the way inside Sterling had his can of Skoal out for him on the counter. 'Not a bad day for it,' Walter said, handing over a bill with fingers stubbed and scarred from a lifetime of lobstering. He spoke with his lips tight together, either because his face was carved that way, in harsh lines, or maybe to hide his tobacco-stained teeth, though he was devoid of vanity in all other ways.

'Wind going to pick up later?' Sterling punched 'sale' and gave him his change.

'You know it. Drop by sundown, though.'

'Fog tomorrow morning.'

'Ayuh.'

'You know what they say.'

'Ayuh.'

Walter left and Sterling sat back down in his chair. Walter looked older than Sterling, because of weather and water, but he'd only been in the class above Sterling and Vee in the Unity school, and Rockport Junior/Senior High on the mainland. He'd dropped out as soon as he legally could, at sixteen, to work. Why would he waste time in a classroom when he could be making a living on a boat? In the Unity school Walter had been good-natured, failing tests with a shrug; on the mainland he'd been sullen, hunched into his flannel shirt and baseball cap, dipping out of class to chew tobacco and spit in the parking lot.

Sterling's memories of Walter's father were also of stained teeth and tough skin. He remembered his funeral. Sterling's parents had gone, along with everyone else on the island, to the mainland to pay their respects at St Joseph's Church. Even as a child, he'd thought it was strange that they had to go so far when everyone knew that the Beottes hated the mainland, ran their boat off Unity, shopped at Ames', didn't talk to summer people, unloaded their traps at the co-op as quick as they could so they could get back home. But there was no longer a church on Unity and almost no one was buried on the island any more. The little cemetery had filled up generations ago.

Sterling's own father had been cremated, and his ashes released off the south side of the island, blown out over the water. It was months after his death; they'd waited for a sunny day in autumn. His mother had worn a silk scarf over her hair. But the

Beottes were Catholic, or Catholic enough that even though they eschewed mass, confirmation and confession, they suffered that final trip to the mainland to church and cemetery. Whereas Sterling knew that his ashes would be released here, just as his father's had been before him.

He settled back in the chair, feet resting on the same shelf that P.J. had used for scrolling. *A lot can change*, his mother had said, but he'd never seen any evidence of that. Nothing changed here but the weather, and even that rolled around the same.

Chapter Three

Rachel

She heard the tyre go before she felt the steering wheel jerk in her hands, sharp to the left as if a ghost had tugged it. Carefully she pulled the truck over to the side of the rutted dirt road, though there wasn't much point; she wasn't exactly going to be in anyone's way. She turned the key in the ignition and sighed.

At least she'd finished all her deliveries, so no one would be waiting and nothing would go bad in the back. She could leave the truck and walk home. Sterling would come and get it, or he'd send someone to do it.

But she'd grabbed the truck keys from the hook next to the till because she needed to get away from the store, away from her house, away from everyone. It was an instinct and a habit from Illinois, where a driver's licence meant freedom, where you could climb in your car and drive and drive and drive without a destination, just for the feeling of the road under your wheels, the music on the radio and the miles mounting up between you and what waited for you at home.

It wasn't the same here. Under her wheels the road bumped and spat. There was only one road and it was made out of rocks and dirt and holes. There was no point paving it for two trucks and a few golf carts and bicycles, and it heaved in the winter and washed out in the spring. And there was nowhere to go but in a circle.

Rachel got out of the truck and inspected the front left tyre.

Flat as a pancake. The sun beat down on her bare shoulders, and her stomach rumbled. She'd skipped lunch. She could be home in ten minutes and back in ten more with a sandwich, sunscreen and her husband.

Then she remembered why she was here. She'd been sitting in Sterling's chair at the till while Sterling met his mom, snatching a few minutes between customers to read her latest book, a biography of Eleanor Roosevelt. Marjorie Woodford sidled up to the counter, so quietly that Rachel didn't hear the old lady until she was right in front of her. 'My,' she said, 'look at you. You've always got your nose in some book or other.'

'I'm a historian,' Rachel said, putting her finger between the pages to keep her place.

'A historian, oh yes, of course. They say you know every single fact there is to know about the island, even the ones that most people want to forget. It must be all that reading.'

'What can I do for you, Mrs Woodford?'

'I've just come for my mail, but I'll get a few things first. Don't let me interrupt you, I'm just another customer.' A light tinkle of a laugh, a nice old lady. 'You won't have so much time to read when you've got a baby or two to take care of.'

Her hands went cold. 'I'll always like reading.'

'That's what you say now, but everything changes when you become a mummy. Your time's no longer your own. You can't be selfish even if you want to.' She cocked her head. 'I bet Brenda's getting impatient now. That woman was born to be a grandma, but she and Tom only had the one boy. How long since you've been married?'

'Excuse me,' she'd said, standing, putting her book down, reaching for the truck keys, 'I've got to do the grocery delivery. P.J. – can you finish up here please?'

And now here she was, stuck on the road less than half a mile from the store and even closer to Marjorie Woodford's house. Some escape.

The jack was behind the passenger seat, wrapped in sacking. She had to get up into the bed of the truck to unbolt the spare. She rolled it out and it bounced on the ground before travelling a little distance on the road and falling to its side.

'I know how you feel,' she told it. She jumped out after it, lugged it up to the front of the truck, and got to work placing the jack.

She'd done this once, before she was married, but it was on her old Camry, not on the truck, which was a lot bigger. And the ground was uneven. Working the foot jack made sweat spring out between her breasts and under her arms. She wiped her lip with her forearm and kept working. The truck rose by fractions of inches.

'Do you need some help with that?'

It was an older man, in his late fifties or early sixties. He had perfect silver-grey hair, a tan, khaki shorts, boat shoes. The sort of guy you'd call a 'silver fox'. She'd been on Unity long enough to recognise a summer person even from a distance. It was more than their clothes and jewellery and accents: they all had some sort of clarity, some polish, that Unity natives never did, even in their Sunday best. Even if every person on the island during midsummer swapped clothes, you'd be able to tell. Of course, Rachel would still stick out from either group like a sore thumb, even in a summer person's clothes. Her face, her hair, her accent, her chewed nails, the way she said 'wait on line' and 'cold pop' and made a mess of every lobster she ate and didn't know the second verses of any Christmas carols.

'Thanks,' she said, 'but I'm fine.'

'Are you sure? It's a big truck and you're a little lady.'

He probably meant 'little' as a compliment, but she bristled. 'I'm fine. It's my truck, and I've done it before. It'll only take me a couple of minutes.'

It had already taken her at least fifteen. The summer person hesitated.

'Well, if you're certain,' he said. 'I don't want to be a chauvinist pig, but I don't want to leave you to it, either.'

'I'm sure.'

'I'm only over there if you need some help.' He gestured to the big house down the road, one of the older ones, rambling, with a wrap-around porch and lilies planted around it. The type that had belonged to generations of summer people. The sun was behind it; she had to squint, because of course she'd forgotten her sunglasses too. 'Or if you're thirsty,' he added, 'my husband makes a wonderful sun tea with mint from the garden.'

She thought about the rules she'd gleaned about summer people. None of them were said out loud, of course, but they informed every interaction between the people who lived here and the people who came here for pleasure. If you lived here, you served the summer people. You sold them what they needed, you cleaned and repaired their houses, you caught their lobsters, you cooked their meals, you took them for rides on your boat. You were polite to them, even friendly. You made them feel welcome, because the income of the whole island depended on them. But you didn't make the mistake of thinking that they were your friends.

She imagined showing up and knocking on the back door, covered in sweat and dust, leaving finger smears on the iced tea glass handed to her by a gentleman equally as impeccable as this one, making conversation restrained by the necessity of having no opinions. 'Thanks,' she said, and waited until he'd strolled off before she turned back to the truck. Hair had fallen into her face; she twisted it up and shoved it into a thick ponytail, though springy strands escaped almost immediately and stuck to her face.

Once she got the truck up on the jack, she wiped her forehead and began wrestling with the wheel nuts. The first one came off pretty easily, making her smile with achievement, but the second one was stuck. Who knew the last time these nuts had been taken off? It wasn't one of Sterling's priorities to rotate the tyres on a truck that only drove a few miles a day. Rachel strained at the wrench, put her weight on it. This spot was sheltered from the wind by trees, and a cloud of tiny black flies hovered around her bare shoulders, neck and face. With both hands busy, she could only toss her head to dispel them, but they kept coming back. She'd seen a t-shirt on a tourist once: STATE BIRD OF MAINE, it had said, over a drawing of a giant black fly. She wished for a hat, a can of insect repellent and a cold bottle of water.

Before she'd come to Maine she'd never known that there were so many insects. They'd had spiders in Highland Park, and flies, and mosquitoes, and grasshoppers outside, and glistening dragonflies in summer. But not swarms of little biting bugs that followed you everywhere in spring and early summer, and got in your hair and your eyes and got caught in your clothes. People who'd grown up here on the island just ignored the bugs, treated them like a minor inconvenience like the way the electricity went out during storms, or all the times that the ferry got cancelled, or the lumps of dirty snow that lingered on lawns all through spring, or the way you couldn't use the beach during peak season because there were too many visitors.

Still: at least she wasn't listening to Marjorie 'Nosy' Woodford. She squeezed her eyes tight shut and pushed harder.

'Hey,' said a voice near her ear, and she jumped and lost her grip on the wrench, which fell to the ground with a clang, narrowly missing her toes. It was Jacob Farmer in his summer uniform of baseball cap, Red Sox t-shirt, worn jeans and work boots. Jacob had no job and every job: he was unofficial handyman and caretaker for most of the summer houses, which meant he always had dirty hands and the latest model of iPhone in his back pocket. 'Sterling said to come out here and help you change a tyre.'

She wiped her dirty hands on her shorts. 'How did Sterling

know?' she asked, but it was a stupid question. Everyone knew everything here.

'Fellow yonder called the store.' Jacob hitched his thumb at the big summer house that belonged to the silver fox. 'Sterling didn't have a minute, so I said I'd walk over. Said I thought it was looking flat earlier when I drove the bags. Budge up, I'll get her changed.'

She stooped and picked up the wrench. 'There's no need, Jacob. I'm fine.'

He didn't seem to have heard her. 'You see Vee Harper when you took the groceries over to Daybreak?'

'I don't know who that is.' She got back to work on the nut.

'Vee and Sterling used to be thick as thieves. Don't think they ever went anywhere without each other. She practically lived at Ames'. We all thought they'd get married someday, but then she lit out. Never saw her again until today when she got off the ferry. If that was her. She looked different, and I was real surprised to see her. Looked like she'd broken her arm.'

'I'm not really interested in my husband's old girlfriends.'

'Not a girlfriend really. She was always in a mess of trouble, and Sterling always got her out of it. I said I'd handle the tyre for you.'

'And I said I can handle it, thanks.'

He stayed right where he was. 'You see her when you went over to Daybreak?'

She had the sensation of going in circles. 'No, I knocked and no one answered the door, so I left the groceries in the shade with a note.' She straightened up. 'Jacob, please let me change this tyre. I'm almost done.'

'It's no problem, Sterling asked me to do it.'

'And I'm asking you to let *me* do it?'

He shrugged and put his hands in his pockets. 'Your funeral. You want me to get Brenda to send your supper out here?'

'I'm not useless!'

She realised she'd shouted it. Her hand gripped the wrench. Jacob shrugged again. 'Just trying to help.'

Rachel waited until he'd walked off before she bent over the wheel again.

After an early dinner, Sterling walked Brenda down to the dock to get the evening ferry. Rachel read her book on the sofa with a glass of wine. Her shoulders ached from straining at the wrench. The small of her back ached, too, though that was for a different reason. It was the middle of the month; after more than two years of counting dates and marking calendars and evaluating mucus, she didn't need an app to know she was ovulating. Tomorrow or the next day a pimple would erupt on her chin or her lip; next week she would cramp and bleed. Rachel's useless reproductive system was as predictable and cyclical as Unity Island.

Last year, she would have drawn a star on the *DownEast* calendar that hung on the back of the pantry door, and Sterling wouldn't have invited his mom. They'd have opened a couple of beers or a bottle of wine, planned a dinner that didn't need to be cooked or that could be eaten in bed or afterwards, standing at the kitchen worktop in their bathrobes, hungry and laughing and eating toast or leftover chicken. A couple of nights every month. At first it was a romantic ritual, a little holiday in their normal life. Then it got to be ... not an obligation, but a habit. A rule. She cooked beforehand so they'd have something to eat. She shaved her legs, put polish on her toenails.

Then they made appointments with the doctor. She had tests. She had surgery. Nothing helped.

Tonight she turned the page of her book. Reached for her wine glass; realised it was empty.

The back door opened when she was in the kitchen opening the refrigerator. Sterling came in with a gallon of milk.

'Your mom get off okay?'

'Yeah. Her hip's been bothering her though. She had a nice

chat with everyone waiting for the ferry.' He stood behind her to put the milk in the fridge as she took out the wine bottle. It was the closest they'd stood to each other all day, she thought. Usually they were squeezing past each other in the store but she'd been gone for most of the afternoon. Sterling smelled like he'd always done, for as long as she'd known him: shampoo, fresh air, something not quite woody and not quite musty, which she knew now was the scent of Ames' General. Essence of bags of flour on the shelves, floorboards underfoot, boxes of lettuce, his creaking leather chair. She probably smelled of it too. Though weren't you supposed to stop noticing a smell if it was your own? Some primitive trick of the brain that kept creatures from being startled by themselves, told them that they were safe.

She thought about leaning back, resting her head on his chest. But he stepped away before she made up her mind to.

She closed the fridge. 'Want some?' she asked him, holding up the wine bottle, which had just enough left in it to share. He shook his head.

'Why wouldn't you let Jacob help you with the truck?' he asked, and she saw the subtle firmness of his mouth: he was angry, or as angry as Sterling ever let himself show. Or maybe he was ashamed. From long habit and self-preservation, Rachel was good at reading other people's moods, but Sterling was not an aggressive man and, on him, the expressions were hard to tell apart. Possibly they were the same.

'I didn't need his help because I did it myself.'

'They were laughing about it down at the dock.'

'Why? Is the idea of a woman changing a tyre so funny?' She refilled her glass of wine, and kept pouring till the bottle was empty. Then she took a gulp. She rarely had more than two glasses but there wasn't any rule about what size those glasses could be. 'Surely the concept of feminism has reached even this far down-east by now.'

'It's not because you're a woman. Nobody cares that you're a woman.'

I thought you used to care. The thought surprised her as much as the way she'd raised her voice at Jacob earlier.

'What's the problem then?' she asked. 'I got a flat and I changed it.'

'It took you hours. Jacob could've done it in five minutes.'

'Did you need me at the store?'

'No.'

'Then what's the big deal?'

'You're always saying that you want to belong here, that you want to fit in. But you don't understand anything about this community at all. It's been years, Rachel, and you don't even try. It's hurtful.'

Carefully, she put her wine glass down. 'I don't know what there is to understand. Is there some rule on this island that only Jacob is allowed to fix the truck?'

'Are you being intentionally provocative?'

Her hands were shaking. She was fighting an overwhelming impulse to flee, to hide, not to have this conversation, to smooth it all over, make everything okay. 'I don't know what to apologise for, Sterling. I have no idea what I've done wrong.'

'I've explained it to you over and over. I explained it to you before you even came here, when we first met.'

'I don't want to argue, but I have no idea what you're talking about, so I guess you're going to have to explain it again.'

He took a deep breath. 'We stick together on this island. If you live here year-round, you're not by yourself. You're part of a community. Especially if you run the store. It's not like the city; none of us could live without each other. You've spent a couple of winters here, you know what it's like. We need each other. We help each other. It's at the heart of everything.'

'But I didn't need anyone to help me.'

'That's not the point, Rachel. If someone offers you help on Unity, you take it. You don't let pride get in your way.'

'It wasn't pride. I just wanted to do it by myself.'

'You were out there in the sun for hours. You said no to everyone who tried. You've got sunburnt, you didn't have lunch, you wouldn't even take a drink. What else is it except for pride?'

'And where was your pride when people were talking about me and then laughing at me for doing something as simple as changing a tyre? Did you defend me?'

'Of course I did.'

But she knew Sterling. She knew how Unity ran in his blood for as far back as anyone could remember. He'd been born here, educated here, grown up here. So had been his parents, and his parents' parents. He would die here, and then that would be the end. He'd defended her, but only so far, because how could you defend your wife against everything that made you who you were?

'Thanks,' she said. 'Okay.' She didn't have the energy to fight any more, or to flee. To be truthful, she had no idea how this had turned into a fight in the first place. She pulled out a kitchen chair and sat in front of her glass of wine, which she didn't want either.

'Just ... would you accept some help next time? Even if you don't feel that you need it?'

'Sure.'

'People like to help. It makes them feel good. Listen, I know you've had to look out for yourself for most of your life, Rachel. I get it. But you're here now, and we can look out for you.'

And when he said it that way, so reasonable, so calm, she did feel foolish. 'Okay.'

He sighed. 'Now I wish I'd said yes to that glass of wine.'

'You can have mine.' She stood up. 'I'm going to bed.'

'Okay. I'll be up in a little while. I've got some paperwork.'

She hugged him and he hugged her back. She'd promised this to herself, long before she'd met Sterling: that when she got married, she would never go to bed angry. She wouldn't let resentment simmer. She would compromise if she needed to. She'd seen all her life what happened when you let bad things fester, unsaid.

It was harder than she'd anticipated, to smooth over cracks between them that were so fundamental to who each of them was that they didn't ever seem to get filled. But maybe that was the work of marriage: to keep on trying.

'I love you,' she told him, because that was the truth and it usually made things better.

'I love you too,' he said. He kissed her forehead and gave her an extra squeeze. From the minute she'd met him, his hugs made her feel safe. 'I'll come up in a few minutes,' he said. He let her go and picked up her glass of wine, taking a sip.

She waited a minute, wanting something more. An apology? Not really, not quite, because had he done anything wrong? Maybe she wanted an acknowledgement that she hadn't done anything wrong either. A confirmation that he had to reach, and change, and keep on trying too.

But he didn't say anything. So she went up to bed by herself.

Chapter Four

Sterling

This was his parents' kitchen, and his grandparents' before that. When Sterling proposed to Rachel, his mom had told him that she would move into an apartment on the mainland and they could have the house near the store. Property on Unity was too expensive for them to buy a new house there. He'd protested. 'This is your home,' he'd told his mom. 'We'll live in the apartment above the store, like you and Dad did when you were first married. Or you can live with us, in the house.'

She had told him all the reasons that he already knew: her arthritis was getting worse and it was safer if she lived in a ground-floor apartment near health care; he and Rachel would need the space for when they had children; if he was running the store all day he should have at least a little space away from it when he came home at night; Rachel should be able to make a place her own and that would be harder if Brenda was living with them; and overall, it was family tradition that the person who ran the store lived in the house. It was what his father would have wanted.

All of this made sense. What didn't make sense was Sterling's feeling of loss, his gut-level fear. If his mother wasn't in her house any more, it was his. His father was gone, and his mother had moved. He was the grown-up now. This was his house. It was all his responsibility and it would be forever, until his own child took over.

But to Sterling, this was his parents' kitchen. A lifetime of meals, childhood tantrums, skinned knees treated at this sink in between his mother baking and washing the dishes. He'd had his first sip of beer here, sneaked out of his dad's glass when Dad went to the bathroom. He'd listened to a million adult conversations in this room, probably a lot of things he wasn't supposed to hear in the first place. Rachel had painted the cupboards and got a new fruit bowl and tablecloth, but the bones and the guts of the place were the same. He could find anything in this room – in this whole house – with his eyes closed and his ears stopped up. The past was always layered over the present.

He'd never heard his parents argue in this room. He'd never heard them argue at all. They didn't always agree, nobody did, but there weren't any arguments, just respectful discussions. He never recalled his paternal grandparents having a cross word, either, though his mother's parents in Rockland used to grump at each other.

After Rachel went upstairs, he sat at the kitchen table and had a long drink of the wine she'd left. *Did you defend me?* she'd asked. It was a good question. And he'd answered *Of course.* But had he?

Sterling, your wife do all the car repairs around here now?

Sterling, I've got a problem with my boat engine, think you could send Rachel over to have a look?

Hey, Sterling, Rachel gonna open her own body shop? Think we could use one of those.

'She likes doing things for herself,' he'd said. Mildly. He said everything mildly. It was another thing his father had taught him. If you showed your feelings too much, it just caused a big mess. It was wiser to keep them to yourself, just like it was wiser to keep quiet about your politics and your religion. And conversation moved on to something else – Vee Harper, mostly – so at the time he'd thought that was enough.

But was it? Did being a grown-up require more than just smoothing it over? What would his dad have done?

It wouldn't have come up, he thought. His mom understood the island, and that was that. She would've taken the help and praised everyone for giving it. She would have told everyone how kind Jacob was to interrupt his lunch to walk over and help her. She wouldn't have got sunburnt and probably risked heat stroke to change a stupid tyre. But if she had... his dad would have defended her. Then they would have sat here in this kitchen and discussed it, and actually got somewhere. They wouldn't have stood here staring at each other, baffled by their inability to communicate at all.

Sterling leaned his head in his hands. He should go up there and get into bed with Rachel, spoon up against her, bury his face in her curls. She'd nudge back up against him. He should go to sleep with his arms around her. That would make her feel better.

But he didn't want to go to bed. He wanted to jump into the shocking-cold surf. He wanted to teleport to the mainland, go into a bar or somewhere that no one knew his name. He wanted to do something with this energy that was battering away inside of him. Push it out. Give it a name. Use words that were neither mild nor wise.

He wasn't going to do that. That wasn't a path that was available to him.

His laptop was on the table already, from answering emails over breakfast. He opened it up and clicked on the search engine. Eyes on the screen, he reached for the wine and took a drink. There were two names he'd avoided searching for years: one out of duty, and one out of anger.

He put down the glass and typed in the second one. *Vivian Harper*. And pressed 'search'.

Chapter Five

Vee

Aside from the ocean, the weather, the scent of the water and the pine trees and the sound of arguing gulls, she wouldn't have known she was on Unity at all. In fact, if she put in a little effort, she could pretend she was on another Maine island, or maybe off the coast of Massachusetts, Canada or Norway. Daybreak was a world of its own. It had gates, a private dock, a tiny private beach that was sandy at low tide. It had a tennis court, an outbuilding with a gym, a garage with bicycles and a golf cart and sports equipment, a media room with a projector and built-in surround sound. It had two generators, plenty of stored rainwater, a septic tank built for twenty people, a wine cellar, three chest freezers. The sailing boat meant that they had their own crossing, if they needed it, without having to use the ferry. It was an island within an island.

It even came with its own social life, because of Mike, of course. Their third morning, he was up at what seemed like the crack of dawn, singing in the shower, getting dressed in that I'm-being-just-quiet-enough-to-make-it-seem-like-I'm-trying-not-to-wake-you-but-really-I-want-you-to-wake-up shuffle that she knew extremely well. She rolled over. 'Where are you going? Making me breakfast in bed?'

'I was going to take the *Dawntreader* out for a little sail. Want to come?'

'Sailing sounds like a lot of hard work before I've even had coffee.'

'There's a coffee-maker on board.'

She closed her eyes again. 'I didn't get a lot of sleep. I'll come later, if you can wait.'

He didn't reply, so she peeked at him. He was biting his lip, hesitating. She knew exactly what was going through his head: torn between desire and duty. They'd come here to save their marriage. Spend more time together, find more things in common. Which meant either he had to give up on a morning's sailing, or she had to force herself to go with him and spend the morning feeling useless and bored. Even when she had two working arms, on a boat her hands became spades, her head a magnet for the swinging boom. Her knots fell apart with the smallest tug.

'It's okay,' she said. 'I'll have a lazy morning and put something nice together for lunch. We can eat on the patio.'

He leaned over and kissed her forehead. 'You need the rest,' he said happily. 'Just let all that stress fall away, and relax. I'll see you later, darling.'

That had been two days ago. Now, permission given, he didn't bother to invite her, and she didn't bother to acknowledge that he'd woken her up. She stayed in bed till he was gone and then got up, made herself coffee, and went back to bed to read. It was what she normally did at weekends at home in New York anyway. And most weekdays, too, before her yoga or Pilates class, while Mike met friends for tennis or squash or golf. Here, she worked on reading a 900-page novel that had won lots of awards and which she had been meaning to get to. She couldn't remember who any of the characters were or why she was supposed to care about them so she kept losing the thread and putting the book down to look out the window.

Maybe this was relaxing, but she felt untethered. All she could think about was being on Unity, and how easy it was to ignore that she was on Unity, and whether she should be ignoring that she was on Unity.

She was flicking back through the doorstop novel to try to

work out whether a character who had just appeared in chapter twelve had previously been part of the plot, when her phone rang. It hadn't rung since they'd arrived; not even her mother had called her, though she had sent a text saying *Call me when you've had enough of your second honeymoon.*

She snatched it up. Mike.

'Are you okay?'

He was on the water; she could barely hear his voice above the wind. 'Great! Listen I just met some people, a couple from South Carolina, they've sailed up here on a gorgeous ketch, hand-built. They're anchored on the other side of the island, visiting friends who have a house there, so I invited them all over later this afternoon for drinks. What do you think? Meet the neighbours?'

I think you are tired of me already, thought Vee.

'Is it a summer house?' she asked. 'This house on the west side?'

'God yes I'd think so, they said they were up from Texas. That is, I haven't met them, but George said something about Dallas. I said five o'clock, and I talked up your clam dip. Completely authentic recipe! They said they wouldn't miss it for the world. Could you put a bottle of Grey Goose in the freezer? We've got olives, yes?'

'Clam dip?'

'Yes, that one you make. I'll be back before then, promise. Vee?'

'Yeah?'

'This is all right, isn't it? I can put them off if you're stressed.'

This was new: asking her for permission.

'No, it's fine. I can make clam dip and small talk.'

'Beautiful.' She could hear the smile in his voice. It was give and take, right? They had to try to make each other happy.

Clam dip, or the clam dip that her grandfather had taught her how to make in their small kitchen, leaking cigarette smoke and burned grease like an ill-built dinghy, had three ingredients in it: canned clams, Worcestershire sauce, and cream cheese. 'You can put some Tabasco in it if you want to be fancy,' Pops told her, but Pops was never fancy, so Vee never tried it. Clam dip was a treat, and you always used canned clams, which were more expensive. Fresh clams were free, if you wanted to put in the work getting up early and digging at low tide. You put them in a bucket, carried them home, scrubbed them, soaked them with corn meal so they'd spit out the grit, slowly, over hours. Then scrubbed them again, steamed them open, picked out the meat, removed the dirty grey membrane over the neck, rinsed them in the strained clam broth, dipped them in butter if you had butter in the house. Fresh clams were rich people food that poor people could eat any time they wanted.

You didn't go through all that work to eat clam dip on ruffled chips in front of the TV. Pops always used Bumblebee clams. They had a little note on the label, almost too tiny to see: Distributed in California.

Vee searched through the kitchen for the ingredients. The cupboards had been well stocked before they arrived; evidently it was part of the rental service to have a wide selection of gourmet ingredients on hand. The initial delivery from the store, the one with the anonymous note, had carried them through up till now, and Vee planned to top it up by sending Mike on errands to the mainland on the boat, or getting him to call through orders to be delivered from Ames'. She rummaged through giant Israeli couscous, dried porcini mushrooms, ancho chilli powder, rosemary flatbreads. They had potato chips – hand-cut, small batch-fried, flavoured with sea salt. The Worcestershire sauce had the same orange label she remembered from childhood and adult Bloody Marys. Maybe there was only one kind. The cream cheese in the fridge was mostly intact except for a dollop, which Mike presumably had used on a bagel.

There were no canned clams. Of course not. Canned clams weren't a luxury to summer people.

*

At three thirty she tried to call Mike, but there was no answer. At four o'clock she couldn't get through. She stood in the kitchen, wearing the silk sleeveless dress she'd put on to welcome company – casual enough for afternoon drinks outside, a little bohemian if worn without shoes, her hair loose, make-up carefully done to look minimal, right wrist clanking with silver bangles that maximised her tan – and wondered if there was time to call Ames' and ask for a delivery.

Delivery of a single can was the epitome of a spoiled summer person thing to do. And anyway, Sterling might deliver it. What would be worse: for her to make herself look ridiculous and cower in her house, hiding and waiting for a knock on the door? Or pull up her big girl panties and go to the only store on the island, for God's sake, a store that she'd spent a good three-quarters of her childhood inhabiting, somewhere she knew as intimately as her childhood home?

'Fuck it,' Vee said. She might have grown up and changed, but she was not going to do something that her teenage self would have scoffed at and mocked. And she was not a coward. It was going to have to happen sometime or other. Might as well be now.

She pulled on tennis shoes without socks, found her sunglasses, put her phone in her purse. Left a note on the table, in case Mike got back before she did (who was she kidding? Mike would motor up at past five o'clock and bound onto the dock, ready for a drink and socialising, ready to show off his summer house and his beautiful, clever wife, expecting it to be all ready for him). She considered the golf cart in the garage, took a bike instead, and cycled down the rutted road, steering with her right hand, her left arm held out bent in front of her. She pedalled towards the ferry landing and the store, the part of the island that they used to call 'town', even though it wasn't a proper town at all.

Sterling's dad Tom Ames had taught her how to ride a bike. She didn't have one; went everywhere powered by her trainers.

Her mom made her wear socks even in summer because it made the shoes last longer. In winter she wore two pairs of socks and second-hand boots with bread bags inside to keep the water out. On Sterling's eighth birthday he got a new black BMX and in the afternoon after his party he tore up and down the road, pulling wheelies, making skid marks in the mud. 'Wanna go?' he asked Vee, who watched him from the top of a melting snowbank that was peppered with dirt.

'Nah,' she said. She'd just fall over. But she wanted to speed, to soar, to get her clothes splattered with mud and puddles. She pretended not to care, and pelted Sterling with soggy snowballs when he rode past. She didn't think anyone noticed her yearning.

But a couple of days later, on a Sunday which was her mom's sleep-in day, when she turned up at the store only to find that Sterling had gone out riding bikes to the other side of the island with the Dunn cousins, Mr Ames got up from his chair behind the counter and said, 'Wait outside a minute, Vee.'

She stood out front, pushing cigarette butts underneath the benches with the toe of her trainer, thinking maybe Mr Ames would pay her in penny candy, like he did sometimes, if she offered to sweep up. Then he came round from the back of the store, wheeling a glossy red bike. After a second, she recognised it: it was Sterling's old bike, which was a plain old boys' bike instead of a BMX, but it had been painted, and it had a new seat and new hand grips, and new tyres with fat treads.

'I didn't like the thought of it just sitting around gathering dust,' Mr Ames told her, and offered her the handlebars. 'I learned how to ride on this same bike.'

'Oh,' she said, shame flushing up into her cheeks despite herself. Not because it was a handout – she was proud, but not about material things, not then. It was because she couldn't ride it. 'No, I think my mom needs me to do some stuff around the house today.'

'You can ride it home,' Mr Ames said. He smiled at her. 'Come out back, there's a flat place where you can practise. I'll give you a hand.'

No one could see her out back except for Mr Ames and, from the kitchen window, Mrs Ames. Within half an hour she was riding circles, pelting out around the outside of the store to sail down the track to the ferry dock, whoops of triumph streaming out behind her like her hair.

There was no one sitting on the benches and chairs outside the store, which was a relief. They'd been freshly painted in forest green; she knew from experience that they had to be repainted every couple of years, because of salt water and weather. In the mornings, fishermen sat there drinking coffee, blowing steam and fog from their fingers; in the afternoons, summer people chattered, licked ice creams. Vee remembered when she used to be the exact length of the bench on the left, at age thirteen – she'd been able to lie on the seat with her head touching one arm and her feet touching the other. The right-hand bench was longer, and by the time she was old enough to measure herself against that one, she didn't much care any more. The window boxes had been painted the same green as the benches, and stuffed with petunias and geraniums. She leaned her bike against the left-hand bench (no one on Unity had bike locks), took a deep breath, shook her hair back, and pushed open the screen door.

She was thirteen, she was seven, she was four.

She put her sunglasses onto the top of her head and channelled a mixture of her mother-in-law, Sarandon Ellis, who had the silver-spoon gift of confidence that she belonged in any space whatsoever, and Vee's own mother, who knew she didn't belong in plenty of places, but had long ago decided not to give a fuck. Vee stood just inside the store for a moment, looking from side to side like she owned the place. The changes were the easiest things to see: the deli counter, the new beer and wine fridge that stretched along the right-hand side, the large display of produce at the front, which in her day was mostly onions and lettuce and cucumbers in plastic wrap, and now contained baskets of shiny aubergines, heaps of green beans, husks of neatly stacked corn, fuzzy peaches, a riot of greens and herbs, heirloom tomatoes. 'It's like Whole Foods in here,' she muttered, but she could see the point of it, the appeal to summer people but also to the person she used to be, someone who'd never seen an avocado, who would wrinkle up her nose at a green bulbous tomato. Sterling had been doing things. And not doing things: the shelves were the same, the three wooden coffee-stained tables with mismatched chairs by the window, the maps of coastal Maine on the wall, the pink-and-yellow sign with a Gifford's ice-cream cone. And the smell. Even if she couldn't see or hear, she'd know where she was.

She didn't glance over at the counter; instead she strode between the shelves of dry goods. She saw giant Israeli couscous, graham crackers, marshmallows, three types of Doritos. The cans were all in the same aisle, no matter what they had in them, which had been Mr Ames's shelving method: fruit, chilli, baked beans, condensed milk, tuna, pineapple juice, refried beans. If it was a can and it was food, it was in the can aisle. Except dog and cat food, which was in the back near the toilet paper. The family story with the reason for this was something to do with a snooty summer lady and a can of Alpo. Vee didn't remember the details, but then again you didn't have to.

The Bumblebee clams were beside the tuna and the clam chowder, which made sense. She picked up two from the shelf, stacked in her good hand like a weapon and, for the first time, glanced over the top of the shelves to the counter. Maybe Sterling had already seen her. Maybe he didn't recognise her, with her earned sheen of money. (She'd recognise him, anywhere, no matter what, though sometimes she couldn't consciously call his face to mind.)

Maybe he did recognise her and was sitting there, mad. Some people had school reunions, old friends on Facebook. Vee had this: a man in a store who she was pretending not to be afraid to see.

But it wasn't Sterling at the counter. It was someone else, a woman, though her head was bowed over something so Vee couldn't see her face. She had thick dark hair, in curls, glossy and undulled by grey. A summer hire, probably a teenager, though that wasn't Unity hair.

Vee relaxed. She was going to have to see Sterling, and his mother too, but not today. She marched up to the counter and put down the cans of clams.

'That it?' said the woman, not glancing up from her book, which was thick and had the title *Bad Women*. She was sitting in Mr Ames's chair, wearing khaki shorts and a black V-neck t-shirt, her sandalled feet propped up against the bottom shelf. Her toenails were unpolished. Her hair, closer up, was glorious: wild, unrestrained, soft and thick, a deep brown-almost-black jumble of curls, a very pale parting in the centre that somehow made Vee think of a young child. But she wasn't a teenager. She was an adult – younger than Vee, maybe not yet thirty – a smattering of freckles across her bare collarbone.

'That's it,' said Vee, almost sang it, so glad she wasn't having that conversation with Sterling yet. She rose on her toes, smiled at the top of this woman's head. 'Just a couple'a cans'a clams. I hope we have an electric can opener because I've only got one good hand.'

The woman looked up, head tilted, smiling. Their eyes met and Vee teetered.

Her eyes were also dark, like her hair, lined in thick lashes, her brows wide slashes, nearly meeting in the middle. Vee felt their gaze like a punch in the chest.

She didn't know this woman, did she? Did she? Who was she?

'Are you okay?' the woman asked.

Slowly, Vee sank down, feet full on the floor with a creak. She did not know this woman: her eyes, her face, her hair, her voice.

Her curled vowels that were not from Unity. The freckles on her round cheeks, the generous dip of her top lip, the long curve of her nose, her awkward, beautiful face. Vee did not know her and she was instantly, absolutely, home.

'I'm Vivian,' she said.

'Hi,' said the woman. 'I'm Rachel.'

'Rachel.' Syllables at the front of her mouth, behind her teeth, settling in her throat. She had never known anyone of that ancient name before. They stared at each other: Vee standing, Rachel in her chair, head tilted upward so her hair fell down her back.

Rachel closed her book.

'Can I get you anything else?'

'Yes. I mean, no.' Vee lifted one foot and placed it over her other. She had the urge to run her fingers through her own hair and imagine Rachel's. What was this?

'I can open the clams for you, if you want,' said Rachel. 'I have a can opener back here somewhere.'

'Are you—' Vee said, and then she stopped. 'You're not from Unity, what brings you here?'

Something passed over Rachel's face. 'I married in.'

Her hands were long-fingered, also without polish on the short nails, blue veins on the back. There was a wide gold band on the fourth finger, no engagement ring.

'I married out,' said Vee, though that wasn't true – she'd met Mike long after she'd left Unity – but because instinct made her think the parallel would make this woman smile, and it did: a faint smile, lips only half-open. 'Where are you from?'

'Illinois, originally.'

'I did my law degree at the University of Chicago. I can hear the accent now.'

Rachel's eyes rolled at that. 'You and everyone else,' she said, and Vee laughed. Unlike normal laughter, it came from high in her throat, and didn't dispel any of the tension squeezing her chest. Rachel picked up a can, then stood and punched numbers into the till. 'Are you Vee Harper?' she asked, looking at the keyboard.

'Yeah. Is everyone talking?'

'You have to ask?'

This time the laughter was lower in her body. Again, Rachel didn't return it, but she smiled. Vee dug in her handbag and held out a bill. Taking it, Rachel met her gaze again. Vee flushed. Rachel dropped coins into her palm. Vee wanted to kiss them: the dimes, the nickels. Metallic taste on her tongue. They stood wordless for a moment. What did Vee need to say? What could she say, were there words for this hunger?

The bell over the door rang. It was the same bell that had always been there, and its sound startled Vee out of whatever she was feeling. She picked up the clams, stuffed them into her handbag, stepped back. 'Nice to meet you,' she said, though it wasn't nice. It was painful, shameful, exciting, none and all of these. Seeing nothing, she hurried through the store and outside, walking straight past her bike before she remembered it was there.

Chapter Six

Vee

What the fuck, what the fuck, what the fuck?

Vee stood on the pedals, gripped white-knuckled on the handlebars with her cast held in the air. She panted, swerved round pedestrians without a word. How long had she been speaking with Rachel? A minute, ninety seconds? It had been a week and a half in her mind. Had she breathed for any of that slowed-down time? Who was this woman, and why? What the *fuck*?

She skidded around the corner through the gate and stopped at the back door of Daybreak, dropping the bike with a clatter onto the ground. She needed water. And then something stronger, but water first.

No, first she needed a shower. Sweat was dripping from her forehead, staining her dress. She changed course from kitchen to their bedroom with its en suite. She was supposed to make appetisers and then have a convivial cocktail with strangers. How?

What was wrong with her?

In the doorway of their bedroom, she collided with Mike's chest, didn't recognise him right away, and yelped. Mike laughed and looped his arms around her waist.

'What are you doing here?' she said. 'I didn't see you.'

'Just got back.' He kissed her cheek. 'Mmm, you're all sweaty.'

'It's hot out there.'

'It's hot in here.' He nuzzled her neck.

'Don't we have guests coming?'

'We've got time.'

'I need a shower.'

'After.' He licked her collarbone. 'God, you're sexy. My sexy wife. I'm a lucky bastard. I've been thinking about this all day.' He slipped a hand inside her dress and Vee had a sudden, strong vision of Rachel's hand on her breast. Long fingers, short nails. Lust swelled in her. She grabbed Mike's hair and kissed him, hard and sloppy, teeth clashing.

'Baby,' he murmured, pleased, and she tugged him by the waistband of his shorts into the room, onto the bed, already parting her legs, hiking up her dress, taking him in.

'Are they good investments, though? The upkeep must be substantial, but I suppose they hold their value.'

'A lot of these seasonal homes have been owned by the same family for generations. In a place like this, you have to balance out the lack of infrastructure with the exclusivity.'

Mike shook a mixer of his famous dirty martinis over his shoulder. The ice swished and rattled. Vee held out two glasses for him, and he winked at her as he poured. 'Extra olives?' he asked Savannah, who said 'Yes please,' and then turned to Vee. 'Love your dress. Is it Nicole Farhi? I've got one in cream, but I think the eau de nil is much more flattering. What happened to your arm, may I ask?'

'I got hit by a bus.'

'No! Did you? You poor thing!'

Savannah had a charming, expensive Texas drawl and a tumble of honey hair. She'd had some work done to her face, but it was subtle, like her gold jewellery. At forty-something she was much better-looking than her husband, who was older and looked exactly like the oil executive he was. Nevertheless, did Vee want to sleep with her? No.

She and Mike had only just finished when there was a knock on the door to the front patio signalling the arrival of their guests.

'Don't shower,' he'd whispered to her. 'I like it when you smell like me.'

The sex had been good. Better than normal, even by the standards of this week. She put on a fresh dress without underwear and she kissed her husband lingeringly. 'Do you think they heard us?' she asked.

'Quite possibly.'

'Good,' she said, and dipped a finger inside herself, rubbed it behind her ears like perfume. Mike's eyes widened.

'Dirty bitch,' he said. 'Let's get rid of them quick.'

Now that their guests were here, though, installed in Adirondack chairs near the dock where they'd moored their motor dinghy, in the perfect spot for watching the sunset, making their way through their second round of martinis, Mike didn't seem in any hurry.

'You're a beautiful couple,' said Savannah. 'Mike said it was your second honeymoon?'

'Something like that.'

'Vee knows what it's like here in the winter,' Mike said, filling his own glass last and adding a slice of dill pickle. He sucked the juice from his fingers.

'Cold,' said Vee.

'I can imagine,' said Bob, the South Carolina wealth management consultant. He was new money; his wife Rusty, well preserved in her fifties, was old money. It was in her rolled-up jeans and white tennis sweater, the way she didn't colour her hair. Vee had developed a sixth sense about these things, though it was easy enough in this case. 'We usually summer in Italy,' she'd told Vee when they first arrived, 'but Bob's mother is getting chemotherapy so we wanted to stay in the country.'

'You came late in the season,' Rusty commented now. 'Are you going to stay for the autumn leaves?'

'We're only here until after Labor Day.'

'Where do you usually summer?' *Summer*, the verb.

'Mike's parents have a place in the Hamptons.'

'Oh, gorgeous. So where did you grow up? It's not in the house *we're* renting, is it? I *love* that place.'

'Eagle's Flight? Yes, that's a gorgeous house. I've only ever seen the outside.'

'Well, you must come for dinner next week, and I'll give you the tour.'

'Which house did you grow up in?' Bob took a big scoop of clam dip on a chip and popped it in his mouth. Vee hadn't touched any. Too many memories. Pops, baseball games on the TV, Scrabble on her bed with her mom.

A new memory. Rachel.

'It's gone now,' Vee said. 'Did you say you were planning to sail up to New Brunswick?'

Mike joined in before she could respond to whatever it was that Bob said, and she settled back in her chair, sipping her drink. Mike did make a good one. His talents: sailing, tennis, cocktail mixing, charm. Born with them all, along with his money. Vodka pooled in her stomach, warmed her. The three couples sat in a semi-circle, men on the right, women on the left. She could see her reflection in the other couples' eyes: she and Mike were the golden ones, younger, still in their thirties, still in love. One day, if they stayed together, they'd be like Savannah and Tim, Rusty and Bob. She was drinking dirty martinis with future versions of herself.

She rubbed her finger against her wedding ring, platinum with matching pear-cut diamond platinum engagement ring. She thought about Rachel, new in the old store, with her untamed hair and rounded body and long fingers, her dark eyes. Her inexplicable appeal. How her mouth formed words. *I married in*, she'd said, and it made more sense than Vee's half a lie, *I married out*, because you could only ever marry in. The person you married was the future you chose.

'Oh,' Vee said, but no one heard her, because they were still talking about sailing and Mike was getting up to mix more drinks. 'I'll get more ice,' she said, jumping up and grabbing the ice bucket, hurrying to the house on her bare feet, because she had just understood the meaning of that flat gold wedding band that the other woman wore.

Rachel was Sterling's wife.

Chapter Seven

Sterling

'Who is Vee, anyway?'

They were sitting on their screened-in front porch, which had a view of the landing, boats on moorings, and the Beottes' stack of lobster traps and pots in various states of repair. The ferry had come and gone, and the fishermen were all in for the night, so the harbour was quiet except for a summer person in a kayak. It was one of the Sorensons with their dog. The dog – it was a little one, a cockapoo or similar – had on a life jacket and was attached to a line. Every now and then the dog would jump off the bow of the kayak and swim for a few minutes, until it got tired and the Sorenson fellow would fish it back in with the line.

They always had dinner out here on warm nights. It was Rachel's turn to cook and they were eating turkey meatloaf, boiled baby potatoes and cucumbers from her garden, and drinking iced tea. He had ketchup on his meatloaf and drank his iced tea with lemon. She sprinkled salt and drank her iced tea with sugar.

'Who's Vee?' he repeated, looking away from Sorenson and his dog. 'I thought I told you all this.'

'Well, tell me again.'

He felt slippery, sometimes, with Rachel: with all of his other relationships with friends and family, he knew where he stood, what other people knew, what they thought. The ground steady under his feet. But Rachel surprised him. She forgot things, or they meant something else in her mind. She could lose a basic fact about life here, while retaining a million different other historical facts about people she'd never met. She was smart, he knew, smarter than him – she had a master's degree – and her intelligence was one of the reasons he'd been attracted to her from the start, even before they'd met, when they'd been texting on the dating site. She puzzled him not because she was intelligent, or because she was seven years younger than him, but because she was other. She'd been put together in a way that was different from how he'd been put together. The building blocks of her world were not made of the same material as his. And that was exciting, sometimes, and sometimes... it meant that he had to tell the same story over and over again to her before she understood what it meant.

Maybe this was marriage, this rebuilding on shifting sands, but it wasn't the way his parents' marriage had been.

'Tell me what you remember,' he said, more patiently than he felt.

'Her last name's Harper. I presume she's descended from the Harpers who had a farm here in the late eighteenth century? So the family's as old as yours. There are several Harpers in the cemetery. But there aren't any Harpers living here now. Did they all leave?'

'Vee and her mother Dottie left. Her grandfather died.'

'What about her dad?'

'Her dad was never in the picture.'

Rachel nodded, and continued. 'You and Vee were best friends when you were kids, and everyone thought you were going to get married and have lots of babies and be the king and queen of Unity Island, but you had a terrible argument and she left and you've never seen her since.'

'We didn't have an argument. She abandoned me for no reason at all. And we weren't planning on getting married.'

'No? Jacob said she was your old girlfriend.'

'Are you jealous, Rachel?' he asked, irrationally sort of hoping she was.

'No, I was just repeating what Jacob said. So she wasn't your girlfriend?'

'More like my sister. Vee was always over here. She didn't have a happy home life. They never had much money, and she lived with her grandfather who was a drunk and couldn't work.'

'You rescued her.' Rachel sounded accusatory, which put him on the defensive.

'Well, yeah. Where else was she going to go? We helped her out in a lot of ways, with stuff she needed and also a safe place to be. Some weeks, she ate most of her meals with us.'

'So she was a charity case?'

'Not a charity case. It was the right thing to do. It's how we do things here. If someone needs something, we get it for them.'

'And she wasn't sufficiently grateful?'

'I didn't require her to be grateful,' Sterling said. 'That's a mean thing to say.'

'I'm not trying to be mean. I'm sorry. That came out wrong. I'm trying to figure out why it hurt you so much that she left, so you're still angry now.'

'Because we were friends. She wasn't a charity case. My parents loved her like a daughter, especially my dad. She didn't have a dad, so the two of them bonded.'

'A functional family is pretty attractive in that situation,' Rachel said, and he knew of course that she was talking about herself, about her own non-functional family.

'I didn't rescue you, Rachel. That wasn't my motivation at all.'

'I wasn't saying that. Just that … I can understand it, from her point of view.'

'You wouldn't do what she did, though.'

'Well.'

'You *had* to leave. You couldn't have survived in that house where you grew up. You had to make a break. What Vee did wasn't like that at all.'

Rachel nodded. Took a final bite of meatloaf, and pushed her plate away. 'Did you care about her?'

'Of course I did. She was my best friend.'

'She was really important to you, but this is definitely the only time you've really told me about her. I forget some things, but I wouldn't forget your best friend.'

'I don't like talking about her.'

'Why not?'

'Because she left!'

It came out more loudly than he'd meant it to, more like a wail or a protest than a statement. Rachel got up and started clearing the table.

'That's a crime?' she said, stacking their plates. 'Leaving Unity?'

'No, of course not. It's *how* she left. Without telling anyone, packing up and leaving their house up there empty to rot. The day after my father died.'

'What?' She paused, crumpling paper napkins.

'Dad had his heart attack in the store on the afternoon of the ninth of July. He was gone before the air ambulance could get here. They took away his body. It was the worst day of my life.' Even now, he couldn't talk about it without his eyes prickling, his voice clogging up. He cleared his throat. 'Everyone knew, everyone was there to help us, the house was full. That's how it always is when someone dies, and my father – everyone knew him. Everyone liked him. But no Vee. I thought maybe she didn't know, maybe she'd been off the island. I mean, she was supposed to be my best friend, like my sister. She was supposed to *love* my dad. The next morning, I went to her house and it was empty. They hadn't even locked the door.'

'Maybe she didn't know?'

'Oh, she knew. A few people told me later that she'd been outside the store when the helicopter landed. But she never came inside. She just packed up and left on the next ferry, apparently, she and her mom both. Her grandfather was dead by that time. I was there for her when *that* happened, that spring, I'd sat through the funeral with her. I'd helped her look after him for a couple of months beforehand, too, and Pops was mean, Rachel. He could be really mean. I stood by Vee all that time, and then when my own dad, my dad who loved her like a daughter—'

He choked. He got up and grabbed the jug of iced tea and carried it to the kitchen, and stood at the sink, ashamed.

His mom had said he should give Vee a chance, that he should think well of her, but when he thought of her, he felt terrible. So it was easier to try not to think of her at all.

Rachel came in after him. She put the plates quietly down by the sink and began wrapping up the leftover meatloaf. She was given away only by the metallic rustle of foil. It was one of her talents, he'd discovered: she could move almost silently when she wanted to. She was able to give other people the sensation of being alone and private, but also to let them know she was listening.

'Anyway,' he said to the tap. 'That's why I'm so angry with Vee Harper.'

'She came into the store today.'

He straightened. 'She did?'

'Uh huh.'

'What did she say?'

'Not much.' Rachel put the meatloaf in the fridge. 'She said she went to law school in Chicago.'

She'd been an attorney in New York, working for a large firm. She'd spoken at a conference in Florida, and she'd had a few articles published with titles he didn't understand. She'd married Mike Ellis, of the Ellises. He'd discovered all that during his clandestine Google search the other night, along with some photographs of her: most with her wearing business attire, with hair pulled back away from her face, and one casual shot, with her hair down, wearing a pink t-shirt, running a 10k race. In that shot, she looked like Vee. In the others, she looked like a stranger.

'Did she ask about me?' he asked, before he could stop himself.

'No. She just bought some food.'

'Fucking nerve,' he said.

'Well,' Rachel said mildly, 'it's not as if there's anywhere else to buy food around here.'

'I've got a mind to go up to Daybreak and ask her where the hell she's been all this time.'

'Will you?'

'Do you think it's a bad idea?'

'I'm not the one who knows her.'

'I thought I knew her, but then I didn't. She's never even sent me an email. No sympathy card. Not a word in twenty years, even though she knew exactly where I was. And then she swans back like some queen.'

Rachel's brow furrowed, but she didn't say anything. She picked up the dishcloth to wipe the table, and went back out to the porch, leaving Sterling with hands clenched. Vee had been to his own store and not asked after him – his father's store, the place where Thomas Ames had died, one summer afternoon while restocking shelves. Sterling had been helping him. His father had taken one sharp breath as if struck by sudden pain, staggered, and fallen. And Sterling, falling to his knees beside him, shouting his name, shaking him, and then, filled with horror and disbelief, pounding on his chest like he'd practised in school first aid lessons when he'd pushed and breathed into a rubber mannequin, except this wasn't a mannequin it was his dad, not breathing, eyes half-open, terribly solid and unmoving under his hands, Sterling not realising yet that this meant that for the rest of his life he would be alone.

Part Two

—

Summer, 2015

Chapter Eight

Rachel

Rachel had never been a gardener before she came to Unity. The house she grew up in, in the Chicago suburbs, had only a lawn and a fence and a single evergreen shrub which grew exponentially bigger every year. She used to mow the lawn so their house didn't stand out as different, and at times she hacked at the shrub, but that was as far as her expertise went. Occasionally in a burst of optimism or foolishness her mother used to buy houseplants. A few months later, Rachel would throw away their shrivelled husks. She didn't see the point of having green things growing. They were only another thing to take care of.

After she fled, aged twenty-four, she shared her brother's third-floor flat in Hoboken. He had a plastic cactus in the bathroom.

The Ames house, on the other hand, had a garden. It took up a quarter of the land on the side of the house, on the opposite side from the store, and when she first came to Unity, Sterling's mom Brenda, that sweet woman, showed it to her with pride. 'We've got green beans, peas, cucumbers, courgettes, and beetroot. Lots of swiss chard because it's easy to grow, but nobody likes it. Maybe you'll like it? Garlic, that's easy. Tomatoes over here on the south end where they get the sun. It's overgrown a bit now. It's hard for me to do the weeding.'

'I don't know what to do with any of this,' Rachel had confessed to her. 'I don't even know what swiss chard is.'

'Don't worry,' said Brenda. 'I'll show you.'

Julie Cohen

And she did. Sterling and Rachel were married in October, and after their short honeymoon in the Green Mountains to appreciate the foliage, Brenda walked her through the garden row by row, bed by bed, pointing and explaining. She put out lawn chairs for them both, got out a Thermos of tea, and talked her through the seasons.

At first, Rachel bristled. She liked learning new things, but why did this mammoth task fall to her? If this was her house now, her land, why couldn't she just rip the beds up, plant a lawn? Why couldn't Sterling take it over, if it was so important? Why was this a woman's job?

But then she came to love it. Brenda's sweet hot tea in a metal cup, her kind, patient explanations. The story that came with every plant. Part of it was because her mother-in-law was a nice person and, before she met Sterling, Rachel hadn't had the chance to spend much time with people who were simply nice. Part of it was the garden itself. It was history: fruits and flowers layered over each other, a tapestry of leaves and tendrils. The peas grew best in this spot. Cover the seedlings from birds. Thank goodness we don't have to deal with deer or raccoons here on Unity. One year the frost came too early; one year all the corn blew down. And Rachel, with her degrees in history, who had lived in her head rather than in her hands, thought about how huge human movements were so often caused by the vagaries of crops and seasons.

This garden fell to her because the movement of history fell to women, the ones who planted, harvested, guarded the earth. The ones who gave birth and nourished, the ones who cultivated the wanted plants, who rooted out the weeds. Eve plucking the fruit of knowledge, Ruth gleaning in the fields. A garden was memory and it was future. The Ames family had grown food here before they had a store. Brenda had given the garden to her because Brenda was also giving her the future of their family. It was a gift of trust and hope. The garden was peaceful. It was her job, now,

64

to shape it with her body and her hands, keep it safe. It was a job that she could do, as compared to all the other ones that she couldn't.

She'd kept everything the same as Brenda had it: flowers on the perimeter, vegetables in neat rows, tied up carefully on canes. This morning, she was harvesting green beans, snapping them off the vine and dropping them in her metal colander, which had been Sterling's grandmother's. Every now and then she ate a sun-warmed bean instead of dropping it.

She had gone to sleep last night thinking about Vee. There was a lot she hadn't said in her conversation with Sterling and, as usual, he seemed oblivious to it. She'd gone to bed thinking about Vee's honey-coloured hair, her nervous laughter, her slim shoulders, her silk dress the colour of the April sea. She'd wondered why Vee had really left, or how Vee had ever fitted into Unity. She'd wondered how much Sterling was leaving out about their relationship.

Vee Harper was a mystery, and very few people on Unity were interesting to Rachel. Very few people aside from Brenda treated her naturally, like a friend. Vee was different, like Rachel herself was. She was well put-together, but her hair was wild from the wind; she was beautiful, but her arm was broken. Rachel had seen all of this within a few moments, and it made her curious.

In a garden, she'd learned, things happened by chance all the time, but there was always a reason for them. A seed dropped by a passing bird. A tomato plant beset by aphids while its sister plant, just the right distance away, stood tall and healthy and free. Gardens had history and even unexpected events had a cause in the past. Deep roots, pollen carried by the wind.

She stretched, circling her shoulders to get rid of the kinks. She went inside to scrub the dirt from beneath her nails. Then she found the truck key and went over to the store to tell P.J. that she'd do the deliveries today.

*

Rachel knocked on the back door of Vee's house and waited, her arms around a bag of groceries. She'd pushed all her hair up beneath one of Sterling's old Red Sox caps. She used to own a Cubs cap, but people commented on it so much she threw it out.

There was a noise from inside the house, so she knocked again. It was a screen door; she stepped up close and peered through it, but she couldn't see much because light was streaming through from the front of the house and it dazzled her. They must have huge windows, she thought. She tried to remember if she'd ever seen the house from the water. She didn't remember it, anyway. She usually only ever saw the backs of these houses.

'Hello?' she called through the screen. 'Hello, Vivian? It's Rachel, from the store.'

A silhouette appeared and Rachel had to suppress a little nervous hiccup. Then it got closer and she saw it wasn't Vee; it was a man. He opened the door and grinned at her. He wasn't tall, but he was extraordinarily good-looking, movie-star good-looking. He had golden skin and white teeth and he wore white tennis clothes. Rachel had seen plenty of super-rich people since coming to Unity and lots of them had this ineffable polished quality, but this man was a few degrees beyond that. He looked like he should be on television: not that he *could* be on television, but that he *was*. As if she could reach over and turn him off.

'Hi,' he said. 'Hey wow, beautiful day, isn't it? Did you say you were Rachel? I'm Mike Ellis, nice to meet you. Here, let me take that from you, it looks heavy. Come on in.'

Because she had no idea what else to do, because she was curious about Vee's life, she followed him into the house. It was a rich people's house of polished wood and white furniture and big windows. Mike carried the groceries into the kitchen, which was part of the open-plan living area. 'It's hot, how about a glass of water?' he asked her, and started getting out glasses before she'd answered.

'Oh, I'm okay,' she said, but didn't protest when he filled a glass with ice from the dispenser in the refrigerator door and poured her a glass of mineral water, the expensive kind they sold in the store and that came in blue glass bottles. He cut a lemon on a little wooden board and popped a slice in the glass.

'So, how's business?' he asked, handing her the glass.

'Oh, fine. It's always really busy in the summer.'

'I bet. Well, we appreciate the time you take to deliver stuff to us. We're getting completely spoiled.' He poured a glass for himself and leaned against the worktop, a respectful distance away, regarding her pleasantly, as if this were a cocktail party.

She sipped the water: it tasted like normal, non-expensive water with a piece of lemon in it.

'So what do you do in the winter, when it's less busy? Do you go somewhere warmer?'

'No, I live here year-round,' she told him, and added, 'I'm not just a shopkeeper. I'm actually a historian.'

'Is that so? What period?'

'I'm interested in all North American history but I did my master's thesis on patterns of nineteenth-century Jewish immigration and assimilation, and the mainstream cultural response.'

'Impressive.'

And she was trying to impress him. Why? Because he was rich, handsome, polished, from somewhere other than Unity? Because he was male? Because he was Vee's husband? She shrugged. 'It's just my thing.'

'Well, I'm in awe of anyone who can stick with any subject for that long. I didn't even finish college, as my dad likes to remind me. What about the history of this island? Do you know a lot about that?'

'I've done some research. It's been pretty quiet here for a few hundred years, but some exciting stuff happened back in the mid-eighteenth century.'

'Oh really? What?'

Once again she felt herself pulled in by his charm, and once again she pulled back. 'There's a museum in the old schoolhouse. You should check it out.'

'I will! Thanks for the tip.' He put down his glass. 'Anyway, did you say you were looking for Vee?'

'Not really. I mean, sort of. We met yesterday, so I was going to say hi.'

'She took the ferry this morning to run a few errands. She'll be back later, though, if you wanted to drop by.'

'Oh! No, that's okay. I'm sure I'll see her around.'

'So you work with Sterling?'

'You could say so, yes. I'm his wife.'

'Ah!' An enormous white smile. 'I didn't want to assume. Well, that makes sense. You know that Sterling and Vee used to be best friends?'

'I've heard.'

He tilted his head and narrowed his eyes, like a man appreciating a fine morsel of gossip. 'Do you know what happened? She's only mentioned that they used to be friends, that's it.'

'I've . . . heard a few things.'

'She won't talk to me about it. She doesn't talk about her childhood at all, if she can help it. Her mother does, mostly to say how awful it is here and how nosy and closed-minded most people are. Have you met Vee's mother, Dot?'

'No.'

'Not surprised. She's got a real vendetta against this place. She's a wonderful woman, though. Completely hilarious and takes no shit from anyone. She's a lot like Vee.'

'If . . .' She overcame her resistance, tumbled into the conversation. This guy was exactly the sort of guy she didn't like: handsome, cocksure, entitled. But there was something about his sunny assurance. And also, she'd come here to find out about Vee, hadn't she? 'If Vee hates it so much, why did she come back this summer?'

'It was my idea. I'm incredibly convincing when I want something.'

'I'd never have guessed.'

To give him credit, he laughed. 'And also, Vee doesn't hate it here. She talks a good game.'

'Anyway,' she said. 'I've got to get going. Thanks for the water.'

'No problem. It's great to meet you.' He took her glass and walked her to the door, and when they were nearly at it, he said, 'Actually, Rachel, I wonder if you can help me with something.'

'What's that?'

'I wonder if you and Sterling would come for dinner?'

No way, she was going to say. All of her careful, keeping-normal instincts told her to say it. *My husband would never agree to that. Also, I'm far too eager to be friends with your wife, and that scares me, because experience has taught me that when I want something too badly, I never get it.*

'Sure,' she said. 'We'd love to.'

Chapter Nine

Mike

Mike first met Vivian Harper at a benefit for something or other. He could never remember exactly what the evening was in benefit of, which in his opinion made him more romantic, not less. 'I was so blown away by your style, beauty and intelligence that everything else has completely dropped out of my mind,' he would tell Vee, after they were married.

She reminded him on every anniversary what the benefit had been for and he still always forgot. Something to do with children? A museum? Maybe racial justice. He'd paid five thousand dollars for his ticket, or maybe it was ten, so it was something or other worthy. He couldn't even remember where it had been. Maybe the Guggenheim. But honestly what did it matter? What mattered was that he'd met Vee.

He'd been single for about six months at that point, because it was by far a lot less hassle, except for the fact that his friends all kept on trying to set him up with women. His last relationship had been with the daughter of a man who owned a lot of hotels but she had suddenly decided she wanted babies, so that was the end of that. He was *not* father material. Since then he'd been on as many dates as he felt like, usually only one or two with the same person, always prefaced with the caveat that the person was very special to him but he just wasn't ready to commit to a woman right now, especially with all the travelling he liked to do, but let's seize this moment together to have an incredibly fun time that you'll never forget, so when we say goodbye, it will be without any regrets.

He realised he only got away with this sort of awful behaviour because he was rich. Sometimes he told his dates this, and they would always laugh and deny it. That was how he knew that although he was charming and reasonably good-looking, they were only with him because of his money.

'You're never ready to commit to anything,' his mother Sarandon said to him, when they met for brunch at least once a month when they were both in the city. 'It's not just women. It's jobs, or cars, or houses, or even your college degree. You're a talented sailor, but you couldn't take that seriously enough. I raised a butterfly. My only child, a butterfly.'

'But a beautiful butterfly,' he agreed, leaning across the table to kiss her. 'And if I'm lucky, one day I might wake up and find that I've become a very homely caterpillar.'

Because he met his mother at least once a month and because the next morning after these brunches he always talked himself into committing to something, by the time he met Vivian Harper at that benefit for whatever it was, he belonged to at least a dozen committees and had invested in several start-ups and signed a two-year lease on his Range Rover. He already regretted them all, so he tried not to think about them.

Mike's father Alonzo had made his first million by twenty-four, which sounded exhausting. When Mike stopped sailing competitively, he'd gone to work for his father, but he was so inept that he only lasted six months. Since then, Alonzo did that thing with his mouth whenever Mike was in the same room. This is why Mike didn't meet him for brunch.

Mike's full name was Michael Paul Richard D'Arcy Ellis. He had been named after his maternal great-grandfather. The first Michael was the son of a property magnate. Despite being bone-idle and, reading between the lines of family stories, colossally inept, while the first Michael was alive he had managed to increase his family fortune exponentially through pure charm and a series of haphazard and blind-luck investments. He'd met his own wife not through the normal social networking done by the one per cent, but entirely by chance, when he rescued a young woman by the side of the road one rainy night when her car had failed, and he'd driven her home only to find that she was minor Dutch royalty and the head of her own fashion house. 'Grandfather Michael always came through,' his mother would say, when Mike did something like drop out of college or date a cocktail waitress. 'You'll do the same. You've got it in your blood.'

Meanwhile, Mike couldn't even keep an Instagram account going. He pointed this out himself; he was always the first one to perceive and mention his own faults. He'd discovered that people hated him less for being self-aware. It didn't make him hate himself less, of course.

He was thirty-two on the night of the benefit for whatever it was, and he'd just decided to give up on a macrobiotic diet. If he'd lasted only twenty-four more hours on it – or, if he'd quit it twenty-four hours earlier – he'd never have met Vee, which, he often said, was as good an argument as he'd ever encountered for eating meat. That night, the catering staff were carrying around silver trays of wagyu beef skewers. When Mike reached for one, he misjudged, stumbled, and tipped the tray over on a woman in a black dress, who was standing on her own.

'Oh gosh,' he said, gaping at the woman. She had roasted tomato salsa all down her front, and cubes of beef on her shoes. 'Oh gosh, I am so sorry.' He squatted down immediately and began picking up the ruined canapés from her high heels. The waiter hurried off.

'I'm not drunk, I swear,' he told her. 'I've only had one glass of champagne, but I've only eaten algae smoothies for the past two days so it went straight to my head.' He looked up at her. 'Have I ruined your dress? I'll buy you another one.'

The woman, now that he looked up at her, was a honey-blonde

and not quite beautiful, more handsome. Even with salsa all down her front, she had a sort of dignity.

'Mike Ellis,' he said, dumping his handfuls of expensive beef onto the abandoned tray, and standing up. In heels, she was taller than he was. He held out his hand to her, then realised it was covered in salsa and meat juice, so he wiped it on his dinner jacket. 'There, now we match.' He held it out again. 'I really am awfully sorry.'

'It's nothing,' she said. 'It's just a dress and a pair of shoes.'

'You say that because you're not the one who looks like an idiot.'

'*Looks* like?' she said. She had a rough, throaty voice, very sexy, although she was dressed modestly.

'Listen, let me make it up to you. Let me take you out to dinner.'

'So that you can throw that all over me too? No thanks.'

The waiter returned with a dustpan and brush and some cloths, one of which he handed to the woman. 'Thank you,' she said, and began to walk off with it.

'Wait!' Mike called, and hurried after her. 'At least give me your number so I can reimburse you for the dress and shoes.'

'I work at Gardner and Gardner,' she said. 'I'll leave the dress at reception. You can pick it up and take it to the dry-cleaners if you want. But there's no need.'

'Dinner would be more fun though. I'm good company, just ask anyone here.'

'Aren't you going to help clean up the mess you made?'

'Oh, oh yeah.' He turned back to help the waiter, and when he looked for her again, she was gone.

Gardner and Gardner was a large law firm on Fifth Avenue. Mike picked up the dress the next day and left two dozen roses at reception, with his phone number. She didn't call, and he found himself thinking about her almost constantly. Her legs, how she tucked her hair behind her ear, the way she'd gazed down at him and dismissed him, the richness of her voice. She'd come across as strong and tough and feminine. Not glamorous, but secure in her skin. He thought about looking her up – her photo was bound to be on the firm's website, and he could find out her name – but he didn't, because that would be weird, and also because Mike had never asked a woman out again if she turned him down the first time. There were too many women out there without having to chase just one.

And besides, they'd never turned him down. Was that because he was irresistible, or because he only ever asked a certain kind of woman?

He was still thinking about her three weeks later when he was standing at the bar at the theatre. Over his shoulder, he heard a laugh that could only be described as dirty. He glanced over at a rangy middle-aged woman with dyed orange hair, standing next to the one who got away. She was wearing another black dress, not the same one that he'd ruined, and her hair was up in a sleek ponytail that made her neck look long and graceful.

He ordered two extra glasses of champagne and took them over. The woman whose dress he'd ruined, who'd ignored two dozen roses, recognised him straight away. She didn't look exactly pleased to see him, but she accepted a glass of champagne without throwing it in his face, so that was a start.

'Mike Ellis,' he said. 'I spilled a tray of meat on you. Most embarrassing moment of my life.'

'Was it the most embarrassing?' she said. 'Lucky you.'

'I'm Vee's mom Dorothy,' said the older woman with the shocking orange hair and the dirty laugh. She held out her hand and Mike shook it. Vee didn't offer hers. 'I'm up from Florida for the week. Vee hates plays and I love them, so she's suffering in silence.'

'Not in silence,' said Vee.

'You spilled meat on her?' Dorothy asked, and Mike explained what had happened, including the algae smoothie and the two dozen roses. 'Are you rich?' Dorothy asked next. Her voice had the same roughness as her daughter's, but it was more ragged, as if she'd smoked every day of her life. She had a deep tan and was wearing a flowered polyester dress, off the shoulder, and four-inch heels.

'Yes, very.'

'I thought so. You look like it. Vee, why wouldn't you go out with this guy?'

This made Mike laugh. Vee didn't laugh. She said, 'Mum, cut it out.' She sounded just like a teenager when she said it, which Mike found charming.

'What did you say your name was?' asked Dorothy.

'Mike Ellis.'

'Ellis? As in Alonzo Ellis?'

'That's my dad.'

'Alonzo Ellis's boy,' said Dorothy, turning to Vee and elbowing her.

'I don't know who that is.'

'She doesn't read any of the magazines,' said Dorothy to Mike. 'How do you like the play?'

'Love it,' said Mike, who didn't really care for it either way, but he wanted to see if Vee would roll her eyes. She did. It was adorable.

'See?' said Dorothy. 'This guy has taste. And he's single. You *are* single, right?'

'I am very single.'

'You should go out with him.'

'Mum, I can choose my own boyfriends.'

'You suck at choosing your own boyfriends. You have worse taste than I do, even. Take his number.'

'I'm sorry about this,' Vee said to Mike. 'My mother is a pain in the arse.'

'You don't have to call him. I think you should, though. Learn from my mistakes.'

'Mum.'

'Give it to me,' said Dorothy to Mike. 'I'll give it to her. She might call you, who knows. She stopped doing what I told her to do when she was about six years old, so I wouldn't hold my breath, but she might. Stranger things have happened.' She took her phone out of her bag – it was in a rose-gold diamanté case – and punched Mike's number in. 'If you're not married, you're an improvement on her last one.'

'They're going to start the third act,' said Vee, dragging her mother away without speaking to Mike again. Mike watched them go. He hoped she would call.

She called ten days later. 'I told my mother I'd go out with you so she would stop nagging me.'

'I'll take it. Dinner tonight?' He was in Aspen. He was already opening his laptop to book a flight to JFK.

'Lunch tomorrow,' she said. 'I'm free between twelve-thirty and one-fifteen. Then I have to go to court.'

He met her in reception. She was dressed in a trouser suit and low heels, but she'd put on lipstick, which he saw as a hopeful sign. He walked with her to a bench in a park round the block from her office and handed her a paper bag.

'Peanut butter and jelly sandwiches,' he said. 'I made them myself.'

'Keeping the expectations low?'

'Are you joking? I never make sandwiches. The stakes couldn't be higher here.'

That made her laugh. It was as sexy as he'd hoped. After lunch, she told him they could do dinner next time, as long as he wasn't cooking.

Nearly eight years later, Mike sat at brunch and used his thumb to twist his wedding ring round his finger. His father had turned up with his mother this time. They'd ordered Bloody Marys but none of them had drunk them yet.

'I don't care why she wants a divorce,' said his father. 'I'm not interested in the ins and outs and what you might have done or what she might have said. None of that matters. Marriage isn't about that, Michael, and it's time you figured that out.'

'It sort of is about that, Dad.'

'That woman is the best thing that ever happened to you,' his mother said. 'Vivian is the only thing in your life that has lasted more than a few months. She is the only thing you have ever had to work for. She's a good woman. She's smart and she's savvy and she's got a foot in the real world.'

'I know that, but she—'

'Stop keeping score,' said his father sharply. 'Do you think your mother and I haven't had our differences? The point is that we have worked them out. We have supported each other and stayed together.'

Mike crossed his arms and slumped back in his chair.

'We knew from the minute we met Vivian that she was the one for you. She sees right through you.'

'You can say that again,' he mumbled.

'That woman could be the making of you,' his father said. 'This could be the one relationship that turns you into an adult.'

'Because you're not doing that by yourself, Michael.'

'God knows that I've tried, but it hasn't worked. Your mother has tried, too. But we're finished now. You're thirty-nine years old, you have to grow up and take your marriage seriously.'

'I do take it seriously. I'm not the one who's asking for a divorce.'

'Have you been having an affair?'

'No.'

His father gave him a look. He saw, to his dismay, the same look on his mother's face. He repeated, '*No*. I was as surprised by this as you are.'

'She hasn't told you why?'

'Does she want children?' asked his mother. 'Is that why? You could give her that.'

'She's never wanted kids. We had that discussion.'

'Then what does she say?'

'The bus hit her, and when she got out of hospital, she said she wanted a divorce.'

'We know why it is,' his father said. 'You do too.'

'I wish, for once, you would stop talking to me like a child. Do you ever think about that? Maybe if you treated me like an adult, I'd stop feeling like a child.'

'Exactly. This is our fault, at root.'

'Finally.' But he didn't like that either. He didn't like feeling about eight years old.

'So, your mother and I have agreed. If you divorce Vivian – if you throw away this woman and this chance – you're on your own. We're through supporting you while you make bad choices.'

He sat upright. 'What?'

'We should have done it a long time ago. Let you stand on your own two feet.'

'Mum?' He turned to her.

'It's tough love, Mikey.'

'This is ridiculous. This is – blackmail.'

'No, it isn't. It's the support you need to get your marriage back on track.'

'But *she* wants to get divorced.'

'Then you've got your work cut out for you, haven't you?'

Chapter Ten

Vee

The cast fell open and Vee lifted her arm, unburdened for the first time in eight weeks. Her wrist looked thinner than usual, and the skin was pale and flaky. 'Ew,' she said, and rubbed at it.

'You've got tan lines,' said the nurse.

'Should've used sunscreen.' She lifted her arm and looked at it. It felt light. There was a distinct line where the cast had started on her forearm, and along the base of each of her four fingers and thumb. 'It's like the adultery line.'

'The what?'

'You know. The line left on a married man's finger when he takes off his wedding ring when he's away from home.'

'Wouldn't know,' said the nurse. 'Never had a thing for married men myself.'

'Smart.' Vee wiggled her fingers in the air. 'This is great. I feel so free.'

'It's healed well. It'll be weak for a little while and you might be clumsy with it yet. I've got a sheet of exercises for you to do. You should bounce right back.'

'I'm good at bouncing back.'

The nurse gave her a photocopied sheet with diagrams and then clicked on his computer. 'Says here that you were hit by a bus.'

'Uh huh. The M4 from The Cloisters to Midtown. It came out of nowhere.'

'Nowhere? Or The Cloisters?'

'Same difference, right?'

'Never been to New York, wouldn't know.'

'Never been to the city?'

'The City,' he said, the ironic capitals clear, and laughed. 'Never been south of Massachusetts. I came from New Brunswick, did my degree at UMPI.'

'You're missing out.'

He shrugged, clearly unbothered. 'I like my hiking and kayaking. Anyway, you're not going to have to worry about getting hit by a bus on Unity Island. Maybe a golf cart.'

'Those things can do a lot of damage.' Vee got up, rotated her wrist again, wiggled the fingers. 'Thank you.'

The nurse was still looking at her. 'What's it like being hit by a bus?'

It's like seeing Mrs Rachel Ames sitting on a cracked green leather chair.

'It's about what you'd expect,' Vee said. 'It hurt, but only after I woke up.'

She was in the waiting room, digging in her handbag for her phone to check how much time she had before the afternoon ferry when someone said, 'Vivian?'

Vee recognised the voice before she saw the woman, sitting in a chair by the reception desk. She had short silver hair, round glasses, blue dangly earrings, a t-shirt with a moose on it. 'Mrs Ames?'

'Sterling said you were in town.' Brenda gestured her over and Vee hesitated because if there was one thing she did not want to do, it was sit in a doctor's waiting room next to the mother of her childhood best friend, practically her foster mom, and explain where she'd been for the past twenty years. But Vee had never, in her life, refused to do something that Brenda Ames asked her to do. She didn't think many people ever had the heart to.

She went to sit down next to Brenda. 'You've cut all your hair off. It looks good.' But Brenda looked much thinner. A cane rested next to her chair.

'Did it when I turned sixty. Ancient history.' Brenda reached over and circled her arms around Vee and hugged her, hard. 'Give your old pretend mom a peck on the cheek.'

Vee kissed her cheek. She still smelled of Avon Skin So Soft and cake, so Vee kissed her again. She never used to kiss Brenda, even when she was a little girl. She was never exactly a kissy child.

'Oh, I like that,' said Brenda, and patted her on the shoulder as she let her go. 'I've been waiting a very long time. So tell me: have you visited Sterling yet?'

'Um, well, I—'

'Why not?'

'Is he mad at me?'

'Are you scared of my son?'

'Hm.'

'Sterling is scary? Sterling? Are we talking about the same fella? My son has as much malice in him as his father did, and there was no malice in Thomas Ames. And you used to be tougher than that.'

'I'm not afraid of Sterling.' She glanced around the waiting room to see who else was in it. Nobody she recognised, thank God, but everyone was certainly interested. 'I don't think he wants to see me, is all. It's good to see you, though, Mrs Ames.'

'Brenda, please. You're all grown up now. Look at you. You look great.'

'Oh.' She waved her hand in the air to dismiss the compliment. 'I finally learned the secrets of hair straighteners and good make-up, that's all. Um ... Sterling isn't here with you, is he?'

'No, I don't like to bother him with routine things like doctor's appointments. How's your mother?'

'She is exactly the same. She lives in Florida and she retired as soon as she could.'

'You bought her a nice house, I bet. I hear you're a lawyer now.'

'Actually, she wouldn't take a penny for it. She wanted something that was all her own.'

'That's Dorothy, all right. How about you? I hear you're married too. Have you got any children?'

'No.'

'Too busy?'

'We've decided not to have them.'

Vee steeled herself for the usual questions, but Brenda only said, 'Well. You have a choice these days, I suppose. I'm incredibly nosy, I'm sorry. It's only getting worse as I get older.'

'It's fine. Does – do you have any grandchildren?'

'Oh, it's so sad, my daughter-in-law Rachel can't have them. When Sterling took over the store, I thought it would be in the Ames family for generations and generations to come. But we get by.'

'It would be strange having the store run by someone who isn't an Ames.'

'Tom had some cousins, though they all left a long time ago. But we don't have to worry about that for a long time yet, of course. I keep hoping Sterling and Rachel will adopt. But I don't like to interfere. Anyway, enough about us. What's it like to be back home?'

'The house we're renting isn't very much like where I grew up.'

'I meant on the island. Once an island girl, always an island girl.'

'You're still living there?'

'No, I'm an inlander now. I've got arthritis, so it's hard for me to get around.' She touched her cane.

'Oh, I'm sorry.'

'It is what it is. I make the best of everything, you know me. So you didn't answer my question.'

'I think Unity looks exactly the same as it always did.'

Brenda let out a long sigh. 'He misses you,' she said. 'He never found another friend like you. And he's one of those men, like his father, who's always alone. Even in a crowd of people, you know? Tom was like that too.'

'It's been a long time,' said Vee, and she got up, but Brenda caught her wrist, the same one that had just been freed from her cast.

'He's stubborn,' she said. 'But all it would take is a little time and effort from you. It's always women who have to put in the time and effort, and the men who get to be stubborn, but that's how it is.'

'He's not stubborn, Mrs A— Brenda. He has a right to be angry with me. I skipped town when he needed me and I never talked to him again. That's a good thing to be angry about. It's something he should be angry about. It's okay. I can live with it.'

'But neither of you should have to. Like you said: it was a long time ago. And he's lonely now. He and Rachel can't have children, and it's breaking his heart every day and he just keeps going on and going on. I can't talk to him about it, he shuts me down. I've never been able to talk to him about any of these things, especially when he's got an idea in his head about what he's going to do.'

'Brenda, I don't think any of this is my business.' She gently disengaged her wrist from Brenda's hand, though she gave it an affectionate squeeze before releasing it.

'Maybe not. And you have to make the right choice for you, dear. But you should know that I'm not angry with you. God knows I can understand why you and Dorothy would want to leave Unity. You always needed to be free, to be yourself. And we loved you while we had you, me and Tom, and Sterling too. Sterling wanted you at his dad's funeral, and he didn't understand, but I did.'

'Mrs Ames?' said the nurse at the door of reception.

'Oh, it's my turn.' Brenda stood up, her hand on the arm of the chair. 'I hope I'll see you again. I play cribbage at the store whenever I can on Thursday nights. Or I've got a flat on Orchard Street. You're welcome any time. I'll make your favourite snickerdoodles. And in case you were worried – for my part, I never held a grudge against you at all.'

Vee fled as soon as Brenda turned to the nurse. Outside the doctors' office in the light of day, she looked around the car park to make sure that Sterling wasn't there. And then she hurried across it, unlocking the Audi as she went so she could duck into it, put on her sunglasses, pull down the sun visor, make herself as invisible as she could in a hugely expensive car, as she drove away.

Because Vee was sure that, as kind as Brenda was, if Brenda knew the truth, she would bear a grudge.

She hadn't seen the bus. She was heading from a yoga class to meet friends for coffee. She had her yoga mat and gym bag slung over her shoulder and was wearing leggings and spotless white running shoes.

She was thinking about the friends she was meeting – both former colleagues at Gardner and Gardner, who still had busy high-paced jobs and who had very little to say about other subjects. At one time, they'd been the only three women working at the firm, and they all had to look out for each other's backs. They'd fought nearly constant battles for equal pay and promotion and the right not to have their points interrupted and then explained back to them by men. They traded tips about how to avoid the senior partner's wandering hands after a late lunch. They'd called themselves, ironically, Charlie's Angels (the lecherous partner was Charles Gardner), and considered themselves the forefront of feminism. Then Vee married a rich guy and discovered that she didn't need to fight those battles any more. She discovered that without the battles, she didn't really like the job any more, either. So she quit.

She had considered these women her best friends, sisters in arms, but now she had nothing in common with them. Charles and his hands had retired two years ago, so these days the Angels mostly bitched about the younger women joining the firm and how easy they had it and how stupid and ungrateful they were. The Angels dissected these younger women's clothes and hair and life choices, the schools they had been to and how 'woke' they were. She wondered if the Angels had always been so boring and petty and she'd never noticed because she'd also been that boring and petty, and she was wondering what it said about her that she hung on to the friendships like a lifeline, even though meeting these friends always frustrated her and she always left promising herself that she wouldn't bother again. But she still did, even four years after she'd left the firm where she hated working every day. She suspected that every time she left them, the Angels bitched about her behind her back, too, for abandoning her feminist principles and depending on a man for financial support.

She considered that she could always make an excuse and leave early, but then how to fill the long afternoon between when she got home and the pre-dinner drinks that she was having with the Voorheeses? Maybe she should give in and take tennis lessons, learn another language, do any of the million and one things she'd always promised herself she would do, but she had been too busy hustling and putting herself through law school and working her way up in the firm and punching through the glass ceiling to do, until she got married and had all the time in the world.

Mostly she took it day by day. It was strange not having a plan any more, or at least not needing to have a plan that stretched beyond the next month or two. At first it had felt roomy, full of space that she could stretch out in. Their life literally took up the entire country. She and Mike had the brownstone on the Upper East Side, the villa in Miami near her mom and the marina, the flat in Aspen for the ski season, the pied à terre in LA, the boat in St Helena. All of them, except the boat, had real addresses with street numbers. Each of them came with a different yet overlapping set of people, a different calendar of social events, a different yoga class and hairstylist and manicurist and personal trainer and chef. They were busy, so busy, all the time being idle, having so much fun, and her mother had never been so happy.

Vee slotted into that life, as she had slotted into her new life in Florida with her mom when they'd moved there, as she'd slotted into her new high school she went to for her senior year, as she'd slotted into University of Florida and University of Chicago law school, all the part-time jobs and internships and side hustles she'd had to take to afford a better life in the future. She fitted in. By the time she was twenty-one she could speak half a dozen languages – not actual languages like her pidgin Spanish or tourist French, but social languages. Class languages. The inflection and abbreviations you used to signal that you were part of a group, that you belonged there. It wasn't just in the words and the way you said them, but it was your clothes, your posture, the way you met people's eyes. She'd always had a talent for it, ever since she was a little girl and she swapped her home language of speaking cautiously when Pops was drinking, quietly when he was sleeping, head down, gaze skittish, for the brighter language of the Ameses' house with its pleases and thank yous and I love yous, spoken without any fear.

Marrying Mike, she had slipped into his world. She had adjusted herself to having multiple homes, many social circles, to owning everything she touched. It was only lately that she had started to feel a creeping suspicion that this life wasn't roomy: it was empty. It only had echoes, like the Angels and their former friendship.

At the exact moment that she stepped off the kerb and into the street, she was remembering the conversation she'd had on the phone with Mike that morning, where she'd mentioned that she wasn't sure if she should meet the Angels or not. He was on the deck of his boat in St Helena; she could hear the water and the seagulls in the background, the clinking of the lines on the mast. 'Do what you want, babe,' he'd said to her. 'It doesn't matter.' And she'd had to bite her lip not to reply, 'Does anything matter?'

She raised one hand to pull her hair out of its ponytail and she heard a whoosh, a wind like a nor'easter but without any force, and she looked up ahead of her and on the other side of the road there was a little girl, her eyes perfect circles, her mouth a perfect circle, pointing her finger at Vee. Vee had time to think, with compassion, *She looks scared* and then the whole world slammed into her, all the jobs all the money all the places all the people she'd ever met and been, and Vee went flying sideways, away from that world, unconscious before she hit the road surface.

When she woke up, she could tell she was in hospital because it looked just like it did on television. She couldn't move her arm or open her eyes more than part-way and her head throbbed with every heartbeat. She was thirsty and her mouth tasted of blood, like when, as a child, she'd lost one of her baby teeth and swallowed it. She looked around for someone, but she was in a private room and the door was closed.

She knew the drill. She was supposed to croak, 'Where am I?' But when the nurse came in, a few minutes after she'd woken up, Vee didn't say that. Instead, she said, 'Who am I?'

The nurse ran to get a doctor who performed a neurological examination which confirmed that Vee did indeed know the date, the current president, her address (the one in New York – they didn't ask about the others), her date of birth and her name, Vivian Gail Harper Ellis. She knew her husband's name and that he was in St Helena sailing for the week but she could reach him on his mobile and when she discovered that her phone had been smashed she told the nurse what his number was from memory; she knew the name of her insurers and of the Angels, who were probably wondering why she never turned up for their coffee date and had most likely spent the entire time bitching about her over their non-dairy flat whites.

It was news to her that she'd been hit by a bus. It hadn't felt like a bus. It had felt like *everything*.

The doctor told her she had a concussion, a black eye, a sprained ankle and two broken bones in her arm, and they were going to keep an eye on her for a little while, but it looked as if she'd been extraordinarily lucky. The nurse told her that she'd reached Mike and he was arranging to fly home. 'Is there anyone else you'd like me to call for you?' she asked. 'Someone to sit with you?'

Vee thought of her wide and varied acquaintance in New York, all the different languages she spoke. She tried to picture any of these people in her hospital room, and couldn't. 'No,' she said.

'Do you have any other questions?' asked the nurse.

Yes, thought Vee. *Who am I? You haven't answered that yet.*

'No,' she said. 'Thank you.'

There was bad weather in the Gulf, and she was discharged before Mike could fly back to New York. She got herself into a cab and up the steps to their house, leaning clumsily on her crutches, and installed herself on the sofa in the den with a six-pack of Diet Coke and a bottle of ibuprofen, her favourite Chinese delivery on speed-dial, and a box set of *Grey's Anatomy*. None of it felt like it was hers: not the sofa or the den, or the Kung Pao chicken or the widescreen television, or her arm in its fresh new cast or her leg propped up on a cushion. She had to plan ahead to get to the bathroom and she couldn't put her hair back in a ponytail because that required two hands.

But it was more than that: more than the bus or the cast or the pain. She was in another world. The bus had sent her sailing out of her life. The cliché was that you got hit by a bus and you suddenly realised that life was short, that food tasted better and nature was more beautiful, that you had to do all the things that you'd been putting off all of your life because being hit by a bus taught you a huge life lesson in mortality. She did not feel that way. She felt displaced. She had taken a step through an invisible wall, or she had been pushed, and now all of her effortless assimilation was gone. Now it was an effort. Everything was an effort, and nothing mattered.

Maybe nothing ever had. Maybe she'd been too busy working, too busy being married, to see it.

Mike came bundling in at about midnight. He'd been sending her texts for hours updating her on his travel progress, though she hadn't answered any of them and had stopped reading them two episodes of *Grey's Anatomy* ago. She heard him unlock the door and call her name, and she heard him drop his bags and rush to the den. 'Holy shit,' he said. 'You really do look like you've been hit by a bus.'

She looked up at him, this man she'd married. He was sunkissed and still wearing shorts. He was carrying a pale blue Tiffany's bag, which he placed on her lap. It was so typical of Mike that he would think that the appropriate response to a near-death experience was to buy jewellery. And also she didn't know that at all. She didn't know why someone would go to Tiffany's. She didn't know what she felt about Mike. After seven years of marriage, she didn't feel anything at all, and she was realising that maybe she hadn't felt anything for a very long time.

'Open it,' he told her.

'I can't,' she said. 'I can only use one hand.'

'I'll open it for you,' he said, and reached for it, but she stopped him.

'I want a divorce,' she said.

And now she was here, in Maine again, the place where she'd told herself she'd never return. She was a summer person, and her husband had rented this huge property, and she was on the ferry that she'd ridden a million times before, going back to Unity because she'd promised Mike that she would give their marriage one more try.

Vee had once thought that life was a line. You had three choices. Either you started in one place and carried on in the same place, going forward with some ups and downs but not really changing, like the Ames family or the summer people or most of the families on Unity, or Mike. Or, you started in one place and you relentlessly slid downwards, like her pops. Or you started at the bottom and went up, as her mother had, or as had Vee herself.

The last time she'd ridden this ferry again, on the way over here a few weeks ago, she'd begun to think that maybe life wasn't a line but a circle, because Vee kept on coming back to the same place over and over and over again. If you were travelling in a circle, if the circle was big enough, you might feel as if you were going in a straight line, until you noticed the repetition of landmarks.

But now, riding back from the doctor with her cast off, she wondered if maybe it was more like a spiral. Most of the time you thought you were going straight or in circles, but every now and then something happened that kicked you up or down another level. Made you stop recognising the landmarks. Made you have to assess reality all over again.

Vee had been kicked this way three times in her life. Most recently, two days ago, when she first set eyes on Rachel Ames. Once, eight weeks ago, when she was hit by a bus. And the first time, twenty years ago, when she left Unity.

Chapter Eleven

Rachel

'We're absolutely not going.'

'Okay.'

'It's cribbage night anyway, so I'm busy.'

'Okay.'

'And there's no one to cover the store.'

'Okay.'

'And also, who the hell is this guy anyway?'

'The husband of your childhood best friend, apparently.'

'I know, but who is he? Why would I want to spend an evening with him?'

'He seems nice enough. Very rich.'

'Well that goes without saying.'

Penny Stewart came up to the counter with a gallon of milk and a loaf of white bread. 'Afternoon, Sterling.'

'Nice weather,' said Sterling to her.

'Ayuh. You got any American cheese? All I could see was that fancy stuff.'

'I put some out this morning,' said Rachel. 'It's next to the Vermont cheddar.'

Penny didn't answer. Sterling got up. 'I'll look out back for you.'

Rachel leaned against the shelves of cigarettes, waiting to see if Penny would make an effort to strike up a conversation. Usually if Rachel was the only person in the store, Penny conducted her transactions in silence. It was so well worn by now that Rachel

91

had never even bothered asking Sterling why this woman who'd grown up a thousand miles from her hated her on sight. At first Rachel had tried to be pleasant, but it had been three years by now with barely a word. Why?

Rachel gazed steadily and in silence at Penny, who avoided her gaze. Rachel had considered that maybe Penny had a crush on Sterling, or she didn't like Jews, or freckles, or people from Illinois. But underneath it all it didn't matter. There probably wasn't even a reason why. It was just a knee-jerk reaction to an outsider. Some people from Unity hid it; some didn't. But they all had it, to some degree or other. They held their insularity as a point of pride.

'Here you go,' said Sterling, returning with an armful of Kraft Singles. 'How many packs do you want?'

'Two. Nice to see the shop so quiet today. Usually in the summer I have to wait in a queue for half an hour.'

Even in peak season, even when there was a line for ice cream and a separate line for the checkout and a third line for ice and bait and lobsters, there were never enough people on Unity to form a line that required more than ten minutes' waiting. Penny Stewart was obviously someone who complained about stop signs or paint drying. And yet she'd lived her entire life on an island which was only accessible to the mainland at set times.

'A full shop's good for business, so you won't hear me complaining,' said Sterling good-naturedly as he rang up her purchases, put them in a paper bag for her, and gave her her change. Penny grunted, told him 'Thanks,' and left the shop without once glancing in Rachel's direction.

'She's a bundle of joy,' said Rachel. 'Also, the cheese was right there.'

'The Stewarts aren't known for being cheerful, and she chose to marry into them, so.'

'Anyway,' said Rachel, 'I'll tell Mike and Vee that we're not coming.'

Sterling frowned. 'Locals don't go to the houses of summer people for dinner parties. That's not how it works around here. Even the families who have been coming here every year for generations, I've still never seen the inside of most of their houses. They come to the store if they want to visit.'

'She was your best friend, though, so that's different.'

'Is it? She's one of them now. Maybe that was what she always wanted. Maybe we were never good enough for her. Maybe they invited us over just to show off.'

Rachel weighed up whether to say anything, and decided to risk it. 'Why are you so angry, Sterling?'

He looked startled. 'Me? I'm not angry. You know me, I don't have a temper.'

'You sure sound as if you are.'

'Having a strong sense of right and wrong isn't the same as being angry.'

'It isn't?'

'No, it's completely different.'

'Okay.' She turned and picked up the clipboard with the delivery lists for the next day and began checking them through. The store was silent, or as silent as it ever got: the hum of the refrigerator, the knocking of the chest freezer out back. Gulls outside, the wind, diesel boat engines, the never-ending susurration of the Atlantic. She liked this about Unity, how it never got quiet, even in the middle of winter. Back when she was a kid she used to keep the radio on all the time for company, loud sometimes to cover up the arguing. When it was quiet, things were wrong. Even when she'd gone to college, she'd worn headphones in the library so it wouldn't feel too quiet. The few guys she'd dated got annoyed when she left the TV on all night. But she didn't need that here. She felt more secure in places where there was constant noise that you could safely ignore.

'If we don't go they're going to think that we snubbed them.

And that's bad for business. We've always been welcoming, you know?'

Rachel understood that by 'we', Sterling meant the Ames family and, by extension, all of the year-round people. She didn't answer, but she didn't need to because Sterling continued.

'I wish they hadn't asked us. What does she think, anyway, that I'm going to drop everything and come over when she crooks a finger?'

'It was only Mike, and it appeared to be on the spur of the moment.'

'Still. What if they say something to the others?'

By 'others', she assumed he meant other rich summer people, as if they had a secret network which you could only access if you had over a million in the bank and didn't have Maine plates on your car.

'It's one dinner, Sterling. I don't think they meant it to be a big deal.'

'Obviously it is, though.'

'It's fine. I'll drop by and say we're busy.'

He creaked the chair back and forth. Then he got up and carried the leftover packs of cheese to the fridge. When he got back, he said, 'There was already cheese there.'

'Yes, I said that.'

He sat down. 'We're going to have to go, aren't we?'

'We don't have to do anything we don't want to.'

By 'we', she meant 'you'. So many codes to get right.

'Do you want to go?'

'I really don't mind, Sterling. You're the one who's up in knots about it.'

'Did you tell him we'd go?'

'I told him we'd love to, but obviously I'd have to check with you.' That last bit was a lie, but it was so automatic for her to placate other people that it hardly counted.

'And what did he say?'

'He said great.'

Sterling sighed. 'That's it, then. We have to go.'

'I know you see this as a whole big-weight-of-the-past and summer-people-vs-island-people thing, but honestly I think it is just dinner.'

'It is not just dinner,' said Sterling. He sighed again. 'I'll ask Sue if she can cover the store.'

Rachel felt a lift of gladness, a little sparkle. 'Thank you,' she said, and leaned over and kissed Sterling on the cheek, which surprised them both. He laughed.

'Am I really that difficult to persuade to change my mind?' he asked.

'You changed your own mind.'

Chapter Twelve

Vee

'You invited them to dinner? What on earth were you thinking?'

She'd found Mike in the home gym, which was in one of the outbuildings and had a glass wall with an ocean view. He was on the rowing machine when he told her about Rachel's visit and his invitation so it was quite natural that she had to raise her voice to practically a shout to reply.

'She seems nice,' Mike said. 'And he's your old friend, right?'

'Was. *Was* my old friend.'

'Well, you'll have a lot to catch up on.' He stopped rowing, reached for a towel, and grinned up at her. The smile of a little boy who had done something naughty but expected to get away with it. 'Come on. You weren't going to be able to avoid him forever.'

'I was giving it the good old college try.'

'And that meant that you were letting things fester. It's better to get things out in the open.'

'Oh, look at you – Mike Ellis, the paragon of healthy relationships.'

'Hey, I have many faults, but hiding my emotions is not one of them.'

'You avoided Ralph Georgiopolos for fourteen months after you didn't turn up to that gala.'

'That's because I avoid confrontation and I hate being nagged. This is different. You said you two used to be like brother and sister. And he's right here, less than half a mile away. It's weird to avoid him.'

'I'm fine with being weird.' She sulked over to the water cooler and poured herself a paper cup full. Mike followed her and took it out of her hand.

'Thanks,' he said, drinking it. 'Anyway, listen, Vee. You said – one of the things you said – when we discussed our marriage. You said that you didn't feel as if you had any real friends. You said you felt lonely. And here's a guy who knows everything about your childhood, who you have so much in common with, who used to be your best friend in the world. Don't you think you'd be happier if you were friends with him again?'

'Ugh.' She turned away from him to pour another cup of water.

'I want you to be happy. That's what this is all about.'

She sighed. She was not entirely certain that all of this was just to make her happy. Mike had a way of making himself happy, or at least amusing himself, which to Mike was more or less the same thing as being happy. But the thing was … he'd listened to her. Not just her random stories about when she was a kid and she and Sterling used to get into lots of trouble, those normal kid stories. When she'd told him how she felt, he'd actually listened. He hadn't said it didn't matter.

'It's probably going to be World War Three over the appetisers,' she said.

'Perfect. I love a lively evening.'

'And I am not cooking for this. It's going to be enough to keep myself from getting embarrassingly drunk. In fact, forget that, I'm going to be drunk before they even arrive.'

'We'll have a barbecue.'

'No caterers or anything. That's summer people bullshit and it will annoy them.'

'I'll do all the grilling myself.'

'And don't buy all the ingredients ready-made from the store and serve it back to them. That's rude.'

'We've got everything we need already in the freezer.'

'You've really thought about this, haven't you?'

'Like I said. I only want to make you happy.' He kissed her on the lips. She wiped her mouth with the back of her hand. 'And I saw that.'

'If you want me to keep your kisses, they need less sweat in them.'

'Deal.' He took hold of her arm and began to steer her to the shower room at the far end. 'You've got a naked arm now. Let's get it all wet and soapy.'

'Mike,' she protested, but it was empty. She'd thought all her protests were empty, but it seemed as if he did pay attention. Maybe he was right. Maybe it was time that she and Sterling became friends again. And also …

'What did you think of his wife?' she asked him, as he was unbuttoning her dress, pulling it up over her head.

'She seems okay. Nothing compared to my wife. C'mere.' He pushed down his shorts and reached for her.

Chapter Thirteen

Rachel

Rachel had spent a lot of time studying maps of the Maine coast before she came to live here. She'd always learned about life from books. She'd chosen to study history partly because her father used to teach it, but mostly because history was all about choosing perspectives. Things were easier to understand from a distance.

At ground level it was difficult to understand the geography of the Maine coast; it was a confusion of bays and fingers and rocks. There were so many necessary lighthouses. But on a map, you could see the Ice Age at work, the direction the glaciers took from the land that still fringes out to sea. All the peninsulas point south and east, and the islands are scattered like tears.

The names told the human history. Some kept their Native American names: Schoodic, Matinicus, Monhegan. Others were named after the settlers who drove the original people away (Baxter, Vinalhaven, Bartlett). Many were named for their geographical features (Long Island, Two Bush, Seven Hundred Acre Island) or animals (Squirrel, Seal, Swan, Deer, Eagle, Hog). Most of their names were reflective of a practical, unitarian worldview, the view of sailors and fishermen and farmers and land-grabbers rather than preachers or philosophers. Some islands had a sort of poetry in their name – Smuttynose, Ironbound – but even then, the poetry was based on the physical.

Only a few were named after ideas. One of those was Unity.

*

When you walked round the island it felt like a circle, but from the air and on maps, Unity was shaped like an elongated oval with jagged edges for the rocky coves. The smaller, uninhabited Brimstone Island with its lighthouse lay off the southeastern side, along with Big Duck and Little Duck, which were no more than lumps of grey rock topped with a few pines. Unity looked as if a piece of clay had been dropped from a height onto a hard surface, and splattered as it landed. The buildings all lay in a ring on the perimeter, following the coast, placed at various intervals and distances from the only road.

The middle of the island formed a hump, covered with pine trees, most of them bowed from the prevailing winds. It was served only by a rocky path and was the subject of constant waxing and waning debate between the islanders about whether a space should be cleared to create a landing strip for small aircraft. Rachel, tending the till in the store, had heard the conversation in various permutations dozens of times. People had talked so much about it that usually it was spoken in shorthand. A minority were in favour, citing convenience, quicker access to medical care in emergencies, better supplies, and greater attractiveness to tourists, especially the ones with money to spend. Most islanders were against it. When she first arrived on Unity, Rachel had assumed that people were opposed to the airstrip because of the environmental and noise impact – which she agreed with – but as the years went by and the same arguments were rehashed with no real definitive solution, she came to understand that the main argument against the airstrip was an inbuilt Unity resistance to any form of change at all.

Rachel was against an airstrip for purely selfish reasons, because she liked how rarely used the path to the top of the island was, even in summer. Day tourists didn't come up here because they wanted the beach; summer people were busy with the water; for most islanders, it was a pointless walk up and down a hill. The trees blocked off most of the view of the water, except for in one spot, a rock-studded clearing. There you could glimpse silvery-blue ocean between gaps in every direction – puzzle pieces that, when put together, might make a view. It felt like the highest point on the island, though Rachel wasn't sure. As a destination, it was an anticlimax.

Her period had come this morning. Even though she'd expected it, it always took her by surprise. She woke up alone, as usual; Sterling was already at the store. The smell of toast and coffee hung ghostly in the air. Other than that you wouldn't know that he'd been home at all. She got up out of bed and saw the red smear on the white sheet, and stood looking at it for a little while. Last year she would have cried. She would have worried about how to tell Sterling. She would have thought guiltily about Brenda. Even before the doctors and the diagnosis, she would have known that there was something inherently wrong with her, that it was all her fault.

It was one of the first questions Sterling had asked her when they started chatting on the app: *Do you see yourself with kids some-day?* And of course she'd said yes. Children were family. Children were part of any marriage. Sometimes Rachel felt as if her love floated around her like a cloud, potent and invisible, waiting. It was in her breath, deep in her lungs, in front of her vision. It got in the way of everything and had nothing safe to attach to. A child would absorb that love, make it corporeal. A child would give her love back to her. It would be hers, finally. Something and someone that was hers. And as soon as she met Sterling she knew he'd be a great father. He was principled, passionate, rational, caring – everything her own father had never been. Just talking to him she felt that her love could become solid, more real. It was something that she could finally touch.

But when she visited Unity for the first time she saw his question meant more than that. It was only the second time she'd met Sterling in person. Her brother was still calling him her 'internet date', even though they'd spent a long weekend together in New

York City, probably the best weekend of her life, a weekend of lazy breakfasts and strolling around museums, people-watching in the park. She drove up Route 1 and he was there at the ferry terminal waiting for her. She'd been afraid she wouldn't recognise him, but she did right away. His hair was ruffled by the sea breeze and his eyes were the same colour as the autumn ocean, and they had little crinkles in the corners from where he smiled. 'You look different,' she told him after he kissed her (so new!) and he smiled and said, 'It must be the Red Sox shirt, I didn't dare to wear it in New York.' But it wasn't the shirt, which was hidden underneath his jacket anyway. It was the way he moved, the way he spoke, unhurried and certain. He knew he belonged here. He was utterly at home.

She had liked him a lot before that moment, but that was the moment where she decided she could love him.

It was May and, as they rode the ferry over, Sterling couldn't stop talking. He was enthusiastic, he knew everyone and introduced her. He pointed out a pod of dolphins in the water, a seal bobbing like a swimming dog. They had lunch with his mother who was – well, she was Brenda, who didn't love her? – and then he took her on a tour of the island. The store, of course, which he showed her with the sort of pride she'd rarely seen in anyone. The man was enthusiastic about a new ice-cream freezer. Who got excited about ice-cream freezers? She found it hopelessly endearing. And then the island itself. It looked like somewhere out of a movie. The sky, pure and blue and enormous. The ever-moving ocean, filling the air with salt. No cars, just the sound of birds and wind, the engine of a lobster boat. The houses were crazy New England quaint: painted clapboard and weathered shingle, with pitched roofs and window shutters. Sterling held her hand. Was this serious? Would she live here someday? Could she?

The school was a one-room clapboard building, painted red with white trim, like a Norman Rockwell painting. 'Did you really go to school here?' Rachel asked, thinking of her own primary school, a squat concrete factory built in the sixties to process hundreds of children.

'Until I was ten, and then we went to the junior high on the mainland.'

'You rode a boat to school every day?'

'I stayed with my grandmother during the week, and came back at weekends.' He led her up to the door, which had a sign on it. UNITY HISTORICAL SOCIETY.

'It's not a school any more?'

'There aren't enough kids. We've only got two families with children living here during the school year.' He opened the door for her and she thought about that 'we', how easily he talked about the entire island like a family.

The front half of the room was still set up as a schoolroom, with desks and a blackboard on the wall. 'I used to sit at this one,' Sterling told her, pointing at a desk in the front row.

'Of course you did,' she said. 'Were you the star pupil?'

'There were only a dozen of us, and I was somewhere in the middle. Here I am.' He showed her a framed photo on the wall: children of various ages standing in front of the school, smaller ones in front, taller ones behind. Their teacher, a woman with permed hair, stood to one side. Sterling was easy to pick out. He looked into the camera with a serious smile and earnest eyes.

'You were so adorable, what happened?' Rachel said, aware she was flirting. Flirtation was new enough to her that she kept on looking at the photographs. They lined every wall, a few in colour but mostly in black-and-white. She walked slowly along them. School year after school year after school year, rows of children in dresses and trousers and shorts gazing at the camera. There were rarely more than fifteen or twenty children, though a couple of photos had as few as six. The hairstyles and the clothes and the film quality changed, but the children looked similar. 'There must be generations of the same families here,' she said.

'Yes. There are some years when most of the photos are taken up by the children of one family. I think this one is nearly all Gallaghers.'

There were other photographs: boat builders, house builders, fishermen, farmers, houses, several photos of Ames' General, women hanging washing, children climbing on lobster traps. But Rachel kept on coming back to the school pictures. There was something about them, the number of them, all of them posed in exactly the same way in front of the same building. At one point the school had been white. She was used to looking for dates; the oldest school photograph she found was 1879. Many were yellowed and faded, and some had spots of mildew. But they had been kept carefully, all framed and hung in straight rows, one after the other after the other. The children gazed into the camera and they grew and then they disappeared and other children took their place.

'That's the history of this island,' she said. 'All these kids.'

'History and future,' Sterling agreed. 'But like I said, there aren't many any more. Most kids, when they graduate high school, want to live somewhere else. There aren't any jobs except fishing and the tourist industry. If you want an education, or if you want to do something else, you have to leave.' He looked around the room. 'Theoretically you could work remotely from here, online, so we could get young professional families, but that's not so easy either because the house prices are through the roof. Unless you've got a house already, handed down from your family, it's unaffordable for most working people. And even those who do have a house here, it's hard to resist the temptation to sell it to developers for a big profit and buy somewhere cheaper or more convenient.'

'You stayed, though.'

'I stayed. Yeah. There's got to be an Ames to run the store, and when my dad died … Anyway, this is my home. Always has been.'

In those days she didn't know Sterling as well as she did now. She didn't know the island, either. It was all new: this man, this image of herself as someone who could find love. To her, 'home' was just as new – not the idea of it, but the concrete reality, a place where you could feel so comfortable, so much part of everything, where you were literally on the walls as part of its history. It sounded so wonderful, so perfect. What she'd been looking for all her life.

And now it was just over three years later, and she was walking up the path to the centre of the island. She had contributed nothing to the history of the island. She had no children. She lived lightly, undocumented in the museum, on the periphery.

At first, early in their marriage she had talked to Sterling about how she felt. 'No one here likes me,' she told him.

'It takes islanders a little time to open up to new people.'

'Donna Orr asked me if I was Jewish and said that she'd never seen a Jew aside from summer people.'

'They'll come round,' he said. 'Give it time.'

Brenda was plainer. 'When you have a baby, you'll feel better. Everyone will pitch in. It's a wonderful place to be a child, and a great place to be a mother, too.'

She and Sterling had tried and tried. And every month, without fail, her blocked and misshapen womb reminded her that she had no reason to belong here.

Chapter Fourteen

Vee

She was lying on a blanket on the grass, eyes closed, letting the sun soak into her skin. She should be getting ready to greet Sterling and Rachel for dinner. Even though Mike said he'd do all the work, even though he had what looked like half a restaurant and most of a wine cellar delivered this morning by boat, she knew Mike. He was better at paying people to do things than actually doing them himself.

But she was nervous, and the Maine summer sun was something rare. As a teen she'd fled with her mother from Unity to Florida and although she was miserable she'd thought this was probably what heaven was supposed to be like. Florida was hot, humid, with movie-star skies and storms that passed on as soon as they came, leaving rainbows and steam behind them. She and her mother would hit the beach, sharing cigarettes and well-thumbed novels and bottles of Dr Pepper. They felt men and boys looking at them. College students, bodybuilders, rich guys between parties, poor guys between shifts. Her mother was still young, and Vee looked older than seventeen. They always laughed when the guys tried to flirt with them, and although Vee sometimes said yes to a date, her mom always said no.

The two of them did that every weekend they could for that first year, even when it was too cold for the locals. They lay out their towels and stripped down to their bikinis. They got great tans and tried to burn away the traces of Unity: that cold house surrounded by colder judgement. The grave they'd left behind and the funeral they had both missed.

Then Vee got her grades transferred and finished high school, and applied to colleges and gave up smoking and magazines and took up sunscreen and studying. But the association had been made. Sunbathing felt like freedom to her. It felt like sex and liberation. And the Maine summer sun was more precious because it had to work harder: fighting through clouds and fog, burning through wind. There was one perfect August day a year, maybe two, before the summer people left with Labor Day and the best you could hope for was a deceptive few days of warmth in September. Warmth in Maine was something you had to seize and conserve. You couldn't assume the sun would be there tomorrow.

She rested her hand on her bare stomach and felt her own hot skin. Her book lay splayed beside her next to her empty iced tea glass. She licked her lips, saw red behind her closed eyes. She imagined there was someone lying next to her on the blanket, shoulder brushing against hers. A hand trailing up the inside of her arm, soft as sunlight. She sighed, turned on her side, breast pressing against the blanket, tilted her chin up to receive a kiss from full warm lips. In her mind she buried her hand in a luxury of curly hair, pulled Rachel closer. Hips against hips. Breast against breast. Her stomach against Rachel's pale skin, her hand slipping into her swimsuit. What would it be like to hear the catching of her breath, revel in softness for once.

'Vee, there's someone here to see you.'

She opened her eyes, turned on her back and lowered her sunglasses. Mike, in white shorts and a white shirt, was looking down at her, blocking the sun.

'Who is it?' Wondering if her desire had pulled Rachel halfway across the island.

'Some guy called Charlie.'

'Charlie Broomhall? Lives in the blue house back from the point?'

Mike shrugged.

'Get rid of him.'

'He said he's already come by twice. I gave him a glass of iced tea.'

She felt overheated and hungry, languid and restless. She spread her legs on the blanket. 'Get rid of him quick so you can fuck me on the lawn.'

'Yes, ma'am.' He jogged back to the house and Vee took off her sunglasses and closed her eyes. She would be happy if she never had to think of Charlie Broomhall again, and tonight was going to be stressful and difficult, but right now she could stay in this feeling, the slow urgency of desire. The sun heated her eyelids; her upper lip was damp. She lay with her limbs weighing her down, aware of her toes, the fine hairs on her arms, the wetness between her legs, until she heard hurried footsteps on the grass. Mike knelt beside her and kissed her stomach, where her hand had been. He licked her navel and Vee pictured looking down and seeing Rachel's brown hair, her dark eyes glancing up at her to check her reaction. Vee groaned and lifted her hips, imagining different hands from Mike's pulling down her bikini bottom, imagining a woman's breath on the inside of her thigh, out here in the open, underneath the sun. She kept her eyes closed.

Chapter Fifteen

Rachel, Vee, Sterling, Mike

'What do you think I should wear?' Rachel surveyed the closet where her and Sterling's clothes hung side by side. She had the left side, like she slept on the left side of the bed. Since getting married, she had collected a lot of flannel. It was hot today, but would it stay hot? Should she do layers? She thought of Vee's silk dress and manicure, and Mike's casually perfect clothes and expensive watch.

'Sterling?' she called. 'What are you wearing?'

'I don't know,' he said, muffled, from the bathroom. 'Whatever I've got clean, I guess.'

'That's no help.' She pushed aside hangers until she found a dress from a while ago, a geometric-print wraparound that she used to dress up with a necklace and earrings and heels. When was the last time she'd worn that? Their first anniversary, maybe, when he'd taken her to a restaurant and a sweet little B&B in Camden. She held it up to herself in front of the mirror and when Sterling came in, rubbing his hair dry with a towel, she asked, 'Do you think I've gained too much weight for this?'

'You haven't gained any weight,' he said without looking at her. He opened a drawer. 'I've got about sixty other things I should be doing tonight instead of having dinner with someone who doesn't want to know me and her husband who I've never met.'

'It will be fun, and if it's not, we can leave.'

'Do you think it will be a sit-down thing? Will there be other people there?'

'I really don't know.' She put on the dress. Actually it fitted okay. A little stretched out along the neckline maybe. Had Sterling done that, in the B&B after they shared a bottle of wine? Past Sterling and Rachel seemed like two different people, characters she'd seen in a movie once. 'What do you think?' She pulled her hair up off her neck and twisted it, holding on with one hand. The dress emphasised her waist and the curves of her breasts. Last time she'd worn this dress, she'd felt pretty.

'You're wearing a dress? That means I have to wear a shirt.' Sterling closed the drawer and went to the closet.

'Do you remember this dress?'

'I don't know, maybe? You haven't worn a dress in a while. I'm not good with clothes, you know that.' He frowned into the closet. 'It's too hot for this blue shirt, I'll have to wear a white one.'

'White is always good. It's classic.'

'We're not trying to impress these people, Rachel.' He pulled his shirt off the hanger. 'Damn, I've got to iron this.'

'I'll do it for you.'

'I can iron a shirt.' He strode out of the room and Rachel looked at herself glumly in the mirror. She hated dinner parties. Someone always drank too much, and she was useless at making polite conversation. She took things too seriously, or she mistook people's meanings. And Vee hadn't invited her; Mike had. For all she knew, Vee had no interest in her, no desire to be friends, and no interest in making things up with Sterling, either, which meant that this evening was a total waste of time.

But it was something new, at least, right? Something *she'd* wanted? She crouched down and dug a pair of heels out from the back of the closet. They had dust on them. Sometimes as a little girl she'd worn her mother's heels, tottered around the house in pointy-toed high shoes because they meant being a grown-up.

These shoes pinched, she remembered. But they made her legs look great, or at least better.

'You're not wearing heels?' Sterling said, pausing in the door. 'We'll be walking there and back.'

'Oh. Yeah.' She put them back in the closet.

'This is ridiculous. I should never have agreed. We have nothing in common with these people.'

'It's fun to go out, though, right?' She found some flat sandals and sat on the bed to put them on. 'Should I leave my hair down?'

'Whatever makes you most comfortable is fine. Oh damn, I meant to bring a bottle of wine over from the store. If you're done getting ready, could you go and choose one? I suppose it'll have to be one of the expensive ones.'

'Sure,' she said. She shoved her hair up into an elastic band and went downstairs.

'What are you wearing?' Mike called from the bedroom.

'Nothing, currently.' Vee reached for her glass of wine on the side of the tub. It was her first. Okay, her second. But only a spritzer, to cool her and calm her while she had a bath.

'I mean later.'

'I was thinking my linen jumpsuit.'

Mike appeared in the bathroom doorway. He had on a pair of jeans and no shirt. Barefoot. 'The low-cut one? Isn't that a little sexy for dinner with your childhood best friend?'

'I'm not wearing it for Sterling.'

Sterling put his burned finger in his mouth and swore. He hated ironing. He hated this shirt, which he usually wore for appointments with the bank. It was too hot to do any of this, too hot to eat food in a stuffy dining room, too hot to be polite and pretend that everything was okay for old times' sake, and now Rachel was probably going to choose a ridiculous wine, either too cheap and he'd look miserly, or too expensive and he'd look like he was trying to impress. And why should he care how he looked? He didn't have to prove anything to Vee. He wasn't the one who'd ever done anything wrong.

He ironed furiously, steam rising around his face. His mother knew he was going to Vee's house. He wasn't sure how she knew, but she'd called him today and said, 'I think it's wonderful that you're giving her a chance. I'm proud of you, Sterling.' And so of course he couldn't say anything to that, and he couldn't back out, either.

He should arrange a secret signal with Rachel if they had to escape quickly. A code word or something, or an excuse. Or he could get Jacob to call him at, say, eight thirty, and say it was something urgent to do with the store so he had to go. He pulled on his shirt, which was unpleasantly hot and stiff, and dug his phone out of his pocket to text Jacob.

The last time he had gone to a summer person's house for dinner, he'd ended up with a broken heart.

Mike buttoned up a white shirt and watched himself in the mirror as he rolled up the sleeves. What a day this was turning out to be. He'd arranged everything perfectly. The weather was fabulous, he'd had time for a sail this morning, the food had been delivered nice and early, he'd had hot sex with his wife on the lawn, and when his mother had called he was able to tell her that he'd invited Vee's oldest friend for dinner. Vee had protested at first, but she was excited now. And grateful, if her enthusiasm earlier was any sign.

He was getting it right. He was building bridges. He was making his wife happy. He was, if he said so himself, really good at saving his marriage.

Chapter Sixteen

Rachel

Sterling didn't speak at all on their walk to Daybreak. Rachel had to hurry to keep up with him, and with every step she got more and more frustrated. If he didn't want to go, he could have said no instead of punishing her for it. She hated the silent treatment. She *hated* it. Her parents had given it to each other for years, when one of them had done something that was so bad that it couldn't even be mentioned. As a child, she almost never knew what the argument was about and she always felt as if it were her fault, as if she could say something that would make it all better but didn't know what it was. The silent treatment was childish behaviour and she was the one who was expected to be the adult: carrying messages, trying to anticipate her silent parents' needs that they refused to express. Then suddenly it would be over, her parents would be laughing and mixing cocktails, and she'd have no idea what she had done, or hadn't done. She was just expected to forget about it.

As they reached the gates of the house, she said, 'At least you could try to enjoy yourself.'

'I can try,' said Sterling grimly, and then he looked at her for the first time in hours. 'It's not your fault,' he said. 'And you're right, I can't keep on avoiding the issue. If Vee wants to apologise, the least I can do is to accept it.'

Was that why they were here? Rachel wasn't so sure; it was Mike who'd invited them, not Vee. But she smiled at Sterling anyway, because at least he was talking to her now. 'Well, we can see how the other half lives. The house is gorgeous.'

'Not bad for a girl who grew up in a shack,' he muttered, and then took a deep breath. 'Let's do this.' Sterling knocked on the back door. Standing next to him, she could feel the tension coming off him. He held himself stiffly, as if he expected to be punched.

Mike answered. He was as impossibly good-looking as he'd been the time before. 'Hey!' he greeted them cheerily. 'Rachel! Great to see you again. You look fantastic.' He surprised her by leaning forward and kissing her on each cheek, and then holding out his hand to Sterling, who towered over him. 'I'm Mike Ellis, great to meet you finally.'

'Sterling Ames.' It was a little strange to hear Sterling telling someone his name. Everyone seemed to know him already.

'Come on in, come on in, welcome. Vee's waiting in the living room. She's been so impatient to see you. This is quite the re-union, huh?'

'Unexpected, to say the least,' said Sterling as they followed Mike into the huge open-plan living space with its floor-to-ceiling windows. 'Wow, this is something.'

'Isn't it? I can't take the credit. Vee, our guests are here.'

Vee stood on the far edge of the room, near the window with the view of lawn and sky and ocean behind her. For a moment, Rachel's gaze met hers and it was exactly like it had been in the store, days ago: a flash of warmth, a little catch of breath, a feeling: oh, I like you.

Then Vee looked quickly away. 'Well, hello, stranger,' she said, and walked towards Sterling, one hand outstretched and a glass of wine in the other. She didn't so much as glance at Rachel, who had the sensation of being doused with cold water.

'Vee,' said Sterling. 'It's been a while.'

'Twenty years, isn't it?' said Mike.

'You look exactly the same.' Rachel watched as Vee kissed each of Sterling's cheeks, just as Mike had done with her. Sterling stood unmoved. He didn't return the kisses.

'You look completely different,' Sterling said.

'Not surprising,' said Vee, and she turned to Rachel finally. 'Rachel, hi,' she said, and held out her hand. Rachel barely touched her fingers before Vee withdrew. 'I'm glad you both could make it.'

'Me too,' said Rachel, feeling foolish, once again as if she had done something wrong without knowing it. Vee had been so friendly before. What was going on?

'Well,' said Vee, 'you both need drinks immediately.'

'I'll get them,' said Mike. 'What's your poison? Wine, beer, mixed drink, something soft? I make a mean dirty martini. I'm sort of famous for them.'

'Though you shouldn't drink them if you want to keep any secrets,' said Vee. 'They pack a punch.'

'Just iced water is great for me, thanks,' said Rachel.

'I'll have a beer,' Sterling said.

'Can you refresh this, darling?' Vee held up her almost-empty wine glass, and Mike took it.

'So,' he said, as he went to the kitchen area and opened the massive refrigerator, 'Vee tells me that the two of you were inseparable as kids.'

'What he means is that I used to drag Sterling everywhere and get him into trouble.' Vee laughed. It sounded completely fake, and Rachel's well-honed instinct guessed that this was her third or fourth glass of wine. Maybe this was a mistake.

'I chose what I did,' said Sterling. 'I was capable of choosing for myself. Still am.'

'Pilsner, red ale, or I've got a blueberry wheat beer that they brew near here I think?'

'Red ale, thanks.'

'Rachel, still or sparkling?'

'Um ... sparkling? Please?'

'Vee? You on the Chablis or the Sauvignon, babe?'

'Don't care.'

Mike brought Rachel a tall glass of sparkling water with ice and lime. She sipped it, watching Vee over the rim of her glass. She wore a white jumpsuit and a pretty jade necklace, understated make-up and a healthy glow of tan everywhere except for her left arm, which had been freed from its cast. Both she and her husband were barefoot. Rachel was intensely aware of her own cheap dress, her dusty feet in practical sandals.

Vee accepted a full glass from Mike and said, looking somewhere to the left of Rachel's face, 'So, how long have the two of you been married?'

'A couple of years,' said Sterling, and Rachel said, 'It's three in October.'

'Time flies when you're having fun,' said Vee.

Mike twisted the tops off two bottles of beer. 'Want a glass, Sterling? Or will we have it the manly way?'

'Manly is fine.'

'Well,' said Mike, handing a beer to Sterling and holding up his own, 'let's have a toast. To friends, old and new.'

'Sure,' said Sterling. His teeth were visibly clenched. 'To friends.' The clink of his bottle against Vee's glass sounded like a rock against a window. Rachel touched glasses with Mike and then with Vee, who glanced at her once, and then immediately away. She blinked back sudden tears.

'So, Rachel, what do you say, you and I go down to the dock and you can pretend to admire my boat, so these two have a little time to catch up?' Mike drew her arm into his. Rachel went with him through the glass door and onto the lawn.

He waited until they were halfway down to the water before he spoke, conspiratorially. 'It's a little tense in there, so let's let them work it out themselves, okay? Sorry to pull you away.'

'It's a good idea,' said Rachel. She swallowed her water. 'I feel a little …'

'…Extraneous?'

She'd been about to use the word *invisible*. But she felt invisible all the time, so why should she be particularly bothered now?

'They've got a lot of history,' she said.

'I get you.'

'You've got a lot of land here around the house. It must take ages to mow the lawn.'

'Wouldn't know, someone comes and does that.'

'Henry. He does a lot of the lawns.'

'Henry, right. Nice guy. Does a really good job. What's it like here after the summer season? Do you get many people?'

'The big houses empty out. Sometimes there are day visitors, or people coming for the weekend. More if there's an Indian summer. Sterling had an idea to attract more people for the foliage season, but the foliage here isn't as good as in the mountains apparently.'

'So it's dead after Labor Day.'

'Well… quiet.'

'It must be a relief after being so busy.'

She shrugged, non-committal.

He tried again. 'You said you were a historian? Do you run the museum you told me about?'

'Uh. No. That's Anita Langlais. It's her domain.'

Mike laughed. 'Oh, I see. She rules over it with an iron fist and woe betide anyone who offers any suggestions.'

'Actually, it is a little like that.'

They'd reached the dock now, out of view of the house, and he guided her towards a white-painted Adirondack chair. She wondered if he was this effortlessly charming with everyone. He must be. How did he do it? Was it something you were born with, like money? Or was it something you could earn… like money?

'So what was the big thing that happened two hundred years ago? The thing that you were telling me about? Because let's face it, I'm not going to go to the museum.' He sat across from her, legs comfortably crossed.

'More like two hundred and sixty, during the French and Indian War. The short version of the story is that the island was settled by the British by then, but it was attacked by the Penobscots.'

'Help me out, I flunked college. French and Indian War? Penobscots?'

'It was before the American Revolution. Basically, the British colonists and the French colonists were fighting each other for territory, and they pulled the Native Americans in. It's where George Washington got his battle experience. The Penobscots are one of the tribes of indigenous people in this area, who sided with the French, which isn't surprising when you consider that the British had a bounty on their scalps.'

'Right. Okay, got it, don't blame them. So the Penobscots attacked Unity Island? Who won?'

'There were about two hundred inhabitants of Unity and they were all fishermen and farmers, and the Penobscots had been armed by the French. The settlers had no hope of winning.'

'Did they all die?'

'No, they nearly all lived. The interesting thing was that the island wasn't attacked in secret. The islanders knew for days that the Penobscots were coming. They'd had news from traders coming down from the north. So the British set fire to everything. All the houses, the church, their stores for the winter. They burned the trees and the fields and they killed their animals and burned them, too. The only things they didn't burn were the boats, which they used to escape. When the Penobscots arrived, they found nothing but ash.'

'Wow.'

She nodded. 'I often think about what kind of mindset those settlers had, that they'd rather burn everything they'd worked for than see it in the hands of someone else.' She took a drink.

'Keeping in mind they stole the island from the Penobscots in the first place.'

'Still. That takes some guts.'

'It takes some guts to live on an island six miles out from the shore, I suppose.'

Mike drank his beer contemplatively. Maybe he was so charming because he let her talk.

'Vee said you're from Chicago,' he said. 'Do you miss the city?'

'I grew up in the suburbs. And no. I'm not really a city person, I guess. I do miss cinemas. There's a single screen cinema in Rockland but I love multiplexes. Sometimes I used to go from one movie to another for a whole day.'

'I have never done that but it sounds great. I would miss coffee shops. I *do* miss coffee shops. There's a state-of-the-art coffee-maker in the house and I can only make espresso. It's a great espresso, but I miss flat whites.'

'You would miss other things than coffee shops, I'm sure,' said Rachel. 'For example, good hair. Between the salt and the humidity, I'm a frizz bomb most of the time.'

'Oh, I wouldn't say that. You have lovely hair.'

'And seeing more than the same sixty faces for weeks on end.'

'I suppose if you like the faces, it's not much of a hardship. It must feel like an adventure living here year-round. Out in the ocean. At the mercy of the weather and wind. You must have to rely on each other.'

'That's what Sterling always says.'

Mike gazed out at the water again. There was a sailing boat moored at the dock, and the lines made gentle clinking sounds against the metal mast as the boat rocked.

'I hope your husband and my wife can patch up their differences,' Mike said.

'Me too.'

'Because this place is good for her. It's really good for her. She's been almost like a different person since we've been here.'

Why doesn't she like me, all of a sudden? What have I done wrong? What's wrong with me?

'What was she like before?'

Mike took a swig of his beer. Despite the salt and the wind, he had great hair.

'Vee finds it hard to relax,' he said. 'She's a very driven person. Very successful, very ambitious. Even when she gave up her job, she was still ambitious. She always has a project on the go. When she broke her arm, it drove her nuts. She couldn't stand staying still. But since she's come here, she's relaxed a lot. She's taking some time for herself, and for us.' He smiled at Rachel. 'Unity is like a kind of magic.'

'I'm so happy for her,' said Rachel unhappily.

Chapter Seventeen

Sterling

'So it turns out you were wrong,' said Vee. 'You said that the bathroom was going to be there.' She pointed at the corner of a room behind Sterling, at a white sofa with carefully placed sea-green scatter cushions.

'No, I said the bathroom was over there.' He pointed in the opposite direction, off to the side of the kitchen, where there was a door. Presumably to a bathroom.

'I remember distinctly. You were sitting on a crate, you had a can of Milwaukee's Best in your hand, and you said the pipes were going to go right there. I think of it every time I see that sofa, that you said that's where the toilet should be. I've never been able to sit on that sofa because of it.'

'I'm surprised you think of me at all.'

'This reunion is going great.' Vee flashed him a sardonic smile, and went to the kitchen area. Her wine glass made a hollow click on the granite worktop. 'Mike ordered way too much food from a caterer in Belfast.' She opened the refrigerator and started taking out plastic-wrapped bowls, lining them up on the kitchen island. 'We've got potato salad, Nicoise salad, green salad . . . I think this is baba ganoush?'

'What's it like being back? Does it even feel like you are back? You haven't talked to anyone.'

'I don't really have a lot to say to anyone. Charlie Broomhall turned up, though. What's that all about?'

'Probably the airstrip. That's what he usually talks about.'

'Yeah, like I'm interested in that.' She took out two more bowls. 'Looks like we've got both sour pickles and bread-and-butter pickles.' She peeled back the film and sampled a sweet pickle. 'Not as good as your mom's. I did talk to her the other day.'

'You did?' He frowned. His mom had gone on and on about him making up with Vee, but hadn't mentioned they'd spoken. 'When was that? Did you come to her apartment?'

'No, I ran into her at the doctors'. She's living inland?'

'Yeah, she insisted that Rachel and I took the house.'

'Is she in a lot of pain?'

He wasn't going to get into that with Vee. 'She has good days and bad days. So, fill me in on your life. You left and became a summer person.'

'Mike's the real summer person. I'm along for the ride.'

'That's funny, because I always thought that someone who came to Unity in the summer was a—'

'You're right. I'm a summer person. Except I'm the kind of summer person who everyone on the island knows all the dirty secrets about. So, basically, the best of both worlds.' She drained her wine glass, and opened the fridge again. 'Want another beer?'

His bottle was still half full. He remembered the way she used to drink when they were teenagers: fast and almost angry, as if sobriety were a burden she couldn't wait to get rid of. 'Sure,' he said, and took a big gulp of beer. 'Why'd you come to Unity for a holiday? I assume you could go anywhere.'

'Again, it was Mike's idea. He thought I needed to get back to my roots, figure out what's important. As if this place is anything like my fucking roots.' She gestured to the house around them. 'The view is a lot better, I'll give it that.'

'So you're a lawyer now?'

'Yes. No. Maybe was? I haven't practised law in four years. But yes, still a lawyer.'

'That wasn't what I pictured for you.'

'Pictured me in jail instead, huh?' She twisted the cap off another beer and slid it over the island to him. 'Or unemployed, single mother, living off cheques from the state?'

'Don't be ridiculous. I know you're smart. You got better grades than I did.'

'I got better grades than almost everyone, despite my reputation.'

'I'm not downplaying your achievements. I just never pictured you in a suit, in that world. I didn't picture you enjoying law.'

'Are you kidding? I spent my entire childhood working out what the rules were, so I could get around them. I'm a really good lawyer. I've got an instinct for it.'

'But you said you don't practise any more.'

She shrugged. 'Not much reason, when your husband has an obscene amount of money. It got to the point where it was too inconvenient to fit the job in with all the other things I'm expected to do. And just because I'm good at something, doesn't mean I enjoy it.' She refilled her wine glass. 'Anyway, enough about me. What about you? Break any laws lately?'

'That was always your area.'

'I had to bring something to the friendship. So you're a fine upstanding citizen. I'm not all that surprised.'

He didn't bother to answer that. He hadn't forgotten what a conversation with Vee could be like, when she was feeling spiky.

'So you went to college,' Vee continued, 'had an epiphany, realised what was important, and came back to Unity to run the family business.'

'No,' Sterling said.

'You didn't bother with the epiphany?'

'I didn't go to college.'

For the first time, Vee looked less than cocksure of herself. '…You didn't? But you'd already been accepted, you just had to choose between California and Arizona.'

'Then my dad died. And my mom was a wreck. She tried to

be strong, but she couldn't cope. And she didn't understand any of Dad's systems, none of his inventory or bookkeeping records, because he'd always taken care of everything. So I deferred for a year, then another year, and here I am.'

Vee was standing with her fists resting on the granite island. 'Oh, Sterling, I didn't know.'

Her pity annoyed him. 'How could you know? You were off living your new life, wherever that was.' He shrugged. 'Anyway, it was no big deal. You don't need a college degree to run an island general store. My dad never had one.'

'But that was always your plan. We talked about it all the time. You wanted to see deserts. You wanted to see Australia and Africa and all the other places beginning with A. Couldn't someone else run the store?'

'That store has been in my family for nearly two hundred years, so no. Not an option. I'm not the type to run away from my responsibilities.'

'Meaning that I am.'

'You had different role models than I did.'

'That's not exactly fair, Sterling. My mom needed me too. Plus, your family were my role models. I had the same role models that you did.'

'I guess that's what makes it so hard for me to understand.'

'What's to understand? You're happy, I'm happy. We both have good lives. That's all that matters, right?'

'Of course,' Sterling said. He clenched his teeth, and turned away to look at the view from the window. Had he been expecting an apology? Or any sort of self-awareness at all, from Vee? He should have known better.

Chapter Eighteen

Vee

She was drunk, and though that had seemed like a good idea before this whole evening started, it seemed less good now. After narrowly avoiding an argument with Sterling before dinner, she'd spent the entire actual dinner not saying what she was thinking, and listening to conversation about the weather patterns and sailing. She had to keep drinking just to stay awake. As long as she could stop herself from flapping her mouth, she would be fine. They'd get through this.

Vee pushed her food around her plate with her fork. As expected, despite his promise, Mike hadn't cooked anything himself, and he had ordered way too much, and none of it was from Ames', which was probably a kick in the teeth to Sterling. But everything was a kick in the teeth to Sterling. So what could you do? You might as well do what she'd been doing all her life, and brazen it out.

'This is delicious,' said Rachel. Despite herself, Vee glanced across the table at her. She thought about picking up Rachel's fork and feeding her morsels of lobster salad. She thought about dipping her finger in her own wine glass, and smoothing it across Rachel's lips.

'Mike's very good at choosing things off a menu,' Vee said, and dropped her gaze back to her plate.

They were eating outdoors, on the patio with the sweeping view down to the water. It had been Mike's idea, even though it would probably be cooler inside in the shade. She was sweating in her linen.

'It's one of my few talents,' said Mike cheerfully.

'I can never make up my mind in a restaurant,' Rachel said. 'Either everything looks good, or nothing does. I don't think I have a very good imagination when it comes to food.'

What about other things? Vee squirmed in her chair. This was ridiculous.

'Oh I wouldn't say that,' said Mike. 'The deliveries we've had from Ames' have been great. I'll be honest, I didn't expect such a wide variety from an island general store.'

Vee glanced at Sterling to see how he coped with this condescension. He kept a stoic face as he replied, 'It's our job to know our customers. In the summer, they come from all over, so we have to be able to supply them with what they're used to, while keeping stock of the everyday things that our year-round community needs. The more we can get summer people to shop on the island, and the more we can serve the permanent residents, the better it is for Unity.'

'The residents have a real community focus, huh?'

'Absolutely. And we provide a lot of services. Plus the store is an important place for people to meet and talk, so I can't just think about profits. I have to think about keeping everybody happy. That means traditional and new.'

'Cribbage night,' muttered Vee into her wine glass.

'We still do that. It's on tonight, as a matter of fact, and it goes on all year. We have horseshoe tournaments, pie baking contests. A few years ago we started doing wine and beer tasting evenings, using local products.'

'It's wonderful that there's such a strong community ethos on the island,' said Mike. 'You don't get a lot of that any more, it seems.'

'Very strong,' agreed Sterling. 'And of course we serve as the island post office, and we've provided computer and internet services for those who have trouble accessing it at home, and we unofficially help a lot of the older folks who are making up more and more of the population. My dad, Tom, ran that store all his life. So yes, we have a lot of pride about Unity and about Ames' General.'

'Yes, we get it, Sterling,' said Vee, reaching for the wine cooler. 'The store is your baby. Anybody else for a top-up?'

No one replied. Sterling was staring at her. Rachel was looking down at her plate. Mike's smile faltered.

She remembered what Brenda had said. *He and Rachel can't have children, and it's breaking his heart every day and he just keeps going on and going on.*

'I mean, it's your legacy,' she said.

'It was my dad's legacy,' said Sterling. 'He was a great man. You might remember him, Vee.'

'I never met him,' said Rachel quickly, before Vee could answer. 'I wish I had. Everyone talks of him so fondly.'

'I wasn't going to talk about this tonight, but now that we're on the subject of my dad,' began Sterling.

'I loved your dad,' said Vee. 'I owed him a lot.'

'You owed him so much that you left the day he died and didn't even bother to turn up at his funeral.'

Right, that was it. She put down the bottle. 'You didn't use to be so self-righteous, Sterling. What's causing it – failed ambition?'

'I live according to my principles, which happen to be the same principles as my father, and his father before him. If that's self-righteous, I'd rather be that than otherwise.'

'Sterling—' said Rachel.

'He wasn't my father,' said Vee. 'I loved him, but he wasn't mine. My *mother* was mine, and she needed me. Pops died, and my mom was escaping this place finally, after a whole life of having no choice. And *you* might see Unity as a wonderful, idyllic community, but she belonged here just as much, her family had been here just as long as yours, and this community was terrible to her. It judged her and whispered about her and called her a slut and a welfare mom, and your parents tried to protect me from that, which I appreciated then and I appreciate still, but it wasn't enough. I deserved something of my own, and so did my mom. So yes, I left without saying goodbye. And in the same situation, I would do it again. You're not the only one who has family loyalties.'

She stood up, steadying herself with a hand on the back of her chair. She was acutely aware of all three of them staring at her: Sterling red-faced, Rachel pale, Mike astonished.

'Well,' she said, 'now all that's out in the open, I'll go and get dessert.'

In the kitchen, she leaned against the sink, head bowed, running cold water over her wrists to cool down. Christ, she'd fucked that up. She'd just confirmed everything that Sterling must think about her: Vivian Grace Harper, Bitch Extraordinaire. Her feckless mother's daughter. A chip off the block of her alcoholic workshy grandfather, who alienated everyone he met. Unity blood was thicker than Manhattan tap water.

This was exactly what she'd wanted to avoid. If she'd stayed at the table, she would have told Sterling a few home truths about his perfect family. She might have even said the real reason why her mother needed her. Why had she let Mike talk her into this?

Oh yes: because she wanted to see Rachel. Who she'd barely dared to look at all night, because she was certain that her desire was blatantly obvious on her face.

'Shit,' she moaned. She wondered if she could pretend to have alcohol poisoning. Or heat stroke. She wondered if Mike would have the good sense to usher their guests quietly home before she could fuck it up even more.

Fat chance. Mike loved drama, as long as it didn't involve him. Why else would he have invited them in the first place?

She closed her eyes, and the room spun. Her head pounded with wine and heat.

'Are you okay?'

Vee raised her head and opened her eyes. Rachel was putting cleared plates down on the kitchen island. Her jersey dress clung to her waist and hips and left her collarbone bare. All night the neckline had gaped a little bit when she moved, exposing freckles and shadows, a hint of cleavage. Her hair was extra curly from the heat. Strands stuck to her neck. Vee wanted to lick them free.

'Are you okay?' Rachel asked again. 'You look sick.'

'I'm not sick. I'm okay. Aside from a case of terminal foot in mouth.'

'Maybe you should drink some water,' said Rachel. She went to the fridge and got out a bottle of water. 'Here.'

She turned off the tap and took the bottle from Rachel, but instead of drinking it, she pressed its cold surface against her forehead. 'Thanks. I guess I've well and truly burned some bridges.'

'To be fair, Sterling's been spoiling for a fight.'

'He's been waiting for twenty years. I can't really blame him.' She laughed without humour. 'Oh well, at least we're leaving after Labor Day. You can all be angry with me in peace.'

'I'm not angry with you,' said Rachel quietly. 'I've had to leave people behind, too. I know what it's like. But ...' She hesitated. 'Vee, have I done something wrong? Are you angry with me?'

'What? No. I hardly know you. You seem great. Why would I be angry with you?'

'It's just that ... when we met before, in the store that time, we seemed to get along really well. I accepted Mike's invitation so we could get to know each other better. But tonight, you've hardly spoken to me. You haven't looked at me, even. I just ... I know you're leaving pretty soon, but if I've done something to upset you, I'd like to know what it is.'

'You're right,' said Vee. 'I haven't been very friendly to you tonight, and I'm sorry about that, but you really don't want to know why.'

Rachel's shoulders slumped. 'Okay, I get it,' she said, fluttering her hands, stepping back, and her voice was so resigned and weary, it made Vee want another drink. It made Vee want to kiss her. 'It happens to me all the time around here. I thought you were different, but—'

'I can't look you in the face because ever since I met you, I've been thinking about you every time I have sex with my husband.'

Rachel had been turning away, but she stopped. Vee carried on, jumping deliberately in front of the bus.

'And I have sex with Mike a lot. So I am thinking about you constantly, and wishing it was you. And I don't know why, or what happened to make me want you this way, because you're right, we hardly know each other, but I can't help it. I can't stop. I don't want to.'

'Oh.'

She didn't say more, and Vee couldn't tell what she was thinking. If she was about to laugh, or to run off and tell Sterling, or if she would come closer. Vee wasn't sure herself which one she wanted. Which would cause the least damage. She had just done something, she knew, which was much worse than anything she'd said outside to Sterling. It could have been a relief to say it, but right in this moment it felt like pain.

'I think,' Vee started, not knowing what words could possibly come after that, but then Rachel said, 'I'll finish clearing the table,' and turned towards the glass door to the patio just as Sterling appeared in it. He had his phone in his hand. Vee felt as *if* she'd been slapped. She leaned back abruptly on the worktop.

'Jacob just texted,' he told Rachel. 'He says there's a problem with one of the chest freezers and we've got to decide what to do with everything before it melts. I've already told Mike I'm going to head back, but if you want to stay—'

'No, I'll go with you,' Rachel said.

'Okay, well.' He put his phone back in his pocket. 'Thanks for an interesting evening,' he said to Vee. It looked as if it caused him actual pain to acknowledge her existence.

'Your freezer has great timing,' she said. She left the kitchen, walked into the spare bedroom, and closed the door after her.

Part Three

———

The End of Summer, 2015

Chapter Nineteen

Sterling

He couldn't remember now how old he was. The memory had become polished from use and retelling. He hadn't started school yet, so he'd probably been around four.

It was night and he was thirsty and wanted a glass of milk, so although he was supposed to be in bed, he crept downstairs to the kitchen. He'd had oyster crackers for his dinner, dropped into his bowl of chowder, and they always made him thirsty. But his mother had sounded final when she'd told him to go to bed, so he half-hoped that they would be in the living room instead of the kitchen, so he could pour his own glass of milk. Daddy let him do that sometimes when he was careful, at lunch sometimes, and Sterling liked it. It tasted better when you poured it yourself, especially when Daddy patted your shoulder and said you were a big boy now.

But the light was on in the kitchen and the door was half-closed, so he paused.

'That's nearly four hundred dollars already,' he heard his father say.

'It was peanut butter and jelly, Tom. And eggs.'

'Eustace was in buying liquor two days ago. If he has money for liquor, she should have money for peanut butter.'

'I don't think it works like that, honey.'

'I know it doesn't. But what am I supposed to do? Not serve

Eustace? He'll just go somewhere else. I feel for Dot Harper. Her choices haven't been great, but—'

'She tries hard.'

'She tries hard now. Yeah, I'll give her that. But I've got a business to run. We're not rolling in money as it is, and we need the boiler fixed and the roof's going to need doing in the spring. I can't feed the island, sweetheart.'

'No one's asking you to feed everyone. But that girl's the same age as Sterling. We can afford to spot them a few jars of Skippy.'

'I know. And I'll keep doing it, though I don't like it. I'd feel better about it maybe if she were a little more—' He paused. 'Hey, son? What are you doing out of bed?'

He got to pour his own milk in front of Mama who said she was proud of him, too, and then he went to sleep. But he remembered the conversation a few mornings later, when he and Mama were waiting for the ferry. They were going to see the dentist and if he was brave they'd visit Grandma after and she'd give him a slice of pie.

When it was busy in the summer, he always had to stay close to his parents at the ferry, because there were strangers. But it was springtime and there were only island people. Mama was talking with Mrs Patterson and there was a girl sitting on the stone wall next to a woman on the other side of the ramp. He knew it was Vee Harper, even though he didn't spend much time with Vee because she never came to his house to play and she didn't go to the birthday parties he'd been at, and she never came into the store to buy penny candy like a lot of other kids did. But he'd seen her sometimes on the beach, picking up shells and seaweed while her mother sat on a rock smoking a cigarette. Her mother was smoking a cigarette now. The last time he'd seen Vee, she'd had long straggly hair, but now it had been cut into the shape of a bowl. Her fringe was crooked across her forehead. She wore shorts and a sweater that was too long for her, and she looked unhappy. Maybe she was going to the dentist, too.

Sterling hopped off the wall and went across the ramp to her. He knew how to be friendly; his daddy taught him always to be friendly to people who came into the store. 'Hi, Vee,' he said.

'Hi,' she said. She kicked her heels against the stone wall. Her mother glanced at Sterling, and then dragged on her cigarette and looked away. The ferry was just coming in.

'I'm Sterling,' he said. She didn't answer that, so he tried again. 'My dad owns the store.'

Owning the store was an important thing. When Sterling told people that his dad owned the store, most people would say 'Wow' or 'I know' or 'You must be very proud of your daddy.' He liked that. He was proud of his daddy, and Daddy was proud of him.

Vee just kept on swinging her feet and kicking the wall, so Sterling thought maybe Vee didn't understand. He explained, 'You know, the store, over there.' He pointed at the building, which was right near the ferry ramp. 'My daddy gives your mom peanut butter sometimes for free.'

Vee did something when he said that. She hopped off the wall, super quick, and she pulled back her arm and before Sterling knew what was happening she punched him in the nose.

For Sterling, it was a sudden burst of pain that made his vision go red and black. He staggered back, hand to his face, too startled even to wail.

'Don't you ever say that again,' Vee said. Her hand was still curled in a fist.

'Oh my God, Sterling,' said Mama, behind him. 'Are you hurt?' He turned towards her voice and her safe arms were around him. He buried his face in her jacket and burst into tears.

They didn't go to the dentist. Sterling's nose swelled up and it was hard to breathe through it, like when you had a cold but worse. He lay on the sofa with an ice pack on his nose and watched cartoons. After the store closed he heard his parents talking in the kitchen, though he didn't get up to listen this time. They talked quietly, like they always did.

After supper on a tray in front of the TV – leftover chowder, and he had to let the crackers get soggy because it hurt his nose to chew – Daddy came into the living room with his trainers and his jacket. 'We're going for a walk,' he told Sterling.

His head still hurt but he got up and put on his shoes and his jacket and he and Daddy went outside. Sometimes Daddy took him fishing after dinner, but they didn't go to the shed to get the fishing stuff or walk towards the dock. Instead they walked past the school and followed the path off the road that led to the middle. It was darker here than by their house, because of the trees, and Sterling held tight to Daddy's hand. They walked for a little while, and then Daddy stopped.

'We're going to Vee's house,' he said. Sterling's nose throbbed.

'Is she gonna get in trouble?' Sterling asked. 'Are you gonna tell her off?'

Daddy crouched down so he was looking into Sterling's face. 'First off, Vivian shouldn't have hit you. No one should ever solve their problems by hitting people. Even if they're really angry. I never, ever want you to hit anyone, especially not a girl. Do you understand?'

He nodded, though he thought he would probably like to punch Vee back, and she definitely deserved it, but if Daddy said it was wrong, he wouldn't do it.

'Secondly, you have to remember that we all live on this island together. Everyone here on Unity is our neighbour, and we have to be kind to them. Even if we don't feel like it sometimes. And you are an Ames. Which means that you have a duty to set a good example, and be kind.' He took a deep breath. 'What you said to Vee Harper was unkind. I know you didn't mean it that way, but your words hurt her. So we are going to the Harpers' house so you can say that you are sorry.'

Sterling's mouth hung open. 'I have to say I'm sorry? *She* punched *me*!'

'I know, son. But you made a mistake. That peanut butter is a secret, and you told it.'

'I didn't know it was a secret.'

'I know, son,' said his daddy again. 'But now you do. She's a girl, and you're a boy, and you have to be a man about it and do the right thing. Mama and I both want you to.' He put his hands on Sterling's shoulders. 'Can I trust you to do the right thing?'

Sterling didn't like this. He didn't think it was fair. He didn't think that Vee Harper was very nice and he didn't want her as his neighbour. But Daddy was looking at him, and he knew that Mama would be waiting at home to hear whether Sterling had done the right thing. He nodded.

'Good man,' said his father, and he stood up again and they walked up the path to the Harpers'. It was getting dark, but there weren't any lights on inside yet, and the yard was full of stuff like old lawnmowers and lobster traps and boat parts and plastic buckets and cardboard boxes melting into pulp. If Sterling weren't half scared and half indignant, he would've been interested in poking around a little to see what he could find. He didn't know yet that in years to come, he and Vee would spend whole afternoons doing that very thing.

His daddy let go of his hand and went up and knocked on the door.

A man answered it. He had a stubbly face and a cigarette in his hand and he wore a dirty John Deere baseball cap. 'Yeah?' he said.

'Evening, Eustace. My boy has something to say to your Vivian. Is it all right if he speaks to her?'

The man shrugged. He went back inside the house yelling, 'Vee!'

Sterling shifted from foot to foot until Vee came out of the door. She was wearing the same thing she'd been wearing this morning except she had a milk moustache. 'Oh,' she said, looking at Sterling. 'Hi.'

Sterling swallowed. He had a sick feeling in his stomach. He looked at his daddy, who nodded at him.

'I'm sorry I told your secret about the peanut butter,' he said quickly.

'Okay,' said Vee. She wiped her milk moustache away with the sleeve of her sweater. 'Wanna be friends?'

Now, Sterling stood behind the counter in the shop his father left to him, where he had spent nearly every day of his life, where he would spend every day of his life to come, where he was not just himself, a bundle of bone and flesh and memory, but something made up of dusty shelves and the sound of a bell over the door. He had no child of his own, and no father either. He was this place, and nothing else.

He watched as Charlie Broomhall walked in the door and poured himself a cup of coffee from the self-service station, like he did every morning. 'Gonna be another hot one,' Charlie said, approaching the counter. As always, he made no move towards his wallet.

'Looks like it.'

'You missed the show last night. Marjorie cleaned house. Double-skunked Anita *and* that feller from New Jersey.'

'I heard.'

'She looked like the cat that got the cream. Never seen that woman looking so pleased with anything. We're never gonna hear the end of it.'

'Probably not.'

'She put her winnings back in the pot and says she's gonna win them all again next week. Anita had a face on her like sour milk.'

'There ya go.'

Charlie leaned closer. 'Heard you went to Vee Harper's last night. You talk with her?'

His lips tightened, remembering Vee, leaning with one hand on the back of her chair as if to keep herself upright, talking about loyalty. 'You could say that.'

'She say anything about that land?'

'No, Charlie. She didn't say anything about land.'

'Because you know we've been trying to get in touch with Dot for years now.'

'Is that so.'

'Oh yeah. The whole airstrip project, you know. You talk about that with Vee?'

'No. I didn't. That's not what we talked about.'

'I dropped by two or three times and she's never at home. I think if she just heard what we have planned, she'd be pretty interested.'

Sterling bit his lip.

'You two used to be pretty tight, huh. Maybe if you go over there again you could just mention it—'

'Vee Harper has zero interest in Unity,' Sterling snapped. 'Give it up, Charlie. You've been going on and on about that airstrip for years. It's a lost cause, and so is Vee.'

Charlie blinked. 'Well. You say so, huh?'

'I do. And the coffee's two dollars seven cents with tax, please.'

He dug out his wallet. 'I don't know that I have any change.'

'No problem.' Sterling took seven pennies from the spare change dish. 'Enjoy your coffee, Charlie, have a great day.'

Charlie wandered out the door, stunned, and Sterling wondered when he was ever going to stop being responsible for Vee Harper, along with everything else.

Chapter Twenty

Rachel

Rachel didn't sleep, and got up at sunrise when the air was pink and grey. She made coffee and sat on the front porch, mug in hand, and watched the waves, the dipping gulls, the lobster boats heading out to work. These were the things that she'd been attracted to when she first heard about Unity. Now she knew the name of every boat, and the sounds and sights had become so ordinary she didn't often notice them any more. But today was different. A few words had made her different.

She hadn't been able to think anything when Vee said those words. That Vee had been thinking about Rachel, fantasising about her. Rachel had only been able to feel, and that feeling was so strange and unexpected and unaccustomed that she had no words for it. A clench in the belly, a thump of the heart, heat in her cheeks and under her hair, hands sweating. No words, nothing rational. But she went over it and over it in her mind as they walked home from Daybreak, as Sterling ranted without stopping about what a terrible evening it was, as she excused herself and went to bed early. Brushing her teeth, washing her face, plaiting her hair, putting on her nightgown. Pretending to be asleep as Sterling came up and lay beside her. Lying, eyes open, as he slept. Rachel thought about the fact that a woman, a married woman, the former friend of her own husband, wanted her. Thought about her intimately. She thought through every heartbeat and shiver, trying to identify it, as if creating a taxonomy of her physical response could tell her how she was supposed to feel.

She could count her breaths and give each one a name.

Sitting on the morning-flooded porch, she picked up a pencil and the hardback spiral-bound notebook she'd bought a long time ago, when she'd thought maybe she'd write a new history of Unity Island. She'd never used it for anything except shopping lists for her trips onto the mainland. Rapidly, she wrote those names down.

Panic.

Shock.

Disbelief.

Fear.

Pleasure.

Anxiety.

Guilt.

And something stronger than any of these, something that caught inside her and would not let her go, no matter how many breaths she took of the air inside this house of her marriage, no matter how she looked out at the sea and inwards at herself. She looked up from her list, traced the route of a gull with her eyes, heard the stirring of her husband in the house behind her. She gave this one a name, too. Shaped it into reality with her pencilled letters.

Desire.

'You're up early.'

She started at the sound of his voice and covered the pad with her spread-out hand. 'Oh, I couldn't sleep.'

He looked tired, too – more tired than she felt, even though she had lain awake all night and listened to him sleeping. He had dark circles under his eyes and his hair was messy from the pillow. Even the t-shirt he slept in was limp, defeated, and she knew that all his anger last night had been a cover-up for pain and loss. He mourned a friendship that never would be recovered, just like his dad was gone forever.

She waited for him to ask why she couldn't sleep, maybe to put his hand on her shoulder, share her coffee, watch the gulls and the sky. Neither of them would lose anything if she told him what had happened. He was so angry with Vee that this would be one more sin against her, one more reason to dislike her. She could recount last night's conversation in the kitchen to him as if it were a piece of island gossip – *And then she said she thought about* me *when she had sex with* Mike! – and framing it as gossip would put the whole thing into context. Vee was like that. A wild cannon, a former Unity person who no longer belonged here, someone impulsive, with no regard for the way you were supposed to behave. A good person to avoid, to chuckle about secretly while shaking your head, thinking about her rich and charming husband who had no idea, or maybe he did. It might bring her and Sterling closer together if they both had a reason to push Vee away. It would remove any need for Rachel to think about how she felt. It would keep everything the same. Maybe a little better. Definitely clearer.

She waited. All he had to do was ask. Acknowledge that she had a reality that was separate from his, so that she could make the choice to share it.

'Thanks for making coffee,' Sterling said. 'I'm going to need it today.' He went back inside the house.

Rachel carefully tore the sheet off the pad and folded it, over and over again, into a tiny triangle that fitted into the palm of her hand, between her love and life lines, a tightly clenched secret.

She put the triangle in her pocket and carried that word, that named breath, around with her all morning. While she watered her garden before the heat of the day, while she helped in the store, while she made up and drove deliveries. Making lunch, pouring iced tea. *She wants me.*

Such a strange idea. If Vee wanted her, she had seen her. Really looked at her, found something to desire, something that no one else saw. Something unusual and special, something Vee wanted to touch and taste. It wasn't about dating or making a life together or planning for any sort of future, nothing practical or sensible or morally sound. It wasn't because their goals aligned and they wanted the same sort of things and wanted to find their place to belong. It was much less than that. But it was enough, more than enough, to change everything.

I think I might want her, too.

The clock ticked past noon. The temperature rose as the sun climbed to its zenith, passed over the island to the west. The store was full of tourists. It was one of the last days of the season. She stationed herself behind the ice-cream counter, but even elbow-deep in tubs of ice cream with cold air kissing her cheeks, she was hot. Sweat trickled between her breasts. Her shorts felt damp; her thighs stuck to each other. She scooped rocky road, chocolate chip cookie dough. The flavours dribbled down the side of the cones as soon as she handed them over to sweaty, eager children. The strawberry wasn't properly frozen and it dripped from the scoop onto her fingers, down her wrist. Rachel stood not twelve feet from her husband and she licked sweet pink from the inside of her arm. She thought about Vee. Tawny hair, golden skin, graceful neck. She thought about Vee's mouth on her and she wanted to melt.

Rachel washed her hands in the employee cloakroom and she caught herself in the mirror. Her cheeks were flushed, lips open, eyes heavy-lidded. How she felt could be read by anyone. No one had ever told her that they wanted her like that. No one had ever made her restless, so aware of every part of her skin and the blood underneath. Her bra felt too tight. Her hair stuck to her neck. She twisted it up, knotted it into itself, and splashed cold water on her face.

There was a queue of people waiting for cones when she returned. Cherry vanilla. Salted caramel brownie. Good old-fashioned maple pecan. Someone laughed, down deep in their throat, and her whole body lit up in flame, flashed with heat and joy and hunger.

What was happening to her?

Chapter Twenty-one

Vee

She woke up to the smell of stale wine on her own breath and the sound of the door to the house opening. Then closing. Footsteps squeaked on the floor down the hall.

'Mike,' she whispered, and poked the side of her sleeping husband. 'What's that noise?'

He grunted, so she poked him again. 'There's someone in the house.'

'Mm?' He raised his head, his blond hair awry. 'What time is it?'

'I don't know. Early. Someone just came in the house.'

'Dunno.' He put his head back on his pillow and was instantly asleep. Vee looked at his tanned arm against the white sheet. Her head pounded. She hadn't locked up the house – why would she? Everyone on the island knew everyone else and thieves didn't ride the ferry over to steal stuff. As soon as she'd hit the age of about eleven, one hundred per cent of the petty theft and breaking and entering crimes committed on Unity had been planned and enacted personally by her. The only people you had to fear on the island were insiders, members of your own family. Not strangers.

Still, her heart beat rapidly as she slipped out of bed and pulled on a robe, and she walked as quietly as she could out of her bedroom and down the hall. The noise was coming from the kitchen, and she supposed someone could have wandered up to the house, walked in, decided to look through the fridge while the summer people slept late. Kids, maybe. It was something Vee would've done. She still remembered the thrill of slipping through quiet rooms, the chill of a pilfered can of Coke under her t-shirt. Sometimes the rich people left messes in their rooms, discarded clothes and half-empty glasses, smeared plates and dirty ashtrays, but Vee liked the tidy ones best, the ones so different from her own home. They were almost like museum rooms. Foreign objects and exotic ways of life, from another, parallel history to her own.

She paused at the end of the hall. She heard someone moving, puffed breaths, and the muffled sound of music, so faint that she could only hear a tinny thread. Headphones. Vee drew herself up to her full height, clutched her robe closed, and stepped into the kitchen, ready to use her most adult voice to tell the kids to get the hell out.

But it wasn't kids. It was a woman with short, sandy, grey-ing hair, wearing ear buds, denim shorts and a yellow t-shirt, bubblegum-pink Crocs. She stood at the kitchen island, polishing the granite with a cloth. From the side, she was solid, her arms strong, one calf tattooed with a butterfly. Her profile was familiar, but it was the butterfly that Vee recognised. She'd used to stare at it, trace its outline with her eyes, its pink and blue swirled wings, want one desperately for herself, one day.

'Bunny?' she said. The woman didn't turn, so she stepped closer and said it louder. Bunny started, her hand going to her chest.

'Jeezum crow you just nearly gave me a heart attack,' she said, and it was the way she said 'heart' – the long wide vowel, the absent letter r – that made Vee rush forward and throw her arms around Bunny, because her mother said that word the exact same way. She hugged the woman hard, breathing in the familiar scents of cigarettes and Lemon Pledge, exactly the same as she used to smell all those years ago when she and Vee's mom came home from work. It hit Vee in the stomach with a terrible longing, a painful nostalgia for something she had no idea she'd even missed, worse than any hangover.

'Is it Vee Harper?' Bunny said over her shoulder. 'Let me go so I can look at you.' She leaned back and studied her. 'Wouldn't have recognised you from a distance. But you never did favour Dottie.'

'We've got the same nose.'

Bunny shrugged. 'P'raps. Anyway you look like a summer person now. I only knew it was you because people been talking.'

'I know they have.'

'Nothing better to do out on this rock, unless you got money. I can see *you* do, now.'

'I've done okay. Are you still working for yourself?'

Bunny snorted a laugh out of her nose. 'That's one way of putting it. Still cleaning summer people's houses. I do most of the ones on this side, same as I used to do with your mom. In the off season I got some work at the canning plant. I spend most winter nights at my cousin's out in Lincolnville.'

'Edith? How is she doing?' When she was in high school, Vee used to board with Edith during the week, and though Dot hadn't been able to pay her much, Edith had been kind. Once she'd taken Vee to the Maine Mall in Portland and treated her to an Orange Julius from the food court. Nothing had ever tasted so sophisticated or delicious.

'Not bad, she had the breast cancer a while back but she beat it.' Bunny turned to the worktop, picked up a bottle, squirted cleanser and started polishing the granite again. The full impact of this encounter hit Vee, at last. It was stranger even than Sterling in her house.

'Wait,' she said. 'You're not cleaning my house.'

'Looks like I am. These granite worktops are good-looking, but they take special cleaner and everything. Pain in the arse. All these houses got 'em now. We have to get the cleaning spray from Amazon.'

'Have you been cleaning this house since we got here?'

'Three times a week. You've been asleep or out. Those windows are a pain in the arse too.'

This had never occurred to her. Somehow she had become one of those people who never noticed the work being done around her: who breezed through life not noticing that windows were cleaned, rugs were vacuumed, floors were mopped, bathrooms were scrubbed, granite worktops were polished with special fluid. She had forgotten how much labour all of these gleaming surfaces required.

'Bunny, you're a family friend.'

'Related, actually. Your mom's my second cousin so I guess that makes you my second cousin once removed.'

'Exactly. You can't clean my house.'

'Sorry to tell you, but I need the money. Some of us en't struck it rich yet.' She said it without apparent rancour, but Vee winced.

'If you need money, I'll pay you anyway. I can do the cleaning. I literally have nothing better to do.'

Bunny stopped rubbing the worktop. 'Vivian Harper, do you think I will take money for sitting on my backside?'

'No, but—'

'You think poor people don't have any pride at all? You forget what it's like?'

'I—'

'You remember my brother John who never did nothing but smoke dope and drink beer? Used to crash out on my couch all summer growing his beard and drawing on his arms, wouldn't even stir himself to take out the rubbish? You think I'm like him?'

'No. I'm sorry, Bunny.'

'Sure, I'd rather sit around on my arse all day and watch *The Bachelor* but what would that make me? Around here, everyone who *lives* here, works for their pay.' She turned her back on Vee to pick up a plastic bucket from the floor. Vee's nostalgia was gone; now she had the distinct feeling that she was seven years old again, and had been told off by her mom's best friend for spilling a whole glass of Kool-Aid on the carpet.

'I'm sorry,' she said again.

Bunny grunted.

'I know you're making a living,' Vee said. 'I guess I just feel funny about having my summer house cleaned by family.'

'Nobody on Unity to do it but family.'

'Yeah, but – you know what I mean.'

'You done good. You got out of here, you made it. Now you live in the big house, and I'm cleaning it. It's no skin off my nose, I'm happy for you. That's the way things are.'

'God, that sounds bleak.'

'You joshing me? If I won the lottery and got a big new house, I'd hire someone to clean it, too. I'd hire Jenny Lassiter. That woman thinks she's God's gift. I'd leave cigarette butts everywhere and "forget" to flush the toilet. I'd leave my jewellery lying around so she could see it and eat her heart out.' Bunny chuckled with satisfaction as she brought the bucket to the sink and started filling it with water. 'That would teach her.'

'You're not Jenny Lassiter, though. You used to swat my bum when I got mouthy.'

'That I did. Not saying you didn't deserve it.'

Vee nodded. She thought about Sterling, last night, and Rachel. She deserved to have her bum swatted, at the very least.

Vee said, 'Listen, how about this. I'll get dressed and help you. That way you'll get done twice as fast and you can watch *The Bachelor* or whatever.'

'With those hands? What do they call that, a French manicure?'

'I'll wear gloves.'

Bunny shrugged. 'Suit yourself.'

In the bedroom, Mike was still dead to the world. She put on yoga pants and a t-shirt, aware that she had nothing old, aware that even this outfit was easily five times as expensive as Bunny's Walmart clothes. She tied her hair back without looking in the mirror because she didn't want to see the summer person reflected back at her: her careful highlights, her skin nourished by serums and night cream, eyebrows shaped, ears sparkling with diamonds. Even her hangover and regret seemed privileged. She slipped off her wedding and engagement rings and put them in her underwear drawer where they wouldn't get lost and where Mike wouldn't see that she'd removed them.

Dorothy Harper had left Unity Island swearing that she would never clean another rich person's house again, and she had made her daughter Vee promise that she wouldn't, either. 'I don't care what you do for money, as long as it's honest,' she told Vee. 'But you're not going to scrub any toilets unless you shit in them yourself.' Dot stayed true to her word, but Vee, away from her mother and working two part-time jobs to put herself through college, cleaned offices early weekday mornings, before her first classes. She didn't mind it. It was boring, but there was a satisfaction in straightening things, scrubbing them clean, emptying waste bins. Unlike the other jobs she took, which were usually waiting tables, she didn't have to deal with customers. It was just her and maybe one other person – always a woman, sometimes a fellow student, more usually an older woman – working in an empty floor of a building, quietly restoring everything to order. She felt no shame in it, even though she couldn't tell her mother. She knew she wasn't going to be doing it forever.

Now, she and Bunny worked together and even though Vee was living in the house, Bunny told her what to do. Bunny put her earbuds back in and the two of them worked in companionable silence. She fell back into the work in the same way that she fell back into being the child in this relationship. Both were comforting. They swept and mopped the floors, ran a quiet vacuum cleaner over the rugs (Vee hadn't even known where it was kept), polished the kitchen surfaces, dusted the living areas, left clean towels in the bathrooms, put the old ones in the washing machine and then the dryer. She found herself being irritated that Mike was still asleep so she couldn't clean their bedroom, but she brought her bucket, mop and cleaning cloths through to the en-suite bathroom and cleaned that. He didn't stir.

'Well, that's done,' Bunny said to her when she returned. 'Just got to fold the towels now.'

'I'll do that, Bunny.'

'You got to do it the right way, like you're in a hotel. These summer people are picky.'

'I'll keep that in mind. You got a cigarette?'

'Sure do.'

Vee grabbed a couple of bottles of water from the fridge and led her out to the patio, where the flagstones had been warmed by the morning sun. They sat together at the table. Bunny lit a cigarette in her own mouth and passed it to Vee before lighting another one for herself. She inhaled deeply, with the zeal of a long-time smoker, the type who was reaching for a second cigarette before they finished their first. She spoke on a plume of outward smoke. 'Well I feel all la-di-da and fancy out here.'

'Want to use the jacuzzi?'

Bunny laughed. 'Yeah, maybe some other time. I en't got my bathing suit and you don't want to see my nudie old lady tits.'

Vee inhaled. She'd given up smoking once she was a grown-up and it wasn't cool any more, but the feeling in her throat and chest were as familiar and comforting as Bunny herself. The nicotine hit her immediately with a rush of dizzy pleasure. 'God, that's good.'

'How's your mom doing?'

'You don't talk to her?'

'Haven't heard a nip from her since she left all those years ago. Not that I blame her. She wanted to leave this life behind, you know? She never talked about nothing else. She knew there was nothing for her here except you and Eustace, and when Eustace was gone, she could take you with her.'

'But she never got in touch?'

Bunny shrugged. 'Figured if she wanted to, she knew where I was. Same house, same phone number, I'm probably even wearing the same undies. What's she up to these days? She doing okay?'

'She's in Florida. After she left Maine, she got a job in a dentist's office as a receptionist. She got her GED in her spare time and got her associate's degree in Business Administration. Before she retired, she was the office manager for a large practice.'

'Good for her. I always knew Dottie was smart. How about you?'

'I got a scholarship to law school and worked in New York for a while until I got married.'

'Rich guy.'

'My mom picked him out for me, would you believe.'

'Oh, I believe it. She wanted you to have the best. Just about used to kill her when she couldn't give it to you.' She tapped her ash onto the patio, and pushed it away with her pink-Croc foot. 'Your mom married?'

'No, she never got married. She hasn't even had a serious boyfriend, as far as I know.'

'Dottie was always real secretive about her men. You ever find out who your dad was?'

Vee felt her face redden. 'No.'

Bunny didn't seem to notice her blush. 'Oh, we had some times,' she said. 'D'you remember that winter when we had one storm after another and we couldn't get off the island to work and we couldn't get our social security checks and all you and Dottie had in the house was Ritz crackers and stuffing? The dry stuff, in a box?'

'I remember stuffing for dinner. We ate it with spoons out of a bowl. She said it was Thanksgiving in February.'

'Dottie told me about it after, a long time after. One day when we were cleaning together. She said it was the worst week of her life. Her pops had spent all the money on liquor. She was afraid she was going to have to go to Ames' and beg for food. I told her next time to come to me first. I don't know what she did. She never asked me, anyway. She went without sometimes so you could have enough.'

Vee remembered Brenda Ames giving her food to take home, when she was a child. It was always things like cookies, home-made rolls, muffins. Things that were presented as treats, as things that she had made extra and had to be eaten. But Brenda knew exactly how bad it was for Vee at home.

Everyone knew.

'Anyway, she never had to go without the cancer sticks.' Bunny laughed, dropped her butt and ground it out with the toe of her Croc. She immediately lit up another. 'John used to get those for us. Said they fell off the back of a truck. Only thing he was good for, truthfully.'

'How's John?'

'In jail. Got to buy my own smokes now.' She offered the pack to Vee, who shook her head. Bunny leaned back in her chair, crossed her bare ankles, butterfly leg on top, and gazed out over the rolling lawn to the sea. 'God, this is the life, en't it?'

'Come over for a beer some evening after work.'

'Nah.' She waved her hand. 'That would be weird. Thanks for your help today, though. Tell your mom hi. Seeing you reminds me how much I miss her.'

'I'll give you her number.'

'Nah, it's okay, I don't hold it against her. When you leave something behind, sometimes you got to leave everything and everybody. Maybe I should've done it too. I think about that sometimes.'

'You're not exactly an old lady. It's not too late.' But Bunny did look old. She'd lost one of her canine teeth, and her eyebrows were over-plucked and sparse. She had the leathery skin of a smoker, the blunt wrinkled hands of someone who worked hard every single day. Islanders – the residents, not the summer people – all had something of this look, as if the constant salt and fog and wind weathered them down, showed the granite in them. Her mom had shaken it, somehow. Most of it. But every now and then the granite showed through, the hard rock under the sun-kissed skin, the pastel clothes, the adopted Florida drawl.

'Even if I won the lottery, it would be too late for me,' Bunny said. 'I still wouldn't feel comfortable in a house like this. But you done all right for yourself, Vee. I'm proud of you.'

'You wouldn't be proud of me if you knew what I was like.'

Bunny shrugged. 'Yeah, same here.' She stood up. 'I gotta get going to my next house.'

'When are you here next? I'll give you a hand again. That was fun.'

'You got a strange idea of fun.'

'Nice, I mean. It was nice spending time with you.'

Bunny nodded. 'It was. But I don't want you to help me again. That's not the way the world works. You make your choices, and you live with them. We all do.'

Chapter Twenty-two

Vee

Mike came onto the patio about noon, stretching and scratching his chest. He was showered and clean, smelling of mint and expensive shampoo formulated for men, carrying a bottle of acai berry and seaweed smoothie. 'Hung-over?' he asked her.

'I've done a full day's work already.'

'Oh, good for you.' He pulled out the chair next to her. 'Hot out here. It's cooler indoors.' He wrinkled his nose. 'Also, you reek of booze and cigarettes.'

She grunted and turned her chair so she was facing the almost imperceptible breeze from the ocean.

'I thought it was fun, last night,' he said. 'It was definitely another side of you.'

'I drove your guests away.'

'It was the booze talking. They'll get over it.'

She thought of Sterling's furious face. She thought of Rachel, scared motionless. 'I don't think so,' she said.

He twisted off the cap of his bottle and took a sip. 'This stuff tastes like shit. Why do we buy it?'

'It just comes with the order. If you don't like it, you'll have to tell them yourself. I'm never setting foot in that store again. Thank God we're leaving next week.'

Mike set the bottle down. 'I think you're making a mistake there.'

Vee, startled, looked at him. 'What?'

'So you had a few too many drinks and you were a bitch. So what. Nobody cares. You've known this guy all your life. Even when you were arguing with him and he was being all passive-aggressive, it was clear that you have a lot of shared history. You don't have that with anyone except for your mom.'

And Bunny, she thought. But she didn't bring that up with Mike. He'd have trouble understanding why she felt so bruised after being rejected by the cleaning lady.

He continued, 'Someone very wise once told me: it's not about keeping score, or who's right or wrong. It's about recognising the people who matter, and sticking with them.'

'Who said that?'

'Well, my dad actually.'

She raised her eyebrows. 'Unexpected.'

'My dad's a smart guy.'

'No, I meant from you.'

'Thanks for thinking so highly of me,' he said, and took another drink of smoothie. 'Ugh.'

'I mean, I would think highly of you, but it's hard to take advice from a dude who can't even remember not to drink something disgusting.' She twisted her hair around her finger. 'I was mean to Sterling, wasn't I.'

'It was sort of *Desperate Housewives*.'

'Oh dear lord.'

'You know me, I have no right to tell you what to do. We're here in Maine to make you happy. Go ahead and keep the feud going, if that makes you feel good.' Mike stood up and wandered off towards the gym building. She could have sworn she heard him whistling.

The problem was, how to talk with Sterling without seeing Rachel. Because Vee had told more than one home truth last night, and telling her private fantasies to Sterling's wife was by far the worse betrayal. If she could talk to Sterling first, smooth it over, then she could speak with Rachel privately and apologise. She could laugh and say, oh, I'm sorry, silly me, I always proposition women when I'm drunk, I hope you didn't get the wrong idea. And then, preferably, swear Rachel to secrecy.

Unless she'd already told Sterling, of course. Unless they'd been up late talking about her. Sitting in bed. Shaking their heads. Pathetic Vee Harper, see, I told you that's what she's like, the way she used to be, always starting drama, trying hard to be outrageous, to be a rebel, to be noticed.

She put on her least summer-person clothes: a pair of grey shorts and a pink tank top, plain white trainers, a baseball cap and sunglasses. Still, she felt conspicuous walking down the dirt road around the island towards the store, and she pulled her cap down as far as she could and avoided eye contact with other people walking along. Odds were they were other summer people, day visitors, but last night had been cribbage night. It would be entirely typical of Unity if Sterling had gone back and bad-mouthed her to every single person with cards in their hands. And news travelled around this island faster than lightning.

When she got to the school/museum, she stopped. What the fuck was she doing? Since when had she ever crept around anywhere? Even before she was born, when she was in the womb and her mother was a sixteen-year-old high school dropout pregnant by some unknown guy, her mother walked around Unity with Vee in her belly and she kept her chin high and she didn't let anyone insult her to her face. That was the lesson that Dorothy Harper had taught her only daughter: no one could put shame on you without your permission.

Vee took off her baseball cap and put it under her arm. She pushed her sunglasses on top of her head. She was six again, going to school with a bunch of kids who knew her family got food stamps. She was twelve, giving the finger to the grown man who commented that she was starting to look trashy like her mother. She was sixteen, marching up from the ferry dock with the Honor Roll list in her hand so she could shove it in the face of Anita Langlais, who had told her that she'd never be more than a C student.

Vee Harper walked along the only road in Unity with her head up and her face bare for all to see. She walked straight to Ames' General Store, pushed open the door and marched up to the counter, where Sterling was scrolling on his phone. If not for the phone and the threads of silver at his temples, he could be his teenage self, the one who Vee cared about more than almost anyone. He looked up when she approached, and before his face could harden into anger, she said, 'Come and meet me under the dock as soon as you're free. I'll wait.' And then, because they weren't their teenage selves any more, she added: 'Please.'

Most of the edges where the island met the sea were jagged granite, except for in two places. One was Unity beach, in a shallow cove on the south side of the island which was covered in tourists from June to September. The other was directly under the ferry dock at low tide. Under the barnacle-crusted pilings lay a narrow strip of what looked like sand, until you got up close to it and realised it was millions of pieces of fragmented shell. Vee picked her accustomed way down over the rocks to this secret place, canopied by trailing seaweed. You couldn't see it from above, only from the water: the perfect place for secret conversations, for games of pirates, for drinking purloined beer and smoking illicit cigarettes. If you weren't careful, anyone standing on the dock would be able to hear you, but you could see their shadows first through the thin lines between boards, and shush each other, clamping your hands over your mouths to stifle the giggles.

Vee sat down on the corpses of numberless creatures and waited for Sterling. She wasn't going to rehash the past, or blurt out any confessions. She certainly wasn't going to go into the real reason why she'd left all those years ago, and why she had to go without saying goodbye. She was going to front it out, like she always did, like she'd been doing since the day she was born. You couldn't take back mistakes, and you shouldn't be made to feel ashamed of them. But you could make things better, sometimes.

She'd given Sterling a black eye more or less directly above where she sat now. He'd forgiven her then.

She nosed the toe of her trainer into the pieces of shell. In all the years they'd come down here, they'd never seen anyone else. Sometimes there was rubbish left strewn on the little beach, but it could have washed up there. Once, when they were – what, fourteen? fifteen? – they'd found a used condom, limp and translucent like a dead jellyfish. Sterling had picked it up with a stick, his face a picture of disgust and fascination, and dangled it as it dripped salt water and … something else. Then he flung it out to sea. Any other boy she knew would have taunted her with it. Said 'Did this fall out of you?' or 'Bet your mom wishes she'd used one of these' or something worse. Much worse. Not Sterling. It wouldn't even cross his mind. There was that one time he punched Danny Salisbury for holding his fingers up in a V to her and licking between them. Danny had ended up with the black eye that time, and Vee'd spent hours consoling Sterling afterwards because he felt so guilty that he'd punched someone, even someone who deserved it.

God, she missed him. She felt the ache of all the years she'd been without him, now that she was sitting here, in this place where they'd spent so much time. Maybe she'd been missing him since she was seventeen, and she'd just refused to acknowledge it. Right now, she thought that the odds were against him even coming down here to find out what she had to say. But she was going to wait. If necessary, she'd wait until the tide came back in and forced her onto dry land.

A footstep crunched on shells and she looked up from her clasped hands. 'Hey,' she said. 'You came.'

'I'm not sure why.' He stepped in further, ducking his head to avoid the festoons of weed. 'I haven't been down here since …'

She scooted over to give him room to sit. 'I wanted to offer the hatchet. Bury the olive branch. However you say it.'

'Did you.'

'I was out of line last night, Sterling. You were my guest, and I was rude to you. I found your tender spots and I poked them. I'm sorry.'

He was still standing. 'That's not what I'm angry about, Vee.'

Shit. Rachel had told him. 'Can you just clarify—'

'I'm angry with you for saying you were my best friend for our entire lives, taking everything my family had to give you, and then abandoning me when I needed you. Abandoning us.'

'Okay. That's fair. I won't apologise for leaving. But I will apologise for leaving you. You needed a friend, and I wasn't there.'

'I didn't even know you were gone until someone else told me. You didn't leave a note, or a message. Nothing. One day we were best friends. The next day, my dad died and you were gone.'

'Yeah. It must have been shitty for you. And I was devastated that your dad died. I loved him. He was probably my most important person, after my mom and you.'

Tom Ames, pushing her on a bicycle. Slipping a Charleston Chew bar into her coat pocket after school when the other kids weren't looking. Handing her his big handkerchief so she could clean up the scrape on her knee.

'He helped me once,' she said. 'In secret. He was like that.'

Sterling leaned against one of the pillars, still at a distance. 'What did he do?'

'It was that last summer, fourth of July weekend. You were doing stuff with your family but I got invited to a party with some summer people, some college kids using their parents' place. I don't know if you remember it, it was in one of their houses. I think it was Dunroamin. Anyway I was there drinking, having a good time, and I suddenly realised I was the only girl there. It was all guys. All older than me. And the way they were talking…'

She swallowed, remembering the creeping awareness, the touch of their gazes, the way one boy kept refilling her drink. 'Anyway, I didn't dare just leave, I didn't want to walk home by myself, so I called you.'

'I don't remember that.'

'No, because you didn't pick up. Your dad did. He said you were asleep, and he asked where I was, so I told him. And less than ten minutes later he was there, with the truck. I didn't even know how scared I was until he turned up. And I was embarrassed that he'd come instead of you, so I asked him not to tell anyone, and he didn't. He didn't give me a lecture, either. He just made sure I was safe, and dropped me off at home.'

And then, in return, Vee had kept a secret for Tom Ames, after he was dead.

'He was a good man,' Sterling said.

'And you are too. I know you idolised him.'

Sterling didn't reply.

'It must have been awful when he died,' she continued. 'I didn't know you had to change all your plans. I had no idea you had to give up going to school. I thought you were off, travelling like you wanted to.'

'You could have called any time. You had my mom's number. She would have told you.'

But Brenda Ames was the last person I wanted to talk to. 'You're right. I could have. I guess I thought it would be best to make a clean break.'

'You thought.'

She looked up at the dock above them, rimed with salt, green with nameless growing things. Somewhere, on one of these pilings, she'd carved her initials. She didn't remember which one it was, and it was all covered with barnacles and seaweed now anyway, even if it hadn't been worn away by the tide.

'A lot of time has gone by, Sterling. And I'm leaving after Labor Day anyway. I did something bad to you when we were kids, I didn't treat you like a friend, and I'm sorry. I didn't do it to hurt you, but I'm sorry anyway. And you didn't deserve it, because you're a good person. Maybe you'll never forgive me, maybe you'll always be mad at me, but you are one of the closest things to family that I have, besides my mom. Even though I haven't seen you for twenty years, you and I still know each other better than almost anyone else. That's why I can make you so mad. And you can get mad at your family and never forgive them, but you can't get rid of them. It would mean a lot to me if we could at least call a truce.'

Sterling sighed. He came over and sat down beside her.

'You smell like smoke,' he said.

'I had a sneaky one with Bunny Phelps earlier.'

'I could use one now, if I'm honest.'

'You still like Virginia Slims Menthol Lights?'

'The girly cigarette of champions.'

She didn't have to look at him to know he was smiling.

'I haven't touched one of those since you left,' he said. 'I even stopped stocking them in the store because they pissed me off every time I saw them. Fortunately everyone else around here had better taste than to smoke them.'

'You were always more of a Marlboro Lights man at heart.'

'I never liked smoking much at all, to be honest. I did it because you did. And seeing your dad drop dead of a heart attack tends to cure you of nicotine cravings.'

'I still miss him,' she said quietly. 'Coming back here, I see him everywhere.'

'Yeah.'

'You must too.'

'Every day.'

They sat, both watching the waves foaming against the shells. The water made a different sound here than anywhere else on the island. It was softer, enclosed; a gentle sound, like breathing.

'What about Rachel?' she said.

'What about her?'

'Do I – do I owe her an apology?'

'About the baby remark?'

'Um. Yeah.'

'It's a tender spot, but it's okay. It's all everyone around here talks about anyway. We've only got four children living full-time on the island, and three of them belong to Penny Stewart.'

'Sour Sadie? Poor kids.'

Sterling nodded. 'I've got to get back to the store.'

'Broken chest freezer again?'

'The chest freezer didn't break. I just wanted to get away from you.'

'Knew it.'

'Today we're busy though. Plus, the tide's coming in.'

'I don't even know what time high tide is any more,' Vee realised, standing up. 'I could've come down here and it was all under water. Where would we have had this conversation then?'

'If it had been high tide and you'd asked me to come down here I would've known you'd completely become a summer person.'

'You wouldn't have come.'

'Nope. So I guess that proves at least part of what you were saying about family.'

As they climbed back up the rocks, her going first with Sterling following, she reflected that this was as close to forgiveness as she was probably ever going to get. She'd feel better if she thought she deserved it.

Chapter Twenty-three

Rachel

Labor Day weekend. A flurry of activity: hot dogs, briquettes and lighter fluid, lobsters, buns of every description, beer, sparklers, ice cream, souvenirs, firewood, more beer. It was busier because it was hot and sunny. During the day, Rachel hardly had time to sit down from sunrise to about ten o'clock at night, when everything was restocked and cashed up. One little boy from a family of day visitors fell on the rocks and came in with his head bleeding, his father hysterical. Rachel patched him up with the first aid kit while Sterling found him an emergency place on the next ferry so he could get checked out for concussion.

'It's not so bad this year,' Sterling told her. 'I remember about seven years ago when we had a broken leg and second-degree burns from a barbecue accident, both on the same afternoon.'

Rachel knew there had been worse. She had studied the archives of this place. Life was hard for the early islanders, even when they weren't burning their houses to the ground, but modern-day Unity still had its share of dangers. Boat accidents, children drowning, lobstermen lost at sea. A cot death. An electrical fire in the dead of winter that killed three members of the same family. Tom Ames, dead of a sudden cardiac arrest before medical help could arrive.

Grim thoughts for a holiday weekend, but at least she wasn't thinking about Vee Harper.

'She apologised,' Sterling had told her on Thursday night.

Rachel didn't have to ask who 'she' was. She'd seen Vee come in and speak to Sterling that afternoon, and leave without so much as looking in her direction. She hadn't breathed the entire time that Vee was in the store. She hadn't really breathed again until she'd taken a shower to wash off the ice cream and sweat and found herself gasping against the tiled wall, her hand between her legs stroking herself, her eyes closed so she could imagine.

She and Sterling had this conversation as they were sitting in bed. Sterling had a magazine open and Rachel's finger was marking her place in her book, though she hadn't taken in any of the words on the page.

'That's good,' she said cautiously. 'Do you feel better about it?'

'I guess it's all I could ask for.'

'Well, anyway, they're leaving on Monday.'

'Right, so everything will go back to normal.' He flipped a page in his magazine. Rachel thought about reaching out to him under the blanket, running her hand up his leg, which had always been their signal for initiating sex. Maybe it would quench this craving.

I think about you when I have sex with my husband.

She put down her book, turned out her light and lay on her side, facing away from him. That was a deception she wasn't capable of.

On Sunday she dropped a six-pack of craft beer when she was weaving between people browsing the shelves. Two of the bottles shattered and a woman standing nearby shrieked. Beer foamed out onto the floorboards; it was in the woman's sandal. 'I'm so sorry,' said Rachel, stooping to collect the shards of glass quickly before anyone stepped on them.

'I'm soaking wet,' said the woman.

'Yes, I'm so sorry, are you okay?'

'What now?' Sterling appeared, looking flustered.

'I dropped a—'

'I have beer in my shoe.'

'How did you manage that?' Sterling asked Rachel.

'It just slipped.' A bit of glass stabbed her finger, and she hissed in a breath.

'For goodness' sake, get a brush,' Sterling said. 'No, forget it, I'll do it, you're tired, take a break.'

'No, I can do it, I—'

'Go, Rachel. You're exhausted and that makes you clumsy. Come back in an hour. We can cover it.' He turned to the customer, to appease her, and Rachel stood up and went out the front door, into the sun, where she scrutinised her finger. It was only a small cut. She sucked her finger, tasted blood and beer.

She considered going to the house to try to take a nap, but their bedroom would be hot in the afternoon, even with all the windows open. She couldn't keep touching herself in the shower. She needed not to be fenced in by her thoughts, not to be anywhere near the store, not to be surrounded by her marriage.

She started walking, not really planning to go anywhere, just needing to escape the people around her, but within a quarter of a mile her feet took her off the road and up the shaded path to the centre of the island. It was cooler here. As she walked, she saw the flash of a bright red leaf that had already turned for autumn. And another.

Soon it would be quiet, and the summer people would go away, and so would Vee and Mike Ellis. The leaves would turn to gold and red and orange and fall, leaving only the evergreens, and Rachel and Sterling would be alone with each other and their marriage and their failure. It would be her third autumn here. The changing season always prickled her with dread. When she was a child, autumn meant that the lies had to start up again, about her home life and her parents' addictions. There was something about the shortening days and the cooler nights, the scent of smoke and leaves, that told her that it was time to put herself away, to pretend everything was normal. She still felt it here, even though she'd left her old life behind.

The scent of barbecues and the shouts of children carried through the trees on the breeze. When she rounded the path to the clearing in the exact centre of the island, she saw she wasn't alone. A woman sat on a rock in the clearing, with her back to Rachel. Her honey-coloured hair was loose on her shoulders and she wore white linen. It was Vee, as if Rachel's thoughts had summoned her.

Rachel stopped. Vee hadn't noticed her. She held a bottle of Wild Turkey in one hand and, while Rachel watched, powerless to say anything or to flee, she unscrewed the top. But instead of drinking from it like Rachel expected, she upended the bottle and poured it glugging onto the ground. Rachel must have made a sound of surprise because Vee turned, bottle poised. Vee's cheeks flushed bright red and Rachel felt hers heating, too.

'Oh,' said Vee. 'I didn't—'

'I'm sorry,' said Rachel at the same time. And then, when Vee stopped speaking: 'I'm just on a break from the store, I was getting some air. But I won't disturb you.'

She should turn around and leave. She meant to, that's why she mentioned not disturbing Vee. But she didn't move, and neither did Vee. The silence stretched out, sticky with bourbon. Rachel couldn't look away from Vee's eyes.

'I used to live here,' said Vee finally.

'Right here?'

'Well. About six feet in that direction.' Vee pointed with the neck of the empty bottle. 'That was the front door, that was the living-room window, that was my pops's bedroom window. The propane tank was around the side, near the kitchen. I slept on the second floor with my mom. It was just one big room up there, but we divided it with a curtain.'

'I didn't know there was ever a house up here.'

'Only ours. And now it's gone. I thought maybe there'd be a few walls standing, but.' Vee shrugged. 'I haven't found so much as a nail.'

'I'm sorry.'

'Don't be. That house was a piece of shit. It wasn't any more fit for purpose than the man who built it. The wood was so warped that the windows didn't open in the summer and in the winter, we had to cram newspaper in the cracks. I expected to find something left, though.'

'What do you think happened to it?'

'Things don't get wasted on an island. The wood wasn't much good for anything but building fires. There were a few things that my mom …' She shook her head. 'No, we took everything that mattered.'

This was a different Vee than the one Rachel had met before. She wasn't breezy and funny or drunk and provocative. She was still and pensive and sad.

Rachel came closer, sat on another rock. 'Where's your grandfather buried?'

'Lincolnville, I think. It's expensive to get buried in Unity dirt, and the cemetery's just about filled up. We couldn't afford a headstone, so I'm not sure I could find the grave even if I looked for it. This seemed like the best place to remember him. This was his favourite.' She showed Rachel the Wild Turkey label, and put the bottle on the ground. 'It's a little offering to him. I wasn't able to give him that much when he was alive.'

'I hear he was a drinker.'

'He was a drunk who couldn't hold down a job, and my mom was a teenage mother, and I was a wild child. We were all clichés, the whole family. Everyone on the island knew it, and they never let us forget it.'

'My parents were alcoholics, too.' Vee looked at her, surprised, and Rachel added, 'Are alcoholics. They're still alive, I just don't talk to them.'

'That's tough. I'm sorry.'

'She was a teacher and he was the superintendent of schools.

So they did all their drinking in private and nobody knew. It was my job to keep everything looking normal from the outside.'

'I know the feeling. Hiding the bottles. Answering the phone before anyone else can. Keeping money away from them.'

'I had to cook for them, or they wouldn't eat. And I set four or five alarms so they'd get up for work.'

'And so you could get up early and clean up their mess, because somehow it's shameful if they see it even though they caused it. Right?'

Rachel nodded. This was, she realised, the sort of conversation she'd wanted to have with Vee from the minute they'd met. This common ground, this acceptance.

'It was my brother's job too,' Rachel said, 'but he left as soon as he turned eighteen so there were quite a few years where I did everything.'

'How old were you?'

'Thirteen when he left.'

Vee nodded. 'You and I both had to grow up quick.'

'It made me good at keeping secrets.'

Their gazes met and held. Vee dropped hers first.

'I was drunk,' Vee said. 'I don't usually drink that much. I was really nervous, and that's not an excuse, I know it's what alcoholics say all the time. But I actually do not have a drinking problem. A lot of other problems, but not that.'

'Sterling said you apologised to him.'

She raised her eyebrows without looking at Rachel. 'You talked to him, then.'

'Yes.'

'Did you tell him what I said to you?'

Rachel's heart was hammering. She didn't know how to answer this question, because if she told the truth in any way, it was going to change everything. And she didn't feel ready to change it all, to detonate a mine in the set and safe path of her marriage.

'I shouldn't have said it,' said Vee. 'I came here with Mike to save our relationship. And you're Sterling's wife. I've said and done enough to hurt him. Also, if none of that were true, which it all is, why would I even think you like women, or that you care about my fantasies? I was an idiot, it was inappropriate and intrusive, and I was drunk. I'm sorry.' She stood up. 'At least we're leaving after the weekend so you and I won't have to run into each other.'

She picked up her empty bottle from the ground, turning to go, and Rachel, without knowing what she was doing, was on her feet, hand around Vee's wrist. It was the madness that had made her run so hot, touch herself at night, catch her breath at the sound of laughter that sounded like Vee's.

'I don't understand what you've done to me,' she said, her voice not her own, or maybe more her own than it had ever been, and then she was pulling on Vee's wrist, drawing her closer, wrapping her other arm around Vee's neck, tilting her chin up, eyes closed, kissing her, letting everything burn.

Chapter Twenty-four

Vee

Ocean and sky reflected each other, each a deep and flawless blue. Vee gasped in the water, then held her breath and dived, letting her feet lose contact with the rocks. Underwater, sound was a faint surrounding boom and the cold was more than the absence of warmth: it was a creature, wrapping around her, touching everything, everywhere, lifting her hair and holding her weightless and unconnected to anything but itself. She came up for air and did it again, and again.

Her teeth were chattering when she hauled herself up on a slippery rock and sat on it, waiting for the sun to warm her goose-pimpled flesh. Swimming in the Maine ocean was more of a shock than a pleasure, even in late summer, even when you were overheated from the air and from the touch of a woman's skin. But that's what it was supposed to be: a shock to the system, a cleansing.

Did she want to be cleansed?

She licked her lips and tasted salt. Rachel's lips had been soft and unexpected, and they tasted of salt too, but from the sweat of her upper lip. Vee had put her hand on Rachel's bare shoulder and the skin was smooth and a little clammy. They had stood close together, breasts pressing against each other as they breathed (did either of them breathe?) and when Rachel's tongue had touched hers Vee shuddered with wanting, so much wanting to touch this woman, to open Rachel's arms, her legs, her mouth, lift her up and crawl inside, not even to do a specific act but to know. Know everything. Be everything and understand.

Water was dripping down her back from her hair. Vee reached for her towel and draped it across her shoulders. That was the best fucking kiss of her life and she did not know what to do.

'You feel this way too,' she'd whispered, when they'd stopped kissing finally, after what felt like a long time and also too short a time. Rachel looked dazed, blurred somehow, her eyes and lips soft as butter, though Vee felt sharper, as if she could cut through anything. Even marriage.

'As soon as you said it,' Rachel said. 'I haven't been able to stop thinking about you. I don't know what's happening.'

'Me neither,' Vee had replied, and then they were kissing again, her hands in Rachel's hair this time, pulling it loose from its elastic.

It only finished when Rachel stepped away, wiping her mouth with the back of one hand, while with the other she still held on to Vee's wrist. 'I have to go. I have to get back to the store.'

'Okay,' said Vee, and she watched her go, stupidly stuck to this spot that used to be what they called the front yard but had really been a collection of junk and salvage and immovable rocks.

When she'd pulled herself together, run her fingers through her hair, wiped her mouth with the back of her hand, she returned to the house. She paused inside the door and listened for Mike. She'd expected him to be out on the boat but she could hear him faintly, talking to someone in a distant room. She slipped into the bedroom to change and then she'd come down here, to the water, to try to process what had happened.

But the cold water, the weightlessness and the shock and the tidal pull, didn't help her process it. How could you process something that had nothing to do with the rational mind? And did she really even want to think too deeply about it, anyway? It had been beautiful. It was a beautiful thing. A perfect moment. If she thought too deeply, she'd start blaming herself for betraying

Mike. She'd start wondering if this meant she was really a lesbian, and she'd been fooling herself by dating men, by marrying one. She'd start to question whether this was a symptom of a dying marriage, rather than a genuine desire for someone else. Did she want to divorce Mike so badly that she had to look for excuses? He was trying so hard to make things better. Could she only walk away by committing adultery, in a way that exonerated Mike from being at fault?

No.

She wouldn't do this. She wouldn't torture herself by trying to figure out why. It was something beyond her, that was all. Like the bus. Her feelings about Rachel weren't an excuse for anything, and she wasn't attracted to Rachel because she was female, but because she … because she *was*. It was just her.

And this didn't have to be a disaster, or change anything. She and Mike were leaving on Tuesday, and they had no reason to come back. Even if she and Mike didn't stay together, Vee wouldn't come back here. She would move on with her life. This could remain her secret, but a precious, beautiful one. Like a fossil in amber that she could nestle in her hand, polish with her touch, bring to her lips now and then to savour the warmth and smoothness, to try to smell the remembered scent.

Eventually one day she would forget that she wanted so much more.

She stared at the dazzling water, reliving the touch of Rachel's mouth, the softness of her eyes, until she felt the salt crisping on her skin and hair and her shoulders beginning to burn. Then she slowly wrapped her towel around herself and made her way up the lawn to the house.

Mike was standing in the large living-room window looking down over the property. He was still talking on the phone but as soon as he saw her, he finished the call and put his phone in his pocket. He was not a private phone call person and fleetingly Vee wondered if he was talking to another woman, if he'd lined up someone else for when they split, which would mean she didn't have to feel guilty at all. Then he grinned at her and waved through the glass, beckoning her to come inside, and she knew she was fooling herself. Mike wasn't that good an actor. He always wore every single feeling plain on his face, and he looked gleeful, not guilty.

'What's up?' she asked him as she stepped into the house.

'Oh my God, babe, you're not going to believe what I've just pulled off.' He kissed her cheek. 'Wait, wait, we need champagne.'

She watched him go to the wine fridge and pull out a bottle. 'What's going on?'

'I'm a genius, seriously.' He lined up two flutes and popped the cork.

'Okay, but why are you a genius?' She accepted her glass.

'Well, for one thing, I chose this house and you like it. You do like it, right?'

'Yes, it's an amazing house.'

'And for another thing, we're having a really good time here. The scenery is perfect, the sailing is great, we're spending lots of quality time together with fewer distractions, you've even made up with your childhood best friend.'

'Well... maybe not made up, but we called a truce.'

'He's a great guy, you'll be friends again in no time. You were saying that you needed more friends, more real friends.'

'I did say that, yes.'

'See, I paid attention. I pay attention to everything, babe. This is why I'm a genius.'

She took a sip of her champagne, because he didn't seem in any hurry to make a toast. 'Are you going to tell me why?'

'Well, you know how we're supposed to be going back to New York on Tuesday?'

'Yes.' For someone who said he paid attention to everything, he wasn't paying any attention to her impatience, or the fact that she was dripping on the floor.

'We're not,' he said. 'We're staying here.'

'…Why?'

He grinned, and spread his arms out wide. 'Because this morning, I bought this house!'

'You … what?'

'I bought this house! I bought Daybreak. It's ours. We live here.'

'But … it's Sunday. On a holiday weekend.'

'The broker was only too glad to be called away from his family barbecue, believe me.'

She sat on the arm of a sofa and put her glass on a side table. 'How long have you been planning this?'

'Almost as soon as I saw the place in person. But I made the offer after Sterling told us so much about how great the year-round community is here. How everyone pulls together and makes a big family.'

'Um. I don't think it's as rosy as Sterling makes it out to be. When I grew up here, it might have been one big family, but it wasn't a happy one. It was pretty dysfunctional.'

'Things change. You've changed a lot since then.'

'Hm. The winters haven't changed. This island is bleak in winter. And freezing.'

'The house is fully winter-proof. It'll be cosy. We can see the icy weather outside, and be safe and warm in here.'

'The ferry can't always run in winter, so we'd be stuck here.'

'If we were going stir crazy, we could use the boat. I bought that, too. And I'm a good sailor, I seem to recall.'

'I don't think you've ever lived six months without going to any parties.'

'Well, I'm not saying we can't go to New York for weekends, and when we need a shot of culture. But this can be our base. Our home. You know?' He came closer, putting his hand on her bare shoulder. 'You're happier here, Vee. I don't know if you've

noticed it yourself, but I have. You're calmer, you seem less…
angry, almost?'

'Angry? I'm not angry.'

'Well, stressed, then. Since we've been here, you've seemed
more comfortable in your own skin. There's a light to you that
I haven't seen for a long time.' He caressed her cheek. 'Unity is
good for you.'

'I don't know if it's caused by Unity, Mike.'

'It's definitely not caused by New York. You're not happy there.
But since we've been here, you've been happy.' He picked up her
glass and put it in her hand. 'We don't have to stay if you don't
want to. But it would be nice to have a home. I've never really had
a home home, just houses.'

'And you feel that this could be a home home?'

'Don't you?'

She thought about Rachel. Who had kissed her, thinking she
was going away soon. Who, if she stayed, Vee would see any
time she went into the store, whenever she went for a walk, on
the ferry. Plus Mike would probably want them round again for
dinner. And what if Mike decided he wanted to join in with cribbage night or get involved with the community in other ways?

This was the moment that Vee could say something. One of a
million things that would change the path she was on. She could
laugh and say, *No, this is a terrible idea, let's go back to New York.*
She could say, *I think it's time I went back to work anyway.* She
could say, *Maybe we still need a divorce.* She could say, *Actually,
I'm very attracted to Sterling's wife and if you and I are going to stay
married I think it's a good idea if I never see her again.*

Or she could give in to the warmth in her belly when she
thought about Rachel and those kisses.

'We could stay and try it out,' she said.

Chapter Twenty-five

Sterling

Sometimes before opening the store, he walked down to the beach on the south end of the island. He'd been doing it for years. In the early morning at low tide, you weren't likely to run into anyone except a few people digging clams. He often brought a plastic bucket with him, but it wasn't for clam digging. His father used to take him down here to fish, but it wasn't for that, either. As he walked to the beach, he'd stoop and pick up loose stones, a few at a time, so that by the time he reached the sand, the bucket was heavy. He'd walk down the length of the beach to the rocks and tide pools, where there was a good view of Brimstone Island and its white-painted lighthouse across the narrow strait that separated it from Unity.

Then he'd put down the bucket, and one by one, he'd throw the stones into the ocean.

If anyone asked, he said it was for exercise. Sometimes he said he was building up muscles for the big horseshoe pitch tournament they had every Fourth of July. But that wasn't the truth. It was catharsis, more than anything. Stone by stone, he threw Unity Island into the sea, and by the time he reached the bottom of the bucket, sometimes he felt lighter, too.

He was still mad at Vee. He thought he'd probably always be mad at her. But if he was honest, he wasn't only mad at her for leaving him. He was mad that she'd left in the first place. That she could leave without caring, without feeling guilty, when he couldn't leave. It was worse that she was here, reminding him of everything he'd once meant to do and never had.

And he knew that he was taking it out on Rachel: grumping at her, correcting what she did. He wasn't proud of that, and yet he seemed powerless in the moment to stop himself from doing it. He knew she tried hard to please him, and he knew that he made her feel inadequate. He might not be as kind as he wanted to be, but he wasn't stupid.

Out here, throwing rocks, it was easier to think about the way he should behave, rather than the way he sometimes actually did. The movement made things feel easier.

It was Lisey who'd taught him that, years ago, long before he'd met Rachel.

She was divorced, ten years older than him, part of a group of women who rented the little cottages in the grounds of Dunmore House on the north point for a month each June and went around the island doing yoga and painting landscapes. None of them were any good at painting, but they didn't seem to care. Lisey was beautiful and she invited him for dinner, one night when the other women in the other cottages had gone to Boothbay to a gallery opening.

They were lovers for five summers. He was pretty sure she was dating other people, and sometimes he did too. All the rest of the year, they rarely spoke. But June was theirs. Every night for five Junes he would come to her cottage and they would lie in bed together with the windows flung open and the air caressing their skin. She was long days, languid nights, midsummer.

And then before the first day of July she would go back to California and her three children, who had been staying with their dad.

'You could stay,' he said to her, that fifth summer. They were sitting on the beach, throwing rocks. It had taken half the bucket before he'd got up the courage to say this.

'My kids wouldn't live here,' she said. 'Anyway, this would never work.'

'Why not?'

'You're a dream,' she told him. 'You're a glorious escape from everything in my life. And I'm the same to you.'

'You're not an *escape*. You're a person.'

'Okay then, how about you come to Los Angeles and get a nine-to-five and become a dad to my kids?'

'I can't do that.'

'And there's your answer. We're different people in real life. Which is why this is so good between us.' She kissed him, and stood up, and held out her hand. 'Come back to the cottage so we can go to bed.'

That was the last summer. She didn't come back the next June, and he knew it was because of the question he'd asked. So in the winter, he decided he would find someone who could stay: someone who would entwine her whole life with his, who would live here year-round. And that was how he joined the dating app, met Rachel, and was charmed by her, and married her.

Sterling threw another rock in the water, as far as he could. His shoulder ached. He could not blame Rachel for not being Lisey. Lisey was sensual and sophisticated and a dream. Rachel was reality. She was quirky and clever and she needed him in ways he did not quite understand, and he had promised to love her forever, just like he had promised to stay on the island and look after what his family had built.

An hour later, he put down the phone. The island grapevine was rarely wrong, and this confirmed it. He attached the list to the clipboard they kept hanging behind the counter as Rachel came in from the back, carrying an empty mug from the house.

'Didn't you say you were going to see your mom today?' she said.

'Ferry's not here yet. I just got a call with a delivery list.'

'Okay, not a problem, I can do it. It'll be quiet today.'

'I can stay if you need me. I'm not doing anything that can't wait.'

'I can handle a delivery and the store, Sterling. You don't need to question my competence every chance you get.' He watched her as she went to the coffee station and put a fresh filter in the machine.

'I know,' he said. He rubbed his shoulder, which was aching from throwing rocks. 'I'm sorry.'

'Okay then.' She began to measure Morning Blend into the filter. He could hear the ferry's approach, right on time as always.

'The delivery's for Daybreak,' he said.

She paused, head bent over the coffee bag, back to him. 'I thought they had left after the holiday weekend?'

'Apparently not. Mike called in the order. He said they've bought the house and are going to make it a year-round residence.'

She switched on the machine and checked the supplies of stirrers and sweetener. 'They bought it, just like that? That house has to be worth millions.'

'It's a decent investment. You know what the prices are like here.'

'If you have the money to spend. Wow.' She'd begun to rummage around in the cupboard under the station, so her voice was muffled. 'So they're going to stay on?'

'Vee knows what it's like, but I give Mike till November, latest. You know what this means, though ... Rachel? Did you hear me?'

'Hmm? What does it mean?'

'We're going to have to invite them back for dinner.'

She pulled out a box of stirrers and appeared to be examining the label.

The ferry was louder; he checked his watch. 'I've got to go. There's a bunch of restocking to do. You sure you don't want me to stay?'

She waved him off, head back in the cupboard.

Chapter Twenty-six

Rachel

She turned the sign on the door to CLOSED and drove the truck to Daybreak. She held her breath as she knocked on the door.

Mike answered. 'Hey,' he said, clearly glad to see her. Vee hadn't said anything, then. He took the box of groceries from her arms. 'Is there more in the truck?'

'I'll get it.'

'Don't you dare. Come on inside and have some coffee.' She followed him inside the house and instantly saw Vee through the windows, sitting on the patio in the shade of an umbrella. He put down the box on the worktop and Rachel stood in the kitchen, awkwardly, as he went through an interminable and self-satisfied fuss with a complicated coffee machine. At one point, this morning in the store, it had occurred to her that maybe this whole thing was a manipulation, a scheme of Mike's and Vee's together to spice up their marriage. 'Go ahead and join Vee outside,' he said finally, handing her a cup of something frothy and fragrant. 'I'll take care of these groceries. We're neighbours now. You heard?'

She said something that Mike seemed to accept as sufficiently enthusiastic and took her coffee outside, to Vee.

She wasn't sure what Vee's response was going to be to seeing her again. They'd left everything unfinished, or rather Rachel had assumed that it was finished before it had begun. She'd walked away from that clearing in the centre of the island without any expectation of seeing Vee again, ever. Every morning since, she'd sat alone on the porch with her notebook, but she hadn't been able to write anything down at all. What she felt was too large and uncontained to be captured by a ballpoint pen on lined paper.

Vee looked up at her approach and Rachel saw her face changing, from surprise to half a smile, quickly suppressed. Vee glanced at the house and then stood up, lips pressed together in a smile that was more cautious. In that moment, Rachel knew that none of this was a scheme, none of it had been planned at all.

'Hey,' Vee said. 'How are you doing?'

She wore shorts and a strappy top that showed tanned shoulders and cleavage, no bra. Rachel remembered how her warm skin had felt under her hands and said, politely, 'I hear you've bought the house.'

Eyebrows up. 'Yeah. It was a surprise to me too. Mike—' She glanced at the house again. 'I see Mike made you a coffee.'

'Yeah.'

'Please, have a seat.'

Was this what it was going to be like? This careful friendliness? She sat across from Vee and sipped her coffee and thought about what she could say. Whether to bother saying anything at all, or whether it would be better to go back to the store and pretend that nothing had happened. 'Are you enjoying that?' she asked, pointing to the thick paperback on the table between them.

'It's definitely thought-provoking. Have you read it?'

'I read it last year when it came out in hardback. The library in Rockland is really good at getting the prize-winners in.'

'Ah, yes, I'd heard it won a bunch of awards.'

'It has a lot of interesting things to say about the limitations of art.'

'Yeah,' said Vee. She looked miserable. 'I can see that.'

Rachel sipped her coffee. She glanced at the house. Mike was nowhere in evidence.

'I'm hating it,' Vee blurted. 'I hate this book. It's boring and I can't work out what's happening and I keep on forgetting who everyone is. I like books with a plot and dialogue and people making horrible mistakes. I know that makes me an incredibly shallow person.'

'I didn't like it either. I only finished it because I finish every book.'

'Why, though?'

'What do you mean, why?'

'Why did you finish it? Why am I trying to finish it?'

'I don't know,' said Rachel.

'Let's go for a walk.' Vee stood up and started down the lawn. Rachel abandoned her coffee and walked with her towards the water. 'There's nowhere on this island for any privacy,' said Vee, as soon as they were out of earshot of the house.

'Tell me about it. Mike said he was going to put away the groceries.'

'That could take anywhere from ten minutes to two hours, depending on how distracted he gets.' Vee ran her hands through her hair, which was loose around her shoulders. 'I had no idea he was planning to buy this house.'

'Really?'

'I know it sounds incredible, given how much this place must have cost, but you don't know Mike. If he wants something, money is no object.'

'Why did he want it?'

'I think he has an idealised view of what this place is like. But really he bought it for me.'

'He doesn't know—'

'Of course he doesn't. We're here to *fix* our marriage.'

'So ... he bought you a house.'

'He gives me gifts all the time, without asking whether I want them. I have to act pleased, or he gets hurt. Sometimes I think he doesn't give the presents to me, he gives them to an imaginary wife who would want what he has to give.'

'You didn't want to stay.' This hurt her, more than it should, if she had been expecting Vee to leave.

'I. Well.' Vee looked over her shoulder back at the house. They'd walked far enough so that they couldn't see in the windows that made up the entire front of the house, offering a view of the whole lawn. It was like a theatre, with Vee and Rachel the show, and an unseen audience inside.

'I asked him for a divorce two months ago,' Vee said. 'Way before I met you, or even knew you existed. So this isn't anything new. But he persuaded me to give us another chance, which is why we came here.'

This was news to Rachel. 'So that's why you ... why we ... because you're unhappily married?'

'No! No, that is really not what I wanted to happen at all. I wanted a change, I felt like our marriage was going nowhere, but Mike deserves a chance. If we end up splitting, it would be because of him and me, not because of someone else. I'm not looking for an affair, or to do anything dramatic to make him divorce me. Because an affair with another woman would *really*—'

'We haven't had an affair,' said Rachel quickly.

'No.'

'That's not even on the cards.'

'No.' Vee said it vehemently, and that hurt Rachel again.

Rachel said, 'So this is – this is fine, we made a mistake, we'll just be friends.'

'*Did* we make a mistake, though?' asked Vee.

It was an entreaty. They stopped walking to look at each other. Vee looked anguished, and Rachel didn't know how to answer that question.

'Let's ...' She gestured to a pair of rocks at the end of the lawn, overlooking the water and clearly visible from the house, but far enough away so that they could see anyone approaching long before they could be heard. Vee nodded and sat on one, while Rachel perched on the other.

'I don't know what to think,' said Rachel. 'This is all completely unexpected. And I thought that you were going away, so we didn't have to deal with it.'

'So we could leave it as a beautiful memory.'

Rachel swallowed. 'But now...'

'Yeah.'

Rachel watched the ocean. It had seen all of these problems before, and didn't care.

'Have you... Have you...' she gestured vaguely to indicate whatever this was between them '...with a woman before?'

'No,' said Vee. 'Not... I mean, growing up, it was pretty much understood that being gay was for summer people.'

'That's still true around here,' said Rachel.

'I'm bisexual,' added Vee, 'but until now that's been theory rather than in practice. I did have a threesome with a guy and another girl, but it was mostly for the guy's benefit. And that was a long, long time ago. I had a huge crush on one of my professors at law school. She was this ice-queen type, incredibly intelligent and hot. But I never said anything. I was focused on getting the grades. What about you?'

'Sara-Jade,' said Rachel. 'Yeah.'

'She was your girlfriend? Before Sterling?'

Rachel shook her head. 'No, she was never my girlfriend or anything like that. But... I've been thinking about her.'

'Tell me about her.'

Sara-Jade, of the braceleted arms, of the winged eyeliner and the deep dimples. 'I was only a teenager. I'm not sure it really counts.'

'Have you listened to Sterling and me talking? Things that happened when you were a teenager shape everything.'

'I haven't thought about her in years. I... didn't have a lot of friends in high school. I couldn't join any clubs and my parents both worked in the school system, so I had to …'

'Watch them.'

'Yeah. I couldn't *watch* watch, but I was vigilant. And of course when you're the child of a teacher, you're not the most popular. My brother was good at sports, so he found it easier, but I was pretty much a nerd. So I had a lot of strikes against me.'

'I would've been your friend. I never gave a fuck about what anyone thought.'

'You wouldn't have noticed me. I tried hard to stay under the radar. But Sara-Jade … we were assigned a project together in history when we were freshmen and we became friends. We ate lunch together for three years. Every day. She always had the same thing: a hot dog with mustard and a fruit salad. Not the fresh kind – it was the long-life kind in the little pots. Every day she made it a game to see if she was going to get a cherry. She said if she got a cherry, she was going to have good luck all day. She used to like Motown and trashy horror movies and skateboarding. She was a really good skateboarder. She was fearless. Like poetry.'

'What did she look like?'

'She had beautiful eyes and she had dimples, and she hated her hair. I loved it, because it was long and dark and looked like silk. But she said she loved mine. And I had terrible hair because I hadn't learned about conditioner for curly hair yet. She used to play with it all the time. She'd flop it in my face like I was a Jewish Cousin Itt. It always made me blush.'

'Did you …?'

'We made out. We used to hold hands, when no one else could see us.'

'What happened?'

'She asked me to prom.'

'Did you go?'

Rachel let out a short laugh. 'I wanted to. But there was no way.'

'Why not?'

'I had to stay normal. I had to stay unnoticed. If I didn't keep everything under control...'

'But lots of girls went stag to prom at my high school. No one would have even noticed you were a couple, if you didn't want them to.'

'Sara-Jade wanted them to. She wanted to come out to everyone. I told you, she was fearless.' Rachel chewed on her lip. 'But I wasn't. I was afraid of what it would mean if I went with her. What it meant about me. I had so many things to worry about at home. I wasn't ready to be different in any more ways.'

'Are you ready now?'

'It doesn't look like it, does it?'

Vee sighed. 'What happened to Sara-Jade?'

'She told everyone to call her S.J. and went to prom with a cheerleader. They were runners-up for Prom Queen. I didn't go.'

'Was there anyone else? Any other girls?'

Rachel shook her head. 'Not until you. Until you said that. Now I'm wondering if I'm really a lesbian, and if I've been denying it so hard for so long that I never even allowed myself to think about it. Because when you said it...'

'I thought you were terrified of me.'

'I was.' She paused. 'I am. Maybe not of you, but what you represent about what I want.'

Another glance at each other, and then back up at the house.

'You're married,' said Vee. 'And I'm married too, but you happen to be married to Sterling. And I meant it what I said to him, that he's my family. So I can't avoid him. Or hurt him.'

'I don't want to hurt him either. He's had enough of it.'

'You've had enough pain, too.'

Rachel shrugged. 'I'm used to it. It's never been any different.'

Vee reached a hand for hers, and then stopped.

'So we have to not do anything else,' Vee said. 'You and I. We have to stay friends and that's it. No more touching, or kissing, or talking about this stuff.'

'Right,' said Rachel. 'And that's good, because I need friends.'

'Yeah,' said Vee. 'I need friends too.'

Part Four

Autumn, 2015

Chapter Twenty-seven

Sterling

When he was growing up, autumn had always been Sterling's favourite time of year: when the leaves turned red and orange, and the sky settled into a deeper shade of blue, and you dug through the boxes in the closet under the stairs for scarves and gloves and knitted hats, even though you didn't need them yet, not quite, but you wanted to be ready for the inevitable day when you did. Autumn meant that Unity was quieter and less peopled. It meant school starting, yes, but it also meant that the store wasn't busy and his father had more free time, so he could take an afternoon off to fish or dig clams or go bike riding, before it got too cold, like it was in the winter, or too buggy, like it was in the spring. Autumn was the time when he felt special: new school clothes and trips to the mainland to visit Funtown USA before it shut for the winter, fresh notebooks and pencils for school, unmarked and unchewed, a new seat in a new place in the island classroom to mark the fact that he was one year older. Vee always sat on his right, Walter Beotte on his left, and Sterling knew he was the buffer between the troublemaker and the kid who needed extra help, but he liked that responsibility, that signal that he was special, he could be trusted.

When he left the Unity school and went to Rockland Junior High, autumn became the time when he rode the ferry by himself, when he stayed with Grandma during the week, when he walked into the big modern building and found his way, when he met people who didn't know who his family was so he had to prove he was worthy by getting his homework in on time and trying out for the basketball team. Autumn meant adventure, new things.

Then his father died and autumn meant not going to college like he'd planned. It meant seeing his mother getting sicker and realising he'd be working in the store for the rest of his life. It meant everyone else going somewhere, his lover leaving him, and Sterling staying here, with the same faces and names, watching the trees change colour, the leaves flutter and fall, and winter creeping in from over the waves.

It was one of the reasons why he and Rachel had planned their wedding for October. It was less busy, but also he'd thought it would mean that there was a special occasion to look forward to. And then afterwards there would be anniversaries to celebrate like they'd celebrate their children's birthdays and the day that those children, too, first went off to school.

Today was the special occasion. This morning, he'd given her a bunch of yellow roses that he'd bought on the mainland yesterday and hidden in the store. He brought them to her in bed, with a card, a cup of coffee and a blueberry muffin. 'They're lovely,' Rachel said, burying her nose in a blossom. Then she got out of bed, knelt on the floor and pulled out a small package wrapped in silver paper from under the bed. 'I got you this.'

It was a bracelet plaited from leather cord and fastened with a silver clasp.

'Three years is leather,' she explained.

'Thank you,' he said. He never wore jewellery, but he was touched by the thought. He put it around his wrist, then kissed her on the cheek, then the lips, and she pulled him down onto the bed with her. It had been a while, and that was probably his fault, because after trying for so long it was difficult not to associate sex with futility. But she gripped her fingers into his back, moved urgently beneath him, and when he kissed her he saw that her eyes were squeezed tightly shut, as if she were savouring this, concentrating hard on it, grasping this closeness between them.

*

Later, he pushed aside the plate with his sixth slice of apple pie and groaned.

'You're quitting already?' his mother said. She sat beside him at one of the store's wooden tables, in the place of honour, a scoresheet beside her. 'You used to be able to try every single pie, and still have room for ice cream.'

'When I was fifteen, maybe.'

She wrote something on the scoresheet, covering the paper with her hand.

'What are you scoring that one?' he asked.

'I'm not telling you.'

'It's okay, I didn't make a pie this year. Neither did Rachel.'

'I'm standing by my integrity as a judge.'

'Wendy's going to win again, isn't she? Those apples came from her own tree.'

'I am *not telling* you.' Brenda turned to her scoresheet, and Sterling sat back in his chair, surveying his store.

They'd held the apple pie baking contest every October for years now. Unlike all the events for summer people and tourists, this was strictly for Unity residents: an excuse to get together during the off-season. At first, it had been his mom's idea, but after she won the popular vote six years in a row, she declared herself ineligible and became the judge instead. She'd still brought half a dozen pies over on the ferry anyway.

Most of the island's permanent residents were in the store, crowded around the tables, leaning against the counters with paper plates in their hands, little Stewarts running between the aisles, hopped up on sugar. More people were outside, under the strings of lights Rachel had put up last May. He hadn't told anyone that this year the pie contest coincided with their anniversary, and he didn't think Rachel had either, but Jacob had painted a big HAPPY ANNIVERSARY sign on half a sheet and that was hung up on the wall over the ice-cream counter. People on Unity had good memories – and they'd got married right here, in the yard of the house next door.

These were people he'd known all his life: talking, eating, laughing, drinking coffee, some of them playing a cribbage grudge match. Mike Ellis was standing by a table, wearing a new-looking flannel shirt. He had made a pie for the competition, the ugliest pie that Sterling had ever seen. The pastry resembled burned shoe leather. Sterling hadn't tasted that one, but he was sure his mother had given Mike a couple of points at least for trying. Now, Mike was surrounded by old Unity ladies, all of them giving him pie-making tips. From here, Sterling could see that they were all charmed by him. Even Marjorie Woodford.

Rachel was in the corner, talking quietly with Vee: his wife, and his childhood best friend. Vee's contribution to the contest had been two McDonald's apple pies, taken out of their wrappers and put on a fancy plate. 'Secret recipe,' she'd told Sterling when she added the plate to the display of home-baked goods near the counter.

'You're working at McDonald's now?' Sterling had said.

'Beats being a lawyer.' She high-fived him. Leaned closer. 'You look happy,' she said. 'You are happy, right?'

He was startled by the question, and he knew that she saw it. 'Why wouldn't I be happy? I'm doing what I'm supposed to be doing.'

'At least you know, huh? That's more than a lot of people get.'

'Right.'

She looked around the store. 'This place never changes, does it? You know, I always wanted to work here.'

'Really?'

Vee nodded. 'I sort of angled for a part-time job but your dad never took me up on it. Maybe he thought I'd lift money from the till.'

'He wouldn't have thought that.'

'Well, I wouldn't have done. Not from him. All of the customers would've been fair game, though.'

Sterling laughed, and Vee laughed too. Rachel wandered over, as if drawn by their laughter. 'I think Mike is fitting right in,' she said.

'No, he isn't,' said Vee and Sterling at the same time, and they laughed again. Rachel looked between them, requiring an explanation.

'He's a nice guy,' allowed Sterling. 'He knows how to charm the ladies.'

'It helps that he's shit at baking and loses every cribbage game,' added Vee. 'That might also be deliberate, but don't tell anyone.'

'If everyone likes him, why do you say he doesn't fit in?'

Sterling and Vee exchanged a glance. How did you explain something so obvious?

'He tries too hard,' Sterling said.

'Oh.' Rachel nodded. 'That makes sense. I tried too hard when I first came here, too.'

And now you don't try at all, thought Sterling, and then suffered a pang of guilt. She did try, and if she'd given up, how much of that was his fault? He touched the bracelet she'd given him, and took her hand. 'You fit in perfectly. Aside from not playing cribbage, of course.'

'You're lying,' said Rachel, squeezing his hand. 'But it's nice of you. I do think it's weird though, that I've lived here for three years, and Vee's been gone for twenty, and yet Vee's slotted right back in.'

'Me?' said Vee. 'I never slotted in here in the first place. Sterling's the Unity man. I'm just a summer person now.'

A Unity man, he thought, later, as he stood beside his mother and gave Wendy the prize. That's what he was: born of the blood. Being a Unity man had been good enough for his father, and it was good enough for him. What other happiness could he be allowed to want?

Chapter Twenty-eight

Vee

'I talked to Charlie Broomhall last night,' she said into her phone.

She could hear her mother's silent disdain all the way from Florida.

'It was the apple pie contest at the store,' she added. 'I didn't let Charlie in the house.'

'That man sets foot on your property, you'll never get rid of him and he'll bore you to death. His father was just like that too. Boring Broomie, we used to call him. How are you getting along with Sterling?'

'Fine,' she said. Crossing her fingers. It was fine, though, wasn't it? It was fine. 'We're going to his house for dinner on Saturday.'

'Brenda okay?'

'Yes, I think so.' She'd avoided Brenda all night.

'What's it like at his house? Is it the same?'

'It looks almost exactly the same, except they painted the kitchen and the living room.' The first time she'd stepped into Sterling's house she'd been able to see Rachel everywhere: the knitted throw on the sofa, the stack of thick books underneath the end table. But the plates and cutlery were the same, the dining table, the kitchen chairs. It was as if Rachel were layered over all Vee's childhood memories.

'Listen, Mum, Charlie said something about Pops.'

'What sort of bullshit was that man spreading about our family?'

'He said he'd been looking at land records for Unity because he's obsessed with building an airstrip in the centre of the island. And he said that Pops owned the land that our house was on.'

Silence.

'Mum?'

'What?'

'Pops owned it. He owned four acres right there in the middle of Unity. Four acres. Did you know that?'

'No, how would I know? Did my father ever act like he owned anything in his life?'

'What did – did you think he rented it? Or he squatted there? There are Harpers in the cemetery.'

'I never asked. I thought... I don't know. I paid all the bills. I can't remember any for rent, but not any for taxes either. I don't know, I never thought about it. I had enough to think about. All I wanted was to get the hell out of there.'

'But he wouldn't leave.'

Her mother didn't reply. Vee pictured her, on the balcony of her Florida apartment, looking out over the swimming pool. There were so many swimming pools in Florida, even for people who weren't rich. Even for people who worked hard and got by after spending their entire life scraping for money and living in a cold, leaky house in the middle of a rock in the sea.

'Charlie said that a group of people were finding investors to help buy the land and build the airstrip. He said he'd been sending you emails.'

'As if I'd open any emails from Boring Broomie.'

'What about regular mail, Mum? Have you had anything about taxes? The land must belong to you now, right?'

'I throw away any envelope if I don't know what it is.'

Vee knew this, having been the person who paid her mother's backdated and ignored parking tickets.

'And I don't want anything to do with that place anyway,' her mother said. 'There was nothing for me there any more, and what was left was too painful. Good riddance. I left and that's it. I'm not visiting if you and Mike stay there, by the way. You're going to have to come to me. Or we can meet up somewhere civilised, like Atlantic City.'

'I know. You said.'

Her mother lapsed into silence again. This was what her mother did, what Vee had learned from her: fight through life, and then refuse to speak about the hard parts ever again. As if you could undo the past by ignoring it.

She and Rachel weren't talking about what they'd done, or what they'd decided. They talked about apple pies, or the store, or books, or world history, or Chicago. Vee tried not to look too closely at Rachel's hands or her mouth. She tried not to stand or sit too close, but even when there was no possibility of touching, she felt Rachel like an electrical field.

With Sterling, though, that was all they talked about: the past. They remembered what they used to do, private jokes they used to have, people they knew in common. That was safer than discussing the present.

And Mike ... he was happy, so happy, pleased with himself and with her, as if the question of divorce had been settled between them, as if they'd agreed to stay together forever. Vee felt the question in the air, all the time. But Mike didn't. Or if he did, he was following his mother-in-law's philosophy: if you don't talk about it, it never happened.

She opened her mouth to ask about Pops, a will, the land deeds, but her mother spoke first.

'If it's still mine, you can have it,' Dot said. 'I don't want it.'

'I have a house, Mum. Houses.'

'Keep it for your kids.'

'I don't have kids.'

'It's not too late. You're only thirty-seven.'

She sighed. 'Mum, we've been through this. I'd only fuck up a kid's life. I wouldn't know what to do with it, and Mike doesn't want his life to change.'

'You never know. I didn't think I wanted kids, but then I had you.'

'I was a mistake.'

'You were never, ever a mistake. Do you hear me? *Never*.'

'Okay, Mum, okay.'

She expected her mother to argue more – it was a favourite topic of hers – but instead she fell silent again.

'He could've been buried there,' Dot said finally. 'If we'd known.'

She dug around in the grass with the toe of her shoe, and felt something hard. It was a piece of metal. When she knelt down and dug it out with her hands, it was a nail. A rusty one. Was it from her old house? Had it been hammered into place by Pops, years and two generations before the wind and snow and islanders tore the house down to nothing?

She picked it up carefully; it would be ironic if she got tetanus and died from the only remaining piece of the house where she'd been born. Her mother never talked about Pops, wouldn't elaborate on what she'd said on the phone, but although he'd clearly been a shitty father he had not always been a terrible grandfather. He took Vee for walks, on days when he was sober and not angry about it. He played cards with her on their scratched kitchen table. He adjusted the rabbit ears on their ancient television so she could watch *Sesame Street*. He'd taught her how to make clam dip and how to imitate the sound of a bald eagle so one would turn its head to listen to you.

After she'd finished talking to her mom she'd called Gina, a former colleague of hers at G&G who specialised in probate. Gina said she would investigate the situation. If the land hadn't been seized already for back taxes owed, it was almost certain that Dot would be better off selling instead of trying to keep it. But her mom didn't want to know, so whatever had to be done, Vee would have to do it.

She curled her hand around the nail. The incredible thing was, even back in the eighties, four acres of Unity was worth more money than Pops had ever made in his life. If he owned it, he could've sold it at any time, moved them inland to somewhere cheaper. Somewhere that no one knew them or would judge them, somewhere that it would be easier for Dot to support them, somewhere he could've got help, or even drunk in bars instead of at home, on the sofa in front of the television, every single day.

But he hadn't. He had stayed right here, on this land. On this rock in the ocean. Something had kept him here, and had kept Vee and her mother here too, looking after him until he died and they could leave. What was it?

She couldn't ask him, and she couldn't ask her mother either. But she thought she knew. It was this. The land. The rock. He'd breathed Unity air every day of his life, drunk water that fell onto this island, slept here and eaten here and taken this place into his very bones. It was part of his flesh. And it was part of hers, too.

She dropped the nail in her pocket.

Chapter Twenty-nine

Rachel

'Good, just hold it steady. Just like that! You're a natural.'

Mike stepped back, leaving Rachel with the wheel in her hands. It wasn't like driving a car; the wheel tugged gently against her palms as the boat rose and fell with the waves, and she couldn't see what was directly in front of the boat because the roof of the cabin got in the way.

'I'm going to crash into something,' she said.

'What are you going to crash into?' Mike gestured at the open sea around them.

'Another boat. A rock. A whale!'

'The whales know to get out of our way,' said Sterling.

'The sharks, on the other hand...' said Vee. She was standing in the door to the cabin. Rachel had been worried about spending a whole afternoon on a small boat with her, but Vee had spent most of the time below. Anyway, the two of them had been just friends for weeks now. They'd been talking about everything (everything except the kiss) and they had so much in common. Not just the fact that they'd both survived alcoholic households: they shared a sense of humour, a taste in films, an interest in the achievements of women. Vee said things that Rachel would never have dared to say aloud, and that made Rachel braver. Rachel didn't have to self-censor about her past, she didn't have to wait for the doubtful look and recoil, she could say whatever she wanted and Vee still liked her. Vee still understood her. And she and Sterling and Vee and Mike were doing couple things together, like normal couples, in a way that Rachel had never done.

Rachel and Vee weren't just friends. They were quickly becoming *best* friends. And that was better than an affair, wasn't it? There were so many ways to have someone be important to you other than having sex with them. Or wanting sex with them.

Vee held up a flask of coffee. 'Refill, anyone?'

'We're going to need to tack in a minute,' Mike said. 'And then we'll be keeling pretty hard. So maybe wait twenty minutes, babe.'

'Okay.'

'You want to help with the tack?'

'Not a chance.' She disappeared back down into the cabin.

'Vee claims she can't sail,' Mike told Rachel.

'She can't,' said Sterling. He was sitting in the cockpit, and he looked more comfortable than Rachel was. Of course he'd been on a million boats in his life, though he'd confessed to her on their way over to Daybreak that he'd never been on a summer person's yacht. It was near the end of October, a crisp, clear day and one of the last before it got cold on the water, and Mike and Vee were still living on Unity even though it was clearly not summer any more.

'Vee's a terrible sailor,' Sterling continued. 'We borrowed a dinghy one time when we were teenagers and tried to sail across to the mainland. She got hit in the head with the boom and knocked herself out.'

'That really happened?' asked Mike. 'I thought she was making it up as an excuse.'

'It really happened,' called Vee from the cabin. 'I still have the dent in my skull.'

'It really happened,' said Sterling. 'I was there. I thought she was dead. She didn't come to until I'd sailed us back to the dock and tied up the boat and was about to run for help.'

'Let that be a lesson to you,' Mike told Rachel. 'When I say "Ready about" make sure you're paying attention. And when I say

"Hard a-lee," turn the wheel fast to the right, and *duck*. Ready about.'

'When you say … ?'

'Hard a-lee.' He put his hand on the wheel next to hers and helped her turn it fast, to the right. The sail started flapping, the boom swept towards her head, and Rachel ducked to let it pass overhead. Mike leaned over, tightened a line, and clamped it off. 'Perfect. Like I said: a natural.'

The sail tightened, the wind caught in it and the boat tilted to one side, so much that it felt to Rachel as if it were going to topple over. They started going much faster.

'Oh my God,' she said.

'You're doing it! Hold on to the wheel. How does it feel?'

They were racing across the bay at what felt like a forty-five-degree angle, cutting through the waves, wind whipping Rachel's hair back, so close to the water she could smell the brine. She'd thought she'd feel vulnerable in a sailing boat, at the mercy of the weather. But she didn't. She felt powerful; as if all of the strength of the water and wind were in her hands.

'It feels great,' she said, and laughed. And then she caught the eye of Vee, who was standing in the door to the cabin watching her, hands braced against the frame to keep her upright, and that was more dizzying, more powerful. She gasped, as if the wind had stolen her breath. But it was Vee.

'I still can't totally trust her,' Sterling had said this morning, when they were choosing layers to wear on the boat, side by side in their bedroom looking in the closet and chest of drawers.

'Vee?' She could just about say the name, now, without feeling like she was blushing, or about to blush. 'It's Mike who invited us to go sailing, and it's his boat. If you're worried about safety, it's him.'

'Mike's fine. Walter said he's seen him on the water and that he knows how to handle a craft, and Walter should know. Anyway,

Mike's easy to figure out. What you see is what you get with Mike. He's a rich man who likes to play with toys. Unity is his newest toy. He'll try to stay the season, and will probably be back in New York by Christmas.'

'You like him, though, right?' She pulled a shirt off its hanger. 'I like him.'

'I like him fine. There's nothing not to like. If he's spoiled, it's not his fault.' Sterling shut a drawer. 'But I don't know what Vee is up to.'

'…What do you mean?' she said carefully.

'There's nothing here for her. If she wanted to build on that land that Charlie says her mother owns, that would be one thing. But to buy a whole new house? Is she trying to prove that she's better than everyone she grew up with?'

'I think, to be fair, that Daybreak was Mike's idea.'

'They're married. Couples decide things together.'

I wouldn't bet on that, thought Rachel. 'It sounds like a lot of people around here used to judge her family. Can you really blame her for wanting to show them that she's done well for herself?'

'Bunny Phelps said that Vee offered to help her clean the house. Despite paying Bunny time and a half to clean off-season.'

'Actually,' Rachel said, 'that sounds exactly like something that Vee would do.'

'You like *her*, don't you?'

'Yes.' Rachel shut the closet door. 'I do like her.'

Sterling sighed. 'I want to trust her. She apologised, and I'll admit that was big of her to do. We called a truce, and I meant it. But she still pretends that she did nothing wrong. And she knows she did. Have you noticed that she won't talk to Mum for more than about five seconds?'

'Really?'

'I know that Vee had a tough time as a kid, and no one trusted her, except for me and my family. She didn't trust anyone, except for her mom, and I thought she trusted us, too. But then she left and I knew she never really trusted us, either.'

'So you can only trust someone who trusts you back?'

'Maybe,' Sterling said.

'Rach, will you help me with the lunch stuff?'

They'd moored at Daybreak and Sterling was on the dock, securing the lines while Mike put on the sail covers. Rachel was collecting the coffee mugs, reflecting on how automatically the tasks reverted to gender lines now that they were near land. But when they'd been under sail, she'd been in charge of everything, once Mike had shown her how. She'd steered, tacked, learned how the wind worked, trimmed the sails, chosen a course, avoided lobster pots and skimmed across open water. She'd learned the language: lines instead of ropes, port instead of left, bow instead of front. Sterling was impressed, and it felt like he hadn't been impressed at anything she had done in a long time. *Rachel* was impressed, and maybe she hadn't been proud of herself for even longer. Mike had said she was a natural, and at first he'd been flattering her along but, by the end, Rachel thought he meant it. He said he'd give her lessons any time she wanted – and it turned out that he'd nearly been on the Olympic team when he was younger. She wasn't bad. She liked sailing. It was technical yet instinctive, physical and intellectual at the same time. It was something that people had been doing for thousands of years. And she felt great: her cheeks windburned, her hair a tangle, her lips tasting of salt, her arms and shoulders aching pleasantly from pulling the lines.

'Sure,' she said, and went down the ladder to the cabin. The interior of the boat was fitted in teak; there was a tiny kitchen (galley) and an even tinier washroom (head), and a seating area whose sofa pulled out to make a bed (bunk). Light filtered in from the door (hatch) and windows (portholes? She didn't know that one). Vee was in the galley, packing the acrylic plates they'd used for their lunch into a wicker picnic basket. Her hair was tied up, except for honey-coloured wisps on the back of her tanned neck.

'What do you need help with?' She stepped off the ladder, and she was immediately closer to Vee than she had been for days. Not on purpose; the galley just wasn't big enough for two. She could smell Vee's perfume, a floral scent she hadn't consciously noticed before but which now her body remembered with a jolt of arousal: a hot breath on a September day, their hands on each other in the clearing. Rachel cleared her throat; their husbands were inches away. She could hear Mike talking to Sterling above them, something cheerful about the weather.

She reached for the bag of uneaten food on the worktop and Vee turned at the same time so they were face to face. A glimpse of Vee's eyes, a coffee cup in either hand. And then Vee stepped closer, pressed against her, pushed her against the galley wall and kissed her. Rachel grabbed her arms and held on tight. Vee's mouth was wet and hot and urgent; their layers of clothing rustled. Instinctively she tilted her hips forward and Vee rubbed against her. Vee's thigh slipped between hers, pressed inward against her crotch, and Rachel moaned, without meaning to, into Vee's mouth.

'You two got everything under control down there?' It was Sterling, calling from the deck above them.

Vee drew her head back but not her body. She gazed into Rachel's face as she called, 'Yes, we're on our way up.' Rachel felt the air from Vee's words on her lips. Heard footsteps right above their head. Their hearts thudded against each other. Vee licked her lips and stepped back. She turned to the picnic basket and began buckling it up.

Rachel picked up the bag of food and climbed the ladder to the deck. Mike was right there in the cockpit; he took the bag from her and swung it over the side of the boat to Sterling on the dock. Had they heard anything? Seen anything? Could they see it on her mouth, her flaming cheeks?

'Let me give you a hand,' he said to Rachel, and steadied her by the elbow as she stepped off the boat. 'You're going to feel like you're still on the boat. It might take you a few minutes to get your land legs back.'

The dock rolled underneath her. She picked up the bag and walked onto the shore, which pitched and moved. Solid land turned to liquid under her feet.

Chapter Thirty

Vee

Fog creeps in on little cat's feet.

Her mother never got her diploma from Rockland High School, but she said that once she learned something, she learned it good. And she had learned the Carl Sandburg poem in Mr Billing's sophomore English class, not long before she got pregnant with Vee, and every single time there was fog, whether in Maine or Florida or New York, she repeated that memorised phrase. *Fog creeps in on little cat's feet.* Vee never studied that particular poem, though she did look it up one time, on a foggy day in Chicago, and was not surprised to learn that her mother had been misquoting it. Her mother was reliable about most things, but she was unfailingly vague about that particular year of her life. In any case, repetition meant that whenever it was foggy, Vee thought about cat's feet too. Padding silently with the stealth of a predator.

But she thought it was a terrible metaphor. The fog on Unity wasn't cat-like. It was not playful or cute. It did not manifest slowly or subtly. It was less like a cat and more like a landslide. On Unity, you woke up to find your house surrounded by thick grey blankness. Or you embarked on the ferry only to discover that you were blind. It rolled in with inexorable silence. It magnified noises, it sent light bouncing in unexpected directions. It was as opaque as dirt and as stubborn as rock.

This morning had been overcast, with a few snow flurries; the type of November day that made you think, *Well, it's winter soon, but not yet.* Mike went out in *Dawntreader* early, wanting to grab a day on the water while he could. Vee almost asked him not to. But what could she say: 'When I'm alone in the house I think too much about the woman I want to sleep with'?

Instead, she kept busy, in the way she'd learned to keep busy since she quit being a lawyer working fourteen-hour days. She slept late, then got up and worked out in the gym, cooked herself an elaborate no-carb lunch which she ate in front of the television, filled the dishwasher, then curled up on the sofa, reading a fat blockbuster she'd taken from the Take a Book, Leave a Book shelf in Ames'. By the time she'd decided she'd read enough Jackie Collins for the day, the house windows were all blanked out by fog. She couldn't see the water, couldn't see the lawn or even the patio. It was as if everything outside of the glass had been eaten up and disappeared.

She wasn't worried about Mike being out in this; she knew he could navigate by instruments. But she called him and she couldn't get through. Sometimes fog played with the satellite signal, and there were some parts of the reach without good reception. So she tried a few more times while she was watching the weather forecast, and only got not-available beeps. *If he's lost at sea, I guess I don't have to worry any more about whether we should get divorced*, she thought, and winced.

On days like these, when the island was cut off, as if the rest of the world had ceased to exist, Unity residents had habits and plans. Between fog and snow, it happened several times a year. If the ferry had stopped running, you sat tight. If you were stuck on the mainland, you found a place to stay. People had emergency back-up family or friends whose spare room or couch was available at short notice. If you were stuck at home, unable to get to work or to school or to whatever you were supposed to be doing, you passed the time. You played cards or watched TV (if you could get reception) or caught up on paperwork or visited your neighbour. On foggy days in the middle of the island, with no neighbours in sight, you could forget anyone else existed.

Pops used to drink. He'd steadily work through whatever liquor there was in the house and, with any luck, he'd fall asleep before he ran out. Vee stayed out of his way. If the fog came in early and unexpected and her mother was stuck at home too, a rare enforced holiday from her cleaning jobs, the two of them would hole up in Vee's bedroom, cuddled on the single bed there under a blanket, and play gin rummy while eating cereal out of the box.

Those days were among the favourites of Vee's childhood. When she was a kid, it was so unusual for her to have her mother to herself. Downstairs, Pops was a low rumble of thunder, a distant danger, but in bed with her mother, Vee felt safe. Which was ironic, because in those moments she was literally trapped. Pops wasn't usually violent, but 'usually' was the key word. You had to watch what you said around him, so as not to provoke him. Fog, though, seemed to pacify him, seep into his bones and weigh them down. She couldn't remember him ever climbing the stairs on a foggy day. Instead, it was whispers and giggles with her mother, a feeling of skipping school and being special. Thinking back, she'd felt safe not because the bad things weren't there, prowling around and below them, out of sight. She felt safe because her mother was there, too.

Now, she was alone. In another house, hemmed in by fog. And she didn't really want to think about her marriage, or what she was doing here on Unity or with her life, or what she was going to do. She didn't want to have fantasies about Mike disappearing and taking all of her obligations and vows with him.

Being hit by the bus had brought her a broken arm and a sort of mental clarity, but time had eaten away at that. Everything seemed more complicated. She'd nearly died: life was short, she should only do what was necessary for her own happiness. She should be free, not safe. Free in a way that she'd thought she was going to be on that night when she left Unity but which she never had been, never in her life, not when she was trapped in the house on an island, not when she was working to prove herself in the eyes of the entire world, not when she was taking vows to love someone forever.

But the months since her accident had taught her that freedom was ruthless and selfish. It left people broken and hurt behind you. It meant you could never go back.

When she first told Mike she wanted a divorce, she hadn't really expected him to object. He was so easy-going, non-committal. Their marriage seemed to skim along the surface of everything and barely leave a trace. He never talked about feelings, which had, up to that point, suited her fine. She'd almost expected him to be relieved: he could move on to the next thing, he could stop trying so hard to please her. But he'd been first shocked, and then upset. He pleaded with her to stay. To give it one more chance. He'd even cried. And she'd seen, suddenly, why people said that their spouses were their 'other half'. Not because they completed you or any of that romantic claptrap, but because you couldn't separate yourself without causing pain to both of you. You were one flesh. Hurting one person felt like an injury to you both.

Her phone rang and Vee realised she was standing at the window, gazing out at blankness. It took her a couple of minutes to find her phone between the sofa cushions, and when she did, she was relieved to see it was Mike, and even more relieved that she *was* relieved.

'Babe,' he said as soon as she answered. 'How about this fog, huh?'

'You're okay? I've been trying to call you.'

'Yeah, I heard the ring but things were a little tricky so I wanted to get anchored up. I'm all safe and sound though. It was fun! Like navigating through candyfloss.'

'Where are you?'

'The chart says I'm in Christmas Cove. I can hear the horn,

but visibility is less than a metre so I might as well be in New Zealand.'

'So you're going to sit tight?'

'Not much choice. It's dead calm. The water's like milk. It's eerie, sort of like – oh hello!' He sounded as if he were greeting someone at a cocktail party.

'Who's there?'

'No one. It's a seal, he just poked his head up by the stern. Anyway, yeah I'm going to stay here. The radio says it's not likely to lift till tomorrow. I've got plenty of snacks though, and lots of water, so I'm good.'

She thought about the boat's cabin. It was fine for one, crowded for two. Unless you were entwined. Kissing. Desperately trying to be silent. Then it was too perfect, and you had to keep revisiting it in your dreams.

'Have you got blankets?' she asked. 'It'll be dark soon, and it'll be cold tonight.'

'Everything I need, babe. And great mobile signal, so I'm going to watch movies and chill with my new seal buddy. You okay there?'

'Yeah, good.'

'You can always call me if you need some phone sex later.'

'And shock that poor seal?'

'Oh, the seal's heard it all before.'

She put down the phone, reassured. Mike was fine, he was having the time of his life, and she wasn't a monster. She was merely a person with doubts about her marriage, with doubts about her sexuality, with doubts about her future. Which made her the same as almost everyone else on the planet. Doubts were as common and boring as misery. She didn't have to act on them. Sure, she'd slipped up on the boat, but everyone slipped up, right? Everyone made mistakes. You just had to choose which ones you would live with, and which ones you would move on from.

Faced with the prospect of a guilt-free evening to herself, Vee put on Led Zeppelin as loud as the living-room sound system could handle, and began dancing across the hardwood floor to 'Fool in the Rain'. Hands up above her head, drumming the air, hips swaying, mouthing the lyrics to her reflection in the window, the bassline shaking the floor beneath her feet. She used to dance like this when she was a kid and no one was watching her. Out in the yard, with her mother at work and Pops passed out on the couch, she'd dance and dance and dance and forget about everything else in the panting of her breath and the pounding of her heart.

She began running in place as fast as she could, hair flying, and suddenly Rachel was standing on the other side of the window. Her hand rested on the side of her neck, as if she were checking her pulse. Her eyes were wide, her lips parted. As if she had been formed out of the fog, or out of desire. As if summoned by Vee's joy and thoughts of freedom and voiceless words about being a fool.

Chapter Thirty-one

Sterling

As soon as he had to switch on his foglights on his car, he knew. But he pulled over anyway, into a nearly empty car park of a Route 1 restaurant, and called Arnie Lunt. Then he called Rachel, and told her the ferry wasn't running, and said he'd stay the night with his mom. Then, finger hovering over his mom's number, he remembered that she was spending a few days with her cousins in Augusta.

He put down his phone. He had a key to his mom's place, so he could just drive there and let himself in. But when he pulled out of the restaurant, he went right instead of left. South, away from Rockland.

During the summer, Route 1 was bumper to bumper with tourists. But tonight he saw few other cars. In the mysterious way of fog, it cleared the further south he drove. Over the Sheepscot River into Wiscasset, over the Kennebec River on the Sagadahoc Bridge into Bath. The Sagadahoc was a precast box girder bridge; it broke ground the year his father died. The old bridge ran alongside it, elegant and rusting slowly away into the water. Sterling had wanted to build bridges once. He had studied maths and physics. He had taken photographs of swing bridges and draw bridges, truss bridges and suspension. He liked the idea of a road connecting two places. It felt like freedom to him.

The noise of the engine and the movement of the car were soothing. At Freeport, he took the ramp onto I-95 South and it was only when he was driving past the twin round towers of the Doubletree in south Portland that he thought: *Where am I going?*

He didn't know. He had hours to himself, unaccountable to anyone. He could drive and drive if he wanted to. He could keep heading south to Boston; keep going to New York or Philadelphia. Hang a right and drive west until he reached the other coast, the one where Lisey was. If she still lived there; he didn't know. He could stop in Portland and get dinner, go to a bar; veer north and go to the casino in Oxford. He could find a hotel, flirt with a woman in the lounge. Bring her up to his room. He could drive over the state line into New Hampshire, buy a bottle at the state liquor store, and find a place to park and drink it. Sleep under the stars. He could abandon the car and take a plane to anywhere in the world.

No one would find out. He could do anything that he wanted to. He could disappear from his own life, just like Vee had done. He could ditch his car and his credit cards. He could throw his phone and his wedding ring into a river. He could never come back.

The thought terrified him. But it excited him, too. What did you do with freedom? How could you make choices if everything was available to you, if your world were not limited by the ocean surrounding you and the duties attached to your name?

If you could be anyone, how did you know who you were?

The moon and stars were bright in the sky. The road widened out to four lanes. He'd been gone for hours, now, and he was still driving.

Just as he couldn't imagine what he would do if he left, he couldn't imagine what would happen to the people who stayed. Rachel would run the store, maybe. Or perhaps as the days stretched into weeks and months, she would give up. His mother would look for him, but how could she look? After a year, or two years, they would sell the store, or get someone to manage it. His name would disappear from the sign. His neighbours would talk about him and talk about him and eventually, though they wouldn't forget him, they'd stop mentioning him, like they had with Vee. And then they would die or move away from Unity and he would be forgotten altogether, without another Ames to take his place.

Another bridge before him: the intricate green arch of the Piscataqua River Bridge that connected Maine and New Hampshire. Four men had died building this bridge when a steel beam collapsed. His father had told him so, as a child, and once they had detoured to see the memorial stone with the men's names. 'We should remember them,' his father had said, but instead of pointing to the men's names, he'd pointed to the bridge soaring above. And Sterling understood what he meant. You were remembered by what you built.

He drove over the bridge and took the first exit to Portsmouth, where he found a Dunkin Donuts and bought a coffee and a muffin. He ate it in the car park, looking at the moving lights from I-95. Then he got back into his car and headed north again, back over the bridge, towards home.

This was his life: crossing and recrossing water. But you couldn't leave a trace on water. You could only leave a trace on land.

Chapter Thirty-two

Rachel

She'd been in the store all day. She'd cleaned the glass refrigerator and freezer doors, restocked the shelves, winnowed out the
produce that was past its best. She swept the floors and replen-
ished the bowl of dog biscuits on the counter. She dumped out
the coffee she'd made this morning and made a fresh pot. She'd
checked the orders, sorted the mail, dusted the shelves, changed
the receipt paper in the till. In between, she'd sat on the green-
seated chair and read her book. The fog was so thick that it looked
like the windows were covered over with grey cotton wool. Not a
single customer had walked in the door.

Sterling called about five thirty. 'The ferry's been cancelled,' he
told her, 'so I'm going to stay with Mum. I'll come back in the
morning so I'll see you then.'

'Okay,' she said. 'See you tomorrow.'

'See you tomorrow. Love you.'

'Love you too.'

The whole exchange was on autopilot; she'd been expecting it
since the fog descended. She put the conversation away with her
phone and got up and turned the sign on the door to CLOSED.
Sterling always told her not to close early; he told her they had a
responsibility to stick to the posted opening hours. Sterling would
never know.

She went outside. She could hear the ocean but not see it, hear
the low boom of the foghorn coming from Brimstone Island,

and everything else was silent. She couldn't see the outline of the white picket fence on the side of her garden, and her house had disappeared. She took a few steps away from the store and looked back: it was gone, too.

She was alone, invisible, in a place with no landmarks. No one to see her or judge her. No one waiting for her. She might as well not even exist.

She wasn't lost. She could follow the path to the unpaved road, turn left and walk for thirty seconds until she saw her own picket fence again.

She turned right.

She must be passing the ferry terminal, the boat landing, the Beottes' house, the Langlaises' house, the old school. She saw none of them beyond distant smears of light. It seemed like someone else was walking, not her. The person who couldn't be seen, who nobody noticed. Whose skin dampened with the fog, whose eyelashes dripped with cold dew, whose hair curled in on itself, whose breath misted out opaque, like the air.

She knew where she was going, of course, even if she couldn't see her way, but her feet had walked this journey in her sleep over and over, and how was this different? She stayed on the right-hand side of the road, watching her feet rather than ahead of her, following the grass verge that was slippery with fallen leaves. She walked and walked and walked, probably past Vee's house, probably right around the island and back to where she'd started from. Though how would she know when she'd got there, either? She could walk in circles forever, until the fog lifted, until she got so tired she had to curl up on the road and fall asleep and be found with the sunrise. That would give everyone on Unity something to talk about.

A white-painted rock appeared on the verge. She stopped, edged forward, and there it was: the gate with the sign, cursive blue letters, saying Daybreak. With a new path to follow, right up to the door.

Now she was here, though, she realised how stupid this was. Vee would be there with Mike. And she could knock on the door, but how would she explain why she was here? *I was lonely and wanted to visit. I got lost between the store and my house. I walked here in the fog, even though I couldn't see, because there is an invisible thread that connects me to you, Vee, an invisible thread that we created when we met, although it was so instant and so strong, that maybe it existed a long time before that. Maybe it is more than a thread.*

The fog thrummed. She put fingers to her throat to feel if this was her heartbeat, echoing, but her pulse was faster. She trailed her other hand along the side of the house as she walked around it, towards where she thought the sound was coming from. The fog in front of her glowed yellow: light from the windows. They wouldn't be able to see her; she'd peek inside, catch a glimpse of Vee, and go back home.

The windows were cold and wet and all of the lights in the house were on and the sound was a drumbeat, a bassline. Music. Within the house she could see a figure jumping, waving, dancing, running, her arms wide, mouth open, performing, framed by the windows, as if alone on a stage. Rachel's pulse and the music beat exactly the same time and she felt that thread swaying, tightening.

Vee stopped dancing and stared at her.

They stood like that for some time, the invisible woman and the one on show, the only two people in the world.

Vee slid open the patio door, releasing a barrage of rock music, breaking the spell. 'Rachel? Is that really you?'

'Yeah. I ...'

'Come in! It's freezing out there. Oh my God your teeth are chattering.'

Were they? She stepped into the light and warmth and noise and Vee shut the door after her. She hurried to the sofa to get a woollen throw. 'Here. No, wait. You need a towel, your hair is wet.'

Rachel stood there dripping, holding the throw while Vee went to fetch a towel. She was herself again: cold, awkward, listening to Led Zeppelin. 'I'm sorry,' she said to Vee when she reappeared with a huge fluffy white towel, the sort that you got in fancy hotels. She had to raise her voice to be heard over the music. 'I should've called first. But I didn't really mean to turn up here, it just sort of happened.'

Vee began to rub the towel over Rachel's hair, something that Rachel knew from experience would result in an enormous frizzy mess. But Vee was close, and when was the last time she had been tended like this? Taken care of? She closed her eyes.

'Did you get lost?' Vee asked.

'No. I wanted to come here. I didn't really choose to. I don't know, it doesn't make sense.' She tilted her head so Vee could get to the back of her hair. 'Sorry, I'm being weird. Ignore me.'

'You're not a person I can ignore. Leave your coat. Come here.' She led Rachel to a big white sofa and sat her down on one end of it, tucking the blanket around her. 'You need to warm up. Do you want a cup of coffee? Some herbal tea?'

'I think I'd rather have a glass of wine.'

'I can do that. Sorry, this music is really loud.'

She turned it off, and in the new silence Rachel watched her walk across the open-plan living space to the kitchen. She felt foolish. Presumptuous. But . . . *You're not a person I can ignore.*

This was different from chance encounters, from secret moments when their husbands weren't looking. What sort of choice had she made, by coming here?

'Where's Mike?' she asked, reaching for safety.

'He's moored in Christmas Cove. Totally fogbound. He's going to stay the night on the boat.'

'Sterling's at his mom's. The ferry isn't running.'

'Oh.' Vee paused, and Rachel saw her own thoughts on Vee's face. 'Um. Red or white?'

'What?'

'The wine. Red or white?'

'I don't mind. No, wait – red.'

Vee took down two glasses with generous bowls. 'Why did you change your mind?'

'About what?'

'About the wine.'

'Because ...' said Rachel, 'because I feel like I should make a decision. I feel like it's been too long that I've been drifting around.'

Vee uncorked an open bottle. She poured two glasses: deep red, more purple than blood. 'Have you changed your mind about other things?'

'I don't know. Not consciously. But I'm here.'

'You are.' She sat down beside Rachel, giving her one of the glasses. 'Did you tell Sterling you were coming over here?'

'I didn't know I was going to, until I did it.'

'Will you tell him?'

'I don't know. Will you tell Mike?'

'I don't know. It depends.'

Rachel knew what it depended on. Was this how her marriage changed? How her entire life changed? Choosing a different path in the fog?

She gulped her wine rather than sipping it. It was rich, strong, overwhelming.

'I don't know what I'm doing here,' she confessed after swallowing.

'I do.'

She watched Vee sip her own wine. Watched her swallow, lick her lips. Remembered Vee's leg between hers, solid heat.

'If I were a man I wouldn't be thinking twice,' Rachel said.

'I'm not sure about that,' Vee said. 'Some men, yeah. But Sterling, and even Mike ...'

'He hasn't cheated on you? I don't mean he's a bad man, but he's such a charmer.'

'I don't think so. It's all charm, he's like that with everyone. No. And he's a terrible liar. I would know.'

'What about you?'

'Me? I'm a good liar.' She smiled, a sad smile that was also incredibly sexy, and sipped her wine again. 'I've never cheated on him. Except for ... that, with you.'

'Yes. Me neither.'

'But I have cheated on other men, before him. If I thought it would get me somewhere. I'm not a good person.'

Rachel put down her wine on the coffee table. She watched her own hand as she took Vee's glass from her and put that on the coffee table, too. 'You're a good person,' she said.

'I don't want to talk about Mike and Sterling,' whispered Vee. Rachel was closer, now, again without meaning to be. The inside of her knee brushed the outside of Vee's.

'Then let's not.' She ran a strand of Vee's hair between her fingers, put her fingertips on the side of her throat. She heard Vee gasp when she touched her skin. Her pulse was rapid and familiar.

'Oh God,' said Vee, grabbing Rachel's arm, pulling her closer. They kissed and their teeth clashed. Rachel heard herself moaning. She grabbed a handful of Vee's hair. This was not what she had planned. It was exactly what she had planned.

Vee fell backwards onto the sofa cushions and Rachel climbed on top of her, blanket discarded, kissing. Pushing up Vee's top, Vee helped her, tugged it over her head, and then Rachel kissed Vee's suntanned chest, the paler stripe of skin, her breast through her bra, which was black and lacy and foreign to Rachel's hands. 'I don't have good underwear,' she said, pulling up her head, looking into Vee's face, wide-eyed, and Vee laughed.

'Then we'll take it off,' said Vee.

'I haven't shaved my legs since September.'

'Shut up,' said Vee, and pulled Rachel down on top of her again and kissed her.

*

Rachel would never, never for the rest of her life, forget the way that Vee tasted. The sensation of Vee's nipple against Rachel's tongue. She was salt and sweetness, perfume and silk. She shuddered against Rachel's mouth and she groaned, long tanned legs falling open, her hand in Rachel's hair. She pulsed on Rachel's fingers, a sticky tang. Vee cried out to the bright room, to the cloud that surrounded them, and then she relaxed, smiled up at Rachel and said, 'Now my turn,' but first kissed her, another taste. She, her, skin, hair, breath, Vee, a pink bite on fair skin.

They rolled so that Vee was on top. She licked down Rachel's body and sucked on her nipples, one then the other. She kissed Rachel's stomach and Rachel had to close her eyes so as not to be self-conscious of her pale skin and too-soft belly. But when Vee licked between her legs, Rachel opened her eyes to see what was happening. It was too important to merely imagine. She had to imprint this image of Vee giving her pleasure, glancing up to see if she liked it. The curl of her lip, blush on her cheek, red of her tongue. Rachel had to see all of it.

It got darker outside, but they kept all the lights on. The house faced outwards to blank ocean, like a stage without an audience. Rachel lay with her head on Vee's belly, Vee lazily combing fingers through her hair, so she heard the rumble.

'After all that, I'm hungry,' said Vee. She disentangled herself from Rachel, kissed her shoulder, and stood up.

'Don't go.' Rachel caught Vee's hand, suddenly afraid, as if after hours on this sofa together, if Vee moved away, she would never come back.

'I'm just going to grab us some food. And water.' She kissed the back of Rachel's hand and went to the kitchen. Rachel pulled the throw over herself and watched her. Naked, she walked the same way as she did when she was clothed: with confidence, head up, hands free at her sides, not covering herself.

'How do you do it?' Rachel asked.

'Do what?' Vee opened the fridge and looked inside.

'Be this way. The way you are.'

'Which way am I?'

Rachel gestured to herself, curled under the throw, and then to Vee, standing naked in front of the fridge, nipples tight from the cold.

'Oh,' said Vee. 'I've never been very modest. Anyway, you've seen it all. You've licked most of it.' She winked at Rachel and began gathering things from the shelves. 'I'm not cooking, so we'll have to eat whatever I can find.'

'I don't mean modesty. I mean ... shame.'

Vee didn't answer that right away. She came back to the sofa with her hands full of food, a bottle of water under her arm, and began to arrange it all on the coffee table. Strawberries, a container of shelled crabmeat, olives, a box of stuffed vine leaves, a bowl of cherry tomatoes. A ready-made post-coital feast. Rachel thought about how Vee had said that she and Mike had a lot of sex.

Vee sat down next to her. 'I have a lot of shame. Just not about my body.' She gave Rachel the bottle of water and took a sip of her own wine.

'You never act ashamed of anything.'

'When everyone's looking at you, you have two options. Hide, or act like you don't care.' She held a strawberry up to Rachel's lips, and Rachel ate it.

'Strawberries in November,' she said. 'You didn't get these from the store.'

'I'll admit it: it's contraband from the Hannaford in Rockland.' She popped one in her own mouth. 'I had some therapy back in college. Shame is a normal response to growing up with an alcoholic. Or, in your case, two. Being in a small community makes it even worse. What are you ashamed of?'

'Everything.'

'You don't have to be ashamed of your body. You're beautiful.'

Vee drew the throw away from Rachel's chest and kissed the side of her breast.

'I feel beautiful with you.'

'That's the idea.'

'But I'm awkward. I'm out of shape. I don't know how to dress. I'm always too clever, or not clever enough. I can't have children. I never fit in anywhere. It's easier not to be noticed.'

'Neither one of us fit in.'

'No, but I'm different from you.'

'You deal with shame by trying to be ordinary. I deal with shame by trying to be extraordinary. Neither one of us can just be ... ourselves.' She offered Rachel a stuffed vine leaf. Rachel took it and reached over and fed Vee a cherry tomato. Vee closed her lips around the tomato and Rachel's finger: warm wetness, the inside of Vee's body. Rachel's breath hitched and Vee lifted the throw and lay down beside her so they were skin to skin, pressed close on the narrow sofa.

'Look at me,' Vee commanded, and Rachel, who had barely looked at anything else, did.

'You bite your lip when you're worried,' Vee said. 'And also when you're aroused. Your second toe is longer than your big toe and your eyes are such dark brown they're nearly black. You close your eyes when you laugh, and when you open them again, you look surprised, as if you weren't expecting to find anything funny. You like to sit with your left leg drawn up underneath you. You prefer lemonade to iced tea, and you drink your coffee with two sugars. You read things – *anything*, books, signs, pizza menus – as if the words are food and you're starving. When you find something you're good at, you get a glow which is so incredibly sexy I can't keep my hands to myself, even though I should. And you lose pencils in your hair. Is that enough?'

'Wow.'

'I see you,' said Vee. 'I notice you. I haven't been able to stop noticing you, from the moment I met you.'

Rachel buried her head in Vee's neck. She wrapped her arms around her and held her tight, and Vee held her tightly, too.

'Are you really so ashamed?' Rachel whispered, her face pressed against Vee's neck. She felt Vee nod.

'I don't tell anyone, though.'

'Except me,' said Rachel.

Vee nodded again. 'Let's not be ashamed of this,' she whispered. She pulled back so they could see each other's faces. 'I know we have to hide it. But we don't have to be ashamed.'

'We can be ourselves.'

'Right.'

Rachel felt herself tearing up, and ducked her head so she wouldn't be seen. This was sex. This was only sex, and it felt amazing and strong and powerful. But it wasn't any reason to cry. It was sex, and maybe the kind of sex she'd been wanting all of her life, but it was still secret. And they only had a few hours of it.

She scooted down the sofa, underneath the blanket, so that she could kiss down Vee's body again. So she could forget about everything else and be herself.

Chapter Thirty-three

Mike

The movie was boring, his phone screen wasn't big enough to show the fight scenes, and all he had to look forward to for supper was protein bars and beer. Mike put his phone in his pocket and went up on deck to see if the fog had lifted at all.

It hadn't. It was quite spectacular, this New England fog. Or, literally, the opposite of spectacular. Visibility was less than three feet; he couldn't see his own mast light. 'Hello,' he called to the blankness, and his own voice seemed to stop directly in front of him, as if he were in a tiny room lined with padding.

He wasn't good at spending time alone in his own company, unless he had something to do, somewhere to go. He heard about other people who went away to find themselves – spending months in some monastery somewhere meditating and not talking to anyone, or solo climbing a mountain or sailing the Atlantic, or living in a cottage in a remote Irish valley while trying to write a novel. Some of his friends had done it, usually dropping vast sums of money in order to have all of their luxuries stripped away, and they always came back saying they felt healthy and rejuvenated and with completely changed priorities in life.

How could you find yourself? Weren't you always already there? Why would you want to spend any more time with yourself than necessary?

Out of sight, something splashed. Probably his friend the seal. He wondered if seals would eat protein bars. He should invent a new type of protein bar, something that would taste decent and exciting. Like ... steak.

He checked his watch. He'd been anchored here for four hours now, and he was bored out of his skull.

His father had laughed when he'd first discussed buying the house on Unity. 'Do you really think you can live a whole winter on an island?' he asked, which had irritated Mike no end.

'I'm saving my marriage,' he told his father. 'Like you said I should do.'

'Your wife is an independent woman. That's why you chose her. She's not going to be receptive to bribes.'

'What is an independent woman receptive to?'

'Independence,' his mother answered.

'Actually, we're doing a lot better,' Mike told them. And he ended the call soon after that, before he got into an argument with them about how little faith they had in him, about how they always assumed he was stupid and spoiled, always assumed that in every situation he was the one who made mistakes, and how was his wife supposed to believe in him if his own parents didn't? And who had he learned the habit of bribery from in the first place, anyway?

Ugh. See, this was the reason he didn't like hanging around by himself. It made him think too much. He squinted at the fog. Was it lifting a little bit? He could see the glow of his bow light now.

He checked his fuel level, and went below and checked the charts. Actually, now that he looked at it, from Christmas Cove to Unity wasn't that difficult a motor. In dead calm like this, he could probably motor the distance in less time than it would normally take to sail. And navigating by instruments was fun. He'd been fair-weather sailing for years now; it would be good for him to have a small challenge like this. He could be back at the house before midnight. Crawl into bed with Vee, if she was asleep. Jump into bed with her anyway, if she was awake.

This was a great plan. He considered calling Vee to tell her, but no. He'd rather surprise her. Because what his parents didn't understand was that Daybreak wasn't about bribing his wife; it was about them spending quality time together. Making a home and a community. He wasn't giving her a house; he was giving her his time, his attention, his effort, his understanding that by pleasing her, he was also pleasing himself.

Maybe that was what 'finding yourself' really meant.

It was only about eleven-thirty and he was running on fumes when he motored up to the dock and jumped out to attach the mooring lines. The first thing he wanted, after surprising Vee, maybe even before, was a large pre-midnight snack. He remembered the cartoons in the Sunday newspapers when he was a kid: Dagwood Bumstead making a three-foot-tall submarine sandwich out of every single thing in the refrigerator, while his foxy wife Blondie, in kitten heels and a shortie robe, looked on in astonishment. Everyday sexism. Still ... he could do with one of those sandwiches. And his wife in a shortie robe.

He hurried up the lawn towards the house. He'd been kidding himself when he'd thought that visibility was any better. Maybe it was clearer closer to the mainland, in Christmas Cove, but the minute he hit the open water he'd been able to see almost nothing, and Unity wasn't much better. Still, he'd made no errors, slipped up to his private dock like a foot into a shoe. Mike Ellis: 1; New England fog: 0. He grinned, picturing Vee's face. Picturing the old-timers down at the store, giving the summer person some grudging respect for boatmanship. See? He was out to impress lobster fishermen. What better sign was there that his priorities had changed?

He had to guess the direction of the house, but as long as he went up the lawn he couldn't go too wrong. But he wasn't too far up before he saw the diffuse glow of lights. Since the summer season had ended, the two of them had adopted more New England habits of early bedtimes, mainly because there was very little to do in the evening, but it looked like Vee was still up. Or maybe she'd left all the lights on for security when she went to bed. Or maybe it was meant to guide him home, like a lighthouse beaming through the fog.

He could see the outline of the windows now; it looked like she had all of the lights on. It was a blur, then he could make out the outline of the furniture, though the fog reflected things, bounced the light around, made them a dazzle. He squinted his eyes. It was weird to see his own house like this, from the outside, and distorted as if through gauze. Strange that he had to navigate just to find his own front door.

Creeping quietly so that he wouldn't frighten Vee, he walked along the windows, peering inside the house. He saw someone lying on the sofa, a flesh-coloured shape, and smiled. She was sleeping naked on the couch. So this was what she got up to when he was away. Then one step further, a clearer view. Vee lay on her back, head on a cushion, her right arm cradling another person. A woman, naked, with dark hair that nestled on Vee's naked breast, with a naked arm that rested over Vee's belly, with naked legs that curled over hers, intimate in a sleeping embrace.

Mike watched for less than a second, his smile frozen. Then he stepped backwards, into the fog, so he could not be seen. He didn't make a choice; his body did it while his mind struggled to catch up.

That was Rachel Ames, sleeping with his wife.

He could not breathe. He felt as if he were being torn apart, from the inside out.

He turned and tried to run back down the lawn to his boat. As if he could escape what he'd seen, as if he could escape the pain. But his feet were clumsy and he couldn't see anything except for the memory, the brightest thing for miles. His wife and another woman. Not a girly sleepover. Not best friends. Not a liberated swinger's party, or whatever they called it these days. She was having an affair with Rachel Ames.

How long had this been going on?

Damp soaked through his shoes. He stumbled and fell to his knees on the grass. Maybe this was just something for fun, something to spice things up? Maybe Vee was going to tell him about it later?

He slapped his palms on the ground. This was not for fun. She had thought he was going to be away all night. How much time had Rachel and Vee spent together over the past few months?

Mike scrambled to his feet. Somehow, walking blind, his ears full of his own broken breathing and not the sound of the surf, he found the dock and the boat. All the lights were off, but he found the hatch by instinct and climbed down into the cabin in the belly of the sailing boat. Here it was dark, not that endless impenetrable grey. He groped in the icebox for a beer, twisted off the cap and stood in the dark galley drinking it all down. Then he dropped the empty bottle on the floor and opened another. The cold beer drove a spike of headache into his temple, but he kept drinking because he did not want this pain. He needed to make it go away.

It didn't go away.

That woman is the best thing that ever happened to you, his mother had said. Right before she said that Mike had to stop Vee from leaving him.

Vee was still there with Rachel. Naked, on their sofa. What did that make him? What was he supposed to do?

He dropped the second bottle on the floor. Beer splashed up his leg and he doubled over, squeezing his eyes tight, his stomach tight, his fists tight. He had never felt so bad. He had never felt so much pain. He could not think of a single thing to make it go away.

Mike understood for the first time, gasping for breath in the dark, that he loved Vee more than anything or anyone in the entire world.

Chapter Thirty-four

Vee

She didn't mean to fall asleep, didn't want to waste a single moment, but then she was waking up with Rachel in her arms and with the wispy fog beyond the windows coloured a dawn pink, as if lit up from inside. Rachel was still asleep. Her head lay near Vee's shoulder, her belly pressed against Vee's hip, her arm draped over Vee's waist. Vee watched her. She felt Rachel's breath whispering out over her skin, saw the faint blue shadows under her eyes, and understood that this moment was just as precious as anything that had happened before. It was different to wake up with a woman than with a man. Their bodies fit together in a way that was forgiving and warm and exciting. Sex with Rachel had been like nothing else she'd ever experienced. It wasn't about performance or even orgasms. It was about pleasure. And then more pleasure. And then Rachel in her arms, on this sofa, with the world brightening around them.

'You're staring at me,' Rachel murmured. Her eyes were still closed.

'You're the best-looking thing in this room.'

'I doubt that.'

'Take the compliment, woman. I could look at you all day.'

Rachel opened her eyes, and squinted. 'Shit. It's morning.'

'The ferry won't be in for a couple of hours. If it's running.' Vee stroked back Rachel's hair and kissed her cheekbone. She cupped her hand around Rachels' breast. 'God, I like boobs. Who knew.

I've missed out on them all these years. I like yours. Yours are perfect.' She stroked Rachel's nipple with her thumb, teased it into hardness.

'I have to go,' Rachel said, but she groaned and tightened her leg around Vee's. She was wet, Vee could feel it against her thigh, and she squeezed Rachel's breast and kissed her with an open mouth. Resuming the conversation they'd enjoyed all night, this journey in delicious circles with no end.

'I really have to go,' Rachel said.

'One minute.' She sucked Rachel's nipple into her mouth, felt Rachel's hands tightening in her hair.

'I really have to. Before the fog lifts.'

'You could just say we had a sleepover. Popcorn and movies. Just a couple of gal pals.' She kissed Rachel's areola, blew lightly on it to see it pucker.

'Or I could say nothing and not have to lie.' Rachel pushed Vee gently away, and sat up. 'Also, we have to talk for a few minutes.'

Reluctantly, Vee also sat up. 'Right. Okay, yeah.'

'This is the best sex I've ever had.'

'Oh God, me too. It's unbelievable, even better than I thought it would be. You don't really have to go, do you?' She reached for Rachel again.

'Yes, I do.' She scooted down the couch, a little further away. 'How are we going to keep doing this without anyone finding out?'

'Oh.' Vee dropped her hands.

'What?'

'I didn't expect you to say that.'

'What did you expect me to say?'

'That this was a mistake, that we shouldn't have done it, that it should never happen again. Why did you think I wanted to shut you up by fucking you again?'

Rachel nodded. 'This is wrong, but it's not a mistake. It can't be. And I know this is the one thing that is guaranteed to hurt

Sterling and make me more of an outcast here than ever, but it is also the one thing that I have wanted for myself, not something that I've done because I was supposed to or because I was scared or didn't know what else to do or because it was the next logical step, but a positive thing that I have reached out for and taken. I'm not going to give it up until I have to.'

'Wow,' said Vee. She felt breathless.

'So. It's nearly winter and we're on an island with fewer than a hundred people living on it. It's impossible to keep secrets here. What do we do?'

'I don't know,' said Vee.

'Me neither.' Rachel stood and began to gather her clothes, which were scattered over the hardwood floor. 'But we'll figure it out. Okay?'

Vee nodded. She watched Rachel get dressed and remembered how she had tugged all of those clothes off her in a frenzy, feeling like she was going to drown if she couldn't inhale Rachel's naked skin like air.

'We have to be careful,' she said. 'I mean this is a pretty traditional place. If we spend time together, the minds of Unity are not immediately going to turn to "they're having a lesbian affair" but … it will be hard not to touch you now.'

'We'll figure it out,' said Rachel again. She pulled on her jacket and sat on the sofa to put on her shoes. 'But Sterling can't know. I don't know how liberal Mike is.'

'He'd do a lot for me, but I'm not so sure he would open our marriage so I could have a lover. It doesn't seem like his thing. Five months ago we were talking about divorce.'

'Don't tell him without talking to me? If you do decide to tell him?'

Vee nodded. 'This is a very grown-up post-coital conversation.'

'Well. We're both grown-ups.' Rachel stood. 'And I've done a lot of damage control in my life. But never when I wanted to keep on doing damage.' She stooped and kissed Vee on the mouth. 'I want to keep on doing it over and over.'

Vee caught Rachel's hand. 'I never want to stop.' She kissed her back, a kiss that said *take your clothes off again and join me on the sofa*, but Rachel drew away.

'Gotta go.'

'Rachel?'

Rachel paused on her way to the back door. 'Yes?'

'It *is* possible to keep secrets on Unity. It's very possible to keep them for years.'

When Rachel was gone, closing the back door softly behind her, Vee wrapped the throw around herself and went through the living room, picking up dishes and clothes, turning off lights. She washed and put away their glasses and put away the wine, and then folded the throw and replaced it on the sofa, plumping the cushions, and walked naked to the bathroom to take a shower. Their night together now erased, she slipped on pyjamas and got into bed and couldn't sleep for a very long time, holding her clean fingers in front of her nose and trying to catch a trace of Rachel's scent. She fell asleep quite suddenly and was dreaming about being in a nightclub packed with people, so many people, pushing through dancing crowds and peering through flashing lights looking for Rachel but never seeing her, when she was woken up by Mike walking into the bedroom, in that way he had of being sneaky without actually being quiet at all.

'Hey,' she said. 'You made it back.'

'I made it back.'

She sat up and yawned. 'What time is it?'

'About eight. I haven't had much sleep.'

He did, indeed, look like someone who had spent a night on an uncomfortable bunk in a small boat cabin. Whereas she should look like someone who spent the whole night sleeping in her own innocent bed alone. She swung her legs out of bed. 'You poor thing. I'll make you coffee.'

'I'm going to take a shower first.'

'You okay?'

He nodded. 'How was your night?'

'Nothing much. I had a couple of glasses of wine and read my book.'

'All by yourself? No visitors?'

'I doubt anyone could've found the house.' She got up and found her robe. She'd said to Rachel that she was a good liar, and she was – she had spent much of her teens and twenties telling bare-faced lies while looking people straight in the face. The trick was to convince yourself in that moment that you were telling the truth. But it was easier to lie to Mike when he wasn't looking at her face. And if Vee believed her own lies, even for a moment, that would be a betrayal of Rachel, too.

Mike nodded and went into the bathroom. She heard the shower turning on.

She was standing at the kitchen worktop putting another pod in the machine when she heard him come up behind her, as usual failing to be sneaky at all. His arm went around her waist and he kissed her neck. 'I missed you,' he murmured in her ear. 'I'm not used to spending the night alone. What about you?'

'I missed you too,' she said to the coffee machine, thinking immediately that if she hesitated, he would suspect something, but if she didn't, would he know anyway? Did she have any marks on her body, bruises or bites? She hadn't thought to check in the mirror last night. Even without any physical traces, would he just know something had changed? She felt different inside, as if Rachel had changed her body chemistry.

He tugged on the tie of her robe, and she said, 'Oh, babe, I'm sorry, I'm having a massacre-level period right now.'

'Oh. Okay.'

'I could take care of you though,' she suggested, hoping he'd say no. Instead, he gently turned her around to face him. His hair was wet, but he hadn't shaved. He looked so tired.

'What would you do if we lost all our money?' he asked her.

This wasn't what she expected. 'I'd go back to work. It wouldn't be a big deal.'

'What would I do?'

'You could be a house husband, I guess. You'd have to learn how to dust.'

He didn't crack a smile. 'Did you marry me for my money?'

'No. My mother told me to marry you for your money, but I married you because you wouldn't take no for an answer.'

'Do you regret not getting divorced in August?'

'No,' she said.

'Do you think we should get divorced now?'

She put her hand on his cheek. 'What's the matter, Mike? Why are you asking me these questions? Is something wrong?'

Could he tell?

'I love you,' he told her. 'I never want to let you go. And all I want, more than anything, is for you to be happy.'

'I love you too,' she said. 'And I want you to be happy.'

She could look him in the face to say that, because it was the truth.

'Then don't leave me,' he said, and pulled her tight to him. She leaned her head on his shoulder. 'Please.'

'Okay,' she said. Not knowing whether that was a lie, or not. 'I won't.'

Chapter Thirty-five

Rachel

'Morning, Edward. Can I get you anything else with your coffee?'

'Ayuh, I guess I'll take a can of "Winstons".'

'Regular or light, Edward?'

'Regular.'

'Here you go, Edward. Is that cash? Thanks, here's your change. Have a great day, Edward.'

She watched the old man as he walked back to the table to sit with the other old men, drinking coffee and eating doughnuts and talking about old man things, like they did every single morning, barring catastrophic weather events.

'Why do you keep on calling him Edward?' Sterling asked quietly, looking up from his laptop.

'That's his name.'

'Well, technically, yes. But no one calls him that.'

'Except for me.'

'Listen, he doesn't mind being called by his nickname. He likes it. Everyone calls him that. It's all I've ever known him as.'

'I can't believe that a grown man likes being called "Turd".'

'I told you, it's a French thing. Edward Poirier the Third, Eddie the T'ird. It's not an insult, it's a joke on the pronunciation. His mother called him Turd.'

'Well, I'm not going to. It's disgusting.'

'I told you—'

'Yes, you're always telling me, Sterling. You're always telling me everything. Every single thing I get wrong, how to do the stock take, how to do the deliveries, how to make the precious coffee, because no one can do anything as well as you can.'

'This is ridiculous. I didn't mean—'

'If I'm not good enough now, after three years, then I'm never going to be good enough. I might as well call people what I want.' She stood up, scraping back the stool. 'I'm going to the house.'

'Rachel, don't be—'

She ignored him and kept on walking out of the store. 'See you later, *Edward*,' she called behind her.

Back in the house, she tidied aggressively. This was the thing. Being watched all the time, everyone waiting for her to slip up. And she shouldn't pick stupid fights with Sterling. But it got so predictable, so tedious, so much so that it felt that she couldn't do anything of her own because if she made too many mistakes everything would tumble down around her.

And maybe she was getting annoyed when she broke invisible rules by mistake because she felt guilty about the big, enormous spoken rule that she was breaking on purpose.

Sterling came in after closing. She'd made a chicken stew. They ate in near-silence, and then Sterling did the dishes and they watched TV together. Normally Rachel would say that she was sorry. But she wasn't sorry for not saying that stupid nickname, and she wasn't sorry for telling Sterling the truth about how he treated her, and even if she could tell him she was sorry for betraying him she couldn't, because she wanted to betray him. Being with Vee had made her feel more whole than anything else had ever done. When she was with Vee she hadn't made any mistakes. She didn't have to walk a tightrope. She didn't feel like a failure. She felt like she had been born to be with Vee, or maybe it was to be with a woman in general instead of a man but, right now, that woman was Vee.

So she said nothing, and then she went to bed, and then he came to bed after she'd turned the light off, and the next morning when they got up they had their regular conversation about coffee and the news and it was as if nothing had happened. As if nothing was going to happen, not for another hundred years, a thousand years.

She wondered if this was how marriages ended: with a whisper, not a bang. Not an argument, which is after all about passion, waves crashing on a shore, but with the small pockets of cold numbness that an argument creates. It's like islands. They don't sink like Atlantis. They wear away, little by little, until all you've got left is a single rock and a light. A warning to safer travellers to stay away.

Chapter Thirty-six

Rachel, Vee

It was near the end of November. Snowflakes drifting around them, Rachel and Vee around the back of the garage where Jacob kept the truck and the golf carts. Rachel pushed Vee up against the wall, unzipped her jacket, shoved her hand down her jeans as she kissed her. Vee gasped against her mouth, their words whispered, making clouds in the air.

'Oh God. Your hand's cold. Don't stop.'

'I've been thinking about this all week.'

'I know. Me too. Faster.'

'We need somewhere warm. You've got too many clothes on.'

'We can – oh God, just there. Yes.'

'You like this?'

'Yes. Please. Oh, that's good. Let me touch you too.' Vee tugged at Rachel's jacket and slid cold hands under her bra. 'We can break into a summer house. I've done it lots.'

'We don't have to break in. Jacob has keys, and sometimes he leaves them in the truck.'

'You are so fucking devious, I love it. Oh God. Don't stop. Faster, I—' She closed her eyes, tilted her head back, bit her lip as she came. Rachel watched her, hungry. There was never enough time, or touching, or orgasms, or kisses. Never enough. Sometimes she felt like this wanting was so strong it would devour the entire world.

She kept on touching Vee whenever she saw her. When Vee

came into the store to buy something: brushing her fingertips against Vee's palm. When the two of them went for a walk around the island: bumping her hip against Vee's as if by mistake, and then holding her hand when they were out of view. When she went over to use the sauna at Daybreak: sitting close to Vee's body, thigh to thigh, shoulder to shoulder, skin sweating and sticking to each other.

It was risky. And yet it wasn't. They were friends, now, and anyone could see that. Friends touched each other. But even if people suspected something, she wouldn't have been able to stop anyway. She felt as if she had spent her entire life not being touched and touching Vee was something she could no longer live without. When Vee wasn't touching her, she felt groundless, unconnected to the earth. How did you even know your body was yours if no one touched it?

Vee hurried around the side of the house on the northwest end of the island. The house was older than she was, painted the same colour grey as a winter sea. It had been built before there was a ferry, when the only people who lived on Unity were fishermen and their burgeoning offspring. It had been smaller then, and probably housed a family of twelve. Now it belonged to a summer person, of course. It had porches added, front and back, a sun room, expensive sash windows with shutters, solar panels, a backup generator on the side. The kitchen would be granite and stainless steel and all the bathrooms would have monsoon showers. However, it had the advantage of not being overlooked by anyone except for seagulls.

Rachel opened the front door before Vee set foot on the porch. She was grinning. 'I've put on the heating,' she said, and brought Vee through to the front of the house, where there was a squat black stove, orange flames in its belly.

'Won't someone see the smoke?' Vee asked, but Rachel shook her head.

'It's propane. Rich people don't want to chop wood.'

Rachel had made a nest of rugs and blankets and cushions on the floor in front of the fire. It was still light outside, but she'd lit scented candles around the room. She undressed Vee slowly, and Vee undressed her slowly, kissing each part of each other in the warm and stolen room.

Afterwards, lying naked and languid, propped up on the cushions, watching the sunset over the water, Vee said, 'Thank you for this gift.'

Rachel raised her head, surprised. 'This isn't a gift. I broke into a house and lit some candles. We have to give it back.'

'It's still a gift,' Vee said. 'Maybe it's even better because we have to give it back.' She traced along Rachel's cheek, her jawline. Her skin was like nothing Vee had ever touched. Rachel took her hand and kissed the palm. The sea and sky in front of them were lit up brilliant orange.

'I keep on thinking,' said Rachel, sleepy. 'Do you know that story about the settlers here who burned their own houses?'

'Um.' Vee cast her mind back to the one-room school, Anita Langlais's high-pitched teaching voice. 'Something about not letting the Native Americans get them?'

'That's it. I was looking out the window earlier and I was thinking, there might have been a house here. And then I was thinking, what was it like for those people to set fire to their houses, and then get on a boat? All that time ago. They must have looked behind them, to see everything they owned on fire.' Rachel gestured with their joined hands to the sky, painted the colours of flame. 'Would you do it?'

'I don't think I would have bothered,' said Vee. 'I've never been all that attached to houses.'

'You've never been all that attached to anything,' said Rachel, still sleepy, resting her head against Vee's shoulder.

'Well. Not things, no.'

'But you married a rich man.'

'I didn't marry Mike for his money.'

'Why did you?'

Mike had asked her nearly this exact same question. Cuddled together with Rachel, in a secret pocket of the world, her answer was different.

'I married Mike because it was easy,' she said. 'And not a lot of things have been easy in my life. He makes things easy. Probably too easy. And I'm still with him because … well obviously I care about him, I *love* him. But also it seems unfair to leave him for the same reason I married him.'

'I love Sterling because he's a good man,' said Rachel. 'That's all he is. There's no darkness in him, no secrets. He's just good. And he offered me a home, and children, and this beautiful place where I could belong.' Vee felt her taking a deep breath. 'And now I find out that I haven't got any of those things. But he's still a good man.'

'Yes. He is.'

The last of the sun blazed across the water. It was ironic, Vee knew, to be talking about their husbands while they were curled up together naked. There was nothing about this that was not ironic.

'Could you set your house on fire?' Vee asked her.

'We're sort of doing it right now,' Rachel said.

'This is secret,' said Vee. 'No one ever has to know about this, if we don't want them to.'

'But I did it once before, too. I left my parents, moved to New Jersey and never spoke to them again. It felt as if I were leaving them for dead. They might be dead. I don't know.'

'What made you leave?'

'Nothing. That is, nothing that wasn't ordinary for them. There wasn't a fight, they weren't drinking more than normal, they both still had their jobs. Sometimes everything was fine, you know. A lot of the time it was fine. And I love them. Just … one day I woke up and I realised, I'm an adult and I need to be free.'

'That must have been hard.'

'I still feel guilty about leaving them,' Rachel said. 'Even though it was what saved me. And then I came here, and I love it here. I love this island, even if it doesn't love me. I don't want to set that on fire. You know?'

Vee nodded. Together, they watched the sun slip below the horizon.

Chapter Thirty-seven

Sterling

The day before Thanksgiving was freezing rain on and off all day, and he'd had the same conversation about it with every single person to set foot in the store. In the afternoon, he went down under the ferry dock for a minute, just to have some quiet and time to breathe. But when he got down there, Vee was there already, collar up on her jacket, looking closely at her phone.

'Hey,' he said, surprised.

'Oh.' She stuffed her phone into her pocket. 'Hey. How're you doing?'

'I'm taking a break. Didn't expect to see you down here on a day like this.'

'I got a sudden urge to see the place where we carved our names. But now that I'm down here, I can't remember which piling it was.'

'This one.' He pointed; it was covered with a thick layer of weed and barnacle. 'Haven't seen you lately.'

'Oh, you know, I've got an enormous house, I can't always find my way out of it.' She went to the piling and started half-heartedly pulling weed off it.

'Are you staying here for the holiday?'

'We're taking the ferry later. I'm just taking a break from packing. We're flying to Florida tonight to see my mom. She likes to have Cuban food for Thanksgiving.'

'Say hi to her from me.'

248

'I will.' Vee dropped a clump of seaweed on the ground. 'Why do you need a break?'

'It's Rachel,' he said, surprising himself.

She paused in her destruction of flora. 'What about Rachel?'

'Oh, nothing.'

'Fair enough. You don't have to talk to me.' She went back to her task.

'You're her friend, though. You two seem to like each other.'

'Yeah, we do.'

'The thing is, it's just ... I don't know what she wants.'

'Women mostly all want the same thing,' Vee said to the piling.

'Do they, though?'

'Sure.'

'I know what my mom wants. I know what you want.'

'I'm not sure I'm interested in *that* opinion.'

'It's exactly the same thing you wanted when you were a kid. You want to prove to everyone that you're good enough, and also that you don't give a fuck what they think. Of course those are diametrically opposite to each other.'

'Well, I never said I wasn't screwed up.' She inspected her dirty hands. 'Do you and Rachel talk to each other?'

'We talk every day.'

'And you haven't asked her what she wants?'

'I have, but ... When we got married she was so enthusiastic about being here, about having a home and a family. She said she definitely didn't want to be an academic or a teacher, she'd rather help with the business. But then she's so resentful of everything. This place, the store, me. We keep on having arguments about nothing.'

'Isn't that the definition of marriage?' She picked at a barnacle with her fingernail. 'How do you get these things off?'

He came over to help her. 'I don't understand her. Maybe I never did. She never even let me meet her parents.'

'From what she says, there's good reason for that.'

'Yes, but how much can you know about someone if you don't know where they came from?'

'Most people don't think like Unity people. I know that might come as something of a shock.'

'She told you about her parents?'

Vee ripped off a clump of bladderwrack. 'Would you look at this.'

It was hard to make out, under here in the shadows, but when he got a little closer he could see it: the name VEE carved into the wooden piling. As he watched, she pulled off another clump and he saw, above it, S.A. He remembered the two of them standing under this dock, passing the knife back and forth, digging at the wood.

'What were we?' he asked. 'Fourteen, fifteen?'

'Something like that. You only managed your initials.'

'Hey, my name has twice as many letters as yours.'

'A lot has changed since then.'

'Has it?' said Sterling. 'Sometimes I feel like nothing has changed at all.'

She picked at the angle of the V with her fingernail. The soft wood flaked away. 'You know, Sterling, you can change things if you want to.'

'What do you mean?'

'You could get off this island. You could go to college and get the degree you wanted to. Remember how you used to talk about it? Civil engineering, volunteering abroad, building bridges all over the world?'

'I'm too old for that now.'

'My mom did it.' She peeled a strip of wood away from the piling, leaving a stripe of lighter colour. 'Even without a degree, you could travel. See some new places, meet some new people. Deserts, volcanoes, mountains. It's a big world out there.'

'Who would look after the store?'

'You could hire someone. To be honest, if you threw in the use of the house for the year, people would probably do it for free. People think it's romantic out here.'

'They wouldn't do it right. Anyway, I can't do that. The store should be run by an Ames. That's what my dad would have wanted.'

'Your choice. If you're happy with things the way they are, then fair enough.' Vee wiped her hand on her jeans, and faced him. 'Listen. I know what Rachel wants.'

'What does she want?'

'She wants a home. She wants you to talk to her. And she wants love.'

Vee's voice cracked on the last word, and Sterling found himself looking at her – really looking at her. She looked tired. Something made him ask: 'How are you and Mike?'

'Mike's great. He's always great.'

Mike had mixed dirty martinis for everyone at the last cribbage night and they were so strong that half the island staggered home, including Mike, who'd had at least three.

'I mean ... as a couple,' said Sterling. 'Do you talk to him?'

'Talking to Mike Ellis is like writing a message on the sand. You think you've got through, but then the next day ...' She shrugged again. 'He only hears what he wants to hear. Not that I can blame him. Frankly, I wish I were more like that. I could've avoided a lot of grief.'

'Everyone here thinks you've got it made.'

'So does my mom.' She gave him a sudden grin. 'Every time we visit, she introduces him to every single person at her apartment complex, including the caretaker and the delivery guys.'

'I bet she does. Why are you avoiding *my* mom, by the way?'

Vee looked startled. 'Um – you noticed that?'

'Just a little.'

'I feel guilty. Really guilty. I feel bad that I let you down, but I feel worse that I let Brenda down.'

'I know exactly what you mean.'

'Because it's easier for you to be disappointed in yourself, than it is for you to feel you've disappointed your mother,' Vee said.

'Ouch.'

'I've known you for a long time.'

'So that gives you the right to drop truth bombs. Just give me a warning next time, huh?' He smiled at her, to soften his words. 'Thanks for the advice about my wife, by the way.'

'No problem.' They began walking, together, to the beach, but Vee paused and Sterling stopped too. 'Since we're talking about feelings,' she said quickly. 'I want you to know that the things I've done, I've done them all for myself. Not to hurt you. Not, in any way, to hurt you.'

'Okay,' he said. 'You're a selfish bitch. Got it.'

'Good. Let's get out of here. I need to wash my hands.'

As usual, his mother arrived on the evening ferry with four boxes of food. For all her talk of leaving the family home to him and Rachel, his mom had no problem taking over what had formerly been her kitchen on holidays. Sterling was assigned the same tasks he had every year: to get the table leaf down from the attic (even though it was only three of them for Thanksgiving dinner this year, they needed the extra space for all the food), to polish the best silver, to carry and fetch whatever was needed from the pantry and the freezer and the storeroom next door. Holidays swept them up, everything familiar, even the same words used every year. His mother and Rachel made the pies the night before; he heard their easy conversation going on in the kitchen as he went about his chores. His mother got up early on Thanksgiving morning to prepare the turkey, while Rachel made them coffee and held the turkey skin closed so his mother could sew the stuffing in. Whenever he walked into the kitchen, he felt as if he were intruding in a world of women, where he didn't speak the language. 'Go back to your football,' his mother would say, and that was the same thing she had said to his father when he was a child.

Vee's words made him notice Rachel more than he usually did. He thought of their first married Thanksgiving. Rachel could cook quick meals, but not a large family dinner with several courses, and his mom took great pleasure in teaching her what to do. Sterling had been so proud, then: sharing his family traditions with his new wife. Now he remembered how she had barely spoken, how she had stirred gravy and peeled potatoes as if her life depended on it. Once, she had been alone in the kitchen, and he'd come up behind her to steal a kiss, and she'd jumped out of her skin, dropping the butter dish on the floor. He'd thought it was sweet that she was so absorbed in cooking. Now, he thought she had probably been frightened of getting everything wrong. Holidays were not happy occasions in the house where she grew up.

He waited until his mother went to make a phone call, then made sure that Rachel didn't have anything in her hands. Then he crossed the kitchen rapidly, hugged her from behind, and gave her a kiss on the cheek.

'Hey,' she said, smiling. 'What's that for?'

'Just because I love you,' he said. And when she hugged and kissed him back, he thought: *Maybe Vee was right.*

So when they went to bed, instead of turning off the light and turning onto his side, he lay down facing her and said, 'How was that for you?'

'Hmm?' She put her finger in her book to keep her place. 'How was what? Dinner?'

'No, the whole thing. The holiday.'

'It was fine. Your mom said the turkey was a little dry but I thought it was all right.'

'I meant ... how did you feel today?'

She put her book down. 'Why are you asking?'

'Because ... because I was thinking about how hard holidays must have been for you, when you were a kid. Especially holidays

253

that revolved around big meals and drinking, like … well, like every holiday.'

'You're right,' she said slowly. 'I never enjoyed holidays. Even if they started out okay, I spent the whole day waiting for the other shoe to drop. Thanksgiving, Passover, whatever. I was on the alert to see how much Mum and Dad were drinking. I was waiting for them to start fighting. One time—' She caught herself. 'It was never relaxing. So I still have trouble with holidays now. Though I guess not as much as Peter. He said he was having a pizza in front of the television, as usual.'

'But was today okay?'

'I'm … learning? To like them better. I guess? At least I can relax and know that we'll be able to eat a full meal together. But…'

'But?'

She spoke quietly. 'That table is so big. For just three of us.'

'It would've been nice to have Peter this year, and Jacob, or my cousins and the kids. But maybe next year. Anyway, I think we made a dent in the food.'

'I meant … without any children. Every time I sit down at the dining room table, I think of how we were meant to have …'

'Oh.'

And he'd been thinking the same thing, hadn't he? He was so used to it now, it was such a normal pain, that he barely even noticed. Or maybe it was still so much more raw for Rachel.

'Your mom thinks about it too. She just catches herself, sometimes, and I know it's because she's being kind, but…'

'It hurts you.'

'Does it hurt you too?'

He nodded. Then said, because a nod wasn't enough: 'Yeah.'

'Are you …' She shook her head, pulled the blanket up. 'No, I'm not going to ask that.'

'Ask what, Rachel?'

'No.'

'Please. Ask me.'

'Are you angry with me? Because I can't have babies? Because I ruined that for you?'

'No,' he said. But was he? Was that what made it so difficult for him to stay still, what made him criticise her when she didn't deserve it, what made him feel, sometimes, like he couldn't breathe?

'Of course not,' he added. 'You can't help it.'

'I wish I could.' She sounded so miserable that he wanted to touch her, soothe her. But she was holding herself stiffly upright against the pillows, the blanket clutched to her chest.

'It's okay,' he told her. 'Come here.'

He held out his arms and she scooted over into them. She lay her head on his chest and he stroked her hair.

'It's all right,' he said, and he felt her relax a little.

'Why are you asking me how I feel?' she said to his pyjama top. 'Did I do something strange?'

'I talked to Vee.'

She didn't answer for a second, then: 'Vee?'

'Yeah. She told me that I should talk to you more. And she was right. I ... this is good.'

'What else did Vee say?'

'She said that I should ask you want you want.'

Rachel raised her head. She looked up into his face. She was frowning, as if she were trying to figure something out.

'What *do* you want?' he asked her.

'I think ...' She smiled at him, a faint and lovely smile. A little shy. It reminded him of when he'd first met her: after months of talking, nothing more than talking by text and phone call, seeing her for the first time under the clock at Grand Central Station, among all the rushing crowds – a small woman with a cloud of hair, a virtual stranger, with a smile just for him.

She said, 'I think I'd like you to hold me some more.'

'I can do that,' he said.

Chapter Thirty-eight

Rachel

December.

They were just two normal women, wearing unmatched wedding rings, sitting across from each other at a table for two at a busy Italian restaurant by the Portland waterfront. Outside the window, Christmas lights sparkled in the street. Around their feet lay bags of Christmas shopping from various shops and boutiques in the Old Port.

'It's our first date,' said Vee, and laughed. 'We should have chosen somewhere more romantic.'

'We should have got a hotel room,' Rachel corrected her. 'A *warm* hotel room. With sheets on the bed.'

'It would be suspicious if we came home from a shopping trip having done zero shopping.'

Rachel shrugged. 'We could've stopped off at the Maine Mall.'

'You forget I'm married to Mike Ellis. I can't just pick him up a pair of slippers from JC Penney's.'

Rachel forgot no such thing. Even in Mike's absence, Vee was so very much a rich man's wife. Ninety-five per cent of the shopping bags were hers. She had spent more money this morning, without apparently noticing, than Rachel had spent since last June.

Vee scooted her chair further under the table so that her knee brushed Rachel's. 'What's wrong? We've been planning this time together for weeks, but you seem unhappy.'

Rachel lowered her voice. 'It's hard to say, exactly. It's like this.' She gestured to the glass of wine in front of Vee, and her own glass of iced tea. Vee's eyebrows shot up.

'Oh no,' she said. 'Does it bother you that I'm drinking? I don't have to, if it makes you uncomfortable.'

'It's not that.'

'Then what is it?'

Rachel tried to put her thoughts into order. 'I don't drink because it doesn't feel safe to me. I don't like to feel out of control, or that I can't react appropriately. But *this* ... this is like drinking. I feel dizzy, I feel out of control. I've felt that way since I met you. It's the least safe thing I've ever done. And I'm not good at it.'

'I think you're pretty good at it.' Under the tablecloth, Vee ran her hand along the outside of Rachel's leg.

'But I'm not. I don't like lying to Sterling.'

'I don't like lying to Sterling and Mike.'

'Sterling's been more open lately. He's been trying harder.'

'Well, that's good, isn't it?'

'It is, but also it makes me feel worse. And you and I—'

'What about us?'

'We're so different,' Rachel said. 'You're so different from me. You make me feel things I didn't expect. Nothing about this is safe.'

'I don't think people start affairs because they want to be safe.'

The waiter arrived. 'Are you ladies ready to order?'

'Not yet, thanks,' said Vee, with the confidence of someone who was used to being waited on.

Rachel waited until he was gone, and then she whispered what had been on her mind for weeks: 'Do you still sleep with Mike?'

'Well. Yes. Don't you sleep with Sterling?'

Rachel didn't answer.

'Oh my God, you *don't*?'

'We haven't that much anyway, not for a while. Not since we found out we can't have children.'

'But not at all?'

'Maybe ... twice. Since you and I ...'

'I couldn't stop,' said Vee. 'I can't stop. He'd suspect something.'

'You said ... you told me ... you have a lot of sex.'

'I'm still married to him, Rachel.'

Rachel chewed her lip.

'This is the way it's always been,' said Vee. 'Are you bothered that I still sleep with him?'

'Well. It's just sex, right?'

'I don't know. Is it?'

'I don't know.'

The waiter brought a basket of bread and retreated quickly. The basket sat in the table between them, untouched.

'I am bothered,' said Rachel. 'Yes. What we do is ... I just can't imagine you being that way with two people at once.'

'It's not the same.'

'How is it different?'

'I don't think that's fair to ask, do you?'

Rachel took a deep breath. She looked at the table.

'If we ...' Vee began. 'If we wanted things to change ... We would have to come out, for a start. Which I'm okay with, but are you?'

'I don't know.'

'Then if I left Mike, because that's what would happen, and you left Sterling—'

'Sterling would leave *me*.'

'Whichever way it happened, both of them would be very hurt, which neither of us want. Which both of us agreed we don't want. Also, people would talk. Again: I'm okay with people talking. I'm used to that, in fact. But are you, Rachel?'

Rachel didn't answer. She didn't know that either. People already talked about her. But being strange, not fitting in, was different from being the person who ruined Sterling Ames's life.

'Are we there, at that point, where we have to change things?' Vee asked. 'Where we have to hurt them?'

'Why is that *my* decision?'

'It's not,' Vee said. 'Not just yours. But I'm asking you because you have the most to lose.'

'I don't know about that,' said Rachel. 'It seems like I'm not the one who told my husband I wanted a divorce but who's still spending his money and fucking him every chance I get.'

As soon as she'd thrown out the words, she wanted to take them back. Vee's mouth thinned, but she didn't reply.

'I'm sorry,' said Rachel. 'I'm sorry. I just feel ... it all feels hopeless. I don't see how any of this can turn out well.'

Vee stood up and began collecting her bags.

'What are you doing?' said Rachel.

'We have four hours before we have to leave to catch the ferry, and this conversation is going nowhere. Let's stop wasting time and get a hotel room.'

Vee paid in cash. Rachel followed her to the elevator. She waited until they were alone and the doors had shut behind her before she said, 'I'm sorry.'

'Sorry for what?' Vee was looking at the digital display saying what floor they were on.

'For ruining things. For being complicated and emotional. I know that this thing between you and me is about sex.'

Vee snagged her finger in the belt loop of Rachel's jeans and pulled her close. 'This is about feeling good. This is about something just for us. It's about feeling alive and knowing what we want, even for a few hours at a time.' She kissed Rachel, open-mouthed and hungry. The elevator dinged and before the door opened Rachel pulled back, wiping Vee's lipstick from her mouth. They walked together through the bland hallway to the room door, which Vee unlocked with her card key. As soon as they got inside, they both dropped their bags and coats and reached for each other. Vee pulled Rachel's shirt off and pushed the cup of her bra beneath her breast, stooping to suck hard on Rachel's nipple, just how she liked it best. Rachel gasped and tugged on Vee's hair, freeing it from its clip, kicked off her boots then unbuttoned her own jeans, pushing them down with impatient hands. Vee didn't even bother with her own clothes. She walked Rachel backwards to the bed, tumbled them both down on it and in a single move pulled Rachel's underwear down. Eyes on Rachel's, she stuck two fingers in her mouth to wet them, and thrust them into Rachel at the same time that she buried her head between her legs and licked her, fast and hard in rhythm with her hand.

Rachel closed her eyes. She didn't know what this hotel room looked like. She didn't know how much it had cost, or exactly how much time they had, or whether she was still wearing her socks. She only knew Vee fucking her, kneeling on the bed between her legs, Vee's hair spread out on her thighs, her breath, her tongue, her lips, even if she couldn't see Vee she would know it was her and no one else. Because this was about pleasure, and feeling alive, and taking what she wanted. She bit her lip and shouted, a hoarse cry to the emptiness that only had Vee in it. Her body jerked and clenched with an orgasm, she pulled Vee's hair so hard that Vee gasped in pain, and this was not about sex.

It was not. It was about pain and freedom and love.

She turned her face into the pillow so Vee would not see the tears. But Vee saw them anyway. She climbed up to lie next to her, still fully dressed, and she pushed back Rachel's hair with a hand that smelled of Rachel, and said, 'Are you okay?'

I'm in love with you, she thought. *And that's wrong.*

'I'm okay,' she lied. 'That was intense.'

'We've had to be quiet. It's good to let it out.'

'Uh huh.'

Her jeans and underwear were still dangling from one leg. She knew they didn't have much time, so she knew she should turn to Vee and start taking her clothes off so they could make the most of this room where they could be naked and loud for a few hours. But this was too much. She didn't know how to be.

Vee kissed her cheek where it was wet. She rested her hand on Rachel's naked belly. 'I could leave him,' she murmured. 'I think I have to anyway. I think this is my way of leaving him. But if I do it here, everyone will know why.'

'How could you do it?'

'When we go to New York for Christmas, then. Maybe.'

'But if you did that, you'd have no reason to come back to Unity.'

'Not without being really obvious, no.'

'So you'd be leaving me, too.'

Vee sighed. 'So we're back to where we were before. If one thing changes, everything has to change.'

Rachel rolled onto her side and kissed Vee fiercely. Love and pain.

'Don't leave him,' she said. 'Not yet.'

Chapter Thirty-nine

Mike

New Year's Eve. Outside, it was snowing. Mike could hear distant shouts and laughter from the New York streets far below.

He watched Vee as she stood in front of their bedroom mirror in the Upper East Side apartment, putting on deep red lipstick before they joined his parents at their party. She had become even more beautiful in the past few months. She had a glow to her, a sensuality in her movements, like a woman who has found a precious secret.

That was one of the reasons he knew that whatever was going on between Vee and Rachel was still happening.

If he hadn't seen them that night, he would never have known. He might've noticed her becoming more beautiful, more alive, and he might've thought that it was because of him, that he was the one making her happy. Because when it came to his wife he was, apparently, blind and shameless and willing to ignore the truth.

Or maybe she wasn't really more beautiful. Maybe he just saw her that way because he'd finally realised how much he loved her, and she was out of his reach.

Because he had to stay quiet. He couldn't say a single word to Vee about what he knew, without losing her.

But wasn't that what he'd always been like? Hadn't he always wanted the thing that was out of his reach? Ever since he was a kid. Once when he was about seven he'd visited a friend's ranch, where they had lots of animals, including cats. There was one cat – it was a pedigree Siamese, all of them were pedigree something – who hated him. The cat hated everyone, to be fair. His friend's mother told him: *You can pet any cat, but not that one.* So of course Mike had to try to pet that one. He stalked it, followed it, backed it into a corner where it hissed at him and when he held out his hand, the cat scratched him, a deep long scratch all the way down his forearm to the wrist. He still had a fine silvery scar, like a spider's web.

'Maybe that will teach you a lesson,' his mother had said. Apparently it hadn't.

Maybe his real problem was that the accident of his birth meant that almost *nothing* was out of reach, so he didn't have any idea of what he really wanted. Except for the thing that would hurt him.

And that was the second reason he knew that Vee was still sleeping with Rachel. That pain in his gut or his heart, the one that didn't go away with alcohol or laughter (though he kept trying both).

He took the necklace out of its velvet box and stood behind her. 'Happy new year,' he said, draping it around her neck from behind. Kissing her ear.

'Oh, you shouldn't have.' She touched the emerald drop on the gold chain. 'Mike, you have to stop giving me presents all the time.'

Despite her words, she held her hair up out of the way so he could fasten the clasp around her neck.

'I like giving you presents,' he said.

'You like your mom seeing me wearing the presents you give me, and complimenting me on your good taste.'

His mother had spoken to him on Christmas Eve, the day after they'd arrived in the city. 'Remember our talk in the summer,' she'd told him. No more, but he knew exactly what she meant. And he wanted to throw it in her face. He wanted to say, *Fuck you. I don't want my wife to stay with me for any other reason than that she wants to stay with me. I'm tired of learning a lesson. Your lessons are cynical and cruel.*

He didn't. He didn't say anything to his father, either. Especially not after the Christmas party, when Vee had hardly left his side, and his father handed him a glass of single malt on the rocks and held it up in a toast, saying, 'Well done.'

He couldn't remember his father ever saying that before. And he was nearly forty, so why did that matter so much? Why did he get a lump in his throat and have to swallow his Scotch all in one, and then immediately order another?

In New York, Vee's affair looked different. Everyone had affairs in New York. It was practically mandatory. He knew a dozen people who would tell him that if his wife had an affair with another woman, it didn't even count. He knew another two dozen who would tell him to go out and have an affair himself. Marriage was a contract, an alliance, your public face to the world. It required lawyers and family and money. Sex, on the other hand, was a human right. You did whatever you could to keep the marriage ticking over, even if that meant playing away.

Maybe what she was doing was to *help* their marriage. Otherwise, she'd have asked for a divorce again.

And his father never would have toasted him and said, *Well done.*

He turned Vee round so they were facing each other. 'I like giving presents to *you*.'

'Well. Thank you.'

'I don't think I told you this, but last summer. When you said you wanted a divorce. It nearly broke me, Vee.'

'Mike,' she said, and hesitated. 'I think I need to tell you some-thi—'

He interrupted her, before she could say the words. Before she could make them both face the reality of what she was doing. 'I put on a good show, because I'm good at putting on a good show, but... I'm glad you decided to give us a second chance.'

She nodded. She touched the necklace and looked down.

'I love you, Vee.'

'I love you too,' she said.

Who cared if she was having a little adventure with her former best friend's wife? It didn't mean anything. She probably found it exciting: the secrecy. Their sex life was still great. Maybe he liked the chase, too. Maybe this pain was just collateral damage, and it would go away when she'd worked this all out of her system.

He tilted her chin up so she had to look into his eyes. So she'd see that he meant what he said. 'I think it would break me if you left me,' he said. 'I will do anything in the world to keep us together, Vee. Anything.'

Part Five

———

Winter, 2016

Chapter Forty

Rachel

There was a bald eagles' nest on the easternmost tip of the island. Technically it was on private land, or rather in a tree that was on land owned by the Guntersons, a family who spent most of the year in Virginia. But the Guntersons didn't put up fences, and they didn't mind if residents came to look at the eagles. So leaving visible footprints in the snow wasn't a problem, unlike many of the other places on the island.

Rachel got there first. She followed the path along the side of the trees to the shore, where she climbed the rocks until she had a view of the nest on the point. As a home, it was less than impressive: it looked like a messy bundle of sticks smeared with white excrement and jammed between the trunk and branch of a tree. She peered at it; it appeared to be empty, so she climbed over the rocks until she was underneath it. Bones crunched under her feet, and she stooped to look. Bald eagles were voracious hunters. Most of the skeletons came from fish, but there were other bones too, of birds and small mammals. She took off her glove and picked up a tiny skull, maybe of a baby seabird of some sort. It had hardly any weight in her hand. She could crush it with a single curl of her finger.

'Hey!' Along the shoreline, Vee was scrambling over the rocks to come and meet her. The sky, rocks and sea were all grey, but Vee was wearing a red parka and white hat and gloves. They hadn't seen each other since before Christmas, and though they'd texted, it had to be discreet; at the sight of her, the only bright spot, Rachel's stomach tightened and her heart thudded.

Rachel loved Vee. She'd known since that hotel room in Portland, and even then it wasn't an epiphany so much as a recognition, an understanding of something that had been inside her all along. Like her sexuality, or the strength she'd found to leave Illinois.

She needed that strength now, today.

'Hey,' she said to Vee. They both glanced around to make sure they weren't being observed, and they kissed: briefly, with cold lips. Then Vee hugged her and smiled.

'I missed you,' she said.

'I missed you. Look, I found this skull.'

'It's beautiful. Poor thing.'

'The eagles aren't here yet, do you want to wait?'

They both sat on a rock, close together, hips and shoulders brushing.

'It's cold,' said Vee. 'We should have met somewhere warmer.'

'Jacob's checking the houses this week.'

'So we're back to sneaking around,' said Vee, but she nudged Rachel with her elbow so she knew it wasn't a complaint.

'Sterling knows I'm here with you to look at the eagles. I'm not sneaking.'

'How is Sterling?'

'We're getting along better. Much better. We're talking more. We even discussed adoption a few times.'

'That's good. I feel less frustrated with Mike, too. Who knew that an affair could improve your marriage? Maybe everyone should have one.'

Rachel didn't answer that. How could she?

'That nest looks like a car crash,' Vee observed. 'It's got to be twenty years old at least. I remember it being here when I was a kid.'

'It's a different pair, though.'

'They probably drove off the previous ones. They mate for life, but they're ruthless. And shitty builders.' She nudged Rachel again. 'How was your Christmas with your brother?'

'It was okay. He doesn't say much. Brenda was nice to him.'

'Brenda's nice to everyone.'

'Families make him uncomfortable. People make him uncomfortable. I think he finds it difficult to trust anyone. Still, it was nice to have another Jew around at Christmas. Back in Highland Park, we used to get Chinese food and go to the movies. I kept wondering what my parents were doing, if they were doing that.'

'None of this,' said Vee, 'is your fault.'

'I used to think I could fix them. Sometimes I still wonder if I could, if I got in touch.'

'You can't fix them. You can only fix yourself. You can only keep yourself alive.'

Maybe, but you're the one who's brought me to life.

'Thanks,' Rachel said instead. 'I know you understand these things. It means a lot.'

'There are things I guess you only know if you've lived with someone with an addiction.'

Rachel nodded. She had planned what she needed to do today, but this conversation didn't make it any easier.

'It's funny,' said Vee. 'While we were apart, I was thinking that I miss kissing you and sex with you, but I also miss talking with you, or just hanging out. I haven't had a best friend since I left here, and I've never had a female best friend. But now I do.'

Rachel tugged off Vee's glove and took her hand, which was much warmer than hers. She put them both in her coat pocket, linked.

'You're the best friend I've had, too,' she said.

'So there's another benefit.'

'We need to end this,' Rachel blurted.

Vee pulled away a little so she could see Rachel's face. 'What? Really? I thought things were going well.'

'It's an affair, Vee. Things *can't* go well.'

'I offered to leave Mike.'

'We both know that's not going to work.'

'But this is great. This is great, what we have. I thought you missed me.'

Rachel had missed her too much. She had felt incomplete without being able to see Vee. She had felt a thrill every time she got a text from her; she had dreamed of her at night. She loved Vee more than she'd ever loved anyone. And though she couldn't say it, that was the reason she had to end it. She needed Vee far too much.

She'd realised it on New Year's Eve, when everyone was gathered in the old schoolhouse which was now a museum. Someone had set up a TV so the islanders could watch the ball drop, while they were watched in turn by the photographs of the island's past children.

She stood there with a plastic cup of sparkling wine in her hand, next to her husband, and all she could feel was how much she missed Vee. All she could think of, when the year turned, was *I don't know who I am when Vee is not here.*

She could not live that way. She'd made up her mind before the fireworks exploded on the screen and she turned to kiss her husband.

'I did miss you,' Rachel said now, resolutely. 'But we have to stop, before someone gets hurt.'

'Sterling and Mike, you mean?'

She did mean their husbands. But really, she meant herself. Rachel was under no illusions; she was selfish and she was protecting her own feelings. It was the same thing she'd done to her parents.

'Yes,' she said. 'We're both married, and we shouldn't be sneaking around. It's wrong.'

'But—' Vee's face was tight. 'You said that you knew it was wrong and you didn't care. That's how we started this whole thing. By you saying that.'

'Things change.'

Vee withdrew her hand, and stood on the rock. 'I thought we were best friends,' said Vee.

'Sterling's your best friend too.'

'I torpedoed that friendship as soon as I started fucking you.'

Rachel flinched at the word. 'Don't blame me for that. You torpedoed it years ago, from what I've heard.'

'So let me get this right. You're breaking up with me, but you're calling *me* faithless?'

'We both knew this couldn't last forever,' said Rachel.

'But . . . I came back for you. I don't have anything else for me here.'

'You think you'll leave?' A flare of panic. She swallowed. If Vee left, that would hurt. It would tear Rachel apart. But it would be for the best. Wouldn't it?

'I might as well. Why would I stay on a rock in the sea if I'm not wanted?'

'Go ahead,' said Rachel, feeling sick. 'Run away again. You don't even need an explanation, right? You didn't have one last time.'

Vee's hair was blowing in the wind from the ocean. She was so beautiful.

'Fine,' said Vee. 'If I'm such a shit, then let's say goodbye.'

Rachel averted her face before she started crying. She blinked hard and stared at the empty eagles' nest, and when she dared to look up again, Vee had gone.

Chapter Forty-one

Sterling

Sterling was sitting alone in the store with his feet up on the counter, watching a National Geographic documentary on his laptop, when the bell over the door rang. It was Mike Ellis, in a drysuit and woollen hat, standing in the doorway, letting all the cold air in and rubbing his hands over each other.

'Hey, man,' Mike called, 'do you mind if I drip seawater all over your clean floor?'

'Not a problem, just shut the door.' Sterling shut the laptop and stood up. 'Why the hell are you so wet?'

Mike left soggy footprints across the store. He went directly to the pot of coffee, took off his gloves, and poured himself a cup, wrapping his hands around it for warmth. 'Windsurfing.'

'In January?'

'Yeah, I got myself a new board for Christmas.'

'You're windsurfing by yourself?'

'Oh yeah. It's straight-up magic.'

'It's lethal, is what it is. Haven't you heard of hypothermia?'

'Nah, water's warmer than the air this time of year.'

'But if you fall in and can't get out?'

'I can get out of anything.'

Sterling shook his head. 'Tourist.'

'You're jealous because I've got bigger balls than you.'

Sterling watched as Mike took a silver flask from a pocket concealed somewhere on his drysuit and poured a good slug of something, probably whisky, into his coffee. 'You sure you should be drinking?'

'Warms you up.'

'I think it does the opposite, in winter.'

Mike shrugged and took a drink. 'Who am I to argue with a St Bernard? Hey, by the way, I saw our wives down on the eastern point, all huddled up together like they were telling secrets.'

'Yeah, Rachel said she was going over there to look at the eagles' nest.'

'Oh, you knew?'

'Sure. Vee must've met her there.'

'I thought you'd want me to tell you what your wife was up to. If she was up to anything. I mean, we're friends, right?' He took another drink, and Sterling wondered how much of that flask he'd had already. Mike was always easy-going, but it felt as if he were forcing it.

'It's not like Rachel can get up to much trouble around here,' Sterling said blandly.

'I think you'd be surprised, my friend.'

'Mike, did you windsurf past the eastern point?'

'How else did you think I got here?'

'It's pretty treacherous around Brimstone.'

'Ha ha, you're telling me. Fortunately, I am an expert sailor.' Mike topped up his coffee from the pot, and added another slug of whisky. 'Listen, I haven't got any cash on me. Can I pay you back for this?'

'Of course.'

'Good. Anyway, obviously I can't tell you anything about how our wives spend their spare time, so I'll get going. Thanks, man. Cribbage tomorrow?'

'Sure,' Sterling said, watching him go, wondering what the hell was going on.

Chapter Forty-two

Vee

January turned to February, and Vee did not leave.

February was when winter really got going in Maine. It started sleeting in October, it started snowing in November, December at least had Christmas, January was just cold, but February was the real deal. February was when things got bitter and icy and locked in, and what little snow there was on the island got dingy, and the days had been short forever, and the trees were black skeletons, and the ocean was unceasing grey, and it was easy to believe that spring was never going to come and you were going to be trapped on this rock forever.

In September, she never would have believed that Mike would last here until February. They'd spent Christmas Day with her mom in Florida and he'd tried singing Unity's praises until her mom shut him down. They'd flown back again to New York the next day and he'd been exuberant and extroverted, catching up with everyone, never saying no to a single party, never letting her say no, either. She'd been expecting the entire time for him to turn to her and say, 'Babe, it's so fun here, let's stay longer.' Or, even more likely, 'Rory and Charlie have invited us for a week in St Lucia, babe, don't you think we could use some sunshine?'

But he didn't. On the seventh of January, when everyone's hangovers were finished and their cleanses had begun, they got on a charter plane back to Rockland and booked the ferry for the next morning.

And then Rachel had ended their affair, and it really was winter.

The sky was lowering and black and the air was thick. February was the month of storms. Everyone who lived on an island felt it when one was coming: deep in their bones, in the pressure behind their eyes.

Why were they here? She had come back for Rachel, of course. Three weeks in New York and Florida, away from Rachel, had made Vee feel as if she were drowning. The parties, the brunches, the concerts, the dinners, the festive everything: all of it so much tawdry glitter. She wanted to be here. On an island, surrounded by slate-coloured water, patched with greying snow. The place she'd sworn to leave forever, with a woman she'd never expected to meet.

And then Rachel had ended it, all of a sudden, and although Vee had threatened to leave, she hadn't. She stayed inside, and gazed at the water and sky through the windows, and pretended to Mike that everything was fine.

Because this was Rachel's island. And she had made it Vee's again, too.

She hadn't meant to spend the night on Edith's couch. But she'd had a dentist appointment on the mainland and decided, spontaneously, to give Bunny a call, and Bunny said, 'We're making White Russians, come over.' It took her a little while to find Bunny's cousin Edith's house: twenty years ago it had been unfinished green Tyvek, with concrete steps going up to the front door, but now it had whiteish vinyl cladding and a wheelchair ramp. It was smaller than she remembered from when she used to board there as a teenager. She opened the screen door, knocked on the inside door, and heard the clamour of countless small dogs.

'Well, look at you,' said Edith when she opened the door, and hugged her, and ushered her through the crowd of shi-tzus into the kitchen, where Bunny was sitting at a table covered with plastic glasses, ashtrays, empty Half & Half containers and a gallon bottle of Allen's Coffee Brandy. They'd clearly been at it for a few hours. Bunny poured Vee a drink, Edith handed her a cigarette, and the dogs wandered off. Vee thought there were five of them, but they kept moving and they all looked similarly fluffy and brown, so she couldn't tell.

'I've only got an hour before the ferry,' Vee said.

The first drink slipped down like a milkshake: cloying, fatty, cut with the taste of ash. It was just like Vee remembered. Sweet booze, smoke, the raspy laughter of the two women and the smell of dog hair.

'What do you do all day out there?' Edith asked, pouring them all another slug of Allen's and opening a bag of salt and vinegar crisps. 'You don't have a job, right? You just work out and watch TV?'

'I was having an affair.'

Vee blurted it out, and then instantly blushed and felt sick. 'Wait. Wait a minute, forget I said that.'

'We en't gonna blab, what do you think? We're your aunties.'

'Anyway,' added Edith, 'we need the gossip, nothing is happening here.'

'Just don't tell us who it is. Tell us everything else.' Bunny turned to Edith. 'Her husband is real good-looking. And rich.'

'Not gonna find many of those on Unity in the winter.'

'Of course it's not someone on Unity,' Vee lied.

'Ah, there ya go. For a hot minute I thought it was Sterling.'

'It's *not* Sterling.'

'Was it good?' Edith said wistfully. 'I'm not gonna lie, I'd go a long way to get something good. All the men my age need a pill to get it up and all the men younger'n me want girls in their twenties. So do the men my age, the dirty fuckers.' She laughed, took a drink, and wiped off her milk moustache.

'I remember sex,' said Bunny. 'Jesus, I loved it.'

'The sex was really good,' said Vee. 'Really good.'

The two women leaned forward.

'It's a woman,' said Vee.

Edith passed her the bottle.

She missed the ferry, and texted Mike that she was spending the night. It was such a relief to talk, unguarded, about Rachel to someone who would not judge her. Bunny and Edith had seen it all before, every permutation of human nature. And they had known her from birth and never sneered at her. She couldn't talk with her mother about her affair, because her mother liked Mike and had a lot invested in Vee's future, but Bunny and Edith only wanted to drink with her and hear the dirt. She may not belong to them any more, because of money and distance and education and lifestyle, but in some ways she always would.

'You gonna leave your husband for her?' Edith asked.

'Of course she en't gonna leave her husband,' said Bunny. 'Have you seen where they live?'

'Prenup,' said Edith wisely.

'Anyway,' said Bunny, 'you got the ideal set-up there. A rich husband and an exciting lover. If it was a soap opera, I'd watch it.'

'Yeah,' said Edith. 'You should milk that as long as you can.'

'She ended it,' said Vee, and she started to cry.

'Oh, honey,' said Bunny. 'Are you okay?'

'All I want to do is touch her,' sobbed Vee. 'And I can't. I can't even talk with her. It's worse than getting hit by a bus.'

In the morning, she felt terrible. She woke up on Edith's itchy plaid couch – probably the same one she'd slept on as a teenager during the school week – and spent an hour throwing up in Edith's toilet. When she emerged, having tried to clean her teeth with toothpaste and her finger, she blanched at the scent of the coffee that Bunny offered her.

'You used to be able to drink a lot more'n that,' said Bunny. 'If I didn't know you're a lesbian now, I'd ask if you was pregnant.'

Vee drank a glass of water, called Mike to come and pick her up on *Dawntreader*, and went to sit in her car. She counted back the weeks in her mind. How could she not have noticed that she hadn't had a period since just after Thanksgiving?

Because for weeks – since Rachel had called things off with her, but before that too, while she'd been away from Unity for the holidays – she'd been trying to ignore the fact that she was miserable, and that meant that she ignored everything except trying to act okay.

She drove to the drugstore, because there was no way in hell she was buying a pregnancy test at Ames' General.

Vee had been on the Pill since she was fourteen. Her mother had marched her straight into the clinic in Thomaston and got her a prescription. 'Don't depend on those pills, though,' her mother told her. 'Always use a rubber. Carry one with you so he can't tell you he hasn't got one. I love you more than anything and I'm glad I've got you, but I don't want you to end up knocked up at fifteen like I did. I want you to have a life.'

Until she got married, she followed her mother's advice religiously. Still, though, this wasn't the first pregnancy test she'd taken. This wasn't even the first test she'd taken in Maine. When she was sixteen, she bought a test in Rite Aid in Rockland after school, which she took in the girls' bathroom the next day. She couldn't risk leaving a test in the rubbish at home for Pops to find.

Instead, Micki Mullins found it in the girls' room rubbish bin. She told the entire cheerleading squad, who told everyone else. No one actually asked Vee, but everyone knew it was hers, everyone whispered about it behind her back, and sometimes even mocked her about it to her face. On the other hand, everyone was fist-bumping Stu Phillips, the guy she'd had sex with after too many cans of Milwaukee's Best.

Fortunately, that test was negative.

So were the two she'd taken since marrying Mike. One after a bout of food poisoning in Kuala Lumpur, and another where nothing had gone wrong, but she didn't have a period for three months. When she went to see a doctor he said it was stress, even though she explained to him that she had nothing to be stressed about, as she never did anything more stressful these days than getting her nails done.

'Maybe that's why you're stressed,' he'd said. For days afterwards, she wondered if this was a surprisingly feminist thing for him to say, or whether it was the normal practice of Upper West Side doctors to reinforce the belief that one-percenters had more difficult lives than everyone else.

Anyway, she'd told Mike about neither of these negative tests. Before they'd married, they'd agreed they didn't want children. Mike said he'd be a crappy father, and she knew she was too selfish to be a good mother. They'd never really discussed it since. Like their prenup, it seemed to be something that was written in stone. It was just another thing in their marriage that they skated around and ignored. Why worry him? It was easier to buy the test, take the test, bury the test at the bottom of the waste-paper basket. Unlike Pops, Mike had no interest in checking through the rubbish to see if he might have thrown away something valuable.

So now she was here, at the same Rockland Rite Aid where she'd bought that first test back when she was sixteen, except it was a Walgreens now. She paused outside the door to look at her reflection in the glass. She looked rough. The winter coat covered up most of her, and she'd tucked her hair up into her woollen hat, but her skin was the grey of winter, and she had dark circles under her eyes.

'Jesus,' she muttered.

She knew that she had managed to get through most of her life by compartmentalising things. She kept her years of poverty separate from her years of wealth; she kept her success apart from her failures. She kept her heartbreak apart from her heart. She was skilled at camouflaging herself without seeming to, at adapting to social situations. Rachel had asked her how she could have sex both with her and with Mike, and that was the reason: because in Vee's mind, these actions were two separate, unrelated things. But that came at a cost of fragmentation. She split herself from herself and it was only in moments like when the bus hit her, those moments of shattering, that she saw that it was possible to be a whole person, but only at the cost of pain.

This could be a moment like that. A circling back to the beginning.

She took a deep breath and went into the store. Here was the make-up aisle where she used to shoplift cosmetics, here was the shampoo aisle where she used to choose the least expensive brand, the one on the bottom shelf. She put Alka-Seltzer and Vitamin C in her basket, in case this was only a hangover, chose a cheap pair of sunglasses to cover her eyes, and then picked up two pregnancy tests. At the till she felt furtive, even though she was a grown woman and she didn't recognise anyone in the store. She added a pack of mint gum and a cherry lip balm, more for misdirection than for anything.

'Don't bother with a bag,' she tried to say cheerfully to the cashier, and stuffed all of her items into her handbag before beating a retreat. She was halfway out the door, wrestling with the plastic tag on the sunglasses, when she heard a familiar voice calling to her from across the street.

'Vee! How are you?'

Brenda waved, her smile cheerful. She was wearing a new down parka in bright purple. She looked as if she were going to cross the street to Vee, but Vee waved her hand to stop her. Then, when it was obvious that Brenda was waiting, Vee crossed over, holding her handbag close to her side to hide the contents.

'Are you on the mainland for the day? Doing some shopping?' Brenda said, after she'd hugged her.

Vee stepped back, conscious of her general fug of Allen's Coffee Brandy and cigarettes and dogs. 'Actually, I stayed the night with a couple of old friends. Mike's going to pick me up in a little while.'

'Perfect! You've got time for a coffee with me.'

'Oh, I don't think – I was going to wait for—'

'It's dead calm today, Mike will have to motor all the way from Unity. Anyway, there's a café on the waterfront, so we can get a seat by the window and watch for him. Come on, no arguments, it's my treat.'

Vee knew better than to argue with an islander when it came to the weather conditions. She walked along beside Brenda, slipping a couple of pieces of mint gum in her mouth and finally tearing the tag off the sunglasses so she could put them on too.

Off-season, the café was nearly empty. They found a table with a harbour view and Vee triple-checked that her bag was zipped up before she put it on the floor. Brenda kept up an easy chatter of small talk about the weather and the island and shopping in Rockland, Vee doing her best to pretend that she wasn't on edge, until they each had a cappuccino in front of them. Then Brenda folded her hands in her lap and she said, 'You've been avoiding me. Why?'

Shit.

'Avoiding you? Of course not, Brenda, you're literally the nicest person in the world.'

'That might be, but you're still avoiding me. It's a small island, and it's difficult to miss.'

She winced. 'Did Sterling say something?'

'No. Sterling thinks I never notice anything that isn't positive. But you were part of my family all those years ago, Vee. And while I'm not surprised that Dottie left it all behind without a backwards glance, you're different from your mother. And you loved my husband like a father, and you and Sterling were like siblings. So I know there was a reason why you never got in touch.'

'That reason could, of course, be because I'm a stone-cold bitch.'

Brenda shook her head and took a delicate sip of coffee. 'No, you're not. Sterling thought you were, and you like to pretend that you are. But I knew you had a good reason for leaving. And because you refused to explain it to Sterling, and since you've been avoiding me since you've come back, I think I know what it is.'

Vee felt cold. She didn't know what to do: laugh it off, pretend she didn't know what Brenda was talking about, get up and walk away. But she owed this woman more than that.

Brenda's already-gentle voice softened. 'It's not your fault, sweetheart. It wasn't your secret to carry. It was your mother's. And Tom's.'

Brenda knew.

'It would've destroyed Sterling,' Vee burst out. 'It still would.'

'That's what I thought, too. But now I'm beginning to wonder if I was a coward.'

'I ... didn't think you knew. I didn't want you to know. He died, so what was the point?'

'And you didn't want to lie to Sterling.'

'Mum wanted to leave, right away. And I knew I couldn't go to the funeral, or stay around, and not say anything. I couldn't listen to everyone saying—'

'What a wonderful man Tom was? He *was* a wonderful man, Vee. You remember.'

Oh, she remembered. The bicycle, the smile, the penny candy slipped to her in a paper bag. The laughter, the fishing trips, the baseball games, the endless debts, the midnight rescue, the way he made Sterling apologise for telling the truth about her family.

'I thought – I used to wish that he was my father. All my life, I did. And then ... I found out. And then he died. It was too much all at once.'

'He would've been proud to be your father.'

'You knew all along?' Vee asked. 'You forgave him?'

'It wasn't easy,' said Brenda. 'But of course I did. I loved him. Have *you* forgiven him?'

'I couldn't believe he would do something like that.' She was aware of her own guilt as soon as she said it. Her own hypocrisy.

The fragments of her life, which made no sense when she pieced them together.

Brenda put her warm hand on Vee's forearm. 'You mustn't feel guilty. You left without a word because you thought it was best for Sterling, and for me too. And for Thomas, and your mother. I understand that.'

'Why are you so kind to me?' she said. She felt tears burning, and was angry with herself. She couldn't break down again: not here, with a pregnancy test in her bag, talking to this kind woman, the mother of the son Vee had betrayed not once but twice. 'I don't deserve it.'

'Oh, sweetheart.' Brenda patted Vee's arm. 'Everyone deserves kindness. Because everyone makes mistakes.'

Mike kissed her cheek and grimaced. 'You smell terrible. What is that?'

'Shih-tzu.'

'Sounds about right. Hung-over?' He tried to take her handbag but she shook her head. Instead he helped her onto the dinghy and climbed in after her.

'Let's just say thank God it's calm.'

He chuckled. 'I made up the berth. You can lie down and go right to sleep.'

She huddled in the bow of the dingy, hood pulled up over her head, as he motored them out to *Dawntreader* on a mooring. Her stale breath fogged around her face and everything felt damp and cold. Mike, of course, was completely at home on the water. Once they'd climbed aboard *Dawntreader*, she felt guilty enough to ask if he needed any help with anything, but he shooed her down below, where she found the berth, blankets, pillows, and a flask of hot tea. Historically, Mike took enormous enjoyment in her hangovers; he never got hung-over no matter how much he drank, and he seemed to think that this made him morally superior. Her irritation with his solicitousness did not make her feel any less guilty.

She toed off her boots and climbed into the berth, still wearing her coat and hat. She tucked her handbag in under her feet, and closed her eyes. Above, she could hear Mike making everything fast, turning on the engine, and casting off the mooring. The sounds should be comforting, but they reminded her of Tom Ames. Not because she'd ever been on a sailing boat with Tom Ames, but because he was the type of man who did things to make you feel looked after: not the showy, expensive gestures that Mike was so good at, but the small things that didn't cost much money but maybe took a lot of effort. Tom Ames was exactly the sort of man she had wanted for a father.

Down here, all she could hear and feel was the engine. It was cold now, but it would warm up soon. In an hour or two, they'd be back on the island. A tear seeped beneath her closed eyelid and rolled down her face.

Everyone makes mistakes, Brenda had said.

Vee had made plenty of mistakes. But before she learned the truth, she'd never believed that Tom Ames could too.

In the womb of the boat, coddled in blankets, tired of crying, she drifted in and out of memories of the day that Sterling's father died.

Chapter Forty-three

Vee, July 1995

Vee was seventeen and had been out partying with a group of college students who had summer work in the restaurants and bars in Camden. One of them gave her a false ID to get into a karaoke bar. She was hoarse and tired and by the time she hitched a lift back to Rockland, it was past five in the morning and too early to wake up Edith, so she went down to the ferry terminal to wait for the morning boat. Sometimes she hung around on the docks instead, hoping to catch a ride on a lobster boat, so she could sneak in before it really got light and pretend to Pops that she'd been back home before midnight. But Pops was dead. They'd buried him three weeks ago. And she was tired, and she didn't feel like coming home smelling of lobsters and bait, and she had no weed left to trade with a lobsterman for a ride. And she hadn't forgotten what had happened recently at the big summer-person house, where she'd felt vulnerable, the only girl in the company of men. So she decided to find a private spot to try to sleep for a couple of hours. In the morning, she'd convince one of the Lunts to break the rules and let her on the ferry for free.

In the unlit field next to the terminal she looked for Tom Ames's truck. Like a lot of Unity people, he often forgot to lock it, and it had a blanket behind the seat. She spotted it right away, even in the dark: he always parked it in the same place, near the back of the car park under a tree. She was almost there, yawning, when she heard voices and she stopped. They were talking too low for her to make out the words. Quietly, so as not to disturb anyone, she crept between the parked cars. As she got closer, she realised that the man was Tom Ames. He was in his truck, and it sounded like he was talking to someone beside him. From here, she couldn't see who was with him – Sterling? Brenda?

Anyway, that was her ride back to the island sorted out – the Lunts and the Ameses always did each other favours. She smiled and approached the truck, ready to knock on the window and give them the scare of their lives.

'I don't like waiting, you know?'

It was her mother's voice. Vee stopped again. Was that her *mother* in Tom's truck? She squinted in the nearly dawn light. She saw two shadows who could be anybody.

'It's your choice,' said Tom. 'You're free now. You can do whatever you want.'

'I'm never going to be free. Because I love you.'

It was her mother. It was definitely her mother. And as she watched, frozen, she saw the silhouettes lean in to each other and kiss.

Vee walked the two miles back to Edith's house where she sat on the front step until Edith opened the door to let her dogs out. While Edith went to work, Vee lay on her scratchy couch, staring at the water-stained ceiling until it was time to walk back to the ferry terminal for the high season midday boat.

On the deck of the crowded boat, surrounded by chattering tourists, she leaned against the railing and pulled her hood up over her head. She was too preoccupied to notice anything. She was still trying to figure it out. How could her mother be in love with Tom Ames? He was happily married, wasn't he? How could anyone cheat on Brenda? She thought back months, years – her entire life – trying to remember if she had ever seen a secret word pass between her mother and Sterling's father, whether she'd ever witnessed a touch or a smile.

She couldn't remember anything – but why would she, if she'd never thought to look for it? They would have had to work hard to keep people from knowing, on such a small island.

All the time, she was aware of a small warm hope, glowing in a secret corner of her chest.

What if Tom Ames was actually her father? What if he and her mother had been in love for years? What if he'd been watching Vee, from a distance, protecting her and helping her, because she was really his daughter?

It was ridiculous. Her mother had been sixteen when she'd had Vee. Dottie hadn't even finished high school, and Tom Ames was already a married man running a business. It couldn't have happened. But …

… But if it had. It would be perfect.

Except that Brenda would hate her. And so would Sterling. If Tom Ames were her father, Vee would be the living embodiment of infidelity and lies, and the one safe place – the one safe *friend* – she had on Unity would be gone.

She was so deep in her thoughts that she didn't notice that the Ameses' island truck wasn't waiting for the ferry. As she walked up the landing she didn't notice the clumps of people standing around talking in low voices, or the lack of teenagers to collect baggage, or the CLOSED sign on the door of Ames' General. Head down, hood up, gaze on the ground in front of her, she tried to figure out what to do next and ran straight into someone standing in the road.

It was Mrs Langlais, her old teacher. The one who'd refused to believe it when Vee's name turned up on the Rockland High School Honor Roll printed in the local paper. Mrs Langlais stumbled back a few steps but she didn't say sorry or start yelling at Vee for being thoughtless and rude. She just stood there, and Vee saw that she was crying.

'What's the matter?' blurted Vee. For a split second she thought that Anita Langlais had learned about Dottie and Tom's affair, and that was why she was crying, because she was a poisonous old bitch who hated anyone to have any joy, even if it was adulterous.

'You haven't heard?' sobbed Mrs Langlais. 'Oh, it's the most terrible thing. Thomas Ames is dead.'

'What?'

'He had a heart attack this morning, right there in the store. Oh goodness, poor, poor Brenda. The helicopter—'

Vee didn't wait for the rest of the story. She took off running.

She found her mother walking between two of the houses she cleaned on the east side of the island. Dottie had her bleached hair tied up in a handkerchief. She wore denim shorts and a t-shirt tied at the waist, and carried a mop and a bucket full of cleaning supplies. She looked young and healthy and, Vee saw for the first time, beautiful. As if she were lit up from the inside.

'You gonna join me for an honest day's work?' Dottie called to Vee, and that's how Vee knew that her mother didn't know yet.

They hardly packed anything – what would they want, anyway? But they were both in agreement: neither one of them could face Brenda and Sterling Ames. Vee had never seen her mother cry, and she didn't see her cry now, not when Vee delivered the news about Tom's heart attack, not when Vee told her mother that she knew about their relationship. Dottie's face merely went dead pale, and she swallowed and chewed on her lips. Then she put her cleaning supplies down, right there in the middle of the road, and said, 'We're leaving, today.'

Vee was stuffing belongings into her school backpack, anything she could that came to hand without really looking, when she remembered her toothbrush and went to the tiny bathroom on the ground floor, at the back of the house. Her mother was sitting on the closed toilet seat. She held a small piece of driftwood in both hands, as if it were precious, and she was rocking back and forth, tears streaming down her face with her mouth open in a silent scream.

Vee knelt beside her. She put her arms around her mother and held her while she cried and cried and cried. Vee wondered if she should be crying, too. But she couldn't seem to, even though she loved Tom Ames, and her mother, and Sterling and Brenda. It was as if once that small glowing hope of finally having the perfect father had been extinguished, she couldn't feel anything at all.

Dottie cried for a long time, and then she sniffed and straightened up, wiping her face with her palms. All of her make-up was gone.

'Let's get out of this shithole,' she said. So they went.

Like their decision to leave, the decision not to use the ferry was by common unspoken agreement. Neither of them wanted to wait, or take the chance of running into anyone. Perry Beotte gave them a lift in his lobster boat. While he drove from the cabin and spat tobacco juice over the side, they both huddled near the stern, next to traps and buoys and the baitbox, and watched Unity receding behind the frothing wake of the boat.

'Was he my father?' Vee asked. She knew the answer, but she had to be sure.

She whispered it, so she wasn't sure if her mother heard over the sound of the engine, but after a minute her mom said, 'No, honey, he wasn't. I wish he was.'

'Did you love him?' She knew the answer to this, too.

'More than I've ever loved anyone, except for you. I'm never going to love anyone like that again.'

Vee thought about Sterling and how heartbroken he was going to be. But that was too painful to think about for very long, so instead she nudged her mother with her elbow and asked, 'Where are we going?'

Her mother stood up straight. Chin up, legs sturdy, even in the rocking boat.

'We're going wherever the hell we want,' she said.

Chapter Forty-four

Mike, February 2016

Mike stared past the bow of the boat towards the horizon, where Unity was growing larger as they approached. From the water the island always looked so vulnerable surrounded by open sea. As if it could be swamped or toppled over at any moment.

Vee lay in the cabin, probably asleep. He should get more sleep, too. He had paced the house last night while she was on the mainland. He knew that she wasn't with Rachel. Last night he'd strolled by Rachel's house, slipping through the shadows to the side of the building. He'd felt both relieved and ashamed to see Rachel in her kitchen window, alone.

Whenever Vee was out of his sight, he wondered what she was doing, what she was talking about. He wondered if everyone in the world knew more about his marriage than he did.

Even when Vee was at home, he couldn't rest. He couldn't focus on anything and nothing felt good any more. Daybreak, the house he'd bought to save their marriage, felt like a stage, a theatre where the two of them were playing roles, badly and without any heart.

He was starting to hate the house. He definitely hated himself. But he couldn't do anything but love Vee, more and more the further and further away she drifted.

'Hey,' she said, and he watched her climb up into the cockpit, rubbing her eyes. 'Are we almost there?'

'Almost,' he replied. She perched on a seat. 'Are you feeling any better?'

'A little.'

He loved her so much. But did he even know her, any more? Had he ever?

'Are you feeling sad?' His heart was in his throat as he asked it. He and Vee rarely ever talked about their feelings, he realised. He almost never did with anyone, because if he started, he was afraid he might not ever be able to stop. He had too many. It was easier to ignore them, and pretend they didn't exist.

Except they did exist, and every day he felt as if he were closer and closer to exploding.

'I'm just hung-over,' Vee said. She pulled her scarf tighter, and looked at the ocean.

'The water's like silk,' said Mike. 'There's going to be a storm.'

Chapter Forty-five

Rachel

People born on Unity could taste the air, glance at the ocean and sky, and know when it was going to rain, when the wind was going to get up, whether or not it was going to be a long winter or a damp summer. They felt storms in their bones. They shut windows when it was still sunny outside, pulled their traps as fast as they could, made sure they were ashore before dark.

Rachel's sixth sense was not about the weather. It was about Vee. As she checked stock, did her housework, worked on the accounts, walked the island, she could feel Vee looking at the same ocean, breathing the same air. She would feel a pull to the window and see Vee walking to the ferry terminal, face turned away from Ames'. She would start to walk towards Daybreak, and turn around in case she met Vee coming in the other direction. She felt Vee's movements like the tides.

She hated how they'd ended it. It was too abrupt, and there had been angry words on both sides. It made her feel empty and breathless.

But what had she had learned from Vee, and what she had learned from Unity Island itself, was this: if you kept your chin up and refused to show any shame, stood straight and true like the lighthouse on Brimstone Island, immovable like a rock in the changeable ocean, things would get better. You would be scarred and beaten, burned and picked over, but you would weather the storm.

Brenda came over on the afternoon ferry, and when Sterling met her, he came back carrying a big suitcase, enough for Brenda to stay for several days. 'Feels like a big 'un,' she said, greeting Rachel with a kiss on each cheek. 'But I'm not going to get a chance to play cribbage again until next month, so I thought I'd come anyway. I hope you don't mind having a visitor for a bit.'

She knew the real reason: Brenda didn't like being on the mainland cut off from her son. Winter or summer, she often came over before a storm, even though Sterling told her not to. Anyway, it was good, especially if they were going to be stuck in the house for a while. If Brenda was here, Rachel had a reason not to think too much, not to get too much into her own head. She helped Brenda unpack her things in the downstairs bedroom, and made her a cup of tea. 'I saw Vee Harper today in town,' Brenda said. 'We had a nice chat.' And Rachel had to stop herself from asking, *How did she look? What did she say?*

'When do you think the storm will hit?' she asked instead.

'About midnight, I'd guess.'

'It feels so calm.'

'Always does. You know, I actually enjoy being on the island in the winter during a nor'easter. It makes me feel so cosy.'

It was after dark when Brenda went over to join Sterling at the store to play cards. As Rachel drew the curtains she could see the lights from Ames' General and the figures of her neighbours turning up. For the most part they were indistinguishable bundles of coats, hats and scarves. Except for Mike Ellis, who walked with a swagger that anyone could recognise a mile away.

Rachel turned from the window, put on some Handel and went to make herself a sandwich for supper. Sometimes she'd gone to Daybreak while Sterling and Mike were occupied with cribbage night. Now, when that was out of the question, everything in her body wanted to walk out the door and up the road to Vee. Maybe she should learn to play cribbage. Maybe she'd ask Sterling to teach her, though he'd be surprised after she'd spent so long resisting. It was just a game, after all. It was better than being lonely, alone in the house while everyone else was in that oasis of light. Better than sitting here thinking about what a mess she was making of her life.

She wondered, lately, if her problem was that she was quick to love, but too tentative about loving. The idea of depending on someone else so much, for everything, was so risky that it meant that she didn't depend enough on anyone. Was this what Sterling meant when he said she needed to remember that Unity people stuck together? That it wasn't so much what she could do for these people, what she could learn about them, but what she required of them?

She'd known from the beginning that she couldn't depend on Vee. It was the nature of their relationship to be secret and chancy. And yet she'd chosen Sterling because he was dependable, and she couldn't bring herself to depend on him, either.

She was slicing bread when her phone rang. Her heart thumped painfully when she saw it was Vee, but she made herself sound casual when she answered. 'Hi, how are you?'

'Rach, I know we haven't really been speaking, but I need you to come over. Now. Okay?'

'It's positive.' Vee was sitting on her bed, near the pillows, while Rachel sat on the end. They had never made love here; they had not even talked here. Not in this room or this bed. Others, yes. This was Vee and Mike's space. As soon as Vee invited her into it, and closed the door behind them, Rachel knew that something was very wrong.

'You're pregnant with Mike's baby,' said Rachel. She felt sick.

'Yes. I can't believe it.'

'It was an accident?'

'A total accident!'

'And yet it's that easy for you to get pregnant.'

'Rachel, I'm sorry. This is not what I planned, at all.'

'How far along are you?'

'I don't know. I haven't had a period since November, but it could be more recent than that.'

'Because you had sex with him so often, even when you were having sex with me.' She hated her own voice, because it sounded bitter and angry.

'Rachel, we talked about this. And anyway—'

'He's your husband. I get it. It's fine.'

'It's not fine.'

'It's just, do you know how I feel right now? When Sterling and I tried and tried and tried, and I felt like such a failure? Like I couldn't do this simple thing, when he'd trusted me to carry on the future of his family, the future of this whole place, and I couldn't do it? And for you, you have no desire for a baby, not even trying, and it just *happens*?'

'I'm so sorry.'

'And why are you telling me this, anyway? Did you even think about how I would feel about it?'

'I just ... I wanted to talk to you. I think about you all the time, and I miss you so much. You're the only person I know who will understand.' Vee wiped her eyes and even in Rachel's anger, she wanted to scoot over to her and hug her. But she didn't.

She had never seen Vee being vulnerable, except in sex. When she had her eyes closed, trembling on the brink of an orgasm. Then she dropped the tough girl act, the confidence and poise and smartness, and became soft and tender. She had not expected to see Vee like this, and she was not prepared for the emotion it raised in her: how big it was, how frightening to have someone depending on her again, someone who had also betrayed her.

'Oh, I understand.' But Rachel took a deep breath, held it, and let it out as a sigh. 'What did Mike say?'

'I haven't told him.'

'You haven't?'

'No. I needed to tell you first, so you could help me figure out what to do. I don't know if I should tell him. He doesn't want kids, but also, if I tell him …' She audibly swallowed. 'I can't leave him if I'm expecting his baby. And even if I do leave him, if I have his baby, I'm going to be part of his family forever. I'll never be free. Maybe I should get rid of it.'

'You're saying that to *me*?'

'I'm sorry. I'm so sorry, that was cruel. I don't know, Rachel. It's all too fucking much. Please.' She reached out and grabbed Rachel's wrist, so hard it almost hurt. 'Please. Tell me what I should do. I never wanted a baby, and you want one so much. You need to tell me how to deal with this.'

'Why do you think I know how to deal with this?'

'Because you're wise, and you're smart, and you care about things. Because you're a better person than I am. This baby should be yours.'

Rachel immediately put her hand over Vee's mouth. 'Don't say that.'

Vee frowned, but she didn't try to speak.

'You don't get to tell me that this baby should be mine. Wanting something doesn't mean I deserve it. And even if I did, people don't get what they deserve all the time.' She felt Vee's lips under her palm and thought about how good it was to kiss them. About how those snatched hours together were the best thing she had ever felt. Rachel would live them again and again and again, if she could. The first and only time she had been in love.

If only the history had been different. If time had unspooled in another way.

She took her hand off Vee's mouth.

'I'm not a good person,' whispered Vee. 'I'm always hurting everyone. I'm always being selfish. How can I be a mother?'

'Mothers hurt people, too.'

'Not my mother. She didn't hurt me. She did everything she could for me. She fought for me. She went hungry so I wouldn't have to. I don't know if I could do that.'

'You don't have to do that,' said Rachel. 'The answer is easy.'

'What is it?' asked Vee.

Chapter Forty-six

Mike

Mike slipped a stick of gum into his mouth before he walked into the store, to mask the scent of Scotch. Jacob hailed him from across the room as soon as he entered. 'Hey, Ellis, where's my fifty bucks?'

Mike acknowledged Brenda, Anita, Wendy, Sue and Marjorie, and then answered Jacob. 'Fifty? I thought it was twenty.'

'Fifty, won fair and square. The Knicks were a disaster. They were giving points away. You gotta stop backing those New York teams, city boy. You're gonna be fleeced.'

Mike laughed, along with the rest of the room, and reached for his pocket. 'Shit, I haven't got my wallet. I forgot.'

'You forgot?'

'That's convenient, when you lose a bet.'

'What kind of billionaire are you, anyway? Can't even hand over a fifty.'

'He pays all his debts in gold Rolls-Royces.'

'Okay, okay,' he said, laughing, holding up his hands in capitulation to the good-natured chorus of teasing. 'I'm a man of honour and I pay my debts. I'll call Vee and get her to bring my wallet down here.'

He stepped outside to make the phone call but before he could, he caught a glimpse of a figure in the perimeter of the light cast by the store windows. He recognised the cloud of hair. She was heading along the road in the direction of Daybreak.

Mike put away his phone and stepped back inside the store. Sterling had started putting slips of paper into the jar to choose partners. 'I'm going to nip over to Daybreak and get my wallet myself,' he called. 'If you leave my name out, I'll join the next round.'

'Fella knows better than to tell Vee Harper what to do,' said Charlie, and everyone laughed.

'Make sure you come back before the storm hits. Even in a nor'easter, a man has to pay his debts. Especially if he's from New York.'

He waved before he left. The smile melted from his face as he headed down the road, following Rachel to his house. Even with the gum, his mouth tasted sour. He spat it out.

A man of honour, he'd said. And here he was, lying, suspicious, trailing a woman. In New York, it had seemed sophisticated and grown-up to accept his wife's affair. But on the island, it was different. Everything he had been thinking, all of the smugness about how civilised and selfless he was being, about how much he wanted his wife so much more now that she had a lover, all his self-regard for the restraint he was showing and how he was putting the marriage above his own pride, all the gratification he felt from finally receiving praise from his father: it was all gone. All of it.

Somewhere along the line he had become someone who listened to conversations, who stood outside windows, who looked for hidden meanings under everyday words. He took notice of every time Vee was texting someone; he checked up on her when she was gone. He needed constant confirmation of the thing he least wanted to know.

This has got to stop, he told himself. He was driving himself mad. This wasn't who he was. He was easy-going, laid-back, everyone's friend. Without judgement, without responsibility, without debt. He charmed people who were intimidated by his name. He made people laugh, smoothed things over. Everyone liked him, because he tried hard to be likeable, because that was his only accomplishment.

God, he hated himself.

Sometimes he dreamed about creeping up to the house that night through the grey fog and seeing Vee and Rachel entwined on the sofa. Sometimes he woke up in the night and leaned over in bed to smell his wife's shoulder, her hair, trying to trace the scent of the other woman on her. He was more deeply committed to tracking Vee's affair than he'd ever been to anything else. He'd had no idea how powerful it was not to care about anything, until he actually started to care.

Well done, his father had said. For the very first time in Mike's life.

At Daybreak, the outside lights were on and there was no sign of Rachel. She must have gone inside already. Quietly, he let himself in, removing his boots as soon as he closed the back door behind him. The house was silent. He crept through it, down his own hallway, past his own guest rooms, until he came to the closed door of his own room. There were voices beyond it. The first thing he heard was his name.

'I haven't told him.'

'You haven't?'

'No. I needed to tell you first, so you could help me figure out what to do. I don't know if I should tell him. He doesn't want kids, but also, if I tell him I'm pregnant … I can't leave him if I'm expecting his baby. And even if I do leave him, if I have his baby, I'm going to be part of his family forever. I'll never be free. Maybe I should get rid of it.'

He stepped back from the closed door.

Vee was pregnant?

His hands clenched.

In that moment, he wanted to break down that door to the bedroom where he'd made love to his wife, where he'd slept and dreamed with her. He wanted to throw the lamp through the floor-to-ceiling window, set the bed afire, shout his rage to rocks and tides, show these two women that he was a person. Not a problem, not a jealous husband, not a charming man, the supplier of money and houses and good times.

He was a *person*.

Instead he turned and went back down the corridor, shoved his feet into boots, and left the house, leaving the door open behind him.

His wife was carrying his baby, and she told Rachel first. And she didn't know what to do. And she wanted to get rid of it.

He tripped over a rock in the dark road and fell to his hands and knees. What were they doing now? Making love again? Making plans to run away together? With his pride, and his money, and his baby?

He had never wanted a baby. Being a parent seemed like just another thing he would fail at. But now that it was a fact, now that Vee was pregnant, he saw that in another world a baby would have been the thing that could have fixed him and Vee. A baby would have made his parents forget about cutting off his income. A baby would have made her realise how good she had it; it would bind them together. Even if Vee didn't love him enough, they would both love the baby. They would have even more in common. They could be great parents. They would love their child unconditionally and never make it feel as if their approval rested on how the child behaved, or whether the child lived up to the family name. A child would be the solution to all of the mistakes that both of them had made, and their parents too, and their parents' parents before them.

Or they would fuck it up. Like he fucked everything up. He'd tried harder at his marriage than anything in his life, and he'd still fucked it up.

But it was his baby. *His.*

Maybe I should get rid of it, Vee said.

Well done, his father said.

He got up and kept walking. It seemed like forever before he reached the store. It was the brightest thing around, with warm yellow light shining through the plate-glass windows in the front of the building; the rest of the building, and all the buildings around it, were almost invisible. He headed straight for the door and burst through it.

'Shut the door!' someone yelled. 'You're letting all the heating out.'

'Are you okay?' asked Brenda, who was seated closest to the door. She struggled to her feet. 'You look like you've seen a ghost. And you're bleeding!'

His face was wet. Had it started snowing yet? He blinked his vision clear and looked around at all the people. Not many, about twenty, but a good proportion of the year-round people on Unity. Charlie, Jacob, Anita, Marjorie, Sue, Wendy, Brenda. Some of them had cups of coffee in front of them. He'd been listening to their life stories and homespun wisdom for months now, while he steadily built a (largely purposeful, but not quite) reputation as the worst card player on Unity Island. And Sterling, who was there too, sitting at the table Mike had abandoned not twenty minutes ago to go back to Daybreak and get his wallet.

They were all staring at him now, not in greeting but as if he were the trespasser, the ghost at the feast, the harbinger of bad news. And he saw how they'd been humouring him all this time. They knew who he really was: the hapless rich guy with more money than sense. The dilettante who sailed a yacht among working lobster boats. The playboy who'd married the black sheep. The fool.

He took a few steps into the middle of the room. He didn't take his eyes off Sterling. And he thought, *If I can't have it, then I will burn it down.*

'Your wife has been fucking my wife,' he said loudly, to Sterling, but also to the entire store full of the population of Unity. 'They've been having an affair.'

Chapter Forty-seven

Vee

Rachel was still wearing her winter jacket as she sat on Vee's bed, close enough for Vee to touch.

'What did you say?' said Vee.

'I said, you should go back to Mike. You should make your marriage work. You should be a family together. You'll be safe, the baby will be treasured, and I think having a kid might make you happy.'

'But – what about you and me?'

'You and I are over,' said Rachel. Though she'd been angry before, she seemed calm now. In direct contrast to Vee, whose hands were trembling, whose throat throbbed from holding back most of her tears. 'We ended things. Remember?'

'But I don't want them to be over.'

'That's not what you said before.'

'That's because – I didn't know. I didn't know what it would be like to live without you.'

Rachel screwed up her eyes. 'What?'

'I don't beg for things. If someone doesn't want me, they don't want me, and that's it. But I miss you so much, Rachel. I only came back here for you. Just to share the same space with you. That's why I called you first when I found out I was pregnant. I think I'm in love with you.'

'You think?'

'I am.' She drew in a shuddering breath. 'I'm in love with you. I love you.'

She reached for Rachel, but Rachel recoiled and stood up, pulling her coat around herself even though it was warm inside. 'It's too late,' Rachel said.

'It's not too late. I've never been in love before, not like this. That's why it took me so long to realise it. This pregnancy is telling me I have to make a huge change. Do you love me too? You do, don't you?'

'It doesn't matter.'

In desperation, Vee crawled to the side of the bed and knelt on the edge, facing Rachel. The words tumbled out of her without her having to think; she only realised how true they were when she'd already spoken them.

'It does matter,' Vee said. 'It's not that I don't want a baby – it's that I don't want one with Mike. It would be like having two children. But with you ... you're wise, and strong, and kind. We could go away, the two of us. We could raise this baby together. We love each other. We don't have to be apart. And you don't have to be without a child. It could be ours.'

'You think that Mike would let that happen?'

'He could be involved. He *should* be involved. He's the father. But you and I could be the baby's mothers.'

And in that moment, she could see it, as if speaking it for the first time made it so. Rachel, in a rocking chair, holding a baby in her arms, her hair falling over both of them. In a park together, pushing a toddler on a swing. A small tear-stained face, and Vee scooping her child up so Rachel could pepper that face with kisses.

She wanted it so badly. A baby with two parents who loved each other, who were both present.

Rachel was picturing it too. Vee could see it in the way her eyes softened, in the way she bit her lip. Then: 'No. It's not my baby. And I'm not going anywhere. This is my home now.'

'But—'

'No. I'm sorry, but no. You should go back to Mike. Try to make it work, for the baby's sake. You and I both know what it's like not to have two decent parents. It messed us both up, in different ways that neither of us are ever going to be able to fix. You should do everything you can to make sure that doesn't happen to this child.'

'*You* could be that parent. With me.'

'No.' As Vee watched, she walked to the door.

'Rachel—'

'Just: one thing.' She spoke to the door, not to Vee. 'Please raise your baby somewhere else. Not here. Not where I can see you.'

Then she left.

Vee knelt on the side of the bed, staring at the closed door, for a long time. Her wrist throbbed where the bus had broken it. She felt the coming storm in her bones. She thought about walking outside, down the slippery lawn, onto the rocks to the ocean. She could wait there, facing east. The wind would come from that direction, and the rain and snow. She would be able to see it advancing, even in the dark. It would eat her alive.

Without being aware of making a decision, she got up off of the bed and pulled a suitcase out of the walk-in closet. She opened it on the bed and began throwing clothes inside. Sweaters, socks, jeans, a silk dress. Whatever came to hand; she didn't care. If she kept the baby none of this was going to fit her soon anyway. She threw in her paperbacks and went into the bathroom to find her toothbrush, her make-up, her expensive face creams. She snatched whatever she could off the shelf and crammed it into her bag. She'd packed so many times. She remembered packing that afternoon when she left Unity, after she'd found out about Tom Ames and her mother. She hadn't paid attention to what she was packing then, either, and later that night when they got a motel room off Route 95 in Massachusetts, on their way south, she'd discovered that she'd packed all of her old schoolbooks and no underwear. It didn't matter. She could always get new underwear. What mattered was that she was finally free.

But she hadn't been, not really.

She dragged her suitcase through Daybreak, glancing out the big windows. The night was overcast, but still calm so far. She had time, probably. She scribbled a note for Mike: *I had to go. I'll be in touch soon. Don't worry.* And then she pulled on her coat and boots and gloves and hat, and left Daybreak for the last time.

The only thing she heard as she pulled her suitcase along the dirt road was the dull rumble of its dragging wheels, and the thudding of her heart, and the sharp pant of her breath. She couldn't think too much. If she did, she would start crying and she wouldn't be able to move. She would start thinking about Rachel's face before she left.

She had to focus on the future, now. It was growing inside her, whether she chose it or not.

The store's windows blazed; cribbage night was clearly in full swing. Mike was inside there somewhere. Vee walked straight by. She counted the houses along the seafront, crowded together here, one, two, three, four, five, until she came to a small one set back from the road, almost dwarfed by the pile of lobster traps and buoys in the yard. It was dark except for the blue flickering light of a television. She dragged her suitcase up the path and knocked on Walter Beotte's door.

It took a good while and more knocking for him to answer, and when he did, he didn't greet her, just stood in his doorway gazing at her, running his thumb over his chin. 'Ayuh, you better come in,' he said finally, and stepped back to let her in.

The door opened straight into Walter's cramped living room. Walter didn't help her with her bag. He settled into a recliner facing the television, which was showing a black-and-white war movie. Clearly he wasn't prepared for anyone to disturb his evening's relaxation. Vee looked around for a place to sit, but the other chairs in the room were covered with newspapers and what looked like engine parts. There was a strong scent of diesel, tobacco, fish and, incongruously, pine. The walls were bare except for a large crucifix over the TV.

'I need a ride to the mainland,' she told Walter. 'Will you take me?'

'Storm coming,' he said, eyes on the TV.

'Yes, but it's not going to hit for an hour or two, and I need to leave. We could run ahead of it. I'll pay you.'

He reached for his can of Skoal, which lay on the side table next to his chair next to a litre bottle of Mountain Dew. 'Ayuh, I could run ahead of it. Wouldn't be able to get back here tonight though.'

'I don't want to get back here tonight.'

'Ayuh, but I do.'

'I'll pay for a hotel room for you. You can order room service and watch movies on a big flat-screen TV.'

'En't spent a night on the mainland since 1998.'

She thought about Mike playing cribbage, unknowing, next to Sterling. She thought about Rachel telling her to leave. She'd made a huge mistake coming back to this island, and now this crusty old salt was acting like she was some flatlander.

'I really need to get away from Unity. C'mon, Walter, it's for me. We went to school together, your dad used to give me rides when I was a kid. Your dad helped my mom and me when we had to leave the first time. He had the fastest boat on the island and I know you do, too. Name your price. Anything. You wouldn't have to work all season. Please.'

He shook his head.

'Fine,' she said. 'I'll ask another lobsterman.'

Walter worked his mouth around his tobacco. 'You can try. No one going to take you.'

'You just said you could run ahead of it! You think everyone else except you is a coward?'

'Can't offer a Unity man enough money to change his ways,' said Walter. 'Seems to me that's the opposite of being a coward.'

He picked up the remote and turned up the TV volume. Vee suddenly saw herself as he did: a woman in a coat that he'd have to pull a thousand traps to afford to buy, with a designer suitcase she'd hauled down a dirt road, standing in his living room surrounded by boat engines and the noise of machine guns, asking him to do something stupid because she could pay for it. Her wrist throbbed with the coming storm.

'Can I have some of that Mountain Dew?' she asked.

'Ayuh. Glasses in the kitchen.'

Chapter Forty-eight

Rachel

She walked out of Vee's bedroom and into a cold draught. The back door was open. She closed it carefully behind her and headed home.

It was still calm outside, and she felt calm too. Maybe later, in the days to come, after the storm had struck and when Vee was gone, she would feel what had happened: how many times she'd walked this road still glowing from touching Vee. How Vee had offered her love, and honesty, and a family, and she had turned it away. She would be able to dissect the choices that had brought her here, and feel regret or maybe even relief. But not now. Right now was too soon. She had to go back to her home, and pretend to her husband and mother-in-law that nothing was wrong.

And maybe, after enough time had passed, it would be as if nothing had ever been wrong.

Though everything she had read and experienced taught her that time didn't heal. New skin might grow over the wound, but the wound remained, festering and deep. Down to the bone.

The door to Ames' General was also open. Light flooded from it out onto the path and as she neared, she could see that no one was making a move to close it, even though it was February. She made a detour to the shop, but it was only when she had her hand on the door handle to close it that she noticed that the inside of the store was completely silent, as if it had been abandoned.

Instead of closing the door, she stepped inside.

She had never done any acting, but sometimes she had dreams where she was in a play and she was expected to act a role without having read the script. The spotlight, the stage, the audience all with expectant and judging faces, her empty hands and panic. Walking into the store was exactly the same as that dream. The shelves had been rolled back for cribbage night and the tables were all occupied with her neighbours. Sterling was standing up, and so was Brenda, and Mike stood in the middle of the room, and as soon as she set foot on the floorboards, everyone was staring at her. Including Mike, who turned around.

'What?' she said. 'What's wrong?'

But as soon as she asked the question, she knew.

'Is it true?' Sterling asked her. His voice was quiet, but it carried over the whole listening room. 'About you and Vee?'

She didn't answer. How could she answer, with the entire population of the island watching her? Every single person who had rejected her in a dozen little ways, and the woman who had been nothing but kind to her? And the man to whom she had sworn to be faithful? There was not one answer that would not reveal her shame.

'Tell him,' said Mike. His voice, in contrast to Sterling's, was too loud. Harsh. 'Tell him how you've been fucking my wife. How the two of you are making plans to get rid of my baby.'

Someone drew in a breath. Someone else tsked. And that was it. That told her how to answer: in the way that Vee had taught her.

'We're not making any plans,' she said to Mike. 'You should talk to Vee about what she wants to do with your baby. That has nothing to do with me.'

'But the rest of it?' asked Sterling.

She raised her chin and looked him in the eye. She saw pain there, which made it much harder. But she bit her lip, and then she said, 'Yes. I was in love with her. And she loved me too. And I'm sorry about that, Sterling, because you deserve better. But I'm not ashamed of falling in love. And I'm not going to be ashamed of who I am.'

'It's true?' said Sterling. He sounded lost.

Someone whispered something and she focused on her audience. She looked every one of them in the face, all of the pale faces that resembled each other: Marjorie, Anita, Charlie, Jacob and the rest. Everyone except for Brenda. She wasn't that brave yet.

'I'm a lesbian,' she told them. 'And that will give you lots to talk about, so fine, go ahead and talk. But everything else is none of your business. None of you have made me welcome here and I don't owe any of you anything. But you all owe it to Sterling to let me talk with him about this in private, so please leave. Right now.'

To her surprise, people stood up and started to walk past her to the door. Mike, though, stepped closer to her. Anger transformed his face, erased the handsome charm. 'What do you have to say for yourself?'

'To you?' said Rachel. 'Nothing.'

'I welcomed you into my home.'

'Mike, what I did wasn't personal to you at all. But you've just made it very personal to *me*, by making it into a drama in front of the whole island. I was unfaithful to Sterling, but you just made sure he found out in the most painful way possible. Please leave, and go and talk with Vee. Sort things out between the two of you.'

He opened his mouth, then snapped it shut. He turned on his heel and stalked out the door, slamming it behind him hard enough to topple over the postcard rack.

And then it was just the two of them. Cards and cribbage boards abandoned, cups of coffee still steaming. Sterling had not moved from the far table. As she walked a little closer, she saw that his hands were in fists on the tabletop, and his face was grey.

'It's true?' he said again.

'Yeah.'

'You and Vee?'

'I'm sorry.'

'For how long?'

'Since August.'

'Since she got here?'

'A little bit after that, but ... yeah.'

'You're a lesbian?'

'I didn't really know before, but ... yeah. That too.'

He picked up his coffee cup. It was a heavy green mug with the store logo on the side. He threw it at the wall, just below the ice-cream sign, where it shattered. Coffee dripped down the painted surface.

Rachel flinched. But she didn't step back. 'I'm sorry,' she said again.

'You're sorry?' Sterling raised his voice. 'You're sorry? What for? For cheating on me behind my back with my childhood best friend? Or for never telling me that you were gay?'

'I'm sorry for hurting you. That wasn't what I meant to—'

'What did you *mean* to do? Did you think that no one would find out? This island is tiny! Where did you do it? In our house, while I was at work?'

'I don't think it's any use to go through—'

He crashed his fist on the table. 'You don't get to decide what's any use!'

'I don't get to decide anything. That's the whole problem.'

'What do you mean by that?'

'You brought me here to be a baby machine, Sterling. To carry on the family line.'

'I brought you here because I loved you!'

'And I loved you too. I still do. But I wanted to fit in so badly and you never helped. You told me what to do and how to do it, but you never defended me against anyone. You just expected me to change. And then when we couldn't have a baby – when I couldn't have a baby – it was like you stopped trying at all. You shut me down. And I tried so hard, Sterling, but you wanted me to stop being myself.'

'So you fucked a woman.'

She swallowed. 'Yes.'

'Get out,' he shouted. 'Get out! Get out of my family's store. Get out of my family's house. Go and pack, get on the first ferry out of here. Go!'

He pushed at the air with his hands, with both hands, as if he were shoving her away from him. As if he could throw her against the wall like the coffee cup. His face was red, his eyes dry, all the pain replaced by anger. But his face wasn't transformed, like Mike's had been. Sterling's was the same as it been for a long time. As if he was only now discovering why he was so angry.

She'd done that to this loyal man.

'I'll leave the store,' she said. She turned and stood the postcard rack up again. Then she went out, closing the door behind her.

The cold outside nearly took her breath. It felt as if it had dropped several degrees since she'd walked from Daybreak. Shoving her hands in her coat pockets, clenching her teeth, she ran across to the house. Brenda was waiting at the door to let her in.

'Where's Sterling?'

'In the store.'

'Are you all right?'

'You shouldn't be worried about me,' said Rachel. She tugged off her coat and hung it up, and then bent to unfasten her boots. 'I'm the one who's done the bad thing.'

'But I am worried about you,' said Brenda. 'I'm worried about both of you. Sterling because he's just had his heart broken, and you because you've had to keep yourself hidden for so long.'

'You're worried because I had a secret affair?'

'Because you've been pretending to be something you're not. That must be terrible.'

Rachel had been calm in the face of Vee's desperation, in the face of her neighbours' outrage, and in the face of Sterling's anger. But Brenda's kindness made tears flood to her eyes. She sat down, hard, on the bench near the door.

'I've been pretending all my life,' she said.

Brenda sat down beside her and put a hand on her shoulder. Rachel shrugged it off.

'Stop it,' she said. 'You're making me feel worse. I can't get through this if you're sympathetic to me, because I don't deserve it. You should help Sterling, not me.'

'I know what it's like to keep a secret. And I know what it's like to love someone who's made a mistake.'

Rachel couldn't ask about that. She couldn't deal with any other secrets tonight. She wiped her eyes with the back of her hand and stood up. 'Sterling has told me to pack my stuff and go as soon as the storm's finished. And I'll move out of this house. But I'm not leaving Unity. I have nowhere else to go. This is my home and I fought for it. I gave up everything for it, even if no one wants me here.'

Brenda took hold of Rachel's arm and pulled herself up. 'You're family,' she said. 'Nothing will change that. Would you get me my stick? I think I need to go and talk with my son.'

When Brenda was gone, Rachel went up to the bedroom that used to be hers and Sterling's. But before she packed a single thing, she sent Vee a message: *Everyone knows.*

Chapter Forty-nine

Sterling

Once Rachel shut the door behind her, the only sounds in the store were his own breathing and the slow drip of coffee off the wall onto the wooden floor. But in his mind he could still hear the echoes of words that had been said. It was as if they were carved on the old walls, dug into the floorboards, printed on the labels of the cans and boxes and bottles.

He slammed his fist on the table again. It hurt but it felt good, too, and it made a noise that he could focus on, instead of the emotions crowding his head. Humiliation, pain, bewilderment, impotence, shame, fury. And relief, too. Relief. Because he had something to be angry about, now. He had a good reason, at last.

And maybe that was the most screwed-up part of all of this. What sort of man felt relief that his wife was cheating on him? What sort of man envied her for her freedom?

What sort of man did this *make* him?

He strode the aisles of the store, seeing nothing. Back and forth. Knowing no way back, no way forward. How to face his neighbours. How to carry on. All the months trapped here with these people. The summer whispers, the knowing looks. The stories that would get told over and over forever, becoming Unity lore. He remembered when Buddy Stewart lost his boat payments on online poker and when Drew Howard was caught siphoning diesel. He remembered Pops Harper drinking his life away, and Dot Harper pregnant with Vee at sixteen. This would be worse. It would become a snigger. A joke. *Oh, the feller who owns the store got his wife leaving him for another woman.*

'Sterling, honey?'

He turned, fists clenched again, expecting Rachel. But it was his mother.

'Mum,' he said. 'I don't want to talk right now.'

'I think you need to, honey.' She made her way across the shop floor with her cane, and he saw maybe for the first time how frail she was, how thin, how her hands had the swollen knuckles of an old woman. This was Rachel's fault too, he realised with another burst of anger. If he hadn't got married, his mom could've stayed on the island and he could've looked after her better.

'She tried to blame me,' he said. 'Can you believe it? She says I wanted her to stop being herself. But all I wanted was for her to fit in and feel safe here.'

'I know, sweetheart.' She stopped a few feet from him, as if his anger created an invisible barrier that she couldn't cross. 'You only wanted what was best.'

'I've been humiliated in front of the entire island.'

'Well. People talk. But they get sick of talking eventually. And everyone will know that you're a good man, and if they don't know that, then they can talk to me.'

'How could she do it, Mum? Did you know?'

'No, course I didn't.'

'I wonder how long that Mike Ellis has known and hasn't said anything. And I knew Vee was bad news, I told you she was! You said to give her a chance. She's come back and ruined everything.'

'I know you want to blame everyone, sweetheart. It's natural.'

Anger flared. 'You think I should blame myself?'

'No. No, not at all. And you're angry right now, which is how you should feel, and how you're going to feel. But eventually, when that subsides, you're going to be able to look around you with a little bit more compassion for other people's mistakes.'

'This wasn't a mistake! It was an affair! It was going on

practically since Vee got here. That's probably why she got her husband to buy her that house – so she and Rachel could—'

His mother reached over and put her hand on his arm. 'Please don't torture yourself, Sterling. It only punishes you.'

He jerked away from her. 'You're always like this, Mum, you're always trying to see the best in every situation and this situation doesn't have a best! You don't know what it's like! All I ever wanted was to have what you and Dad had. Dad would never have put you in a situation like this. He was decent, and responsible, and—'

'He had an affair.'

She said it so quietly that when he stopped talking he wasn't sure if he'd heard her correctly. 'What?'

'Your father had an affair. For … I don't know how long. Two years? Three? He was in love. And yes, when I found out, I was angry like you are now. I'm still angry, sometimes. But I came to understand that he felt trapped, and this was his way to save himself.'

'No.' Sterling shook his head. 'No, Dad would never do that.'

'He did. And you know … I felt sorry for her, when Tom died. I was losing a past, but she was losing a future.'

'What … what are you talking about?'

'I think, now, that I was wrong not to tell you. You were old enough to understand. But then your father died so suddenly, and all of our plans just dissolved. And I got sick. I still think it was the shock. And I was grateful that you kept everything going, and so proud of you, and I couldn't take your home away on top of everything else. So I cancelled the sale.'

'The sale? Mum, you're not making any sense.'

She folded her hands on the top of her cane. 'We were going to sell the store. We had a buyer lined up. And Tom was going to start a new life, and I was going to stay here for a little while, and then maybe move to Portland, once you were all set.'

'But – the store is our legacy. Dad always said that.'

'Legacies change, because people change.'

'No.' He shook his head and backed away from her. 'No, I don't believe it. Dad would never sell the store. He would never take up with – some woman.'

'She wasn't just some woman. He loved her. That was hard for me to accept at first, but … you can't control other people. You can't control life.'

'I don't know why you're lying to me, Mum, but it's not making me feel any better.'

'I'm trying to tell you that people make mistakes. Good people, too. But it all worked out okay. I thought you might prefer college, but you were so insistent that you wanted to keep the store in the family. And you've made it thrive. You've turned into a wonderful man, and some day—'

'Get out of here,' he gritted. 'Mum, leave me alone, okay? Just – you're not helping me.'

She nodded. 'I know this is a lot to take in, and I probably shouldn't have said any—'

'*Leave me alone!*'

His shout seemed to reverberate through the store. In the silence afterwards, he could hear the drumming of sleet on the windows, like a battering of pebbles against the glass. The storm had started.

'All right,' his mother said. She bowed her head and turned. When she opened the door, the wind tore it out of her hand and flung it back against the outer wall.

'Let me help you,' he said, and she shook her head.

'It's only just begun. I can walk down the path by myself. I lived here before you were born.'

He stood in the doorway and kept his eyes on her depleted figure as she made her way along the path and to the house, through icy snow. It was falling fast enough that she left footprints, and tiny round prints of her cane. She went inside the house and didn't look back once.

He pulled the door shut. And there he was: alone again. In this legacy. With this legacy. Which had been an illusion.

An illusion he'd sacrificed his life for.

He started with the newest things. The wooden produce stand toppled over and tomatoes, apples and onions squashed under his boots. The wine rack, with French for summer people and Californian for Marjorie and Anita, smashed to the ground. He opened the freezers and swept food out onto the floor, upturned ice-cream tubs, kicked glass refrigerator doors until they buckled and shattered. Threw bottles of microbrewed beer at the wall, a third of a six-pack at a time.

Sterling upended cribbage tables, the cards fluttering like snowflakes. He pushed at the standalone shelves of dry goods and forced them crashing down. He jumped up and down on packs of cereal, flattened loaves of white bread, crunched a plastic bottle of vegetable oil under his foot so the yellow oil sprayed out over the fragments of mugs and scattered cribbage boards. He dropped the big jar full of names and watched the people of Unity landing in the mess he had made.

All of this was a lie. He drop-kicked bags of potato crisps and pretzels. All the decency and the respectability and righteousness. He aimed a can of tuna at a ceiling light fixture and hit it, bullseye, plunging the front of the store into shadow. He tried for another with a can of pumpkin pie filling and missed. He had lived here all his life, cared for all of this, held it up as a model of tradition and goodness, and what was he? A servant to the summer people. The butt of his neighbours' jokes. Someone who never spoke a controversial opinion, who never allowed himself opinions at all. A shopkeeper, and nothing more.

And his father was a liar and a cheat.

He tore down the maps from the walls, plucked off the vintage soda and diesel signs and threw them like frisbees. The shelves on the wall were harder to dislodge; his grandfather and great-grandfather had built them. He tugged at them, hard, putting his weight behind it (the weight of the male line of the Ames family) but in the end he had to settle for sweeping their contents off onto the floor with the flat of his arm. Shampoo and soap and laundry detergent, paper cups, paper towels, tampons and toothpaste, fishing lures and crabbing lines and plastic buckets and spades.

He had not even noticed his wife falling in love.

Outside, the wind battered against the windows. Sterling didn't hear it, or if he did, he thought it was his own breathing, his own act of nature. Sweat soaked through his clothes and dripped from his forehead.

This was just stock. This was what moved through his hands and into others'. He stood on a toppled shelf and tugged the bell down from the top of the door. It clanged in protest but then lay dead and muffled. Then, panting, he went round the back of the counter, the place where his father had died, and there it stood: his father's chair. He wiggled his finger, almost delicately, into the small tear in the green upholstery. With a jerk of his hand it unseamed itself, tore down the middle, exposing the soft and ancient padding, the dingy and creaking place where his father had talked with his customers, had taught his son what was decent, had dispensed penny candy and wisdom, had been the centre of Sterling's world.

Chapter Fifty

Mike

The wind came up quickly on his way back to the house, and by the time he reached the drive, he had to lean forward to make headway. Almost the minute that he stepped inside, his phone rang. He checked; it was his father. He disconnected the call. 'Vee!' he yelled, but he knew already that she was gone. Her note and the empty hangers in the walk-in closet only confirmed it.

'Fuck,' he said.

He'd thought letting it out would make him feel better. In those minutes between his closed bedroom door and the middle of Ames' General, he thought he'd be the accuser, the righteously angry, a man wielding the fiery sword of truth.

It took only a word and a look from Rachel to show him who he really was: someone determined to cause as much harm as possible, as long as he got to be the centre of attention. Someone who'd known about his wife's affair and tried desperately to hang on to her anyway, not just out of love but also out of greed.

They could have had a baby together. Not to fix things, not to carry on the Ellis line, but... for no reason but to have a baby. They had never discussed it. He had been too scared of failing. Of feeling.

He sat heavily on the bed. He wasn't angry any more. He was empty.

He'd come to Unity with a wife and a fortune and a future. And he would leave it with nothing at all, not even his self-respect.

'Fuck,' he said again, to the empty room. 'Fuck, I am such a fucking loser.'

How had Rachel, the woman who'd been having an affair, sneaking around behind everyone's back, made him feel as if she were better than he was? She'd stood in that store in front of everyone with her chin high and her eyes blazing and she had said that she refused to feel ashamed.

She reminded him of Vee, when he'd first met her. Before she'd changed to be the person who was married to him, before he'd pushed her and pulled her and folded her into someone smaller who could fit into his world.

I'm not going to be ashamed of who I am.

Mike stood up. He pulled out his phone and called his father back.

'Son? I called you just now, why didn't you answer?'

'I've been too busy ripping my world apart.'

'What did you just say?'

Mike raised his chin. He caught a glimpse of himself in the mirror and he deliberately turned his back to it. He said, 'Vee and I are getting divorced.'

'Oh. I'd been hoping I could say I was wrong.'

'Congratulations, you can. You were totally wrong.'

'Michael?'

'You were wrong about my marriage, my intelligence, my integrity, and my capacity for emotion.'

'Pardon me?'

'You were right about one thing. I do need responsibility. But you assumed that the only way I could love someone was if I was paid to do it. Which says a lot about the way you've treated me over the years, as your child who loved you. You threw money at me like that's all I was good for. Like I was a problem to be fixed.'

There was a short pause, during which he could imagine his

father's exact expression. 'To be fair, Michael, you have been a problem to be fixed.'

'Not by you. Not by Vee. Not even by a baby. You can keep your money. I'm through. I'm fixing myself.'

He disconnected the call just as snow and ice pelted against the windows from the sea.

Chapter Fifty-one

Rachel

Rachel lay awake all night in the smaller spare room that used to be Sterling's childhood bedroom, listening to the storm. It battered the house all night; sometimes she felt the building shake. Every time she closed her eyes she could see the waves that surrounded them. Black and fierce and tall enough to sweep over all of Unity, wash all the houses and the people out to sea. Sweep it clean so someone else could start over. Eventually she sat up and turned on the light and just stared at the walls, as if by looking at the building, she could keep it from collapsing.

She used to do this as a little girl, too. Not during storms but during a normal night, any night of the week. She spent her childhood awake and staring, hoping that her vigilance would stop everything from tumbling down. It did, for a while. Until she couldn't preserve that house any more and had to find one of her own.

She'd borrowed a house instead, and now it wasn't hers any more. Maybe she'd blown it to pieces.

The wind died just before dawn. One minute it was blasting and the next: gone. Rachel listened to the silence for a little while, which was not really silence, but just the absence of the storm. She could still hear the clock in the hallway, the drip of the bathroom shower, the everlasting susurration of the sea. All the everyday sounds you started to take for granted, until they were overwhelmed by something larger.

Sterling's old room still had a poster of Smashing Pumpkins on the wall, and the wallpaper that had been put up in the eighties, with baseballs and bats on it. They had been planning to redecorate when they'd need the room as a nursery. She opened the curtains. The room looked out towards the water, which was solid grey. She counted the lobster boats that she could see, each cabin capped with a layer of snow. It didn't look as if any of the boats were missing: they rocked gently on the water, as if the storm had never happened. But it was still too quiet.

She hadn't got undressed, so she put on her slippers and went down the hall. Brenda's door was closed, but the door to her and Sterling's room was open. When she looked inside, the bed was still made. There wasn't any sign of Sterling downstairs.

Dread sharpened inside her. She checked her phone: nothing. She opened the front door and the path was thick with snow, with no footprints. It was tinged pink from the sunrise in a clear sky.

'Sterling?' she called. Her voice was muffled by the snow. A large branch had fallen from the tree in the yard and lay half-submerged in white, surrounded by smaller dark twigs. It had missed the house by a couple of feet at most.

This was what everyone on the island was going to do today: look for what they had lost, and be grateful for every narrow escape.

She thought about Vee, in that house with the huge windows facing the storm, and then forced her thoughts away. She pulled on her boots and coat and went outside. Her feet crunched in the snow, which covered everything in a blanket. It lay heavy on the tops of houses and along tree branches, hid the road and the paths in white perfection. She knew from experience that snow didn't last long on an island: it would melt into water that froze and refroze, rimed everything with dirty crystals.

Her breath puffed out in front of her. Had Sterling spent the night in the store? She walked across the yard to Ames' General, not sure what she should do. He probably didn't want to see her today, but there was no way to avoid each other. They might as well start talking.

Then she saw that the top half of one of the store windows had a big hole in it, and that the bottom half was a cracked cobweb. None of the lights were on inside.

'Sterling!' she said, alarmed, and rushed inside.

She didn't see him at first; she just saw the devastation. All the freestanding shelves toppled over, food spilled and crushed on the floor. And the scent, strong enough to make her eyes water, of stale beer and raw onions, fish and soap and ammonia. As if a giant had picked up the store and shaken it. Something crunched under her foot: a pair of sunglasses, lenses cracked, with a price tag dangling from the nose piece.

The storm had got in. But when she looked up, the ceiling was intact; there was only that one broken window; there was no snow in the building.

It was not the storm. It was Sterling.

She found him behind the counter. As usual. But he sat on the floor, among splintered wood and scraps of green material, next to a slippery pile of spilled cigarette packets and broken glass. He was leaning back against the wall, knees drawn up to his chest, arms curled on top of knees, head bowed, as if he were trying to make himself small. Carefully, she squatted beside him. She could see that his hands were bloody and the fingers swollen and bruised.

'Sterling,' she said gently. She didn't touch him because she wasn't sure if she had the right any more. 'Are you awake? Are you okay?'

He raised his head. He had some sort of white powder in his hair, flour or talc or plaster, and a cut under his eye. He looked around him, as if he was seeing for the first time what he had done.

'Oh God, Sterling. I'm so sorry I did this to you.'

He licked his lips. Looked at her, as if he were seeing her for the first time, too.

'I don't have to do this any more,' he said. 'I don't have to stay here. I'm free.'

She helped him stand up. He was stiff and sore, he'd done something to his foot and his shoulder, and he leaned on her as she took him through the snow to the house. He was heavy, but she could handle it. She was strong enough. Brenda was up, in her bathrobe, waiting in the hall. 'Oh, darling,' she said, and opened her arms. He walked into them and leaned his head on his mother's shoulder, though he had to bend to do it. Rachel waited on the doorstep until they both limped towards the kitchen, where she knew Brenda would find the right ingredient to warm and soothe. Then she went back to Ames' General and turned the sign to CLOSED.

Now that the first shock had passed, as she picked through the wreckage she could see the trajectory of Sterling's anger: how it spread from the temporary to the permanent, how he had ended in the place where everything had begun. That chair, where Tom Ames used to sit, where Sterling learned to be a man, was where she had first spotted Vee. It was built sturdily, to last. She knew what force of fury it would have taken for Sterling to break it.

She had lit the match. This was her responsibility, now.

This was *her* freedom. The one she'd chosen.

She found a board, hammer and nails in the storage room and covered up the window. She unplugged the empty freezers and chilling cabinets. Then she put on a pair of the gloves they used to stock frozen food and moved through the store picking up the broken glass: beer bottles, wine bottles, mayonnaise bottles and pickles, all the shards in a plastic bucket that they used for mopping floors. You took care of the dangerous things first. She stripped off her coat to right the tables and the chairs. She knew where everything went, its proper place, without thinking.

This store belonged to the Ameses, but she was also part of it. She had breathed in it, eaten in it, laughed and cried, cut her hand and bled. Twice she had fallen in love. The dust was made up of her skin. She could walk the aisles in her sleep, point to an empty space in the air and tell you that was where a cormorant had once blundered in, understand the pale patches on the walls and the paths worn in the floors by generations of feet. Even if the store were swept out to sea, flattened by a wave, it would still be haunted by the memory of her voice. Others' voices, yes. But her voice too. She had earned that.

She found an intact wine bottle and put it on a shelf. Next to it, a jug of laundry detergent. An unbent postcard. There were things that remained. There were things that could be salvaged.

Sometimes they were the things you least expected.

Rachel was kneeling on the floor, wondering where Vee was now, and gathering dog biscuits to put back into the unbroken jar when she heard a noise from the other side of the shop and saw a woman with a mop, cleaning up a yellow pool of broken eggs. It was Marjorie Woodford.

'Marjorie, how did you—' she began and then the door opened, bell-less, and Charlie came in. He stamped his boots to get rid of the snow and immediately righted the produce stand, pushing it to its accustomed place.

'Rachel,' he said, and nodded to her. A minute later Jacob came in and without speaking, the two men began to right the standing shelves.

Rachel went back to gathering dog biscuits. One by one, the people of Unity came into the store with brooms and rags and hammers. Wordlessly, by her side, they began to make it right again.

Chapter Fifty-two

Vee

Vee walked across a transformed landscape. Walter's lobster traps had been blown over, there was a tree down in the Fishers' yard, and it looked as if half the shingles had come off the schoolhouse roof. One of the front windows of the store had been boarded up. Everything was layered in snow and, though footprints criss-crossed the ground, she didn't see any actual people.

After the howling of the wind and pelting of ice on the little house, after the constant noise of Walter's war films, everything was so quiet. Vee went down to the ferry dock. She had to watch her step in the snow and slush, but most of that had already melted off the dock itself, leaving bare wet boards. Unsurprisingly, there was no sign of the morning ferry on the horizon. But it would be here later. It always was.

Vee stood on the end of the dock, next to a piling. In the summer when they were kids, she and Sterling and the others, Unity kids and summer kids, used to climb on top of the pilings and jump into the water at high tide. Sometimes they'd do it when the ferry was setting off, so the people in the stern of the boat would whoop and cheer. She'd been doing it for as long as she could remember. Some of the other kids were scared, because the pilings were high and the ocean looked like it was solid far below you, but she was never scared. She loved it: the jump, the soar, the shocking embrace of the cold water, plunging down and down and down. And then you swam up to the light and surfaced, laughing, shaking the water from your hair. You climbed up the ladder on the side of the dock and you got up on top of another piling, shivering, and you did it again.

Every time, you felt free. Every time, afterwards, you came back to solid ground.

She stomped the snow off her boots as she shut the door behind her. 'Mike?' she called, hanging her jacket on the hook, rubbing her hands together for warmth.

'In here.'

He was sitting on one of the sofas, looking out at the snow and the slate-grey water. Like her, he was wearing the same clothes he had last night. After everything that had happened, she was surprised that she was glad to see him.

'You came back,' he said.

'I never left. I spent the night on Walter's couch. My suitcase is still there. Mike, I'm pregnant.'

'I know,' he said.

'I've been having an affair with Rachel.'

'I know that too.'

'I tried to tell you, but—' Her stomach growled loudly, and she realised all she'd had for dinner last night was Mountain Dew. 'We need to talk, but first I need to have some breakfast.'

'Have a smoothie too, it's good for the baby.'

'Those things are gross,' she said, but she took one out of the refrigerator and drank it while she was making buttered toast. Then she took her plate over to the sofa and sat beside Mike. 'Do you want a piece?'

'No thanks.'

Despite their polite words, she felt as if they were balanced on a soap bubble.

'How did you find out?' she asked.

'I came back early that night when there was fog, when you thought I was in Christmas Cove. I saw you then. And then last night I overheard you talking with Rachel. And I went straight to the store and announced it to everyone, because apparently I'm a pissy drama queen, and I'm not proud of that, but Vee. You cheated on me, and that hurts a lot.'

He was speaking quietly, and without his usual smile. Had she ever seen him vulnerable before?

'I thought you were invincible,' she said.

'Well, I'm not.'

'And I'm sorry. I didn't do it to hurt you.'

'You did it without thinking about me at all, which is why it hurts more.'

'I think I have form for that.' She didn't want her toast any more; she pushed it away.

'It was selfish and cruel. You made me feel like I wasn't even a person. And I *am* a person, Vee.'

She nodded, gazing at her lap. They sat in silence for a moment. They never sat in silence. Which was ironic because in some ways, the ways that mattered, their marriage had been almost entirely silent.

'You've known for months,' she said finally. 'Why didn't you say anything?'

'I was hoping it would end. I hoped maybe it was a phase.'

'It did end. But it's not a phase. I'm in love with her.'

He winced, and then took a deep breath. 'And also. My parents said that if you and I got divorced, that they were cutting off their financial support and I would have to fend for myself.'

'Ouch. That's cold.'

'I called my dad last night and told him to fuck himself.'

'Also cold. But deserved. And to be honest, Mike, I think you should've done it a long time ago. You can't depend on them and still be your own person.'

'Screw the money. I loved you. I still love you.'

'I love you, too.'

He folded his arms. 'Funny way of showing it. "My husband is moving heaven and earth to make me happy, so I think I'll cheat on him." That's not love.'

'I asked you for a divorce. And instead of counselling or mediation or even asking me why and listening to the answers, you whisked me off here and bought me a house.'

'You're blaming *me* for your affair?'

'No, and I should have insisted that we get counselling or something, but when you've got an idea you're like a force of nature. You're very hard to resist.'

'So was Rachel Ames, apparently. Are you a lesbian now? Were you lying this whole time we were married?'

'No, and no. I just fell in love. I didn't mean to.'

'You were supposed to be in love with *me*!' He got up and strode to the other side of the room. 'That's *my* child you're pregnant with! Mine. And yet you decided to tell Rachel first, not me! What the hell, Vee? Why wasn't I good enough for you?'

'We never talked! We talked about skiing and wine and gossip! For seven years, I was trapped, because you never admit to having any feelings and that meant I could never feel anything either!'

'What were we supposed to talk about?'

'*We were supposed to fight!*'

She yelled it. Loud enough so that it echoed against the vast windows, in the shocked silence left behind.

They stared at each other. Vee realised she had her hand against her stomach, as if she were protecting the baby that was barely there, from the angry words of its parents. She'd done it out of an instinct that she'd never known she had.

'Well,' Mike said. 'I guess we've fought now.'

'I guess we have. Finally.'

He came over and sat next to her again. 'What do we do next?'

'Next,' she said, 'we talk.'

Chapter Fifty-three

Vee

The sun was low in the grey sky and snow crunched under Vee's feet as she climbed the steps to the Ameses' house and knocked on the door. She'd knocked on this door hundreds of times and yet not once had she ever wondered if this would be her last time. Now, she did.

She had to wait a few minutes, hands stuffed in her coat pockets and her breath clouding around her, before someone came to the door. It was Brenda, leaning on her cane, her glasses slipped part-way down her nose.

'Vivian,' said Brenda.

'Hi, Brenda. Are you okay?'

'I'm fine. Is it true that you're expecting?'

'It's early days, but … yeah.'

To Vee's surprise, Brenda threw her arms around her and hugged her. 'Oh, congratulations. So many congratulations to you, dear.'

'Um … thanks.'

Brenda leaned back a little to look up into Vee's face. 'You've got to promise me one thing. You need to let me fuss over that baby. And make clothes for it. And show it how to grow seeds. You hear me?'

'All right, Brenda. Yes. Of course I will.'

'And I will babysit for you any time. I know you can afford

nannies but they won't love a baby of yours like I will. You just call me.'

'I will, and thank you.' Vee gave Brenda a quick hug back. 'But I have to talk to Sterling, if that's okay.'

'I'll get him. You'd probably better wait here.' Brenda shut the door behind her.

It took long enough that Vee was hunching her shoulders and jiggling up and down to stay warm, but finally Sterling appeared in the doorway. He had a cut on his cheek and stubble on his chin.

'Rachel isn't here,' he told her.

'I'm not looking for Rachel. I'm looking for you.'

'Why?'

'I came here so you could give me a black eye.'

He sighed. 'My dad taught me never to hit women.'

'You literally owe me one. No one would blame you. Most people around here would probably applaud.'

Sterling shook his head. From inside, Brenda called, 'Either let Vivian in, or go outside with her. We're not heating the whole island!'

He stepped onto the porch. 'What did you want to say to me?'

'I'm sorry,' she said. 'I've betrayed you over and over again. And you don't deserve it.'

Sterling ran his hand through his hair. He had some threads of silver in it, like Brenda's. 'Yeah. You did. But I'm all out of anger. I'll probably be angry again, soon, but right now I'm too tired.'

She nodded and dug her toe into the floorboards. 'Okay. Well, you get a free punch whenever you need one. And also, Sterling, I need to tell you this. Maybe sort of warn you. Whatever you and Rachel decide to do, I'm not leaving. I'm staying here. I'm having a baby, and I want to raise it here. I want to build a house – not a summer-person house, but a real house, on my grandfather's land. I want my kid to belong somewhere, and know everything about that place, and be able to hold up their head and say "This is mine." Like you, and me.'

'Not me,' said Sterling.

She'd been expecting him to argue with her, or yell at her. Not this.

'What do you mean?' she asked.

'I've leaving Unity. I'm going to travel. Then maybe go out west for a while.'

Her heart was in her mouth. 'With Rachel?'

'On my own. I need to figure out who I am. Without this place, and without anybody else.'

She gazed at Sterling, who she'd known all her life. Who, in another world, could have been her stepbrother. He looked different, somehow. Tired … but lighter.

'I really am sorry,' she said.

'I don't forgive you,' Sterling said. 'I never really did. Maybe one day we can be friends again, but not today.'

'I'll wait.'

She watched as he went back in the house, closing the door firmly behind him. Then she took another deep breath, and she walked across the yard to the store.

She didn't know what she'd find here, either.

The lights were on, and the door opened without the familiar sound of the ringing of the bell. Inside, the place was totally different. Many of the shelves were empty, the tables were gone, and the walls were missing decorations. The refrigerators were dark. A strong scent of bleach and alcohol drowned out the familiar odours of dust and wood.

But Rachel was standing behind the counter, writing something in a notebook. She looked up when Vee came in.

Vee felt like she could not breathe. She crossed the shop floor like a ghost or a memory, herself when she was a teenager or a child. Or six months ago, when she saw Rachel for the first time.

Rachel's dark eyes, her pointed chin. The wonder that was her hair.

Vee stopped in front of the counter. She swallowed hard. She wanted to launch herself across the counter, drop to her knees. Plead for a future.

'What are you writing?' she asked instead.

'A new history of the island,' said Rachel. 'I've been thinking about it for a while.'

'Looks like this place got hit hard in the storm.'

Rachel put down her pen and shut the notebook. 'I thought you were leaving.'

'Mike is leaving,' said Vee. 'He's packing up and going back to New York tomorrow morning. We're still talking about custody arrangements. But we'll work something out.'

'What about you?'

'The baby and I aren't going anywhere.'

Rachel said, 'Neither am I. This is my home, and I fought for it, and I'm keeping it. Under my own terms, not anyone else's.'

Terrified, uncertain, Vee reached out her hand. Rachel took it. Her fingers were soft and warm. To Vee they felt like home.

'You and I have a lot of work to do,' Rachel said, 'if we're going to get this place ready for summer.'

Acknowledgements

Unity Island doesn't exist. But it is an amalgamation of various islands off the Maine coast, which I have visited by car, sailing boat and ferry. I wrote most of this novel while the pandemic kept me away from Maine, and so the story reflects my yearning for these very special places. My very special thanks to my parents, Jerry and Jennifer Cohen, for sharing their love of these islands and showing many of them to me. After being apart for far too long, we spent a magical day on Monhegan Island together, which I'll never forget.

Rowan Coleman helped me figure out this novel's conflict; Kate Harrison helped me figure out the structure; Angela Clarke helped me figure out the climax; and Melissa Lenhardt helped me figure out the ending. All of these things, as it happened, were figured out in France. So thank you, also, France. And speaking of France: thank you Janie Millman and Mickey Wilson and Rory and Charlie of Chez Castillon for sharing their home in Castillon-la-Bataille, which is the most nurturing and fun place to write and teach.

Thank you to Sara-Jade Virtue, who donated to Young Lives vs Cancer to have her name included in this book, and who ended up being Rachel's first love.

Thank you to Charlotte Mursell, Cait Davies, Leanne Oliver, Helena Fouracre, Sanah Ahmed, Francine Brody, Jane Howard and every single person at Orion whose name is listed in the credits at the end of this book.

Thank you to Harriet Bourton, who helped birth this story.

As always, thank you to my agent, Teresa Chris, who is fierce in telling me what works and also what doesn't. You are a lighthouse in treacherous waters, Teresa.

Thank you to all the writers whom I have coached and taught, at retreats and online and in workshops and in classrooms. You're inspiring.

And thanks to my son, who spent most of a year indoors with me and still kept his sense of humour.

Credits

Julie Cohen and Orion Fiction would like to thank everyone at Orion who worked on the publication of *Summer People* in the UK.

Editorial
Charlotte Mursell
Sanah Ahmed

Copyeditor
Francine Brody

Proofreader
Jane Howard

Audio
Paul Stark
Jake Alderson

Contracts
Anne Goddard
Humayra Ahmed
Ellie Bowker

Design
Joanna Ridley
Nick May

Editorial Management
Charlie Panayiotou
Jane Hughes
Bartley Shaw
Tamara Morriss

Finance
Jasdip Nandra
Afeera Ahmed
Elizabeth Beaumont
Sue Baker

Marketing
Helena Fouracre

Production
Ruth Sharvell

Publicity
Alex Layt

Sales

Jen Wilson

Esther Waters

Victoria Laws

Rachael Hum

Anna Egelstaff

Frances Doyle

Georgina Cutler

Operations

Jo Jacobs

Sharon Willis

She wanted to break free.
But what price will she pay?

Viola has an impossible talent. Her photographs seem to capture things invisible to the eye – only a leap of faith could mean they are real. Until one day a woman arrives in Viola's life and sees the truth – about her pictures, and about Viola.

Henriette is a celebrated spirit medium, carrying nothing but her secrets with her as she travels the country. The moment she meets Viola, a dangerous connection is sparked – but Victorian society is no place for reckless women.

Meanwhile, across the world, invisible threads join Viola and Henriette to another woman who lives in secrecy, hiding her dangerous act of rebellion in plain sight.

Faith. Courage. Love. What will they risk for freedom?

Their love was unstoppable.
Their life was a lie.

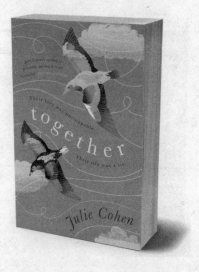

Robbie and Emily have been together for decades.
Now, their joints are creaking and their eyesight is
failing – but their love for each other is as fresh and fierce
as the day they first met. They have had children and
grandchildren, lived full and happy and intimate lives.

But they have been keeping a secret since the day they met,
when their lives changed forever. Over the years, the sacrifices
and choices they made have sealed their fates together.

Did they do the right thing? Read their story, and you decide.